Best k

THE
LIGHTHOUSE
KEEPERS

Dodie Hamilton

Dodi k

x

Other books by Dodie Hamilton

Fragile Blossoms

Reluctant Angels
Prequel to A Second Chance

A Second Chance

Letters to Sophie
The Sequel to A Second Chance

The Spark
Prequel to The Lighthouse Keepers

Perfidia

Fragile Blossoms

To Cressida and Amy

'In My Father's House there are Many Mansions, if it *were* not so I would have told you.' John 14:2

Note from a soldier in Afghanistan

Hello Girl with Green Eyes. It seems I am required to leave a note for my nearest and dearest telling my last wishes. Sad to say I don't seem to have any nearest or dearest – I guess I lost them on the way, and even if I did you would be the one I'd want to say goodbye to. I don't know you and you don't know me but don't be afraid! I'm no stalker. I saw you once and never forgot. Your lovely face has kept me going through a year of hell. I want to thank you and tell you that my wish is for you to know that, alive or dead, in heaven or hell, I will look out for you, and I will find you, and I will love you.

God bless and keep us both.
your wanna-be Guardian Angel.

Part One

Girl with Green Eyes

CHAPTER ONE

Robocop

Daisy Banks doesn't worry about what happens after you die. Here and Now is what matters. Those that do worry, you know, tarot cards and people knocking on tables trying to contact the dead, they are surely the lost and lonely.

Sexy Missoni on her body and Jimmy Choos on her feet Daisy is neither lost nor lonely. A gorgeous redhead with sparkling green eyes and the longest legs in Europe, she's senior exec in a City investment house. She owns a two bed-roomed house in Richmond that she shares with Oscar, her boyfriend, and a three-legged cat called Boffin. An opera buff, much of her spare time is given over to a local am-dram society. Her voice a little basso profundo for a woman, she's no singer but helps painting scenery and handing out concert programmes. The third Sunday of every month she's up to her elegant knees in ooze doing her bit for the planet reclaiming inland waterways – add to that a weekly cookery class at a local college, Daisy, thinking toward the future and a hotel cum donkey sanctuary somewhere in the West Country, and you find a busy girl.

An only child Daisy arrived when all but her mother had given up hope. She had a pampered childhood: William Banks, a retired solicitor, and his Australian wife, Isla, (author of the *Blue Roo* books beloved of children throughout the world) indulged their daughter's every whim.

Along with Mother's Titian hair and sculpted cheekbones

she inherited Father's stubborn streak refusing Uni to backpack Asia. For a time she drifted, dabbling with interior design in an antique shop off the Fulham Road, and then, offered a job in the City, she found a greasy corporate ladder she wanted to climb.

Friends say she's a tad judgemental. Colleagues think her fair but exacting while her lovers know her a tricky mix of fire and ice. Everyone agrees she was born lucky. Daisy doesn't believe in luck, sees it all in the mind along with spooks. The only affiliation she has for things that go bump in the night are the bewitching *Ghost* frocks she wears to the opera. Imagine her surprise then when the Holy Variety came to stay.

Spring of '06 she went to a wedding in Scotland and there in the drizzling rain fell in love. Six Chimneys was a seventeenth-century farmhouse of blue slate and misty mauve wisteria. Ideal for an animal sanctuary, it had seven bedrooms and attic space, and while close enough to the village for comfort, it was far away for privacy.

A tennis court and swimming pool, stables that can be converted to guest apartments, a stream with fishing rights bottom of a meadow, she was surprised to learn it had been on the market for years, the owners having decamped to the Costa del Sol in the nineties. Refurbishment already carried out, new bathrooms, central heating and extensive rewiring, there have been numerous enquiries but none followed through. Thus year-by-year the price has dropped, until now, according to any realtor, 'it's an absolute steal.'

'Oscar.' Daisy peered through a chink in the boarding. 'Look at the window.'

A stained glass window dominated the further wall of the

stairs. More a doorway to the sky than a window, the central panel depicted a mediaeval knight complete with chainmail and sword.

Sunlight shone through the window, sparkling rails of dust upon a staircase of light down which the knight seemed to want to descend.

'Lord! Isn't he something!' breathed Daisy.

Oscar nodded. 'And still in one piece.'

'Have we time to get the key and look inside?'

'We need to be on our way. I don't fancy negotiating these goat tracks at night…unless it's to come back with a lorry and remove Robocop there. I could get a good price for him on E-Bay.'

'You'd need more than a crowbar. That's his home he's guarding.'

'He doesn't seem to have held on to the last owners.'

'That's true. I wonder why they left.' Daisy gazed about the garden, breathing in the heady scent of roses. 'What could be better than this?'

Oscar contemplated his muddied Prada boots. 'A little sunshine maybe?'

'Rain or not, it's my idea of heaven.'

'Forget it. This place will swallow you whole, your money and your soul.'

* * *

Daisy wasn't able to forget. Months passed and the house took root in her mind. She dreamt about it every night, found herself on the stairs talking with Robocop, discussing next season's roses and whether to plant beans.

'I want that house,' she told friends.

'Then get it.'

'Oscar's a city man. He wouldn't want to live there.'

Daisy met Oscar at a Millennium party. Tall, with a lithe muscular body, thick dark hair and liquid brown eyes, he is undeniably gorgeous. Women crowd about him on stage buying him booze and tucking phone numbers top of his boots. They love him and he loves them back, playing them hot and sweet like he plays sax. He is droll and with a ready wit but not the easiest of men; when up he's a hot wire buzzing, when down, the world is a piss-pot.

The week after Christmas Daisy found him staring out the window, the sax cradled to his chest. Sensing broken glass she trod carefully. 'Everything okay?'

'The usual fuck-up.'

Oscar teaches alto sax at the Royal College. It's a job with considerable clout but he hates being tied down, preferring to play gigs in local bars. A night flight to LA and recording sessions, he'll disappear for days. Then there are weekends in Amsterdam with his drinking buddies. He'll call in the early hours, reciting Shakespeare sonnets and dirty limericks, his Scouse tongue mellowed by whisky and weed. Broke, forever on the scrounge – late for appointments, leaves his dirty pants on the floor – Oscar 'Blues' Curran is a selfish son-of-a-bitch but Daisy loves him.

Christmas break cut short, Daisy was recalled to work. Rumours have been flying about for months, the dreaded outsourcing! She has forty people on her team and likes every one but knows someone will have to go. Thursday she left work early, a meeting tomorrow, she wants to be up early. A woman in the City needs to be on the top of her game, for Daisy that means wearing a favourite Donna Karan suit.

'Oscar, did you remember the dry-cleaning?'

'Oops!'

'I needed that suit! Tomorrow is important. People's jobs are on the line.'

'And what you wear will make a difference? Daisy, you could walk in that place naked and with a daffodil up your arse and it wouldn't change anything.'

'Don't be crude.'

'I'm not being crude. I'm saying it as it is. The Asia thing is a done deal, and nothing you say, or do, will make a difference.'

'Maybe, but I have to try.'

'Why do you? They wouldn't try for you. It's a dog eat dog world out there, every man for himself! And if heads are to roll then you and all the other overpaid wankers in that place will have to bite the bullet.'

'You don't say?' Daisy was stung. 'Well, Mister Cliché, let me tell you, if my head is to roll I won't be the only wanker in this house biting the bullet.'

'Is that you having a dig at me and the lack of readies?'

'It might be. The water rates are due and the car tax. Did you get paid for the gig at the Marquis of Granby?'

'I owed a guy.'

'You always owe a guy.'

Oscar never has any money, if you got it spend it, if not borrow, being his motto. With that credo he's forever dodging someone. CCJs against him and creditors on the phone Daisy chauffeurs him everywhere, debt recovery having repossessed his Merc months ago. He's not bothered, a modern Micawber he hourly expects something to turn up.

'Come on, Daze!' he'll wheedle. 'I've a cheque due that'll pay the rates *and* dinner at the Savoy. Slip me a note and I'll nip to college to check the exam roster.' He left and the phone rang. As with creditors there are girls: girls from bars and clubs, girls from college – waif-like beauties, they hover, eyes on the door and saxophone cases held out like cumbersome invitations.

Daisy takes it in her stride, the guy can't help being gorgeous. Her mother is not so inclined. 'Trust that long streak! I'd sooner trust Hannibal Lector.'

Isla is on the phone now, bent over an illustrating board, a *Bluetooth* in her ear and her eyes narrowed against cigarette smoke.

'That you, babe?' As usual she's coughing.

'I thought you were cutting down.'

'I am, beginning on Monday.'

'You're always beginning on Monday!'

'Hey, don't you start! I get enough from your pa. And why are you in work when you're supposed to be on holiday?'

'The usual fuck-up,' muttered Daisy, thinking of Oscar. 'People wondering whether they have a job, people with mortgages and kids.'

'And what about your mortgage and your kids?'

Here we go! Isla's always banging on about kids. *Isn't Daisy leaving it a bit late? Look at all her married friends and their children? She should get a nice boyfriend and stop wasting time with that layabout!*

'Don't let's go there, Mum, not today.'

'Yes, let's go there! Why aren't you married with children? You'd make a great mother. I can't bear the idea of you alone with no one to love.'

'I have someone to love. I have Oscar.'

'The world has Oscar. You have leftovers. Where is he now, out playing in some bar while you're home washing his boxers? Dammed if I'd do it! Let him cook his own meals and wash his own stuff. He doesn't know how lucky he is having a girl like you to run after him.'

'I don't run after him.'

'You all but wipe his backside. And what does he do? Sweet Fanny Adams! So he's good-looking? There's more to life than looks. You need a man with heart, someone who'd lay down his life for you.'

'Men like that don't exist.'

'They do! Okay, they're few and far between but still here if you're willing to look. Look at your pa! You used to say you wanted someone like him.'

'And how old was I when I said that, six?'

'You had sense when you were six, knew goodness when you saw it.'

'I don't want goodness.'

'You don't want badness.'

'Other than to keep my job I don't know that I *want* anything. I'm pretty much my own person. You and Pa help but by and large I do it myself.'

'Good job too because if you're looking for help from Mr 'Blues' Curran you're wasting your time. I know the type. Great when things are going well but trouble and you don't see their arses for dust. I shouldn't criticise. 'Til your pa came along I spent my life running after men like him. He's your choice. I should accept it. I can't. I want someone strong for you, a hero not a fake!'

Daisy was done. 'Sorry, Mum, I've got to go. I've things to do. And please stop worrying about me. I'm doing fine!'

Next morning at the bank among sagging paper chains and artificial Christmas trees she learned she wasn't fine, swingeing cuts made across the board and her job among them. Furious, she glared at her boss. 'Why?'

'Your particular function was best placed elsewhere.'

'Then place me elsewhere.'

'There isn't a suitable slot.'

'There was a suitable slot for Gary Turner and his cronies. How come they've a place and I haven't?'

'Gary has experience in acquisitions and Matt is due for a more senior role. Both men are married and have children. They have commitments.'

'I have commitments. I may not have children but I've a whopping great mortgage. I don't see the distinction.'

'There is none.'

'Then place me. I've worked hard for this bank.'

'And you'll find acknowledgement of that reflected in the compensation.'

'You might have warned me.'

'We had to keep the situation under wraps.' When Daisy continued to stare he waggled his hands. 'It's a company decision. It's not personal.'

No, she thought, had this been personal – had I frequented lunchtime booze-ups along with the rest of your crowd, and allowed your sweaty personal hands to maul my uptight personal bum – it would be Gary standing here.

* * *

The humiliation of it! And, boy, was Oscar ever right! If she'd hoped for support from the rest of the team none was forthcoming. Relieved not to be heading for the dole queue, they buried their heads in their desks. She left with garden leave and a monster pay-off designed to keep her quiet. She tried calling Oscar but only got his service. By the time she was home she was in tears.

'Oscar!' she called. The house was empty, the remains of breakfast still on the table and Boffin yowling at the door. She cleared the mess, threw pots in the sink, and then desperate to talk called the college. 'May I speak to Oscar?'

'Mr Curran isn't available.'

'Could I get a message to him?'

There was a pause before another voice came on the line: 'Oscar no longer teaches here. He and the college parted company some weeks ago.'

'Parted…? You mean he was sacked?'

'It was a mutual decision.'

'But why?'

'I'm afraid you'll have to ask him.'

Stunned, she spent the rest of the day wandering about the house. Left his job and never a word! Lied! Yesterday when asked how things were going he replied, 'usual fuck-up,' the implication he was there to observe said fuck-up.

This is Oscar, never saying what he's doing or why. He is as closed mouth about the past. Sometimes after a jam session he'll speak of his childhood, how he was abandoned by his mother. He'll tell of foster homes, shipped from one family to another until he won a scholarship and made his way in the world. A sad potted history, she hadn't the heart to ask for more.

That evening the phone rang, girls giggling down the phone. 'We wish Oscar a shaggy new year. We wish Oscar a shaggy...!' Daisy pulled the plug. In the past she's ignored Oscar's wanderings but lying about his job? What else is a lie? He'll shrug. 'There'll always be girls. It comes with the territory. But trust me, Daze, I'm no hound dog baying for the moon. I am a cool cat walking the line.'

Cool cat. From the first there was an agreement, no screwing around. All or nothing! Seems nothing is what she has.

Just before dawn he returned, feet like ice and hair smelling of Floris Roses, French cigarettes, and sex. He pulled her close. 'How's my sleepy girl?'

Nails scraping the sheets like Boffin's claws, she went.

He slid his hands up under her vest, cupping her breasts.

'Don't! I don't feel like it.'

'Yes you do,' he whispered, thumbs caressing her nipples, his breath smoky on her cheek. 'Come on, Daze, a nice lazy fuck then I can get a good night's kip.'

She threw him off. 'Judging the smell you should get a great night's kip.'

He sat up. 'What's up, Daisy gal, still bitching about me not helping out?'

'Why didn't you tell me you'd been sacked?'

'What?'

'The College! I rang them. Apparently you've been given the boot.'

'I didn't get the boot. I walked.'

'Why didn't you tell me?'

'It slipped my mind.'

'Was that before or after you went to check the exam roster?'

'Chrissakes!' He turned to look at her. 'What's with the third degree? Do I have to tell you about every decision I make?'

'No but you don't have to lie to me.'

'It wasn't a lie. I forgot. Is that what it's all about, me not telling you I jacked the College, because if it is you're out of line; nobody tells me how to run my music. I do what's right for me.'

'Don't I know it! Everything you do is right for you. Breakfast things on the table, stuff left on the floor, me always stumping up cash and then left on my own, not to mention having to defend you to my mother...'

She paused for breath and he leapt off the bed.

'What's this, a major bout of PMT?'

'It is not.'

'Then you must be sick or something.'

'I'm sick of waiting up for you.'

'Then don't wait! Nobody asked you to. Don't look to me to run your life. You're a free agent. Do your own thing!'

'Free agent?'

'We're both free agents. Free to do our own stuff and not have to come home to the third degree.'

'And free to roll around with whatever bit of spare is going?'

'Ah, for fucks sake! What's got into you?'

'Never mind what's got into me! What's got over you? You stink of sex.'

'I'm out of here.' He pulled on his pants. 'I don't need this at four in the morning, where I've been and what I've been doing.'

'Fine, go! And take your stuff with you. I'm putting an offer on that place in Scotland and I don't want your rubbish cluttering the place.'

'What offer?'

'I've been made redundant!'

'Redundant?' He stared. 'Can they do that?'

'They've done it.'

'You've been there years. You must've got a tidy pay-off.'

'Enough to get me that house.'

He sat back on the bed. 'If you must use the cash get something decent. Forget that Scottish dump. It's too small. You'll never make it pay. I got buddies in Croatia who're buying old chateaux and turning them into goldmines. If not Croatia then France! Better yet let's go to LA!'

Mutinous, she stared at him.

'No, not you!' he sneered. 'That's way too sensible. You'd sooner carry out some crackpot scheme of a cat shelter.'

'I want a donkey sanctuary not a cat's home.'

'Same difference! You'll still end up an old woman stinking of cat piss.'

'Animals smell yet they have their own innate good manners.' Daisy scrubbed a tear from her cheek. 'You've no manners at all. You had sex tonight and couldn't be bothered to wipe her stink off your face.'

'You're paranoid! I had sex with no one! But if I did do you wonder? Who wouldn't go elsewhere if all he's got at home is a tight-ass bitch moaning about him not paying his way.' He stuffed his feet into shoes. 'Women and their hormones? Who needs it!' He was out and down the stairs. The front door slammed, footsteps retreating down the road.

'Here!' Daisy ran to the closet, pulled a jacket from the hangar and tossed it out of the window. 'Take your stuff! I don't want it or you cluttering my life!'

When he didn't return she went nuts, rampaging through the closet, flinging his Christmas presents out the window, hand-tailored shirts floating into the night. Curtains twitched but not a light in the nearby houses flickered. Back to the sitting room she went. What about his jazz collection, thousands of pounds of vinyl? Now that would hurt. Out went Miles Davis, Frisbee-like, across the road and then Charley Parker. Guilt reined in her arm. Clothes he can replace but he's been collecting vinyl for years. It would break his heart.

It was snowing. She went out into the icy road on her knees collecting records, a bleak dawn chorus serenading her tears.

Upset, ears and nose stuffed up, she didn't hear the car rounding the corner. It sped toward her, a boozy Santa at the wheel swigging from a bottle of JD.

Daisy looked up, and seeing it wasn't gonna stop scrambled to her feet.

Arms filled with records she made a dash for the house, but when she looked back Boffin was in the road. 'Boff!' she cried. 'Come here, boy!'

He turned, his eyes shining through the dark like luminous plates.

'Boffin!'

She dropped the records, dashing into the road and snatching him up.

Feet skidding on ice she turned, but wasn't quick enough.

There was the sound of glass breaking, a screeching of metal, and Noddy Holder singing: '... *and here it is merry Christmas, everybody having fun, look to the future now, it's only just begun...*'

CHAPTER TWO

What Future?

'He's up there again,' said Nurse Janet.

'Who's up where?' said Yusef, the physio.

'The weirdo with the hat. He's up on the mezzanine floor.'

'So what? There's always some weirdo. This place is full of 'em. Now, come on Daisy!' Yusef crouched, his hands about Daisy's left ankle. 'Push down!'

Daisy pushed down on the parallel bars. Pain ripped through the crown of her hip, down to the ball of her foot and back again. 'I can't do it!'

'Yes, you can. You've walked six paces. You can do another six.'

'But it hurts!'

Janet yawned. 'We know.'

'How do you know?' Daisy said, tears running down her cheeks. 'They are my legs, not yours.'

'We know because you keep telling us.'

Daisy glared at Janet. Bitch! You and your attitude! One of these days...!

'Okay.' Yusef's hands were steel clamps. 'One more step and we'll call it a day. One more. That's it. And another? Good! Another? Excellent! Another?'

'No more!' Heart pounding, Daisy slumped over the bars.

Nurse Janet started laughing.

'What's so funny?'

'He is,' Janet pointed to the mezzanine balcony.

10 am every morning Daisy is wheeled to the gym. The big man with the knitted hat pulled low over his eyes is always sitting overlooking the gym. When they first arrive he's quiet. Then he gets agitated, punching the air like a boxer and shouting. Nurses were at first alarmed, and then puzzled, and then amused when it became apparent the shouting was aimed at Daisy.

'Come on, wee Daisy! Ne'er mind the old dragon! Put your back into it.'

Since the accident Daisy's hearing is tricky, sound cutting in and out. When she's tired her vision is blurred, everything seen in soft focus. Yet she could hear her name shouted and could see him punching the air.

'Do you know him?' they would ask.

Daisy didn't know him – didn't want to! It's enough with these two having a go never mind a stranger. Today the weirdo seems even more agitated.

'It's like being at a football match,' said Yusef.

Janet grinned. 'Or a ringside seat at Crufts.'

'What's he saying?'

'He's saying he can't stay forever. He'll have to go without her.'

'There you go, wee Daisy,' Janet helped her into the chair. 'He's saying he can't stay forever so better get a move on or he'll leave without you.'

Daisy let them have their little joke. They can do what they want, she doesn't care. Oscar came yesterday. All spiffed up, hair slicked back and a Calvin Klein jacket, 'hello, darling,' he says, kissing her cheek. (He doesn't kiss her lips any more. Put off by a neck-brace and smell of antiseptic he leans away.) The darling is new; normally, it's his blanket term for the groupies on the dance floor, their smoky eyes turned toward Oscar, their Musical Mecca.

He's going to dump me, Daisy could feel it coming. 'How are you, Oscar?'

'Pretty good as it happens. I got a gig in Stockholm.'

'Did you?'

'Yeah, a real cool gig at the Sturecopagiet.'

'Wow! When do you leave?'

'Well, that's why I'm here.' Smile fixed, he hovered. 'I fly out tonight. I didn't want to leave without saying goodbye.'

'Goodbye? That sounds rather final.'

'Don't be silly, darling, it's just a manner of speaking. I'll never say goodbye.'

He did exactly that. That evening Isla, eyes red from weeping, tossed his note on the bed. 'He's cleared out and taken half the furniture with him.'

'Doesn't matter, Mum.'

'It bloody well does matter. Not the furniture! I couldn't give a rat's arse about those bits of rubbish. It's the way he crept away.'

'I knew it was coming. Oscar hates to be tied, and you can't get more tied than looking after a cripple.' The note was brief. *I have to go. I'm no good with sick people. Can't handle it. You deserve someone better. Ciao, angel.*

At least the note was honest if not the man.

There was also a letter from Dad's notary friend in Scotland. It too told of disappointment. *...regarding Six Chimneys. The house in question is for sale and at today's market a reasonable price. However, I refer to a letter from a Scottish notary that may explain the low asking price and why the house remains on the market. It seems the land on which it stands is governed by certain rather archaic Border* *laws. I won't bore you with the details only to say that because of this any changes relating to the house and outbuildings must be agreed by a local land-owner, one Captain Lucian Nairne. Entailment is always a problem inasmuch as any structural alteration, even the banging of a nail, has to be approved. You will be handcuffed, Daisy. Your life will not be your own. While I understand you've set your heart on this house, having known and served your family for years, I urge you seek another option.*

'Tell him to go ahead.'

'Are you sure? This is your pa's friend. He's true beer, none of your froth and wind. If he says it's a no-go, it's a no-go.'

'Tell him to make an offer.'

'But babe, how can you think of living in Scotland? You can't walk never mind start up a donkey sanctuary.'

'If what he says is true it's going to take time. Time is the one thing I have.'

'But Daisy...!'

'Mum, please!'

'Alright. I'll speak to him. Don't upset yourself. You're for surgery tomorrow and need to be calm; me and your pa will be here waiting until you get back.'

* * *

The surgical team came to collect her at four, whiter- than-white surgical gowns and incredible eyes showing over face masks. Daisy had her pre-meds and was as loose as a goose. 'You people must have the same genetic link.'

'Why is that?'

'Your eyes – you look like extras from the *Village of the Damned.*'

The eyes smiled. 'Not the damned, Daisy, more of the other kind.'

'As for your laundry bill it must be phenomenal.'

'We use the right kind of detergent.'

'Good,' croaked Daisy, 'it will help ward off C. Dificile.'

The smile deepened. 'We don't have that here Daisy. We're of the Old School, cleanliness next to Godliness. So do you understand what's happening?'

'I have a hole in my head.'

'It's not a big hole. It just needs a little support.'

'And the rest of me doesn't?' she said – ironmongery protruding from her left foot and right leg, a neck-brace and heavy strapping about her ribs.

The eyes twinkled. 'You think this is bad? You should have seen Brother George when he came in. Not an inch of skin intact. It's his own fault. He will keep fighting dragons.'

'I always thought it was Saint Michael did that.'

'There are plenty dragons to go round. Now, in a moment I shall be asking you to count back from a hundred. You'll feel a cold sensation through the back of your hand and hopefully have a nice long sleep.'

'Only hopefully?'

Smile, twinkle. 'Okay then, here we go! One hundred, ninety-nine...'

'Ninety-eight, ninety-seven, ninety...' She yawned. '...ninety-six...'

'Let go of it, Daisy. Give in.'

She let go, drifting up and away like a titanium embroidered balloon. Bumping along the ceiling, she didn't get far. Silly thoughts went through her head, it's the metal in my legs, it's too heavy. 'Oh, there I am.' She looked down at her body. 'Is that chap really going to drill through my scull...Oh, he is!'

An odd feeling of being both the observer and the patient, and of wanting to fly through the ceiling but of being restrained, tethered, as it were, to the ground but by no physical restraint she could see. 'Unless it's that ribbon coming from my body.' A silken thread attached the Daisy on the surgical table to the Daisy playing footsie with overhead lighting. I've read about this, she thought. It's a life-line to the soul that if it gets broken I'm dead.

Oops! A buzzer sounded!

Something is wrong. People began to run about. The ribbon was no longer there, neither was the ceiling. It vanished along with the surgical team. Instead there was angel on a motorbike. 'Hello, darlin',' he said.

* * *

Daisy pulled herself up by an overhead strap. 'He called me darling, Mum.'

'And he shouldn't! You're not one of those silly girls calling on the phone. You're Daisy Banks. And why are we talking about Oscar?'

'I'm not talking about Oscar. I'm talking about the Angel.'

'I don't want to hear any of that!' Isla laced Daisy into her boots. 'There was no angel. It's as the surgeon said, you lost consciousness for a minute or so.'

'I didn't *lose* anything ...unless it was my life.'

'Don't exaggerate.'

'I died, Mum, no getting away from it.'

'You did not!'

'I did! For two minutes I was gone from here. Zippety-doo! Riding on the back of a Harley Davidson with my arms about an angel!'

'How did you manage that,' said her father. 'Didn't his wings get in the way?'

' A couple of times I had a mouthful of feathers.'

'You sure you weren't chewing a pillow.'

'Ha-ha, Daddy.'

'So what did they taste like, the feathers?'

'Strawberry mousse.'

'Strawberry mousse? Hah! At least it perked you up, whatever it was.'

'I don't care if it did perk her up.' Isla began dragging a brush through Daisy's hair. 'I don't want to hear about it.'

'Ouch! Careful with the scars, Mum! You're hurting.'

'Serves you right, talking rubbish. And you're no better!' Isla pointed to William Banks. 'You shouldn't encourage her. It's weeks since that happened. Doctors hear her talking rubbish they'll send for the shrink. Talking of rubbish!' She dug in her bag. 'Here's the latest letter from that miserable sod in Scotland.'

Miserable is right! If anyone could put her off Scotland it's Lucian Nairne. Talk about putting obstacles in her path! It's obvious he didn't want her buying the house. Every letter, and there have been plenty, is a list of does and don'ts.

Last week Dad took her for a whiz along the M3 to Edinburgh. 'I shouldn't be doing this,' he said. 'Your mother's going to kill me.'

'She doesn't have to know.'

'She'll know. Old Moore's Almanac, she knows everything.' They pulled into the drive. Six Chimneys was exactly as remembered. It's the new owner that's changed: the sawdust limbs of a puppet and head in tune with Mars.

There were vans in the yard and men laying in ramps for the wheelchair. Her father wheeled her to the door. 'We can't go in 'til the floors are finished.'

'You could carry me.'

'Yes, since there's nothing of you.' He lifted her out of the chair. Dodging barrows and concrete mixers they went to the back entrance. A workman saw them coming and opened the door, 'Morning, Miss. Morning, squire.'

It was at Daisy he looked, the same expression seen these days in everyone's eyes. She could've wept. Is this how she's to be seen from now on, the poor little crippled girl? 'Put me down, Daddy.'

'You're not ready to stand.'

'Yes I can. I do it all the time when you're not there. I have to be self-sufficient. I can't keep calling you and Mum.'

'You can as long as I'm around.'

But that's just it, Darling Daddy, she thought. You won't always be around.

He set her down. 'Put your weight against me.'

'I'm alright.' Standing on cotton-wool while balancing on nails isn't easy but she managed. 'Look!' She looked down at the stone quarried tiles and a faded mosaic. 'I appear to be standing on a dog.'

'You're standing on two, Missy,' said a workman. 'There's her over there looking a bit like my old Lab Molly, and if you look left where the lino's coming away you'll see a tail and hind quarters poking out.'

'So there is. Do you think there are more mosaics under there?'

'I fancy there may be. Once rid o' this rubbish lino you'll have a nice bit of stone. Lovely workmanship! Makes you wonder why people cover it up.'

'The back door guarded by dogs and front stairs by a Knight Templar?' said Dad. 'I'm feeling better about leaving you already.'

'Stone dogs are okay but I'd sooner have the flesh-and-blood variety. What about the Knight, Dad? Can you find me a flesh-and-blood version of him?'

'I don't see why not. This is Scotland. There'll be a Jock somewhere nearby who can fill that role.'

'I like your optimism. I'm just glad the window is still here.'

'Did you think it wouldn't be?'

'I wasn't sure I'd imagined it.'

'It's big!' said Dad.

'It's beautiful.'

'It's filthy!'

'There's a glass chap in Melrose can help wi' that,' said the workman. 'You want I should gi' him a call?'

'Please, and a chair, if you would.'

'There's this ratty thing,' the workman returned from the kitchen with a wicker rocking chair. 'We were going to burn it.'

'Don't burn it!' said Daisy. 'In fact, don't burn anything, no matter how ratty!' The chair was ratty, yet it was part of the house and therefore precious.

The angel said everything in Six Chimneys belonged to her. Much of what happened during her trip to Other-worlds slipped away with her return to consciousness yet she remembers the angel saying the house had always been hers. 'How can it be?' she asked. 'Until last May I didn't know it existed.'

'Human beings!' He'd removed his glove and sat astride the bike examining his nails. 'You're so literal.'

It's true! Until Jenny Miller's wedding she'd not set foot on Scottish soil and yet...yet...she gazed up at the window ...this house seems so familiar.

'You've an attic full of rubbish,' said the workman. 'We'll leave it for you.'

* * *

Dad and the workman went into a huddle, talking a skylight for the outhouse. Daisy sat on the wicker chair. Ten months have passed since the accident. Friday, she's in court, the driver of the TVR2 claiming damages, saying Daisy was drunk and shouldn't have been in the road. He's claiming compensation for damage to the car and post traumatic stress.

Until the summons Daisy had never heard Dad swear. When he read this the air turned blue. 'You have got to be ---! kidding! I'll give him ------! post traumatic stress!' As for Isla, the chap better hope they never meet.

So it goes on, the aftermath of a silly deed. Had she not been so jealous and hurt she wouldn't be putting her parents through this, neither would she be about to be humiliated. As it is she's up in front of a judge.

Friday, refusing to present a pitiful spectacle Daisy hobbled into court on crutches. There was lots of arguing, her father red-faced and angry and the opposition smooth and smarmy. 'It was in the early hours of the morning,' said the lawyer. 'Miss Banks was on hands and knees in the road. New Year's Day, I suggested she'd been overzealous in welcoming the year. She replied she was trying to rescue her cat.' He turned to Daisy. 'How is your cat?'

'Dead.'

'Oh.'

'He was killed that night.'

'Ah.'

'Knocked down by that car.'

'I see. That is a shame. We are sorry for your loss.'

'Enough of that, Mr Jackson,' said the judge yawning. 'This is a British bench. We don't want any of your American cop show CSI nonsense here.'

The judge found for the driver yet recognising police evidence – the results of a breathalyser test and empty Jack Daniel's bottle in the car – damages were kept to a minimum. Daisy was urged by council to seek an appeal but thinking her parents had been through enough chose to bite the bullet.

The court case went by in a dream. Nobody gained except the lawyers.

So unreal. Daisy kept pinching herself wondering if she was in some third-rate farce. One man came to watch, the big fellow in the knitted hat, at least Daisy thought it was him sitting at the back. If it was, he was quiet. No shouting, one moment here, the next gone – a bit like life.

CHAPTER THREE

Biting the Bullet

They arrived in convoy: two furniture vans, William's Rover and Daisy's modified Estate. Five minutes, and Isla was ready to drag Daisy back home. 'We must have been mad thinking you could live here. You've mice in the egg-house and a tomb in the rose garden.' There's nothing Daisy could do about the tomb, but her neighbour did offer to rid her of the mice.

After all the correspondence between the two countries – letters back and forth across the border, dos and the don'ts regarding the house – Daisy was sure the Captain would be on the threshold to meet her. No such encounter. He sent greetings via the telephone. An old-fashioned Bakelite phone in the hall rang. 'Daisy Banks?' enquired a deep male voice.

'Speaking.'

'Lucian Nairne.'

'Good day, Captain Nairne. What can I do for you?'

He didn't bother with pleasantries. 'With regard to the mice in the egg-house you'll oblige me by doing nothing. No traps or poisons souring the land. Leave things as they are. I'll have somebody deal with it.'

Daisy was shocked. 'I wouldn't dream of putting poison down. There are more humane ways of dealing with mice. I'll get cardboard boxes and coax...'

'Coax nothing!' He cut her short. 'The mice will be dealt with, though there'll be nothing humane about it, as you, a cripple, ought well to know.'

Bang! Down went the phone.

'What a horrible man,' said Daisy.

'Aye, that'll be the Captain,' a removal man was heard to mutter. 'Arrogant wee sod still thinks he's on the parade ground.' Daisy can vouch for arrogance. In order to buy Six Chimneys she's had to agree to abide by all manner of ancient by-laws, judge and arbiter of the laws, the 'arrogant wee sod.'

Owner of the land all-but surrounding Six Chimneys hostilities commenced the day she made an offer, a letter return of post and map of the house and land, plus notes defining management of house and land even to the keeping of pets, an issue with the Captain, who, '*couldn'ae have the cattle bothered.*'

Daisy ached to tell him to shove the rules up his regulation kilt but pressed by an inexpressible need soldiered on. Over time rules became a list of local facilities – where to purchase the best beef or hire the most able plumber.

Guidelines, the Captain called it. A damn cheek, Daisy called it.

No sooner did she replace the phone than it rang again: 'A chap by name of Oakes will arrive tomorrow at 1300 hours. He'll deal with the rodents.'

'Thank you, I'm perfectly able to deal with them myself.'

'Maybe, but I'm no taking chances. Don't want the countryside overrun.'

'Control freak,' muttered Daisy, replacing the phone. 'And he has the nerve to call me crippled.' Turning away she caught her reflection in the mirror, the crutches, the awkward stance and stiff back. It's true. She is a cripple.

For what seems an age she's crept about like a snail. Only now safe at last in Six Chimneys can she look back on the accident that early New Year's Day all but killed her. Crushed pelvis, fractured skull, breaks to right and left legs, it seems she died on the way to hospital and again undergoing surgery.

There were other losses along the way – none visible as the scars on her legs yet equally debilitating. Rather than be obligated she refused offers of help, phone calls ignored until the phone stopped ringing and no one called.

Six Chimneys has a vigilant watchman fighting a battle against centuries of wear and tear. Despite its age, walls and roof are watertight, the grounds well kept, the grass close cut and the roses free from mildew. Daisy has a tin plate in her head, is dependent on painkillers and crutches, yet she too has an inner watchman that refuses to give up.

* * *

'We'll have to go soon, Isla, if we're to miss the traffic.' Isla and William Banks are returning to Surrey. 'I'm not happy leaving you,' said Isla. 'What if you're ill? You're ace with those crutches but if you fall who' will you call.'

Daisy tugged the sentinel alarm about her neck. 'I can always sound this.'

'I still think I ought to stay. You're alone in a strange house in a strange country!'

'This is the Scottish Borders, Mum, not the Planet Zog. The people here wear kilts and sporran, not a bone through the nose.'

'No. They keep bodies in the backyard.'

The tomb is one of the serendipitous whimsies the house has in store for its new owner. Isla found it behind a curtain of wild roses. 'I don't approve of it being here, but you can see why. It's more peaceful than the council tip we call cemetery. '

'It's a woman's grave – *Mary Gray, loved beyond life and death.* Daisy rubbed the stone. 'There's a date of birth but that's all.'

Isla shuddered. 'Gives me the creeps! Oh my God!' She jumped away. 'There's a grave too! I nearly trod on it.' Indeed, there was a mound of earth alongside the tomb. 'That's recent,' Dad said. 'You can see spade marks on the turves.'

'I wonder who it is.'

'Whatever, it's got to go! You can't have dead bodies cluttering your yard.'

'I don't mind it.' Daisy was reluctant to disturb so peaceful a place. 'I have a feeling Mary Gray and co will be a lot less trouble than other neighbours.'

Isla sniffed. 'If you mean the Captain I must say I'm disappointed with him. I had hoped living so close he might come in handy. But what kind of a bloke knowing a beautiful girl lives next door can resist checking her out?'

'Don't worry about that. He can stay away forever as far as I'm concerned.'

'Come on, Isla!' William Banks heaved the last suitcase into the car. 'Say goodbye to Daisy and let her rest. She looks about dead on her feet.'

Daisy wasn't sorry to see them go. It's hard living with their anxiety. When Dad asked why she couldn't be home with them she said she had to live her own life. 'Yes,' he said. 'But why here?' Truth is, she doesn't know. There are more convenient places but once started the process was a runaway train. If anyone was to blame for her folly it was Lucian Nairne – less antagonistic and she might've dropped the idea. Now with evening drawing on she's alone with Siamese cats, a canary, and a house as mysterious as Scottish laws.

If asked to describe the mystery she'd say things are always on the move. Nothing she can pin down! If there is movement it's always beyond line of vision, the air itself seeming to vibrate. It's particularly noticeable at night when as well as movement there's a humming sound, subterranean, barely audible, music or the drone of conversation. Mainly it's the sound of breathing, the house taking in air, walls inflating like huge bellows.

Here's another thing, since the move she's become forgetful – that or objects here have a life force of their own. Last week a trowel went missing. It was found in the cistern of the outside loo. Friday she mislaid her watch and gardening hat. While the hat is still missing the watch was discovered in the attic, tied by ribbon to a rocking chair. If she were honest Daisy would admit to being terrified.

In Stoke Mandeville she met soldiers from war-zones and victims of road traffic accidents – men and women who'd suffered terrible injuries. They met together talking of fashion, of love-affairs, and the latest story on *East Enders*. They laughed and cried. They were real! She must learn to be as real or die.

* * *

She woke from a nap to find rain seeping through the skylight. Having left a message on the glazier's service she sat gazing out of the window. Thai and Ming, the Siamese cats, lie on the sofa. Inscrutable bookends, at this time of night they watch the canary. A present from Isla, sapphire-eyed icons of an Egyptian tomb, the cats are beautiful but not a patch on her former moggie.

Boffin came from a rescue centre. Poor fellow, didn't have much of a life yet bore no grudges. At night he'd creep under the duvet, squiggling up until he lay on the pillow, a purr in her ear and fishy Kit-e-Kat breath on her cheek.

Boffin is dead, killed by a drunken Santa Claus in a TVR2. 'Sorry, old boy,' she whispered. 'I wasn't quick enough.'

Memories of that night are unreliable. Sound is what she mostly remembers, brakes screeching and Boffin's pitiful cry as he was dragged from her arms.

Earlier, Dad referred to her as 'dead on her feet.' What Daisy feels when she wakes in the morning is not her idea of dead. Death isn't unsightly scars and lurching about on crutches. Nor is it the anxiety of parents. Death on that snowy morning was laughter so wonderfully buoyant it lifted her out of her body.

The world fell away to music on a car radio, the lyrics imprinting the clouds as coloured vapour trails. First stop was Nanny Banks who sat on a cloud knitting, Freddie, the Dachshund, beside her – 'staying, sweetie,' she said, 'or passing through?' Nanny died when Daisy was six, Freddie, a month later.

The memory is comforting but strange. Strangest of all was the angel. The first thing Daisy did when regaining consciousness was to ask for paper and pencil. 'I mustn't forget what the angel said,' she'd croaked through bruised lips. Dad had squeezed her hand. 'Forget that. Concentrate on getting well.'

Her parents don't want to talk of angels. Angels are unsettling.

Daisy's angel was very unsettling. You'd think an angel would fly through the night on majestic wings. Not this one! Dolce and Gabbana leather pants hugging his crotch, a leather jacket with the letter G emblazoned on the back, he sat astride a Harley. Engine thrumming, he'd barred the way, talking as if he'd lived his celestial life in the sound of Bow Bells. 'Hello treacle. Where d'you fink you're goin'?'

'To heaven.'

'I don't think so. It ain't your time.'

'I'm dead, so it must be.'

'Who said you're dead? Do you feel dead? Do you look like a corpse and stink of formaldehyde and them cheap fags the undertakers stub out in coffins?'

'If I'm not dead, and this isn't heaven, then where am I?'

'You're between worlds. Get on the bike.' She'd climbed aboard. Arms about his waist, his wings tasting of strawberry mousse, she rode until arriving at a house, a younger Six Chimneys, the vine barely grown. 'What year is this?'

'I told you, darlin', we're between worlds. Mortal rules don't apply. But if you need to think hours and days, you could say we're movin' through a time-portal, observin' life middle twentieth century.'

'Why have you brought me here?'

'For the same reason I brought you last time.' He'd pointed. 'So you can do somethin' about that.' Daisy followed his finger. 'Oh, the poor things!'

Who or what were the poor things she can't remember. The rest of the near-death experience – dream as Isla prefers to call it – is a blur. Two years on and the memory of the ride is clear, except that now Daisy feels as though she's permanently out-of-body, and the comings and goings of life are the stage directions of a play in which Six Chimneys is the Leading Lady.

* * *

Eight o'clock that evening there was a rap on the door. 'Yoo-hoo!'

Kate is one of Lucian Nairne's better ideas. Knowing Daisy would need help, Isla ran an ad in a local newspaper which brought a letter from the Captain: *you could do worse than Kate Khan. She's an awful gossip but a good woman.*

Kate Khan arrives every morning at eight to help with chores, stays until noon, returning for an hour in the evening. A voluptuous forty-year-old with purple dreads and ear-piercings, she fled a violent relationship some years ago and now lives in a trailer with her five children, her horses and her goats. Isla loves her. 'She's the reason I'm able to leave you in this miserable backwater.'

So far Kate hasn't proved a gossip yet with Mum and Dad gone a barrier was lifted. 'Was it that no account Dougie Fairbrother did your skylight?' she said, a Mancunian accent fighting Border brogue.

'It was.'

'Did you no ask the Captain whether he was worth the hiring?'

'I did not.'

'Don't you like him?'

'I don't like his telephone manner.'

'He's no good with words.'

'I might feel better if we were to meet.'

'He's no good at meeting people either.'

'What is he good at apart from interfering?'

Kate grinned. 'Aye, he comes over strong but inside he's a real pussy cat. He's been pure gold to me and mine. When me and the kids came he was the only one willing to help. All right, he's a might sharp but he's a human being unlike some other bastard I could mention.' Conversation swerved sharply, Kate chewing an ancient cud, Jason, her ex-lover. Daisy mused on her own ex-lover. Oscar tried being the caring boyfriend for a time but left taking most of the household appliances with him. Latest heard, he's shacked up with a student from College working bars in Dublin. 'Ciao, ass-hole,' she muttered. 'I hope your balls drop off.'

'Daisy?' Kate was staring. 'Are you listening to me?'

'Sorry, what were you saying?'

'You wanted to know about that grave? Seems everybody knows about the tomb, all manner of gossip, but nothing about the grave.'

'A bit odd don't you think, an unmarked grave?'

'No more odd than the woman in the tomb. It seems Mary Gray, or Minna, as they call her round here, ran this as a boarding house during the war, billeting guys from the local airbase. One woman and all those men, she was the talk of the village. The Captain won't have a bad word said against her.'

'What is he Captain of?'

'Scot's Guards.'

'He's a miserable so-and-so.'

'He's had his reasons. He was let down by a girl.'

'Hah! Aren't we all but that's no excuse for taking it out on other people.'

'It's not just her. He was hurt in an explosion.'

'I didn't know that. How could I? I've been here two months and never set eyes on him. Why is that d'you suppose?'

Kate shrugged. 'He keeps himself to himself. I clean his place, not that it wants much doing, a man on his own. He's polite wi' me. I'm polite wi' him. We don't stand about and gab. If he wants anything different he leaves a note.'

'He's good with notes.'

'He's had a bad time, poor feller. Got a medal for it, though what good a fecking medal is when your brains are screwed I don't know.'

'Are his brains screwed?'

'There's something, shell-shocked, I suppose. Susie, his ex, didn't help running off with Ziggy from the petrol station. Bitch! No wonder he's short tempered.'

* * *

That evening Daisy took the lift to the bathroom. Dad wants to convert the small sitting room to a bedroom. No way! Ground floor bedrooms are for invalids. After seeing what she's seen at Stoke Mandeville she can hardly regard herself as that.

Getting into the bath is okay. It's getting out that's a problem, the bath deep and the electronic seat sticking. Having washed her hair and soaped and shaved the bits that matter she pressed the button. The chair rose half an inch and stopped. The battle began to get out. Half-way through she was tempted to activate the sentinel alarm but the woman in the control centre with such a snotty voice she'd sooner drown. Bruises adding to bruises, she crawled over the side, changed into pjs, plugged the chair into the charger, and got into bed. No sooner in than she had to get out. She'd forgotten the canary.

Trilby is another refugee. It was found half dead on the conservatory floor one day. Isla hung a cage in the kitchen to hear him singing but so far he hasn't piped a note. At night wary of the Siamese Daisy brings it upstairs.

Recreating a girlhood dream of her own Isla has the bedroom into a Seraglio, filmy drapes at the window that billow in the breeze. Tonight the drapes follow a dynamic of their own, billow out, pause, and then fall back – which is all very nice except there's not a breath of wind.

Daisy lay watching. 'Must be a draught somewhere,' she muttered. I ought to get up and close the ...' She slept and dreamed she sat under the stained glass window. During the day the window is a nuisance – she can't think why she admired it. Impossible to clean indoors or out without the aid of a long ladder, it casts a Stygian pall over all. Composed of three panels – the Knight occupying the centre, the sides twisted green and brown glass meant to resemble branches of a tree – during the day the branches are dirty barley sugar. In the dream the tree is a living laurel, buds bloom and birds sing, rabbits and mice – faded facsimiles of the day – scamper among the roots, while the Knight's vivid blue eyes stare through a visor, the cross on his tunic as red as blood.

Still in the dream the branches of the tree become liquid, and with the sound of a stopper pulled, the angel steps through the Knight onto the landing.

'Wotcha, Daisy!'

What is it about a dream that allows the miraculous to be mundane? Had this happened in waking life she'd have run a mile. Now she's only mildly curious with the thought 'he is an angel and though his manner bizarre – his accent more so – he is God's messenger and therefore to be trusted.'

Daisy settled dark glasses on her nose – she wears them all the time, even in dreams. 'Does the Knight mind you using him as a doorway?'

'Nah!' The angel flicked non-existent dust from his sleeve. 'The bloke's in a daze most of the time. He wouldn't hear if the Last Trump was sounded.'

Daisy was horrified. 'You mean the poor man is locked in glass day-after-day with snow and rain and flies buzzing over him and nobody cares?'

The angel smiled. 'Somebody cares but as yet she doesn't know she cares.'

'What?'

'Never mind, Daisy. It will come to you.'

'So who is the Knight? I mean, is he, er...was he...a man?'

'He has the memories of a man.'

'Why is he in the window?'

'He's guarding the Gate, monitorin' comin's and goin's.'

'The comings and goings of what?'

'Souls in transit.'

Souls in transit! Such words! Daisy's heart was filled with wonder.

'He believes it's his job is to make sure no one gets through that shouldn't.'

'You mean like demons and zombies?'

'Daisy, you've been watching too many late night movies.'

'What then?'

'Those that have strayed too far: the innocent and the foolish, the sick and the comatose, the adventurous and the drug takers, the out-of-body seekers and the lunatics – in other words your average mortal. If such a wanderer arrives at the gate then he or she has lost their way. He sends them back. We've enough with the legitimate dead without overloadin' the system.'

'Does he need a sword to fend off sleep walkers?'

'No, that would be for the demons and zombies.'

Aware of the angel's scrutiny she hung her head. 'Why are you staring?'

'Why d'you wear those specs?'

'I feel better with them.'

'And the crutches? Feel better with them, do you?'

'I can't walk without them.'

'Really?'

'What d'you mean really? Are you suggesting I'm playing at being crippled? I didn't ask to be run down! I shouldn't have been in the road but he shouldn't have been drinking and driving! He ruined my life! I might as well be dead.'

'Maybe you are.'

'What!'

'Maybe you are dead.'

'You said I was between worlds. You said nothing about dead.'

'I didn't say you were alive. When in transition a soul can pass either way. It's a matter of choice. You haven't made yours yet.'

'Dead?' She shuddered. 'What kind of an angel are you to scare me so?'

He laughed. 'Never mind who I am. It's time you remembered who you are.'

'I know who I am,' she said sadly. 'I'm Daisy Banks, or what's left of her.'

'Is that all you are? Is there no more to you?' Sound dropped away and with it a charade. A man in white shirt and pants sat on the stairs. Tall and elegant, with hair and eyes as golden as the sun, he was so pure and so beautiful Daisy could barely look at him. He removed her glasses, her face reflected in his eyes. Transfixed by the image, she wanted to turn away but couldn't.

'Don't look at me,' she said. 'I'm not a nice person.'

Electricity passing from his fingers into her skin and thence throughout her body, he stroked her cheek. 'You are a nice person. You are beautiful.'

She trembled under his touch. Her face reflected in his eyes was forever changing, one moment her own and then the face of another woman.

'My cat died,' she whispered.

'And you are wounded.'

'Why must things change? Why can't they stay the same?'

'Life is about moving on.'

'Why do things move in this house?'

'Such events are reminders. The house is trying to jog your memory, telling you you're in a place where anything is possible.'

'When I was on the bike you said I was to help but you didn't say who.'

He shrugged, the D&G leathers and the cockney accent back in situ. 'I did tell you, treacle, but you keep forgettin'. But that's okay. It'll come. All you 'ave to do is make a start. You can begin with this little bloke.'

'What little bloke?'

'There.' He pointed to where once was a window but is now darkness. The darkness filled Daisy with such fear that even in sleep she tried covering her eyes. A point of light grew in the darkness. The angel walked back through the window, boiling glass reforming around the Knight, the window intact but not before the point of light leapt through the void.

'Thump!'

Daisy woke.

A cat had jumped on the bed! It couldn't be the Siamese. They were downstairs.

Up the bed he came, padding softly, his breath smelling of fresh catnip.

'Miaow!' He paused at the pillow and seeking permission patted her cheek.

Eyes tightly closed, afraid to open them, she lifted the sheet. Under he went, icy fur brushing her knees. He twisted round and round until with a sigh settling in the curve of her knees.

Trembling, she reached down. She touched two velvety ears, a sleek back, a familiar soft belly, and one, two… three paws!

Daisy began to cry.

The cat began to purr.

And the canary to sing.

CHAPTER FOUR

Reminders

Sadly, when Daisy woke the following day dear Boffin was not curled about her knees. Nor was the window on the front stairs a doorway to heaven and the Knight a Guardian of the door. All was as it ever was, except for the canary.

'What's up wi' that bird?' yelled Kate over the constant cheeping.

'Don't ask me,' said Daisy, aware of the dream, the angel, the cat and canary, but loathe to connect events. 'It started in the night and hasn't stopped.'

'We didn't know when we were well off,' said Kate, who was suffering a hangover. 'Bung a sheet over it, noisy wee devil.'

Daisy yawned.

'Did you no sleep last night?'

'Tricky dreams.'

'Dreams? Don't get me started! When I was with Jason I did nothing but dream. Same every night, the kids dead and him setting fire to their coffins.'

'How horrible.'

'So it was! Night after night regular as clockwork and that *before* he tried to kill us, you'd think I would've put two-and-two together and realised somebody was trying to tell me something.'

Daisy used to be a real dreamer. As a child she'd scurry to her parent's bed every morning relating the latest adventure, Isla maintaining most of her *Blue Roo* characters were of childhood reporting. As Daisy grew so dreams diminished, yet moving to Chimneys barely a night goes by without a Cecil B De Mille production acted out before her inner eyes.

* * *

The day grew hot and oppressive.

'I reckon there'll be a storm later,' said Kate.

'I'd better ring the glazier... again.'

'It's your own fault, Daisy. You should've got a name from Lucian. The man's lived here all his life. He knows who's worth employing.'

Kate's off again, yet another verse in the never ending eulogy, 'Praise to Superman Lucian and His many blessings upon her children.'

'If it weren't for him we'd be up the creek. Sure he's a bit of a recluse, but only because he wants peace and quiet. I mean, wouldn't you be the same if you'd been over in that country getting shot at twenty-four-seven?'

'He was in a war-zone?'

'Aye, some place out East.'

'And now?'

'I thought he'd retired but seems not.' Kate sighed. 'I love a man in uniform and he looks reet good in his. The kids worship the ground he treads but then with Jason Myers for role model no man need do much to impress my bairns.'

'Where is Jason now?'

'Doing a twelve year stretch.'

'Do you worry about him coming out?'

'Do I worry? I'm *paranoid* about him coming out.

'It might be okay. You never know he might've changed.'

'No way! He'll never change. I saw his face when the polis took him. He blames me for it. He doesn't forget and he doesn't forgive. No matter where we go he'll find us.'

'Twelve years? What did he do to get that long a sentence?'

'Robbed a garage; put the bloke behind the till in hospital. He's an animal. Twelve years might seem long to you but there's only one sentence long enough to keep that psycho from doing harm and that's a death sentence.'

Daisy took up the crutches. 'I'll pop out for a minute. Get a breath of air.'

'D'you want me to wheel you?'

'I'll take a crutch and go slowly.' Daisy slid her glasses over her nose.

'Why d'you wear shades? You're out in the garden. Who's going to see?'

'Who indeed?' A walk out midday to try retrieving junk from the stream is a midday ritual taking her away from the house and Kate's obsessions. Daisy has worries of her own. The house is paid for and there's some money left but not enough to live on. Isla's books a top earner, she's ever willing to help but Daisy prefers to be self-reliant. A guest house was the original plan but the thought of entertaining strangers is too daunting. Whatever she does it will have to be from home, sewing mailbags or whatever prisoners do.

Limbs aching, she rested by the stream. Closing her eyes, she dozed.

'*Wake up, Daisy!*'

'What!' She's awake and on her feet. Someone called her name. Thinking it was Kate she turned to go but saw movement among the reeds, a sack lying half-submerged in the stream. It moved! There's something inside.

Down she went on her backside, the faster to slide. Nails breaking on the rough weave, she grabbed the sack and pulled it to the bank.

'Oh God!' Kittens dumped in the stream, and all but one dead!

She tucked the little creature inside her bra, a fragile heart beating against her own, and staggering to her feet lumbered back to the house, every clump of grass and every pothole threatening to bring her down.

'Kate!' she stumbled through the door. 'Help, Kate!' She passed over the kitten but unable to abandon the rest hobbled back. She was exhausted by the time she was back, her elbows raw from the crutches.

'It's alright.' She wrapped the tiny bodies in her blue shawl. 'I'll bury you in the rose garden. Minna Gray will take care of you.'

She sat by the kitchen fire. Kate offered a cup of warm milk. 'Try dripping a little of this down its wee throat.' Daisy dipped a milky finger against the tiny mouth. The kitten took three or four swallows and then lay exhausted. Tiny head a broken daffodil, it hung on, sucking and sleeping.

Kate left. An hour passed and then another, Daisy's supper untouched on the table and silence but for the ticking of the Grandfather clock. More dusty wreckage in the attic, the clock was here when she arrived. It works but will only ever chime four. Isla wanted to dump it but Daisy found it restful – so restful that despite the need to stay alert she set the kitten in the wood box and closing her eyes slept.

...And woke to a thunderstorm, a power cut, and the house in darkness.

Lightning ripped across the room. The wood box was empty!

'Thai! Ming!' The Siamese were nowhere to be seen. Visions filled her head, the kitten ripped to pieces. 'You cats!' Panic stricken, she hobbled into the breakfast room. 'If you've hurt that kitten you're in trouble!'

Blundering about in darkness she tripped over a lead and fell. Cursing, she crawled along the passage and into the long sitting room. Halfway through the door her left foot caught on the jamb. Grabbing the pyjama leg, she tried flipping her foot free, but the silky material slid through her fingers. She fell, cracking her head on the door frame.

It was no distance to fall yet like *Alice Through the Looking Glass* she fell forever, down and down until with a smack she hit the floor.

Dazed, she lay still. When she opened her eyes it was to another time and another audience. The room was lit with lamps, a soft glow falling on her face. A group of men crouched about her. Young and old, differing sizes and uniforms, they all shared the same puzzled expression.

'What's going on?' said one.

'Blowed if I know, padre,' said another.

'Looks like she's fallen,' said a third.

'Move back a bit, can't you?' A fair-haired man, silver RAF wings glinting on his jacket, pushed his way through. 'Give the girl some air!'

The circle of faces rippled, moving outward.

'That's better,' he said, 'colour coming to her cheek.'

Daisy struggled onto her elbow. 'I say, old chap,' she said, imitating his cut-glass accent. 'D'you mind not talking about me as if I'm not here?'

'Minna?' he said. 'Can you hear me?'

'Of course I can hear you,' said Daisy. 'Am I deaf now as well as invisible?'

He leaned down. 'Take my hand.'

His hand was warm. 'Oh!' she gasped. 'You're alive!'

He laughed. 'Of course I'm alive. Darling, do wake up. Anyone would think you are talking to a ghost.'

'But I am talking to a ghost!'

'Is that what I am, a ghost! Then what's this beating?' He pressed her hand to his chest. 'Is it my heart? Am I still alive? I have been a little under the weather.' Then seeing her confusion, he grinned. 'Never mind, love, if it makes you feel better I'm happy to be the original skeleton in the closet.'

'So you're not a ghost?'

'Not if you don't want me to be.'

She held onto his hand. Oh, that hand! It was the strongest, most loving hand, and she could have held on forever, but there was a noise, a banging and crashing. It was making her lose concentration.

'Hold on!' he said. 'Dearest, don't let go!'

'I won't! Not ever!' But she was letting go. Her grip was loosening and the hand was thinning, vanishing, gone!

'No!'

Daisy reared up. She was alone and in darkness with only

the cat's faces staring down, and the kitten nestled safely between Ming's paws.

Shuddering, she dragged upright. Blood dripped onto her hand. She'd cut her head. Outside the storm raged. There it was again, that damned banging noise. Someone was battering the door. Someone was shouting!

'Daisy Banks! Are you all right?'

When she didn't answer Lucian Nairne kicked in the door.

A hail of wind and rain blasted through the room. Boots squelching and oiled raincoat flapping, he crossed the room and knelt beside her. 'Are you okay?'

'S..silly question,' she stuttered. 'Do..do I look okay?'

Cussing under his breath, he gathered her into his arms and carried her to the chaise. 'Have you first aid?'

'There's stuff in the downstairs loo.'

Even in pitch black he knew his way around. Returning, he knelt over the chaise, rain from his hair dripping onto her breast. He was breathing hard. He'd been running and was angry, a pulse in his wrist pounding against her cheek.

'Why are you on the floor? Fell over yon mangy cats I suppose.'

'I tripped over a lead.'

'Aye, well, they should be tidied away not left to trip you. You need to take your time with those crutches. No good rushing. You'll only do more damage.'

'I wasn't trying to rush.'

'You were scootin' hell-for-leather when I saw you earlier. Crashing about down by the rill, it's a wonder you can sit ne'er mind stand.'

'There's a reason for that. I found this kitten and I... Oh, forget it!' She set her jaw. Why bother explaining? Who is he with his Scot's accent and bad attitude? And why angry? If anyone had cause to be angry it was Daisy. Barging in uninvited, he drove the men away. Drove...? What...? Who...?

Trembling, she fought to understand. Hallucination! A knock on the head would do that. But would a knock on the head allow her to hear words when words couldn't be spoken and to hold warm flesh where flesh could not be?

Sadness tore at her heart, a yearning so deep it made her bones ache. It was their yearning she felt, a yearning for life. 'Oh, the poor things.'

'What did you say?'

Daisy shook her head. She wouldn't explain, couldn't, not to this man.

Lucian Nairne was not as expected. In early letter-writing days she had a mental image of a weedy little man, a born-again Hitler with toothbrush moustache and halitosis. A tall, well-built thirty-something with dark hair, blue eyes, and the longest lashes ever seen, this man was as Kate said – beyond gorgeous. He was incredibly gentle, but Oh, so angry.

The cats were anxious. Ming settled the kitten in the box, and then, hackles like delicate sea anemones, tried getting between Daisy and this man.

'Calm down,' Lucian batted them away. 'I'm no going to hurt her. She's danger enough to herself without me lending a hand.'

The cats weren't alone in their anxiety. Close to a stranger, and with no place to hide, every nerve in Daisy's body screamed. Despite her fidgets, or because of them, he carried on tending the cut. Then he turned her to face him.

She shied away. 'I can manage.'

He twitched her round again. 'I haven'ae finished.'

Then, bloody hell! Would you believe it but the lights came back on! The hall lights *and* the overhead candelabra blazing, Daisy lit up like the Fourth of July.

She buried her face in her hands. 'Don't look at me!'

Finger tips gentle, he lifted her head. 'Why not?'

'I'm ugly!'

'You're not ugly. You're beautiful.'

A hush fell over the room, such a strange feeling, the house was listening.

Tears slipped under her lashes. 'My cat died.'

'And you're grieving.'

Déjà vu. I've done this before. I've said this before! 'I miss him.'

'I bet you do.'

'I have three cats now. Thai, Ming, and a kitten I saved earlier.'

'Ah! That's why you were running.'

'I can't run.'

'Maybe not run but you got him back.'

'I did and if I don't get some food down him he'll die.'

Click! The feeling of familiarity vanished.

Lucian straightened. 'Okay now?'

'Yes, thank you.'

With that he was gone, striding off into the darkness without another word.

She shuffled into the kitchen. Passing the window she saw her reflection, wild hair and a red nose beautiful? I don't think so.

She collected the milk pan, and sighing, sat with the kitten on her lap. Then Lucian Nairne was at the door again, an aging Labrador with heavy teats and toothy smile beside him. 'I've brought my dog.' He lifted the dog into the wood-box. 'She's had her pups and still lactating.'

'What's her name?' Daisy laid the kitten beside the dog.

'Biddy.'

'Come on, Biddy,' she whispered. The dog flicked an encouraging tongue over the kitten's head. Sensing food, it nosed the dog's belly and after a couple of false starts began to suck. 'Thank God,' breathed Daisy.

'I doubt God had much to do with that.'

'You don't believe in Divine intervention?'

'I believe in myself,' he said, stuffing his hands in his pockets. 'That way if anything goes wrong I've only myself to blame.'

'I'm not sure about God but wouldn't want to think we're alone in this world.'

'Until you came along that kitten was alone.'

'I might be one of God's angels,' said Daisy, trying to smile.

'You might at that.'

'Oh yes, some angel.'

He frowned. 'Why do you do that? Make so much of your injuries, the shades and all? Every time I see you you're hiding behind the things.'

'You've seen me before today? How come I haven't seen you?'

'I've been busy.'

'Too busy to say hello?'

He shrugged. The shrug annoyed Daisy. 'I suppose you wanted to make sure I wasn't breaking the rules.'

'Rules?'

'Yes, the house, what not to do and when not to do it.'

Amused, he pushed his fingers through his hair. 'I wouldn'ae worry about the house. It's well able to take care of itself.'

Suddenly, she wanted him far away. She stuck out her hand. 'Thank you for bringing the dog.'

Icy fingers crushed hers. 'Should I call somebody?'

'No thanks. My parents have had their fill of scary midnight calls.'

He stood at the door, tall and silent as the figure in the window.

'You remind me of Robocop,' she said.

He frowned. 'Robocop?'

'The figure in the stained glass window.'

'Robocop? Lucian Nairne, part man and part machine?' He opened the door, the scent of rain-sodden roses oozing in. Then he nodded bitterly. 'Aye, that sounds about right.'

CHAPTER FIVE

Open House

Daisy might have given up on the idea of Six Chimneys as an animal sanctuary – Six Chimneys, as she was to learn, had not.

The first claimant arrived the next morning via the cat flap. At breakfast there was a scrabbling sound at the kitchen door. Ming heard, and hissing, snatched up the kitten and sprang onto the chaise. 'What is it?' whispered Daisy. When Thai followed Ming's example, she took up the poker. 'Come on out, whoever you are!' Out it came, a ferret, one ear chewed to the gristle.

Daisy laughed, but when more animals arrived trailing broken wings and hobbling like their benefactress, she stopped laughing.

Monday a basket of emaciated rabbits was left on the step. Tuesday, a pair of guinea pigs, *deaf* guinea pigs. Friday, a wall-eyed goat was tied to the rain-barrel. By the end of the month Noah had decanted most of the Ark's redundant creatures into Daisy's backyard. 'Somebody thinks you're a meal ticket,' said Kate leading a half-starved greyhound to the stable. 'While you're paying the vet bills poor little sods like this will keep coming!'

Maybe, but Daisy suspected the influx to be her doing. Having always wanted a sanctuary the wish had become father to the deed. Thinking back to the night when she fell, did she not invite said poor little sods?

It was his fault, Lucian Nairne. The moment his tall figure passed out into the night she wanted to call him back. Alone in a house where she didn't know whether she was awake or asleep she was afraid. Those men? What were they, figments of her imagination? Can you hold a conversation with a figment? Do figments have clean fingernails? Can a figment make her body leap?

'What the hell is a figment!'

Again, it's obvious. It's the wretched plate in her head. Kate said Lucian was injured and his brain scrambled. Maybe it's the same with Daisy, the plate pressing on her brain. Suppose nothing untoward occurred that night, no amiable ghosts, just Daisy going crazy.

Ghosts or madness? What would you choose? That night she'd dashed into the yard, shouting. 'Come on then! Let the house be a sanctuary for the odds and ends of life! Let every ghost from every age step right up! Bienvenue! Willkommen! I'd sooner have goose-bumps than egg for brains.'

It would seem the wounded animals accepted the invitation. Sanctuary is on-going.

* * *

Another week gone by and still no sight of Lucian. As a fox hunts by night so he's gone to ground. More animals arrive but as yet no more ghosts, still, it's odd that no matter how many lamps are lit there are always shadows.

There was a knock on the door. No one there, at least, no one human, just a duck with fishing line about its beak whereupon a tussle developed, the duck honking and Daisy screaming until she managed to shut it in the barn.

Finding it increasingly difficult to cope she asked Kate to come earlier and leave later. Kate shook her head. 'Sorry, hen,

I'm here too long as it is.'

'What about that Fairbrother chap? Would he give me a hand?'

'Are you serious?' yelled Kate. 'See that bucket over there catching rain? That's Dougie Fairbrother. Call the big feller! He'll sort it!'

No way will she call that miserable man, yet she can't keep up this manic pace. Late to bed and up at dawn, she has time to shower, to dress, and then out. The Gucci shades, however, are the first thing reached for when waking. 'You must think me vain,' she once said to a surgeon.

'If keeping the world at a distance helps, who am I to say nay.'

'My surgeon thinks I hide behind my specs.'

Kate sniffed. 'That's a man talking. Only you know what helps you get through. With you it's shades. With me,' she lifted her shirt, 'it's this.'

Kate never wears a bra. When she lifted her shirt there was an explosion of colour, her torso covered in tattoos, fantastic images twining about her midriff while scarlet blossoms clambered about her breasts.

'Wow! Whoever did this is very talented.'

'Yeah.' Kate observed her back in the mirror, 'a talented smack-head who couldn't wait to put his mark on me.'

'Jason did that?'

'Who else?'

'Did it hurt?'

'Of course! That's Jason. He gets off on pain.'

Daisy stared. All that exotic strangeness, she wondered if Kate's hero was barred from private viewing or merited dispensation. 'How did you two meet?' she said, trying to understand the relationship, an uptight military recluse and bohemian lover of life.

'Jason's mum knew mine.'

'Not Jason! How did you meet Lucian?'

'Ah.' There were secrets in that Ah, even more in the hesitation.

'We're not having an affair!'

'I never thought you were.'

'Yes, you did,' Kate stuffed the shirt into her pants. 'You're the same as the rest, bloody nosy!' Later that day Daisy sat trimming beans. Kate came to the kitchen, and leant on the table. 'I didn'ae mean to be huffy.'

'You were right. I was being nosy. But can you not see why? Talk about a mystery! Last night I was in the attic. You can see his place from here. Not a light on anywhere. Is he alone in that awful pile? No family?'

'None that I know of.'

'No brothers and sisters?'

'I guess not.'

'Girlfriends?'

'How should I know? I'm his cleaner not his pimp!' Clang! Off she went, and then, as though compelled, she returned. 'I don't know much about him. He keeps himself to himself.'

'I suppose he spends a lot of time in barracks,' conjectured Daisy, still thinking of the darkened windows in the house.

'Maybe. As I said I did think him retired.'

'Oh yes an explosion. Was he badly hurt?'

'So folks say.'

'Left with psychological problems, I think you said.'

'Aye,' snapped Kate, 'and I was wrong to say it.'

Okay, thought Daisy, change of subject. 'How came you to live in Scotland?'

'I came once on a school trip and fell in love with the land and the people. I've wanted to come back ever since.'

'Me too!' sighed Daisy.'

It was peaceful in the kitchen. The two Bs, Biddy who lives here these days, and Basil, the greyhound, cured of his sores, stretched out on the floor. It had stopped raining. The sun was breaking through and yet suddenly cold, as though Daisy had stepped into a fridge.

'We met at the bus station,' said Kate.

Daisy looked up. Kate was staring into space. A statue or mannequin in a shop window, she was absolutely still, a pastry cutter in one hand. When she began to speak it was with the same Northern directness but devoid of emotion.

She might have been reading a bus time-table.

'We met at the bus station. We'd been travelling all night, the kids trying to sleep and me fighting off drunks and piss artists. God knows what we looked like, dregs of the world I shouldn't wonder, Sean puking and Leon in dirty breeks. Lucian was in a taxi queue toting an army bag. I asked for a light for my ciggie. We were exhausted. I was broke but I had one currency left.'

'You don't have to explain,' Daisy was desperate for that voice to cease.

Kate carried on, speaking faster as though the words soiled her lip. '"Wanna quick poke, soldier?" I said. "Only cost you a tenner." Lucian gave me fifty quid. "There's a pub in the village, the Wayfarer," he said. "Tell them I sent you."

'Next day he offered me work as a cleaner. I thought, oh aye and what else. Nothing else, cleaner he said and cleaner he meant. Then he offered the trailer. Never took advantage of me or the kids. I don't know who he is and I don't care. I only know but for him my kids would be dead.'

The words stopped. For a shuddering minute Kate sat with the same empty expression on her face. Then she picked up her bag and left.

It was a week before she came again. One day she arrived, took up her duties as though never away, no explanation offered and none required.

* * *

Daisy found a battered wooden chest in the attic and dragged it down to the yard to use as a rabbit hutch. A drawer sticking, she was about to take a screwdriver to it when a jeep pulled into the yard. Lucian Nairne stooped under the lintel. 'Yours?' he said holding out a straw Panama hat.

'Where did you find that?'

'In the back of the jeep.'

'How did it get there?'

'No idea.' He leant on the door. 'What are trying to do?'

'Make a rabbit hutch.'

'I remember that chest. It was a gift from one of Minna's admirers.'

'From what I've heard she had more than a few.'

'She did.'

'She kept a guest house of sorts, airmen and so on.'

'She looked after folk.'

'I bet she did.'

He frowned. 'Don't want to believe everything you hear, Miss Banks. Try keeping an open mind. There's always folk willing to fill your ears with dirt. There's gossip, and then there's the truth.'

'I'd like to think I can recognise the difference.'

'I'd like to think the same but it doesn'ae always pan out.' He leaned on the door. 'Me, I'm gullible. I tend to believe everything I'm told. Like the time I heard a pretty woman with a pretty name was moving in next door. Turns out she's more than pretty but doesn'ae live up to her name.'

Daisy bit her lip. Let it go! He's winding you up.

'Now what does the name Daisy Banks evoke?' He continued. 'Maybe some squaddie holed up in the desert, the sun burning a hole in his ass. What does he imagine hearing the name? A summer day, bees humming, long grass, a bottle of JD, and the woman he loves in his arms.'

'It would be an imaginative squaddie that gets all that from two words.'

'Aye, and disappointed when he finds the honey bitter and the bank full of thistles.'

Daisy glared at him. 'Was there something in particular you wanted, or are you just here for a little target practice?'

'I heard you needed help with the zoo.'

'Don't believe everything you hear, Captain. Try to keep an open mind. There's always those willing to fill your ears with lies.'

'Ouch!' He clutched his chest. 'You got me.' He strode away, heading for the house, Daisy scrambling behind. In the kitchen he grabbed a chair. 'This skylight is driving me nuts!' he said, prizing the hatch off the loft.

'Leave it alone! The glazier did the damage. He should repair it.'

'Then you'll have nae roof. You should've used Archie Stubbs like I told Kate.'

'Unlike Kate I don't do everything I'm told.' She grabbed the leg of his jeans. 'I said leave it!'

'Let go my pants. Control yourself, Missy, or you'll have me thinking bad thoughts.' He leaned closer. 'What, no dark glasses?'

'It's not that sunny.'

'Didn'ae stop you before.'

'That was before.'

He smiled. 'Brava, Daisy.' T-shirt parting company with jeans to expose a muscular midriff, he flipped the trapdoor and swung up into the roof.

* * *

It wasn't only the skylight he fixed. He brought coops and cages. 'These have been kicking about the yard for years. I thought they'd come in handy.' Stables cleared and cages stacked inside, he made a bonfire of rubbish, smoke drifting across the yard and soot marks on his cheek. I should offer lunch, thought Daisy. 'There's a casserole if you're hungry,' she said, grudgingly.

'I'll pass, thank you.'

Miffed, she set about the animal feed. He came by the kitchen. 'What is that smell?' he said. 'Not the casserole, I hope.'

'It's for the animals.'

'That's as well. Gi' me the bucket.'

'You don't know where things are.'

'I know this place better than my own. As a lad it was my hidey-hole.' Tiny Tim, she stumped after. He talked but not to her. It was to the creatures, questioning, chastising. 'What have you done to yourself?' he said to a rabbit. 'That's a badger bite if ever I saw one. Come here, you dope.' Ears flopped, the dope approached. 'Look at that ear! Jesu, another day you'd have lost it.'

So it went, cage after cage, a man talking to his buddies. Daisy was beguiled. So were the animals. Even the goat was putty in his hands. Then Basil appeared and the atmosphere changed. Poor Basil, he arrived in such a state Daisy wondered whether he'd be better put to sleep.

'Why would he?'

'What?'

Lucian's eyes were storm clouds. 'Why would Basil be better off dead?'

Daisy gaped. She hadn't said a word.

'Come on,' he said, fists clenched. 'Tell me who gains by it. And don't give me that putting-to-sleep crap! We're talking killing not lullabies.'

'Why are you having a go at me? I didn't beat him.'

'No you wanted to pass the buck. Let's stick a needle in the dog! Let him go bye-byes and then we don't need to think about it!'

'Excuse me!' Daisy was livid. 'Basil is my dog now. He lives in my house under my care. See his bed in the kitchen next to the Aga? See his bowl of water and toys? Does it look like I'm thinking of putting him down?'

Lucian wasn't listening. He was on his knees, hugging the dog to his chest, berating someone only he could see. 'Wake up you idle sons-of-bitches!' he muttered. 'Why sleeping? Come on, Beings of Light! Raze 'em to the ground! And don't do it cheap! Trip the Exocets! Beat the living shit out of them! For what are they worth, these mortals, but to die as they wish all else to die!'

Tears dripped on the dog's muzzle. As he cursed he wept. Daisy wept with him. Time passed. The world turned and all was as before. Basil ambled toward the house and Lucian frowned. 'Why are you weeping?'

'I suppose because you were.'

'Me! You thought I wept over the dog?'

'Weren't you?'

'I have trouble with my eyes. My tear ducts get blocked. Weeping over a dog?' he snorted. 'I'm a soldier. Take more than that to make me cry.'

'What a horrible thing to say.'

'What's horrible about it. I'm merely stating a fact.'

'Fact or not I don't want to hear it.'

'No,' he said, lips tightening. 'You'd sooner bury your head in the sand.'

'If it's more on the subject of euthanasia save your breath! Why am I surprised you feel nothing? Sensitivity is a no-no in your line of business.'

'Shut up!' Eyes blazing, he raised his hand and a wall of anger passed through Daisy causing the fence to vibrate. 'What do you know about my line of business? You and your fragile face and Lady Di ways! You're a lamb in the fold while me, and others like me, are among the wolves.'

'Don't lecture me! I'm not Kate blinded by feelings for you. To her you're a combination of St George and Brad Pit. To me you're a bully. I wish she'd see through my eyes then maybe she wouldn't be so touchy.'

'There's nothing touchy about Kate Khan. She's a great human being, tough and resourceful. You obviously don't know her.'

'She's more than touchy, she's paranoid. I put that down to you. Six years of living next door to you can't be good for anyone.'

'Away, Daisy, you're so funny!' he said laughing.

'You go away! I can't be bothered talking to you.'

'I'm gone.' He strolled off into the sunlit day. 'If you're concerned about Kate try looking at life through her eyes. Her and her brood crammed together in a trailer is enough to make anyone touchy. You've room. If you want Kate and yourself to feel better, give her a home.'

* * *

All evening his words rang in her head. Daisy sat on the chaise, Basil stretched out at her feet. Poor old Basil. Why would anyone hurt him? Surely if you did it would scar your soul forever? She pulled up a pj leg scrutinising her own scars. Lucian said she was pretty. He's another Oscar, flirting. Oscar would meet a girl at a club. He'd name-drop all night, Daisy refusing to rise to the bait.

Oscar wasn't the best of the bunch but she misses the fun of chocolate in bed and quick, joyous sex. Life is so very heavy. Not much to laugh at unless it's the kitten running up the curtains. Let Kate and the kids move in! It will be good to have them. Then maybe Lucian will stay off her back.

Strange man, there was a moment in the yard when she thought she knew him. She almost said, 'You're the weirdo in the bobble hat.' Ridiculous idea yet she does equate Lucian with the memory of a man sitting by a bed, reading a book, tears in his eyes.

It's this house. This crazy, mad, Haunted House!

Shoving the cats aside she cued a CD and using the conservatory doors for a mirror began lifting weights. This house is tricky. It offers glimpses of other worlds while acting as a sleeping draught. 'Don't worry,' it says soothingly. 'Curtains dancing are okay. Dead pilots in the attic are okay. Soldiers in stained glass windows are okay! Relax and enjoy!'

'None of it is okay!' she panted. 'It's a madhouse and if I am to stay sane I need to keep my feet on the ground.'

The phone rang. 'I found what was making the drawer stick. It's what Chimneys was meant to be, a home for the homeless not a badly run rescue centre designed to make you feel better about yourself.'

'Are you done?'

'I'm done except to say this, Kate might confuse me with Brad Pitt but never St George.'

'Why wouldn't she?' said Daisy, sighing.

'Georgie is patron saint of England. He fought wee beasty dragons. I'm a Scot. St Andrew is my man.'

'Ho-hum!' Daisy yawned into the phone. 'And what did he fight?'

'Nothing much, a couple of demons maybe and the Power of Darkness.'

'As you say, nothing much. So is that it?'

'That's it other than to say watch out for the house. Keep the

doors locked and the rooms filled.'
    'Why? Will I save on gas?'
    'No, heartache.'

CHAPTER SIX

Obligations

The problem with the drawer turned out to be a wallet of photographs stuck at the back. Group shots of men in uniform smiling into the camera, half a dozen photographs, different men, and yet always the same smiling woman. That night Daisy dreamed she was checking the coops, making sure they were fox-proof. Rounding the corner of the Italian Garden she collided with that same woman. 'Sorry,' said Daisy. 'I didn't know you were here.'

'I'm always pulling weeds,' said the woman. 'Where this place is concerned a Light Keeper's work is never done.'

'Can I help you?' said Daisy.

'I hope so,' said the woman. 'Your name was given.' She stuffed a handful of weeds down the front of Daisy's pjs. 'Make sure you get to the root.'

Daisy woke at five to the kitten prodding her cheek. Eager to look at the photographs, she went downstairs. There was also a faded air mail bluey and a post-card in the wallet. The postcard showed a picture of the Taj Mahal, a message written on the back in strong male hand: a *man built this in memory of love. I bivouac in mud. Mortar fire rages overhead. Yet the memory of my time with you brings peace to heart.* There was an airmail bluey: *Thanks for the weekend and the bees. Where I'm going the only buzzing I'm likely to hear is anti-aircraft guns. I'll trundle about in my bucket doing my bit but it'll be you I'm thinking of. Keep a place for me in your kitchen and your heart.*

Both the postcard and airmail were unsigned. So much for Minna's critics! If the woman inspired that kind of affection she can't have been all bad.

Daisy called Kate. Her oldest picked up the phone. 'Jasmine, is your mum there?' The phone was snatched. A dual conversation ensued, Kate no longer orbiting Saturn, her feet firmly fixed on planet Earth. 'Just a minute, Daisy...Leon! Get those trainers off and your school shoes on! And don't think I didn't see that, you cheeky wee bugger! What's up, Daisy?'

'How would you feel about you and the kids moving in? There are masses of room. You'd be doing me a favour.'

'Seriously?'

Daisy crossed her fingers. 'Totally.'

They arrived that weekend, their menagerie adding to waifs and strays. At first all was quiet, the kids minding their manners for their landlady. That lasted a week, and then, unable to contain itself noise burst upon the scene. 'Get back here, Jassy! You're not going out with that muck on your face!'

'Mammy, I told you not to call me Jassy!'

'Jassy! Jassy! Jassy!'

'Shut your face, Leon!'

'Shut yours...Jassy!'

It was weeks before Daisy could tell one child from the next. As the mass expanded so individual personalities began to emerge. Jasmine was fifteen and fabulous, with hazel eyes and inky curls, who wore heavy make-up to mask a shy nature. Next is Sharonda, a rotund thirteen-year-old who giggled a lot but whimpered in her sleep. Sean is a spindly child with pebble glasses and tombstone teeth who regularly bunks off school, slipping back to Six Chimneys dividing his time between *Studio Ghibli* and a rat cage secreted in his room; thought to be twelve, he glued his skinny body to Kate during a stay at a women's refuge. Badass Leon wears Armani jeans over a non-existent bum, a diminutive eleven-year-old, and the worry of Kate's life, he spends his time shoplifting. Tulip, seven last February, is blonde, beautiful, and partially deaf. Nothing is said of the fathers: Sean parents as mysterious as Sean, Leon's father worked a hot-dog stand by night and Kate as punch bag during the day, and Tulip's father – the dreaded Jason – at Strangeways.

Lately, Kate is quiet about Jason. One evening, her tongue softened by Beaujolais, she started again. 'Handy with his fists was Jason.' She pulled down a punctured lower lip. 'I got that giving him a cold cup of coffee.'

When Daisy shook her head she nodded. 'You're wondering if he was such a shite why stay. I suppose it was for the same reason I stayed with others, looking for love in the wrong places. I was three when Pa crept into my room spinning his lies, "do it or your mammy dies." Mammy couldn't have cared less; as long as he brought home his pay she turned a blind eye. I couldn't wait to leave home and went with the first man who treated me kindly. Jason was the worst. He came home one night drunk and set about Tulip. I went for him with a poker, his teeth flying like Polo mints. He fled, but when we were a-bed, came back with a can of petrol setting fire to the house.'

'Oh Kate!'

'We landed in hospital and him on the run.'

'Do you think he knows where you are?'

'Nowadays you can't keep anything secret.' Having railed against the worst Kate must praise the best. 'Girls nowadays don't know a good man when they see him. If I were younger I'd be onto that bonnie lad like a limpet!'

Since the Basil incident Daisy hasn't seen the 'bonnie lad.' Once again he's retreated to the shadows. Biddy is here, a living mosaic. Of her master nothing is known until Monday when Kate laid a wad of notes on the kitchen table. 'He knew I'd want to pay rent so sent my wages in advance.'

'I hadn't thought of you paying rent.'

'I had.' The stoic Northern attitude bothered Daisy. For a time she kept out of the way, limping up and down stepladders dislodging spiders from centuries old webs. As the days went by she grew used to ferocious arguments and to boots pounding the stairs. Once again mortal flesh has been brought into sanctuary – things will never be the same again.

* * *

A man from Melrose cleaned the window. 'Wonderful piece of work', he said, from his scaffolding heights, 'unique of its kind.' He then presented Daisy with a bill which in itself was unique clearing all her spare cash.

'I'm expecting great things of you,' she polished the Knight's spurs. 'So you'd better do something, not just stand there looking hopeless.'

Empty purse aside, the window is beautiful, every wipe of a cloth revealing new detail, panels left and right depicting pastoral images of men working in the fields. Lower borders show battle scenes while the upper panel suggests The Day of Judgement. Sunlight pours through the window. Poor fellow trapped behind glass, she can't resist giving the Knight a friendly pat but must be careful since seeing him she thinks of Lucian. Too much of that and she'll go down with Kate's disease.

Wanting to know more about the house she went to the local library. The librarian was scathing about Minna. 'The woman had no shame. Young fellers from the American air-base ask about the house. I had one here last month, "did I know where Pa was stationed during WW2. He'd talked so much of Minna before he died I need to see it." I was appalled. He made Six Chimneys a shrine rather than a bawdy house.'

'Was it a bawdy house?'

'My mammy wouldn'ae let me walk by the hoos ne'er mind call.'

'So you set the young fellow straight.'

'I did. I said the house is respectable now and we didn'ae want a repeat of the other stuff.' Daisy was on her way out when the woman whispered in her ear. 'I didn'ae mention the drug business.'

'Drug business!'

Directed to back copies of a local newspaper Daisy discovered Minna ran a column in *Gardener's Weekly* on the medicinal uses of ancient herbs. The column didn't last, Minna arrested for cultivating marijuana, the headline, '*Gardener Grows Own Brand of Magic*.'

* * *

Daisy flew from Edinburgh for a check-up leaving Sean in charge of the animals. 'Nae worries, Daisy, I'll treat 'em like my ain rattys.' Having seen the love lavished on said 'rattys' she felt she couldn't ask more.

The orthopaedic surgeon talked of the scars on her legs. 'I'm afraid these will always be a blot on a lovely landscape yet you're alive. We must be grateful for that. You're not as buoyant as you might be. I think you might benefit from a chat with Professor Wilkinson.'

'And who is he?' said Isla.

'The professor is a psychoanalyst.'

'Blot on a landscape!' hissed Isla, as they left the surgical wing. 'I wanted to wring his scrawny neck. To whom should we be grateful, God?'

Daisy waited in the hospital cafe while Isla went to the pharmacy. The cafe overlooked the physio wing where every day she was put through hell and where only a chap in a bobble hat believed she'd walk again.

* * *

On the pretext of picking up a prescription Isla leant on a receptionist before parking Daisy with an equally startled analyst. 'I'm sorry about my mother,' Daisy apologised. 'She's a force to be reckoned with.' The analyst shrugged. 'I have a mother-in-law of similar nature. She lays waste to all before her.'

Specs on his nose, he clicked on a console. 'I've had little time to acquaint myself with your case, so, why don't you tell me about Daisy Banks.'

Minus a few omissions, namely houses that move, phantoms in the attic and medieval soldiers trapped in glass, she offered a potted history of her life.

'And Mr Curran, has he been in touch?'

'No and he's not likely to. Whenever Oscar feels he's let himself down, which in all honesty isn't often, he'll run in the opposite direction.'

'How did he let himself down?'

Daisy thought about it. 'He's a brilliant musician but never gets beyond the thought. He'll set a couple of bars down. Someone will call, Amsterdam or the States, and he's gone. Pretty much as he did with me.'

'And how did that make you feel?'

'Worthless.'

'And is that how you feel now?'

'Yes.'

'And who have you let down?'

'I'm not sure that I've let anyone down, unless it's those in the house.'

'You mean the family you've taken in, Mrs Khan and her children?'

'No, not them.' Daisy stared at him. Why, she thought, is he wearing white? What is it with doctors, nurses, and surgeons, that they must wear white? And what's with the golden eyes? 'You have extraordinary eyes.'

'Have I?' He took off his specs and rubbed his eyes. 'It's been a very long day. I wonder they're not pink with orange spots.'

Daisy felt sorry for him. 'You could've done without this.'

'Not at all! You're an interesting case.' He replaced his specs reminding Daisy that she did that, put glass between her and the world. 'You need to feel useful, Miss Banks. The human spirit needs to create. Maybe you and Ms Khan should create together.'

The next day, watching Kate turn another perfect chocolate sponge onto a tray, Daisy made a suggestion. 'We don't we start a cookery business?'

'What?'

'You and me and cookery? We've got a kitchen and time to spare. At least, *I* have time to spare. We could be missing an opportunity.'

'Doing what exactly?'

'Making cakes and puddings and selling them.'

'I don't know about that. My stuff is good enough for me and the kids. I'm not sure anyone else would want to eat it.'

'You're a fabulous cook. Better than anyone I know. I could do the savoury stuff, soups and pies. I might as well make use of that diploma.'

'How would we sell it?'

'From the back of my wagon.'

'What about you? Are you ready for something like this?'

'Ready as I'll ever be.'

'Will we...you...be able to cope?'

'If I take my time, and not panic. See?' Daisy caught up Basil's paws, and slowly and carefully waltzed him round the kitchen. 'Onward and upward! No more hiding behind the past. We'll start with the Bistro in the village.'

'That's an Italian restaurant,' said Kate dubiously, 'but then I ken Italians eat pudding same as anyone. We could call the stuff by appropriate names, say Verona's Vermicelli or Firenze's Flambeaux?'

'Or Daisy's Dumplings.' Daisy saw her reflection in the mirror. She'd regained a little weight. Her breasts were back, as proved by the cleavage.

'Or Padua's Puddings,' countered Kate, standing behind her, observing a similar reflection with her own more generous breasts.

* * *

It was a month or more before they believed in the plan. Then having burnt a few trial dishes and binned many more the Pudding Club was launched.

They sold the first batch to Ziggy at the petrol station.

'Ziggy?' Daisy rubbed the car window, heat from the puddings steaming up the glass. 'Isn't he the guy that ran off with Lucian's fiancé?'

'She dumped him. He crept back home with his tail between his legs like the shite he is. If he wasn'ae living next door to the gas station and handy for the pumps he'd no have got his job back.'

'Shall you tackle him?' said Daisy, hopefully. 'You know him.'

'It's no good me talking to him. You go. Looking the way you do, all helpless and lovely wi' your wee crutch, you could sell shit to a shovel.'

Daisy limped up to the garage. The man, Ziggy, rushed to the door.

'Good evening,' stuttered Daisy, cheeks flaming. 'I wonder if I might interest you in the latest list of our cakes. I have samples in the car if you...'

...minutes later they were stacking the last carton into the shop fridge, Kate breaking open a box of shortbread biscuits and passing them and business cards, about the forecourt. The Pudding Club was off to a start.

* * *

Daisy couldn't sleep. They'd had a busy evening with an order for an old people's rest home, three dozen Angel Heart cookies and economy size Monsoon Curry sauce. She sat watching the moon rise. Now the holly trees are clipped she could see Minna's Tomb from the window.

Unhappy about the grave, Daisy had planted a holly bush as a marker. It's likely it holds the remains of the RAF pilot whose love for Minna held him in thrall. As for the men in the photographs, the soldiers and airmen, Daisy wondered if they returned to Chimneys hale and hearty or only as memories, the woman they adored breathing them in as bittersweet perfume.

Thinking this way she was suddenly cold, breath misting the air. Then with a humming in her ears, and the sound of wings flapping, a porthole appeared in the bedroom wall. Skin prickling, she bent peering through the hole to what looked to be a hospital on the other side. A man sat by a bed reading a book, she could hear him, '...*when a child loves you for a long, long time, not just to play with, but really loves you, then you become real!*'

The words faded, the hole closed up, the ends drawing together like a purse.

Pop! It was gone. Instead, there was Jasmine in the doorway, a scarlet G-string above her jeans emphasising a tiny waist. 'Hi Daisy.'

For a moment Daisy couldn't speak. Then she nodded. 'Hello, Jasmine.'

'Can my friend stay over? We're doing this play and we gotta rehearse.'

'Sure. What is it you're doing?'

'I'm like this spirit attached to cables and have to fly around. It's a good part but I'm no keen on the name Ariel. People will think I'm a washing-powder.' 'No-one would ever think that. You're far too beautiful.'

'Wicked. And Daisy, I don't mind you calling me Jassy.'

'No, you are Jasmine. I couldn't shorten your name. It's far too lovely.'

'It was my grandma's name. She like got cancer and died.'

'I'm sorry. You must miss her.'

'I still see her. She comes when I'm asleep.'

'She comes when you're asleep.'

'Uh-huh. She tells me to get on with my hairdressing course and not mess with Robbie Baxter 'cos he's like using skag.'

* * *

Daisy told Kate of the porthole. Kate suggested she was remembering when she was in hospital. 'And the man reading a children's fairy tale?'

Kate whacked dough onto a floured board. 'Aye, that is a bit weird.'

'I seem to be dreaming all the time. The other night it was about Minna.'

'You sure it was a dream and not Minna herself?'

'Huh?'

'Oh, come on!' She laughed at Daisy's face. 'A little old lady-ghost flitting about weeding borders cann'ae be so bad.'

'Does she do the laundry as well?'

'Stay here much longer and maybe you'll find out.'

'How long did the other families stay?'

'Long enough not to want to come back! It's well known she wanders about. Folks say she really loved this house. Maybe this is her idea of heaven.'

'I wish I'd known before I put in my ten cents.'

'Would you no have bought the place if you did?'

'No! Yes! Probably! You'd think, though, if anyone was going to haunt the place it would be the chap in the grave.'

'It is a feller then?'

Daisy shrugged. 'I don't know. I'm only guessing.'

* * *

Afternoon wore into evening until a face on the TV took Daisy's attention.

'Oscar Curran!'

Kate glanced over spoon. 'Is that your ex?'

'That's him.'

'What's he doing on *Richard and Judy?*'

'That's what I'd like to know.' Daisy turned up the volume. Richard was speaking: '...*play it so viewers can hear a little of Oscar's latest composition.*'

Music faded in, dancers in the background weaving about.

'I know that,' said Kate. 'The kids play it all the time.'

'I heard it too but didn't associate it with Oscar.'

'It's major. He must be raking it in.'

Daisy sat glued to the set. Oscar was at his most amusing, cracking jokes and making Richard laugh. Then eyes sombre, and

Liverpudlian accent thicker than Daisy remembered, he spoke of his childhood. 'Four-years old and at the mercy of the world,' he was saying. 'If it hasn't happened to you then you can't begin to understand. You're never free of the ghetto. That's why I call my song 'The Playground.' It's what me and kids like me never had.'

'Nice looking,' said Kate as the ads rolled.

'Yes,' said Daisy, shaken to think that in that five minute interview she'd learned more about the man than in years of sharing a bed.

'Great body.'

'Yes.'

'Lying through his shiny white teeth though.'

'Lying! About what?'

'Quite a bit I'd say. Some of what he says has a ring of truth but I doubt it's really his life. Ten to one there's a guy in front holding up an autocue.'

'No,' Daisy protested. 'Oscar's mother abandoned him when he was little. He told me about it.'

'Sorry, hen, but it doesn'ae smell right. It's too tidy. And the figures don't add up. I had my kids in care. I know what goes on.'

'What happened to you, Kate?'

'Men happened.' Kate's expression was bleak. 'I didn't leave my kids because I didn'ae love 'em. I left because of what they might find at home, some drunk ready to slap them about the head or show them his willy.'

'You've had a rough time.'

'I've drunk too much booze and dreamed too many foolish dreams.'

Kate lit a cigarette and talked of her life in Salford. None of it said in a lilting Scottish accent, straight Mancunian, her chin settled in a stolid line – no embroidery, hard facts and work-worn hands playing with a fag packet.

She spoke in the same zombie-voice, as though it was the only way she could relive such times. 'Another thing, I don't get the accent. I spent years Moss-side and know the real thing when I hear it. He may have been born in Liverpool but with decent parents. I'd like to bet that right now some poor cow is staring at the TV wondering what she did to deserve a scumbag for a son.'

Daisy protested. 'What about the saxophone and his time in Music College? He told me his foster parents helped him get a scholarship and that he worked nights in a hotel kitchen to help with fees.'

'And I'm fecking Gloria Gaynor! This is some PR's notion of a Profile. He's being packaged and sold to the punters as the ghetto kid made good. As for foster parents, how many in his supposed neck of the woods can afford to buy their kids dinner ne'er mind a saxophone. Sharonda's pestered me for years to let her do music. I've nae money for a kazoo never mind a cello.'

'Why would anyone want to project that image?'

'Because bland doesn't sell! He's a hustler! If you could travel back in time you'd find the exact moment when he and the PR feller chose to reinvent Oscar Curran. It's likely he did go to music school. Whatever, it worked for him. Come on, Daisy, wake up and smell the bullshit! You lived with him. Did you never think he was a phony?'

'No, never.' She looked out of the window. Some weeks ago she told Lucian Nairne she could recognise the truth when heard. It seems she may well be blind as well as deaf. 'I never did meet the foster parents. Come to think of it I don't believe he ever sent or received a Christmas card, nor for that matter a birthday card. I thought it was because he'd sooner not remember the past.'

Kate smiled grimly. 'He doesn'ae want to remember. The ghetto is fashionable. I bet if he could change the colour of his skin he'd do it! This is the man. Get used to it. You couldn't prize him away now from the image even if you tried. He not only believes the lie. He is the lie.'

CHAPTER SEVEN

A Thousand Names

They were in the High Street, Lamar's Hair Studio, Kevin with scissors poised.

'Are you sure about this, Jasmine?' said Daisy.

Jasmine nodded. 'It'll be mint.'

Daisy was in a state of panic. Why is she thinking of having her hair cut when Oscar liked it long? 'Don't you dare,' he used to say whenever she suggested a shorter style. 'Short hair is for old women and dykes.'

Time is supposed to be a healer but where Oscar is concerned neither time nor distance lessened the hurt. Seeing him on TV brought old feelings to the surface along with new, and painful, intimations of fraud. It's true she can't recall him phoning or visiting his foster family. At the time she thought his memories were too painful. Now she doesn't know what to think. Not that it mattered. Her opinion, like her love of him is irrelevant.

'Well?' said Jasmine, breaking into Daisy's thoughts.

'Hack away! I'm sick of the old me.'

The makeover was decided yesterday. Daisy only said d'you think a bob might suit me? The next she knew she's under the microscope.

'What d'you reckon, Shaz, layers?'

'Yeah and lose the boring colour.'

'I'm thinking spiky bits about the eyes. She's got Kate Moss cheekbones so she can handle it.'

A lamb to the slaughter Daisy waited to be shorn by an effete shepherd with pink Mohican. Two hours later her hair is transformed into a layered cut with bags of movement and shine, the stylist adding golden highlights while whizzing the curls about her ears into a delicate shade of apricot.

'Wicked,' said Jasmine.

'Aren't I?' beamed Daisy. Thrilled, she took the girls to lunch and on to the mall where she bought boots for Jasmine and sandals for Sharonda.

'Check these out!' Jasmine proffered a pair of scarlet *Kurt Geiger* heels.

'Too high.'

'Don't stress it, Daisy. They're wedges. They would spread your balance.'

She didn't buy. There is a limit to courage.

They took the escalator to the Teen-Scene department. 'If you're going to be a star, Jasmine, you'll need something luminous.'

'I've already got my dress. The needlework teacher made it.'

'Don't tell me, three yards of dirty muslin and bent tinsel wings.'

Jasmine nodded gloomily. 'Minging.'

'We can do better than that.' Daisy rattled through favourite labels. 'If we don't find a suitable outfit here I'll eat my crutches. Now this,' she said, pulling out a froth of pale green lace, 'has fame written all over it.'

'O-Mi-God!'

'Doesn't it make your mouth water?'

'And this for Sharonda?' a white leather mini-skirt with tassels.

Amid shrieks of excitement the girls retired to the changing rooms.

Daisy then bought a top for Kate, a phone for Leon, a brace of terrapins for Sean, and a vanity case for Tulip. She returned to Teen Scene and was matching a sweater to a skirt when Lucian stopped at her elbow.

'Afternoon, Daisy. You're looking well.'

So did he! Six-three of honed muscle, hand-tailored khaki jacket and pants that fitted like a glove, skin a sexy burnt copper and hair streaked by the sun, Lucian was as the girls would say – wicked! What's more he knew it.

'Everything tickety-boo at the house?'

Tickety-boo? 'Fine, thanks.'

'Bairns no driven you out of your mind?'

'Not yet.'

'I'm sorry I haven'ae been in touch.' He flicked nonexistent fluff from his jacket. 'I'm no in control of my life. The army whistles and I jump.'

Daisy could only stare. To confirm her opinion three women, who until they saw him were heading in the opposite direction, switched route, and like synchronised swimmers, arrowed back to crowd about him.

When Daisy went to move away he took her arm. 'I don't believe you've met my neighbour. Miss Banks owns Chimneys.' Here it comes, thought Daisy. In a rolling movement three pairs of eyes passed down her body, paused at the crutch, and then they looked anywhere but the crutch.

'And how are you finding it?' said one.

'Fine, thank you.'

Like butterflies their glances flickered back and forth before settling on Lucian. 'Lucian, darling, do come to the ceilidh next month.'

'I don't know about that.'

'Come! You owe it to us. There's an awful shortage of men.'

'Maybe, but only if my neighbour agrees to come with me.'

Daisy regarded him blankly.

'A ceilidh is a local hop, you wee Sassenach,' he said, grinning. 'You know, where folk jump up and down and make fools of themselves.'

'I don't think so, but thank you.' She grabbed a skirt off the rail. 'Excuse me. I need to try this on. So nice to meet you all. Have fun at the hop!'

She perched on a stool in the fitting-room and then poked her head out. Lucian was still there, leaning against the counter. 'You didn'ae need to hide, Daisy,' he said. 'I would've defended you against the ravening hordes.'

'Were they ravening?'

'Aye and then some! You're probably used to it. Beautiful women come up against that kind of hostility all the time so I'm told.'

Daisy grimaced. 'How long have you been waiting to say that?'

'Since May 12th 2006.'

'May 12th...? But that was when Oscar and I came to the wedding.'

He nodded. 'You were outside the house peering in. I was peering out.'

Daisy squirmed. 'You must have thought us a right pair of fools.'

'I thought you were beautiful.'

'What were you doing there?'

'Taking care of a couple of things, fixing windows and doors, mending tiles on the roof, keeping body and soul together.'

'You love that old place.'

'Yeah, for my sins.'

'Were you surprised when it turned out I was the one wanting the house?'

'Not at all. I knew you'd come back. It was only a matter of time.'

A matter of time? The world shifted. Reality came adrift. Once again Daisy was gazing through a peep-hole in time to a hospital bed. A monitor ticked. There was pain and a medicinal smell. A man was leaning over the bed, his mouth was moving. He was saying. 'I know this is neither the time...'

'...nor place but there are things I need to say.'

Click! She was back in the Mall. It was Lucian speaking.

'Are you listening to me?' he said.

'What is it?' she whispered, gripped by a sense of urgency.

'I get it you've no fondness for me. Why would you? I'm a miserable man who spends time teaching other miserable men how to maim and kill. Even today with the fancy duds and gleaming smile I'm a bad risk. All the same, I need you to know I've been waiting for you all my life.'

There was passion in his voice. His eyes dark and intense and his face white beneath the tan. 'You're all I think about. Night or day it makes no difference.' Nails digging into her palm, he held her hand. 'Finding you here I took a chance to tell you how I feel, that if you need me I'll come. Does'nae matter where or when. Day or night, heaven or hell I'll be there.'

The words were known. They'd been said before and by this man!

'Do you hear what I'm saying?' he was demanding, his voice coming through a fog. 'Are you listening? Am I getting through?'

'Hey, Lucian!'

The girls stood watching. Snap! The moment was gone. Nothing had happened and yet everything was changed. 'Love the buzz-cut.' Jasmine tossed her hair. The army man again he took the banter. 'Good isn't it.' Sharonda giggled. 'You're awful brown. You been fighting a war some place?'

'I don't do wars. I'm a geezer. I do a little bit of this and a little bit of that.' His manner sharpened. 'Talking of geezers, tell Leon I'm back. He'll know what I mean. And take these,' he passed a couple of packages. 'They were bought for you so you might as well have them.'

The girls ran to the changing rooms. The spell broken, he shrugged. 'I'm sorry,' he said, eyes bleak. 'I shouldn't have spoken.'

Daisy shook her head. He had no right to be sorry, not after that.

A cross-shaped stud in his ear caught the light.

'You wear an earring,' she said, inane comment. 'Doesn't the army have rules about that sort of thing?'

'They do but I don't always follow them.'

'I thought Kate said you had retired.'

'Kate wouldn't know what I do.'

'Are you staying a while or moving on to places unknown?'

'I'm here for a couple of days then I've business in London.'

'Anywhere exciting?' Horrible conversation!

'The army reckons I'm Humpty Dumpty and a shrink the one to put me back together again. The army loves a challenge.'

'And can he put you back together?'

'I doubt there's glue strong enough.'

* * *

There was a fearful row earlier, Kate determined the family should be at the school to support Jasmine, and Leon determined not to be there. 'I'm no having a sister of mine make a fecking laughing stock of me!' he yelled, whereupon his mother scrubbed his mouth with soap. 'I'm gonna tell Esther Ranzten of you,' he wept. 'She'll call the polis on you.'

'Go ahead! Esther Ranzten can have you.'

When everyone was calmed down and Kate promised to find money for a holiday in Benidorm – and Daisy to video *Enders* – they left. 'What a performance,' she said to Tulip who was excused because of a cough. Out of the corner of her eye Daisy saw Sean – also excused – sidle past the door with the aquarium. 'Don't you think they'd be better in the garden room, Sean?'

'They're best with me. Terrapins get lonely.'

Daisy loved Sean. So ugly, bless him, ugly and devoted to the ugly.

'When they were handing out beauty our Sean was back of the queue,' said Kate. 'He's one of they hobgoblins that naebody but his mammy could love.'

With the coming of the Khans the menagerie trebled – Trilby a flash of yellow in a twittering world. Animal and human partnerships are formed. Jasmine takes care of L'il Kim, the pony.

Sharonda has the wall-eyed goat. Sean caters for the slimy stuff. Tulip bunks with a house bunny and Boff-Two with Daisy. The Siamese and Leon remain aloof, Leon preferring *Kill-a-Cop* in the arcade.

Earlier this week there was a difference of opinion, Daisy concerned Tulip struggled with deafness. 'What about Lucian?'

'I'm no asking him.'

'What if I phone Isla? She had trouble with her ears a while back and swears by this guy in Harley Street. I'm sure she.....'

'Forget it! The kid's been messed about enough.'

Alone with Tulip, the child's nose touching the TV screen, Daisy decided to risk Kate's wrath. The number was on the fridge. Not that she needed it. It was imprinted in her brain. 'Yes?' shouted some old buffer.

'Could I speak with Lucian?'

'Who?'

'Sorry, wrong number.' She tried again.

'The offices of Somerset and Painswick are closed. Business hours are...'

'Damn!' She tried one last time. It was picked up.

'Lucian Nairne.'

'At last! I thought you might be the Chinese laundry. I got everyone else, an old man woken from a nap and the service for the offices of Somerset and...'

'Painswick. That's my notary. What are you doing calling him?'

'I have no idea. It was only you I wanted.'

A long silence.

'Hello?' Daisy thought she'd been cut off. 'Anyone there?'

'Yes, I'm still here.' Sound boomed, his voice crystal clear. 'I'm just shocked that any woman – ne'er mind the one woman in the world I care about – would speak to me after the way I behaved the other day.'

Daisy's toes curled. It was a good start. 'You did say that I could.'

'My God, yes! Any time! Any place! Anywhere!'

'It's about Tulip.'

'Is it only about Tulip? It's okay to talk about Tulip. I'm willing to talk about Tulip all day and every day if it keeps you with me.'

Daisy's toes curled tighter. 'It's her ears. She's not getting better and Kate being busy I was wondering if you might suggest a course of action.'

'If it's medical advice you want Kate knows my thoughts on the matter.'

'But someone needs to do something.'

'What would you like me to do?'

'Help her.'

'Why don't you?'

'I would if I knew what to do. I had thought of a course in lip-reading. Or perhaps I could even learn to sign?'

'Where is she now?'

'With me in my sitting-room. That's why I'm whispering.'

'Go give her a hug. A hug from the lovely Daisy will make her feel good. And if there has to be a use for the lips, let your lips kiss her good night.'

It was Daisy's turn to be silent.

'Modern medicine can perform miracles. A shrink trying to piece together a broken man has merit, yet a kiss from you would set my soul alight.' The line went dead. She redialled but got Somerset and what's-it, finally leaving a message suggesting where they could shove their crossed line.

Tulip was brushing Boff-2. A couple of months ago that little spark of life was almost extinguished. Now even with stunted paw he is Master of the Universe. 'Pre-natal,' the vet had said examining the paw. 'It ought to be amputated or he'll have trouble when he's older.' That paw gave Daisy the shivers. Boffin's three paws and now Boff-Two! She asked Kate what she thought about animals and reincarnation. 'If it means Jason Myers a Dung Beetle shovelling shit all day I'm all for it.'

Daisy sat beside Tulip. 'Sweet, isn't he?'

'I don't like his name.'

'What would you like to call him?'

'Kylie.'

'That is a good name. I like Kylie. I used to play her song all the time when I was little. Do you know the one I mean?'

Tulip jumped up and began to sing and dance. '*I should be so lucky.*' Daisy joined in, stomping about, floorboards rattling. The attic door pushed open, and eyes alight with curiosity, the Siamese slid into the room followed by Basil and Biddy. It was when Sean's ferret arrived, and a stream of moths through the open window, that Daisy stopped dancing.

'What's happening?' said Tulip.

'I don't know.'

The dogs wagged their tails and barked. The ferret rolled over and lay on his back, furry belly exposed. The Siamese, barometers of all things weird, puffed out like Michelin Men. Then in a living wreath of white the moths encircled Tulip's head. She ducked and squealed. 'It tickles.'

Daisy was next, moths clinging to her sweater, their tiny forms emitting pulsating energy that surged from her head down to her toes.

Gradually the lovefest ceased, the moths leaving as silently as they came, and the animals heading one-by-one out the door.

'I'm tired,' said Tulip, feet dragging. 'I'm away to my bed.' Daisy crawled to the bedroom and stripping to bra and pants fell into bed.

Four in the morning she dreamt she sat on the tomb alongside Minna.

'...the trick,' Minna was saying, 'is to not take any of this seriously. Believe in what you do yet maintain a healthy disrespect for all things "spooky".'

Daisy offered a piece of ginger-snap. 'Is that what you did?'

Minna ate the cake. 'No, more's the pity. I started cocking a snook at all things medical. Bad mistake! These guys study for years. The last thing they need is an Oxbridge blue-stocking telling them where they went wrong. We're none of us wrong; we look through different ends of a microscope.'

'So what should I do here in this house?'

'Three rules – listen to the Boss, stay real, and watch out for Shadows.'

'Shadows? You mean devils and things?'

'Away, Daisy, you and your demons, though you do need to be aware of such things. They do exist. There are many in this house hidden away in dark places and many more where you'd least expect to find them.'

'What does a demon look like?'

'There's no standard variety. They're not like a bag of spuds, small, medium and large. They come in all shapes and sizes.'

'How will I recognise them? '

'You'll recognise them. They usually introduce themselves.' Minna jumped down. 'Anyway, I'm off. Stay real, Daisy. Stick with the business in hand. Forget about demons and with a bit of luck they'll forget about you.'

CHAPTER EIGHT

The Shadows

Kate pulled the curtains and sunlight flooded the bedroom.

Daisy shielded her eyes. 'What time is it?'

'Half past seven! If we're to get that order ready for the ceilidh you need to be up and doing.'

'Don't fuss,' said Daisy dragging the duvet over her head. 'They don't need the stuff until Saturday so Friday's plenty soon enough to start.'

'It is Friday.'

Friday! What happened to Thursday? There's a vague recollection of tea-trays placed by the bed and of Kate and Jasmine leaning over her, their faces filled with light, and Jasmine saying, 'leave her, Mammy, she's dreaming.'

Twenty-four hours she slept, and as Jasmine said she dreamed, and as she dreamed the angel walked down out of the window.

'Hello Daisy. How are you?'

'I'm okay.'

'Okay? What kind of a word is that?'

'It's a word. I suppose it means I'm fine.'

'Fine? That's another useless word, though thinking about it, it sums up the human race, bland while hiding a multitude of sins.'

Oh dear! His Holiness is in a bad mood. Then he is a grouch, always making you feel less than worthy. And last night... yesterday...whenever, the scowl on his face said she was not to enjoy the cosiest of dreams.

'Where's the Harley?'

'I don't need the bike. We're beyond symbols now.'

'Symbols?'

'Yes, symbols, you know, bike + movement+ brmm-brmm = what?'

'Travelling?'

'Right. You are dreaming therefore you occupy a teensy-weensy portion of the astral world, which means your slightest thought, correction, *my* slightest thought, will provide all the momentum we need.'

The cockney accent had been replaced by crisp county tones.

'What happened to the bovver boy?'

'Gone along with the rest of the useless data,' he'd replied, his huge white wings shrivelling like discarding snake's skin.

'Your lovely wings!'

Golden hair flying he shook himself. 'Yes lovely but heavy as hell and cumbersome to steer. I wear them merely to enhance the image.'

'What image?'

'The heroic fighter pilot.' He spoke and trappings of an angel morphed into an RAF uniform. The beautiful face remained, his hair, however, in keeping with the '40s, and the only visible wings those embroidered on his jacket. He doffed his cap. 'Squadron Leader D'angelo at your service.'

'Oh, really?'

'Not really. Just getting into the role. Loosening up,' he rolled his shoulders and flexed his fingers. 'Method acting, a little Stanislavski touch, you dig?'

Daisy yawned. 'Is that it now or are you going to become

someone else?'

'I can be whoever and whatever I choose. Watch!' A multitude of images overlaid his form, man, woman, and child, a house, town and city, one vision giving way to the next. 'I can be all things, a bird, a plane, Superman! But today by way of making you smile, I am C for...' He unbuttoned his jacket to reveal a vest with golden C embroidered over the heart. 'Charley.'

'Charley! That can't possibly be your name.'

'What's wrong with Charley? It's a good name and easily remembered. Now look, Daisy, if this is to work we're to have a relaxed attitude, none of this bowing and scraping.'

'When was the last time I bowed and scraped?'

'You never do. And why is that, exactly?'

'You don't inspire it. Well, you do, but I didn't want a C on your jacket. I'd hoped it was a G, as in guardian angel. I mean, isn't that what angels do?'

'Some do, some don't. Some would spit in your eye sooner than save your life. You'll have to wait and see how I turn out. Let's go. The future waits.'

He slid his arm about her waist and Daisy was lifted up out of her body. Looking back she saw a pale woman asleep in a bed. 'Is that me?'

'Well, it ain't chopped liver.'

'Phew! You are in a bad mood.'

'So will you be when you see what's on the programme.'

'Bring it on,' she said, sighing. 'I'm as ready as I'll ever be.'

'It's already here, Daisy,' he said sadly. 'All you have to do is look.'

'Daisy!' Kate's voice broke through the recollection. 'Are you getting up or do I have to cook these pies on my own!'

'I'm on my way!' Daisy swung her legs over the bed. 'What's the rush? Anybody would think there was a fire.'

Fire………….!

The word exploded in her head. They died! Every one burnt to death, skin crackling like bacon and skeletal hands clawing at the air! She ran to the bathroom and threw up. 'God's sake!' Kate pounded up the stairs. 'What's the matter with you?' Daisy shook her head. How d'you tell your best friend that last night you saw her die and her children with her.

Last night the angel took her to where children lay sleeping, the Khans as they were some years ago, side-by-side their faces haloed by light.

'What is that light?' Daisy had hovered above the beds.

'The light of love watching over them.'

'It is beautiful. Can I touch them?'

'Wait and watch!' Darkness filled the place. A snakelike shape slid into view. There was the stench of petrol. A match flickered and flames roared!

She'd screamed. 'Why are you showing me this?'

'This is fear, Kate's fear; a living force that left undefeated becomes a prison. The day will come when she, and you, must face up to fear.'

* * *

Jasmine talked of her play. 'My teacher said I was the best Ariel and that I could wash his whites any day.'

'That's great.'

'You okay? You seem a bit down?'

'Too much sleep has given me a headache.'

'Tell me about it! We thought you and Tulip were dead!'

'Tulip overslept?'

Responding to her name Tulip appeared.

'Hi, sleepyhead.' Daisy patted her shoulder. 'You okay?'

'Mint!' said Tulip tucking into a bowl of cereal.

Tulip might be none the worse for her hibernation. Daisy felt very frail and phoned home. 'Hello, Mum.'

'What's wrong?'

'Nothing.'

'Yes there is. I can tell by your voice. Aren't the new crutches working out?'

'I'm managing with one now.'

'Should you be doing that? You don't want to bugger up the system.'

'It's okay, Mum, my legs are fine,' said Daisy realising it was true. Her psyche may be rock bottom but the rest of her was doing fine.

'And what does the Galloping Major say about that?'

'He's a Captain not a Major and he doesn't gallop, he ambles.'

'Hold the phone! Do I detect a hint of admiration?'

'Admiration?' Torn between the need to slap or kiss him, Daisy didn't know what she felt.

* * *

The photographs showed of what was left of the mosque after the IED. The shrink shook his head. 'To get out of that in one piece a man would need to have either phenomenally quick responses or to have led an exemplary life.'

Lucian shrugged. 'Can a modern soldier lead an exemplary anything?'

'It must be difficult. What is your particular expertise?'

'I'm what's called an ATO – Ammunition Technical Officer.'

'And what does that entail... layman's terms, if you please.'

'I do my best to make noisy bombs less noisy.'

'And from this photograph am I to understand there was a failure on your part to make a bomb less noisy?'

'Doc, what I'm about to say is bullshit of the first order, but for security reasons – and because we're both too long in the tooth to do anything else – let's go with the party line. Hence I was part of a task force sent to deal with unstable armaments in what was considered an unofficial war-zone. As a result of hostile action on the part of patriots, for that read insurgents, I suffered injuries which led me to your door.'

'Ho-hum.'

'As you say, ho-hum.'

The psychiatrist perused his notes. 'Details are sketchy.'

Lucian gazed out of the window. Details are more than sketchy. He has minimal recollection of the operation. What he does know is what he's told, that on December 31st 2006 SI trackers reported multiple IEDs, that the team came under fire, and before the escort could take out the sniper, one Captain Lucian Nairne, taking a round in the head.

That's it; the rest is damaged CCTV footage, great chunks of it missing.

'I mean Hogmanay, for Chrissakes, doc!' he hissed. 'We should've been running about wi' our pants on our heads not dancing wi' death!'

That Lucian walked away from that incident doesn't mean he survived. The bullet to his head left him with impaired memory function and still whole sections of time go AWOL. Minutes, hours, even days will pass with only a clock as proof of passage, Lucian waking as from a dream to find he's talking with the CO, or in the Mess eating lunch, or even at home in bed yet with no memory of how he arrived at that point.

In panic he will freeze, but then, finding those around him seemingly unaware of his confusion, he will adjust; it is terrible, Dante's vision of hell could be no less tormenting. And who can he tell? David Gilchrist, the Medical Officer, is a friend but Lucian is sparing with the truth. If he confessed the true situation he'd be hauling ass down Civvy Street faster than you can say God Save the Queen. So he offers a sanitised version of events. David refers him to a shrink, who in turn refers him to another shrink, who suggests Post Traumatic Stress Disorder.

Bullshit and guts get him by. Sober, correctly attired – and therefore fulfilling his function as an officer and gentlemen – he sleeps his way through the days. Memory, what's that? He can quote 14th century Scottish history, but ask of life circa New Year's Eve, 2006 and he can't tell you.

Carrot and stick, ask the right question he'll give the right answer. Every day he loses more, his life reduced to photograph albums.

Two aspects of life remain constant, a woman and a sound. The sound he hears waking or sleeping, the kick-start of a jet engine or the flapping of wings, he doesn't know what it is – only that it brings despair.

* * *

On his way out Lucian saw the guy that dumped Daisy hiding behind a copy of 'Variety News'. Daisy Banks is Lucian's true constant. May 2006 she was in Jedburgh for a wedding. Had he been more sociable they would've met face-to-face, but choosing to unblock a flue rather than 'drink and be merry' he missed the chance. They were outside the house, she with her beautiful face alight- he should've spoken if only tell her how beautiful she was.

The day he saw her at Chimneys he straight way phoned Kieran Wallace asking who she was and for her phone number. But then he had to go on tour to Afghanistan and getting shot put all thoughts of romance on hold. Even so, bullet or not, he couldn't get her green-eyes out of his mind.

First thing he heard getting out of hospital was that she was looking to buy Chimneys, and more shockingly, she was querying wheel ramps.

What the fuck? Why would she want wheel-ramps? He searched the web. That's when he saw the headlines, *best-selling author's daughter hurt in crash*. That scared him! Her address in his pocket, he made the trip to Surrey in time to see her dad lifting her from a taxi into a wheelchair.

Jesus that hurt! That's when he became a stalker, following her progress even to the hospital and physio unit. Signed off on sick leave himself – the Invisible Man in a knitted hat – he would sit in the hospital cafe overlooking the gym. She would huff and puff and he huffed and puffed with her!

Curran was supposed to be her guy in those days. He was supposed to be supportive! Useless bastard was never there – too busy shagging bits of spare. So, why was he in the waiting room back there?

Lucian did an about-turn, was that Oscar Curran, the saxophonist, and what did he want? The receptionist was not a lover of jazz or Oscar Curran, but adored handsome soldiers. 'He's here for absolution.'

'Absolution?'

'He wants a neck lift but needs to be told its okay to have one.'

'Is a neck lift a good thing to have?'

'Only if your brains are sagging.'

* * *

Daisy was hacking at a hedge when she heard hooves. Oh, please, not another animal? Only this morning someone left a box of free-ridden pups at the gate. Now some chap is leaving a pony here that looks as if it hasn't been fed in weeks. 'Hey!' shouted Daisy. 'What are you doing?'

The chap grinned. 'Hi gorgeous! You talking to me?'

'Well, I'm not talking to St Francis of Assisi that's for sure! Where you going with that pony? It looks to me like you're dumping him.'

'I wasn'ae dumping anythin'. I found him back of my place and hearing you took in strays thought to bring him.

Daisy saw welts on the pony's neck. 'That pony's cheek is raw.'

'I know. I used a rope to get him here. I wouldn't normally do that but....'

She didn't wait to find out what he wouldn't normally do. Children burnt alive and kittens left to drown, that's enough pain for one day. She thought to dish out a bit of her own pain and drawing back her hand slapped him.

After supper, ashamed of her behaviour, she crept to the attic, and there dreamt of the front stairs and Charley stepping onto the landing.

'Oh, not again!' she cried. 'Once is enough to see friends die.'

'You've witnessed the passing of these friends more than once.'

'What, Kate and her children?'

'Daisy!' He rolled his eyes. 'Quit with the deaf, dumb, *and* blind. Choose one of the options and stick with it! Once again you're avoiding the issue. But then what's new, imitating the Ostrich is a human trait.'

'Charley, can I ask a question?'

He sighed. 'If you must.'

'Do you actually like people?' Today with jacket unbuttoned and tie askew today he looked more human which allowed her to be argumentative. 'Only I can't help noticing you're less than flattering when speaking of us.'

'Like human beings? Let me think.' He counted on his fingers. 'Weapons of mass destruction, random violence, murder, famine, and the destruction of an eco system that was another Eden, what's not to like?'

'Then why on earth are you here? If you don't like us how can you as an angel function properly?'

'Ah, Daisy.' He took her hand. 'My directive is not to like you, it is to love you, and I do love you, every one of you.' Warmth spread from his touch, a love so profound it pierced her heart. Everything that had hurt, Oscar's betrayal, her own lack of self-worth, the abuse of animals, human pain and degradation, all welled up inside, while at the same time remembrance of things she'd done to others – petty deeds, unloving acts – rose up to spill out of her eyes.

'Don't cry, little Daisy! God loves you. Besides, your mascara's ruining your nice, new chair. ' He hugged her. 'Come on! You've had a bit of a day. Why don't we take a trip?'

'What sort of trip?' she snivelled. 'I couldn't bear anything like the last.'

'We won't do that again. As you say, the death of a friend ought only to be witnessed once. Come! We'll take a little whiz around the world.'

A flick of his fingers and the staircase became Jacob's ladder with a hint of Blackpool illuminations. 'I thought you said only the dead can pass through.'

'You're with me so you're asbestos clad.'

'Is it safe? I mean, are we likely to meet ghosts and ghouls?'

His lips twitched. 'Human life moves among ghosts and ghouls every minute of the day. You don't recognise them. You think such beings should be slavering corpses. That they might be too beautiful to behold never occurs to you.'

Then they were out flying through space caught up in what at first appeared to be a meteor shower or rather stream upon stream of shooting stars rising from a blue depth that may well have been the earth toward the brightest sunrise.

And there was music, such music, a wild and wonderful sound that enchanted the soul. 'What is it?' She gripped his hand. 'What am I seeing?

'Souls in transit.'

'Souls in transit?' Such words! 'Where are they going?'

'Home, Daisy!' he said, eyes ablaze. 'Home to their loving Lord!'

'Let me go!' The need to be with them was overwhelming. The pull of music and light was so strong she could hardly bear it. 'Please, let me go with them!'

The lights vanished and there was a sense of hovering in an empty sky.

'Why can't I go?'

'You can but not yet. You have things to do, one of which is to drop in on another lonely soul and make him less lonely.'

'What do you mean drop in?'

'Share consciousness.'

'Can we do that?'

'What d'you think is happening here? Are you seeing through my eyes or your own? Can mortal eyes, in or out of the body, sustain a glimpse of heaven?'

'How do I know? I'm only human!'

'Or so you pretend,' he said, disparagingly. 'But to answer your question we may share another's consciousness if invited. You don't have to do it, although the one who invited is in dire need.'

'I'll do it if you say it's right to do it.'

'Then you must be calm and quiet and not try to influence the host even though you may long to do so. If you do impose your will you'll be withdrawn and this will be remembered as a dream.'

'Close your eyes.'

Daisy closed her eyes. There was a rushing in her ears, a slipping into darkness, and then a strange new body to inhabit. Tiny and fragile, she crouched in the corner of a brooding presence. It was intimidating, like being locked in a cage with a dangerous animal. Were it not for Charley she would have panicked. But remembering his words she remained quiet, and gradually the feeling of claustrophobia disappeared only to be replaced by terrible sadness.

'Oh,' she sighed. 'And I thought I was lonely.'

'He does think he is alone. It is a mystery. Every man, woman, and child is born knowing they are never alone. Alas, almost all die believing they are.'

They were in a dusty room piled with junk. Dirty and covered with cobwebs, it was oppressive, the walls and windows hung with blackout curtains.

'If this is human consciousness, how come I see dust and cobwebs?'

'If a human being decides his life is a train wreck, neither he, nor anyone else, can hope to see it another way.'

'It reminds me of the attic in Chimneys.'

'It would. The attic was where as a child this man felt most safe, and where else would you hide your treasures if not in a safe place.'

'This junk is treasure?'

'Since when did memories become junk?'

'But it's covered with cobwebs.'

'That's what happens when a man ceases to hope.'

There were toys in the room, a rocking horse, a cricket bat, and a gun.

A memory of her own tugged at her mind. 'Do I know this man?'

'It would be more true to say he knows you.'

Daisy tiptoed about. It was a Tardis, never ending. In one

corner there was a car, an old-fashioned vehicle yet well maintained. The windows were dark. She cupped her hands trying to see. There were shapes inside like stuffed cushions. She went to open the car door and Charley shouted, 'Come away!'

Glad to leave it, she went to another room where hung a life-sized portrait, a woman, the hem of a gown peeping from under a dustsheet.

'Why is everything covered up?'

'He cloaks his memories in the hope of keeping them private.'

Daisy peeled back the dustsheet. 'It's me!' Startled, she stepped back nudging the painting. An earthquake rocked the room. 'What's happening?'

'He doesn't want that memory touched. He's afraid of losing it.'

'Why is it so dark?'

'He believes he doesn't deserve to be in the light.'

An ornament sat on a table, a glass paperweight in the shape of a hand-grenade, and inside a tiny snow covered church. There were figures, mechanical soldiers, standing by a church. 'For a toy this is incredibly heavy.'

'It's not a toy. It's a chapter in this man's life, though having said that, since it represents all he's been taught to believe, it's more of a book.'

'My goodness!' Her hands closed tight about it. 'No wonder it's heavy.'

'It is heavy. It so weighs on his heart and soul he cannot bear to look on it, and mindful of his mortal profession confines it within a bauble.'

Daisy gently shook the paperweight. Silver sparkles whirled

and the scene changed to the soldier fixing a visor over his eyes. She shook it again and saw that the soldier was leaning on the back of another writing a letter. Then he was walking down a red-soaked path, and then lifting his visor, his face clear.

Lucian!

'Be careful,' whispered Charley. 'It's not your will that directs you.'

'He knows I'm here?'

'He's trying to make you understand.'

'Understand what?'

'That you hold his life in your hands.'

'His life!' Daisy all but dropped the ball. Glass broke, silver shards whirled, and she was the soldier – tension in every muscle and dark hopelessness in his head. There was gunfire, a bullet passing so close to her cheek it scored the visor. There was shouting, a crowd of people in a confused din. She could feel him moving, hear his thoughts. Then, he was running and shouting.

'Get out...!'

'...of here!' she screamed.

Boom! There was a sheet of flame; Daisy woke with the smell of cordite in her nostrils and a vague memory of someone else's nightmare.

CHAPTER NINE

Climbing Mountains

Lucian's going to the ceilidh. He takes a chance on blacking out but has heard Daisy is providing the buffet and seeing her again is too tempting.

Right now he's trying on his best duds except he doesn't seem to have any. Every item in the closet looks, and smells, as if it hasn't been worn in years.

There is the family tartan. Heavy weighted kilts are hell on the knees but the lassies like 'em. The velvet jacket he'll take to a do-it-yourself cleaner on the by-pass and then get a shirt in Edinburgh.

Why are his duds in a mess? Irritated, he slammed the door. It wouldn't happen if Basset was here. Clyde Basset was his aide in the Gulf. Jowls and sparse comb-over, closet gay and prone to massive hissy fits, how in hell could he forget that guy?

Lucian gazed into the mirror. A tall man gazed back, eyes shadowy and hair glinting with silver. If this is how it's going to be, post traumatic stress erasing everything that matters, then to hell with it! Cinderella shall definitely go to the ball.

* * *

The Pudding Club is up to their necks in hot ovens and chicken vol-au-vent. 'Why am I doing this?' groaned Kate. 'I could be home with my feet up.'

'Couldn't we all,' said Daisy, kicking the door shut.

'Mind what you're doing with that leg! You know what the doctor said. You can try with one crutch as long as you take it easy.'

'Waking every three hours to feed puppies is hardly taking it easy.'

'It's your own fault. You will take in strays.'

This from the mother-lode of stray-catchers! Daisy let it pass. They've been at it all night, even press-ganged Jasmine and Sharonda to help. Swaddled in aprons, 'Pudding Club' embroidered across their caps, the girls were not happy. 'I'm no wearing that cap,' said Jasmine. 'I look a right fecking eejit.'

Daisy popped a raspberry into Jasmine's mouth. 'Don't let Mammy hear you swear. She'll think it my fault.'

Kate overheard. 'It is your fault. You got us into this.'

Daisy sighed. 'Aye, so I did.' They all fell about laughing.

Two hours later no one was laughing. The janitor was late opening the hall which meant the champagne didn't get into the chiller. Then they'd to erect tables, fiddle with a boiler, and clean out a filthy tea-urn. Daisy's wagon conked on the by-pass so the cheeses came via taxi. Add to that Sharonda dropkicking a tray of meringues, and you'll get the picture.

They sped about with only minutes before the first guest arrived.

By nine-thirty the tables were a war-zone. 'I don't know why we bothered,' muttered Kate. 'We might as well have dumped it on the floor and let 'em get on all fours.'

'They're not all like that.'

'No,' Kate followed Daisy's gaze. 'There's one a cut above the rest.'

Magnificent in a kilt – a bottle green velvet jacket smooth across his broad shoulders, white lace at his throat and a dagger in his stocking – Lucian could have been auditioning for the *Monarch of the Glen*.

'And I thought him boring.'

'Boring!' Kate was scandalised. 'You wee bat, you cann'ae see beyond your dark glasses.' At that the man in question finding them staring acknowledged their presence with a courtly bow before being swooped away.

'He seems to be enjoying himself.'

Lucian was enjoying himself. He'd chatted with folk, remembered who they were, danced a reel or two without treading on too many toes, and laughed. Then a woman spoke of his paternal grandparents, saying how she served on committees with Lady Pamela and the '*darling*' Brigadier.

Lucian couldn't relate to her memories. As far as he knew Pamela Nairne and Andrew Archibald Urquhart Nairne were darling to no-one.

A veteran of two world wars – Edward Elgar look-alike minus moustache and musical genius – Andrew was a bully and a snob. Sure of his opinion, and with the hide of a rhino, he couldn't get through a day without giving offence.

'Too tight,' he'd say of Lucian's jeans. 'Too long,' of his hair. 'What are you, a Frog poof?' Grandfather Nairne – you couldn't call him Grandpa – didn't care for people. His weakness was for thoroughbred hunters. Gassed in the battle of the Somme, he didn't ride but spent hours buffing them to a shine.

Unbending as her corsets, Grandmother Nairne was a thin woman with stick-like legs and a lilac perm. A keen hunter, preferring to bait her own snares and throttle her Christmas goose, she was mute most of the time but would break out at Hogmanay, a glass of port in her hand and the 'Erinskay Love Lilt' on her lips. As grandparents they were a washout. The only time the Brigadier played with his grandsons was to fight the Battle of Waterloo in the attic, his hand-painted hussars lined up against the boys' French mercenaries, and where terms of surrender demanded the docking of pocket money.

If he'd left his detestation of the French in the attic the family might've survived but wary of her beauty he poured contempt upon Lucian's mother: she was too foreign, her accent thick and her clothes too colourful, plus she was too familiar with village folk and too soft with the boys.

Eloise Nairne stuck it out for a while but after a decade of tyrannous relatives, and a husband with no backbone, finally left – taking Ian with her. Even after all this time it hurts; was Lucian not as precious as his brother? Ian was able to cut adrift. It didn't matter what went on around him, curse or slap, he would smile. The Brigadier said Ian was a disgrace to the family, a moron. Ian was no moron. He was gentle and pure and Lucian loved him.

The elders lived out their latter years in a bungalow in the grounds of Drummach Hall, the big house passed to Alistair Nairne as too expensive to run. The bungalow's gone. Shame the Hall didn't go with it. Raised in an atmosphere of rigid self-restraint Lucian's father felt compelled to pass the same opinion on to his sons, stiff upper lip and cold showers.

'*Dinna trust yesterday's footholds, they will let you down,*' was Alistair Nairne's philosophy. Critical and prone to sneak attack, he needed to be chief in all things. He was a bully, words the preferred weapon, the blow coming when least expected, after mother's kiss at bedtime or at the Lido in front of your mates: '*What d'you mean cann'ae swim? You can paddle. If a dog can do it, Ian, so can you.*' He saw Ian a weakling. '*If the army was good enough for your grandfather it's good enough for you. Forget the Sorbonne and the rest of the fancy nonsense your mother's crammed into your head. You'll join the army. I'm no subsidising you for the rest of ma life!*'

Strange how even in the uncertainty of Lucian's memory Father's anger survives whereas moments with Ian are as precious jewels among ash.

* * *

On the dance-floor lads throw Jasmine and Sharonda about like a couple of gorgeous dolls. One lad caught Lucian's attention. Golden hair, and a way of flinging about, no skill yet plenty enthusiasm, brought Ian to mind. He loved to climb and the Isle of Skye a favourite bolthole. In the early days Father went with them but plagued by ill health soon left them alone. Ian revelled in the climb of Cuillin Ridge – even the Brigadier couldn't fault him in that.

Lucian stood watching the dancers and thinking of the past when there was a sound in his head, a hiss of air, as though a pressurised door opened. Walls melted! He was on a rock face, the wind in his hair and cormorants wheeling overhead, and racing ahead a slight figure in a scarlet jacket, scuttling over the rocks like a gaudy daddy longlegs.

It was Ian. '*Get a move on, Luca!*' a call floats down the ridge. '*I'm waiting.*'

The glimpse of yesteryear didn't last. He was back and among the dancers, gripping the lad by the wrist. Aware of startled glances, Lucian released him. 'I beg your pardon. I seem to have lost the thread.'

The dancers moved on. Lucian glanced at his watch. The last time he looked it was ten. Now it's almost midnight. Two hours have passed! What was he doing during that time, leaping about with the others or lost in the vision, a drooling creature from the Black Lagoon?

God almighty! His heart beat like a hammer but not for fear of looking a fool. It was the intensity of the experience that blew him away, the certainty of granite under his boots and his beloved brother alive and well.

Trembling, he leant against the wall. The ceilidh staggered on. The band was playing a Rod Stewart number, people forming a chain. A girl, tipsy and happy, caught his hand to pull him into the swell. At first he resisted until caught up in the maelstrom he complied. Up and down the hall they went, '*sailing over stormy waters,*' Mardi gras with Lucian Nairne as chief clown.

* * *

Daisy and Kate stood in the kitchen taking nips from their own private bottle of Moet. 'Lucian's quick on his feet. I didn't think he had it in him.'

'He's drunk.'

Daisy didn't think he was drunk. Earlier he looked so lost she almost ran to help him – not that he needed help, a leggy blonde huddling against him.

'He's certainly popular.'

'Aye, the hypocritical sods!' Kate spat. 'Not so long ago they'd cross the road sooner than speak to him.'

'People don't mean to be cruel. It's discomfort. When faced with sickness or scars, or whatever, they feel awkward and don't know what to say.'

'It does'nae excuse them!' Kate was a terrier defending her pup. 'You saw him earlier, that dazed look and folks giving him a wide berth. How do they think a soldier gets this way if not from trying to save their skinny arses!'

'Lucky the man that gets your love, Kate. He'll never find better.'

'Tell that to Jason!' Kate stomped into the kitchen. 'I loved him and look what he did, set fire to the fecking hoos!'

Daisy slipped outside and sat on a wall wondering if she'd made a mistake buying Chimneys. The nightmares are no better. At first they were fun, but children burning and soldiers dying isn't fun. In the clubhouse people are having fun. Daisy wants that kind of fun, not climbing stairways to the stars – and she certainly doesn't want to fall in love with an angel, no matter how beautiful. 'So forget it, Charley,' she whispered. 'It's not happening.'

'Who's Charley?' Lucian stood before her.

'Someone I know.'

'It didn'ae sound like you were overly fond of the guy.'

'You can't be fond of Charley. That's too feeble a feeling. You can be fond of your aunt, or your dog, but not Charley.'

'Wisht!' He perched on the wall beside her. 'Whoever he is he's made an impression. How long have you known him?'

'All of my life, so he says. Not that I necessarily believe what

123

he says. He's a tricky character, changeable, if you know what I mean.' Daisy changed the subject. 'I've not come across the name Lucian before. Is it Scottish?'

'It has Scottish connections. My mother chose it for me.'

'Your mother was French.'

'Parisian.'

'You seemed to be having a good time out there.'

'Hah! Is that how it looked?'

'Were you not having a good time?'

'I was making the best of a bad job. I had hoped we might have a wee shuffle, but you didn'ae come out of the kitchen.'

'I thought it the safest place to be. All that screaming and shouting! I had thought you were a reserved nation.'

'We are, which is why we lean toward excess when breaking out.' He folded his arms, blocking that line of conversation. 'Why are you out here and not whooping it up with Sharonda and the rest of the girls?'

'Are they whooping it up?'

'They were the last time I saw them. A couple of lads were flinging them about the floor. They'll be lucky if they come out alive.'

'Poor girls.'

'Poor lads I would say, blown away by Jasmine's eyes.'

'She is beautiful. A couple of months and Sharonda will be as stunning.'

'I understand she's taking music lessons and the little one ballet lessons.'

'You mustn't call her little. As of yesterday she is to be known as Tulsa.'

'I thought that was a city in the States.'

'It's also Tulip's new name.'

'And she can hear her new name when it's called?'

'It appears so, a mended stirrup the doctor said, or is that the ponies?'

'Ponies?' He frowned.

'Excuse me. I've horses on the brain. We've new additions to the Ark. In fact we've so many we're in danger of sinking.'

'Have you indeed.'

'Now look, I know we're breaking the rules but if you'd seen the state when they arrived! Disgraceful! What sort of person does that?'

'If you mean Bram Roberts who owns the Wayfarer pub on the green then I'm no sure what sort of person he is. I do know they weren't his ponies. Some naebody left them on the spare lot behind the pub.'

'Then why didn't he say so?'

'I understand you didn'ae give him chance.'

'It's true. Oh hell! I'd better go and apologise.'

'I told him to make allowances. New Age folk are inclined to be hysterical.'

'Hysterical?' This was the Lucian she hated, the autocratic know-it-all putting his oar in where it wasn't required. She was about to sock it to him when silence made her glance sideways. 'You nearly had me going.'

'Are you not going to have a go then?' he said, grinning. 'I like it when you explode. So emphatic! You're eyes open up and your hair stands on end. Talk about pyrotechnics! It's better than any firework display.'

'I'm glad you find me amusing.'

The grin slipped from Daisy's face.

'You told me that I reminded you of the Knight Templar. RoboCop you called him,' said Lucian. 'Do you still feel that way?'

'Did I say that? How ill mannered of me.'

'Never mind your manners,' he brushed it aside. 'Do you still see me as the iron man or have I gained ought in your sight?'

'I don't know you well enough to make a judgement.'

'So you don't have an opinion?'

'I know you've been helpful to me and kind to the Khans.'

He slid off the wall. 'Kate was here for me when others turned their backs. It's nae difficult being kind to her. She'd do the same for me if I were on the losing end.'

'I'm sure of it. She's very fond of you.'

'Fond.' He grimaced. 'There's that word again.'

Pressed into a corner, she could only shrug.

'Ah well, goodnight then, Daisy,' he walked away. 'It seems you do have an opinion of me, but unlike your man, Charley, it's no worth recalling.'

CHAPTER TEN

What Reality

Late summer and the drapes flattened against the windows like exhausted moths. Evening is the best, a breeze blowing off the rill. Daisy walks the grounds, breathing in the night-scented stock and collecting the chucks. Isla is often at the house, arriving laden with packages. She follows the kids, listening in on their conversations and making notes. 'I hope your mam's no writing about my kids,' said Kate, dragging a comb through Sean's hair. 'I don't want folks thinking them freaks.'

'You've got Kate worried. She thinks you're stalking the kids.'

'Maybe I am,' said Isla. 'There's such stuff in them, especially Sean. I love that kid but don't like the way he gets shoved around.'

'It's because he's shy.'

'He won't get shoved anywhere if I've anything to do with it. Your pa's investigating the kid, trying to find out who he is. Talking of stalkers,' Isla veered away from the subject. 'Your ex is suing some blonde bimbo who's been harassing him. He phoned home the other day wanting your number.'

'You didn't give it to him.'

'I wouldn't give him the drippings off my nose. How are things with you and the Captain? And don't look at me like that! I'm only asking.'

'Well don't! I know what you're doing, matching the strong silent type with the cripple. I'm no cripple. I can walk, drive a car, *and* ride a horse.'

Horse riding is Daisy's latest thing – pony riding, actually, Begonia too small to be called a horse. 'She's not very friendly,' she said when first presented.

'Baggy thinks with her belly. Offer her a Mars bar and you've a friend for life.'

The owner flung Daisy aboard. 'There you are, safe as houses.' Bram Roberts is the chap who brought the pony and got slapped for his pains. Nothing lost, he returned with Baggy and his own horse, a high-stepping hunter named Connor. Today they jog along the canal path, Bram fishing for a date and Daisy for news of Lucian. 'You show a keen interest in that guy,' said Bram.

'Of course! He's single and still has hair.'

'That's the upside to Luca Nairne. There is a downside.' Daisy would've asked more but Bram was keen to press his own interest. 'How about thinking of me as single, my own hair and crazy about redheads?'

It was a pleasant way to spend an idle hour. On return, Bram helped her down, kissed her hand, and jogged away. Jasmine and Sharonda were watching.

'Luca Nairne won't like him hanging around,' said Sharonda.

'Why not?'

'He fancies you.'

'Who, Bram?'

'Him too but I was talkin' about Luca.'

Daisy wasn't averse to Bram. He is amusing and not bad looking in a Ben Affleck sort of way. These days she's glad of the male company, because she thinks she's being followed. When it first happened...footsteps behind her... she thought it might be Leon and mentioned it to Kate.

'Why would it be our Leon?'

'I don't know that it's anyone. It's the feeling of being followed.'

'I know who it is,' said Sean. 'It's the lady ghost under the lilac. I've seen her. She waves to me when I'm out grubbing for ma rats.'

'Weren't you scared?'

'Scared o' what?'

'Well, you know, a ghost?'

'She doesn'ae look like a ghost. She wears a hat like yours and digs wi' a fork.'

Lucian at that time was waiting to take Leon on a fishing trip. 'Your ghost, Sean?' he said. 'Was she tall, blonde, and with her hair in braids?'

'Braids!' Daisy had freaked out. 'You know how a ghost wears her hair?'

Lucian had laughed. 'Minna's the one supposedly walking the grounds. I wondered if Sean's spook looked anything like the photographs.'

'If you have photographs of Minna I'd like to see them.'

'I'll drop them by. Better yet come and look. There's a heap of stuff belonging to Chimneys. My mother saved it all when Minna died.' When Daisy looked sideways, he shrugged. 'It's okay. Naebody's going to jump your bones, living or otherwise.'

Daisy thought she might take him up on the offer. Meanwhile, she walks the meadow and is not alone. It's not exactly that she hears footsteps. It's more the knowledge of a person alongside, walking, breathing…. and talking.

'Hello, Daisy,' said a voice in her head.

'Hello, Charley.' She crouched beside the rill, watching a

school of minnows swim through the water. 'I thought it might be you.'

'Are you disappointed?'

'Not at all.'

'My, aren't you polite!'

'I thought you wanted me to bow and scrape.'

'I ought to blast you with a thunder bolt.'

'Do you do that sort of thing?'

'Frequently, but never to beautiful mortals and never before supper.'

'You eat?'

'Of course! How else do I survive?'

'You're an odd sort of angel.'

'And you're an odd sort of helper. What happened to the promise you made to help free those trapped in time.'

'Did I make such a promise?'

'Twice. Once in '37 and then New Year's day 2007.'

'Phooey! I might've said something in '07. If you recall I was on life-support at the time and likely to say anything, but 1937? I wasn't alive.'

'Really? Then who is that sitting on the bank?'

Daisy looked up and there she is sitting by the duck-pond, a book in her lap, and the same battered Panama on her head. Robbed of speech, she stared. They are alike except the woman was taller and her hair a golden shade. 'That's Minna Gray.'

'Are you sure? You look the same to me. What about the man with her?'

Another figure appeared on the bank. Cap thrown down on the ground, he sat with a smile on his lips and his fair hair ruffled by the breeze. It was the RAF officer who held her hand when she first came to Chimneys.

More figures appeared, some in shirtsleeves, some with jackets unbuttoned. Jobbing actors taking a break from a wartime movie, they sat relaxed and easy. Yet as she watched the scene solidified. A moment ago birds sung in the trees and clouds scudded across a sky. Now all is silent, no life, no breath in her lungs, a swallow poised over the water. The vision faded but not before Minna turned to stare, a question in her eyes. 'What?' Daisy leapt to her feet. 'What is it you want?'

There was only the riverbank and a lark singing. She burst into tears. Warm flesh and blood arms came about her, Lucian. 'What's the matter?' Squashed against his chest, she sobbed. 'I don't know what they want. I keep asking but no one says.'

Heart pounding, he held her until, discomfited, she pushed away.

'What are you doing here? I thought you were fishing.'

'Leon was driving me nuts so I shipped the wee sod back home.'

'I thought boys liked the great outdoors.'

'Leon thinks he's a hard case but when it comes to home comforts he wants a duvet on his bed and fried fish from the chippy.'

'At least you tried.' She turned toward the house. 'I'd better go.'

'What was going on earlier? You looked like you'd seen a ghost.'

'I had.'

'Come on.' He took her arm. 'We'll take a walk up to the house and have a glass of something. Then you can tell me about it.'

* * *

'This'll put colour in your cheeks.' He pushed a glass into her hand. 'Brandy, lemon, and a shot of old and filthy, it's called a Bazooka.'

She took a sip. Fire streamed through her veins. 'It's a good name.'

'Excuse me.' He took to the stairs. 'I stink of fish.'

She prowled the room trying to gain information on the man. The house was stark and worn, smoke-stained walls and a patched leather sofa. A golf bag stood in the corner and a bucket of fish on the kitchen table. There were military books in the bookcase, biographies and manuals. His musical choice leaned toward choral music, Monteverdi and Palestrina, before veering sideways to James Brown, and Queen.

There were no family bibelots and no mementoes of school-days on the shelves. There were two photographs, a man and woman and a young boy – Lucian and his parents, perhaps, and of Lucian and a young soldier, but that was all. Daisy once had a fling with a chap from the 'Blues and Royals'. You couldn't move in his flat for memorabilia, trophies from college and a picture gallery of his stint in the Gulf, guys in tanks giving thumbs up. Where are Captain Nairne's proud moments?

A thought was presented to her mind. What if he's another Oscar, the past an illusion and the present makeshift-and-mend? No time to ponder. He was on the stairs in fresh khaki and his hair wet from the shower. 'Feeling better?'

'Thank you.'

'What was going on back there?'

'I'm not sure I want to say. You already suspect me of being off my head.'

He refilled her glass. 'I figure your temperament to do with the colour of your hair. By-the-by I like the hairdo. It's bonny, or is bonny an insult to a modern girl?'

'Do you know many modern girls?'

'Thousands.'

'And they object to the word?'

'I never thought to say it to them.'

It was on her tongue to say, 'not even to Sexy Sue,' but having heard Sue was back in town she held back. 'Gorgeous would be nice but I'll settle for bonny.'

'Good. I wouldn'ae want to offend. So what was going on back there?'

Daisy tossed back the drink. 'I caught a glimpse of the past, Six Chimneys circa 1940, RAF boys sitting on the grass waiting for a signal to go.'

He raised his eyebrows. 'RAF pilots?'

'Yes, RAF, and men from other branches of the service sitting with Minna. And you're right. She does wear her hair braided.'

'You look like her.'

'So I'm told.'

'How clearly did you see her?' he said, refilling her glass.

'Better than I'll be seeing you if I drink much more of this.'

'The men in these sitings? Would you recognise them if seen again?'

Malt liquor was revving up the works. 'What d'you mean recognise? They were psychic phenomena, not an identikit of a bunch of old lags!'

'Why are you so angry?'

'I'm not. I'm puzzled and more than a bit scared.'

'What did they want?'

'I wish I knew,' she said, gazing into the bottom of the glass.

'Come on!' He pulled her to her feet. They took to the stairs, half open doors giving glimpses of bulky shapes draped in dust-sheets. 'This place is full of rubbish. One of these days when I've time I'll boost the lot to the Salvation Army.'

Daisy was shivering. 'This is a big place to keep warm.'

'I stick to the east wing. As you can see the rest is locked off.' As they went he gave a brief historical resume of the Hall, an oak settle carved in 1565 and a sword carried at Culloden by a chief of the clan with a blood stock line going back to William Wallace. 'By rights you and me shouldn'ae be talking.'

'Why's that?'

'Your father's a Surrey man. In 1297 the Earl of Surrey was hacked to pieces not far from here. Your forefathers may have been among his men.'

'Kate reads Scottish history. She says the Nairne family is kin to Robert the Bruce.'

'Kate's in love with Scotland. She finds *Braveheart* under every stone. It's no difficult to understand why. She needed a safe place to hide and found it here.'

The guided tour continued. An ugly house with high ceilings and large fireplaces it would be draughty in winter and hot in summer, and with dodgy plumbing if the lavatory is anything to go by. The tour ended at a cubbyhole full of ancient tea chests that contained letters, the pink ribbon a giveaway. 'Love-letters?'

'When the lawyer knew Six Chimneys was up for sale he

brought the tea chests to my mother, he didn'ae want folks prying.' He took a scrapbook from a box. 'Every person who's ever slept under her roof is in here.' It fell open at a marker, and a photograph of people standing under willow trees. 'Is this what you saw?'

She nodded. 'Some of them.'

'There you are then. You're no going off your head.'

'Surely a photograph of men who now are extremely old or extremely dead proves I'm off my head? Why am I seeing them? Should I book a booth at Southend Pier and lay in a fresh supply of crystal balls?'

Lucian took her glass away. 'Maybe a black coffee might be a start otherwise you'll need to be carried home.'

'What a fabulous idea. I am tired and it would be a great way to travel. Plus, it's in keeping with my mother's notion – you Tarzan and me Jane.'

He gazed at her. 'What are you doing?'

'Doing?' She gazed at the photograph, her finger tracing the RAF pilot's handsome face. 'I'm not sure I'm doing anything.'

He stepped aside, inviting her to pass into the corridor. 'It's time you were home. I'll bring the rest some time tomorrow. They belong to you anyway.'

Daisy touched his arm. 'Sorry.'

'What for?'

'Trying to seduce you.'

'Is that what you were doing?'

'I think so...and clearly not making a very good job of it.'

He bent, laying his cheek against hers. 'Don't worry, Daisy. If you're not up to scratch I'll allow you plenty practice.'

On the way home he kept his distance. Daisy could've wept. At what point did she decide bazookas were fuel for romantic seduction. She may as well have ripped off her knickers, leapt on the table along with the salmon yelling, 'come on, big boy!' He'd obviously found finding her seduction routine unattractive.

Stone cold sober she pushed through the door and into the kitchen where Kate was putting finishing touches to a treacle tart. 'You still up,' said Daisy.

'There's plenty to do.'

'It is warm.' Daisy sat fanning her face and wiping her cleavage, reddened lips and t-shirt slipping off her shoulders suggesting a woman hot from a steamy bed.

Kate was fiddling with the tart. 'We need to talk. I'm not happy with the thought of battening on you. You've got your life and don't need us messing it up.'

Daisy snapped to attention. 'I didn't know you were unhappy.'

'It's not a question of happy. It's about what's right. You've been a good friend to me, but I cann'ae stand to be beholden.'

'I didn't know you felt beholden. We share costs. Business is great with orders in the pipeline, or are you feeling awkward about that too?'

'I was hoping to carry on wi' that.'

'So it's only me you find *awkward.*'

'I think you might show a little more consideration. Take this evening, me worrying about you and in you waltz large as life and twice as drunk.'

'I am not drunk.'

'Maybe not but smelling something awful.'

'I am not drunk, Kate Khan, and you are not my mother.'

It was getting heated. Voices raised and Biddy and Baz scratching to get out.

Kate shooed the dogs out and rounded on Daisy. 'It's as well I'm not your mother. If I were you'd get a slapped arse. Coming in stinking like a brewery and not the decency to tell those who are worrying where you were!'

'I said I was sorry.'

'You did not.'

'I am sorry. I should've called. But there was this thing by the rill and it gave me a scare. I was coming home but Bram was late and so Lucian and I we...!' She ground to a halt. 'This is about Lucian.'

'It is not.'

'It is too! You're angry because I was with him.'

'Bollocks!'

Daisy lost her temper. 'You're mad at me and cover it with crap about being beholden and getting in the way. It's nothing to do with that. You're jealous!'

'Jealous? What have I to be jealous about?'

'I don't know because if ever a woman had his grace and favour it's you. Think of all he's done? You couldn't get a sweeter love anywhere.'

'I know what he's done. I don't need you telling me.'

'Then what is this? I come in with whisky on my breath therefore I must be having sex with the man you adore?'

'You've got a big idea of yourself,' snarled Kate. 'I'm no interested in your dirty doings. You could be shagging SpongeBob Squarepants for all I care!'

'Mammy?' Tulip stood at the door.

'What? And here's another thing, Daisy Banks, where do you get off telling me what I feel? You haven't been in the place five minutes. Don't judge my feelings for Lucian or his for me on what you think you see. I've told you stuff but not all.'

'I've never enquired into your past. Anything I've learned I've learned from your lips. And if you have secrets you can bloody well keep them!'

Tulip called from the doorway. 'Mammy, why are you yelling?'

'Because I'm fed-up wi' people asking questions! And you better go back to bed or you'll be hearing more!'

Tulip climbed up on the chair and laid her hands over her mother's mouth.

'What are you doing?' Kate knocked the child's hands away. Tulip began to weep. Kate, put her arms about her. 'Sorry, hen, but I don't know what you want.'

'I don't want you to shout. Daisy magicked my ears and I can hear you shouting.'

'You talking about your poorly ear? The one the doc said is better?'

'Uh-huh. It was Daisy made it better, no him.'

'Okay, off you go. Take a bit of the pie but don't get crumbs in the bed.'

Daisy went too. 'We'll talk tomorrow if there's anything left to talk about.'

Kate began on the dishes. What a waste, she thought, looking at the treacle tart. I should've waited til the morning. 'Idle hands make work for the devil!' her father used to say while his idle hands were creeping into his daughter's nappy.

'No!' She threw the thought away. 'I don't need to remember

old pain!'

But *he* is always there with his bald head shining in the bedroom light! How can you lay a ghost to rest when the cause of the nightmare still haunts you? Yes, he's still around, festering in a tenement flat and sending begging letters. A year after she settled in Scotland, Rajeev, who knew how to work the system, wrote to Lucian. *Captain Sir,* he wrote, bad spelling and childlike scrawl. *I drop you a line seeing as Mahonia's living with you now. She a good girl, genrous to her old pa. I want to say best luck, Captain, and come by say hello. PS. Can you lend us a couple of quid? I to have an operation. Doctor say no hope. Best wishes. Rajeev Khan.*

Lucian brought it to the trailer. 'I know it's none of your doing but do you want me to help?' She battled with her conscience wanting the bastard to die without a crumb. The note vanished into history. Only once did Lucian make reference to it. They were sharing a ciggie. 'Mahonia?' he said. They laughed until they cried.

Kate's past is a minefield – few places to tread in safety. If she gets by the abuse there is the booze, vodka in the early years and later cheap wine. At fifteen there was an abortion. The rest is roach-filled squats and Jason. There are a few happy memories, good friends were mercy ships in the night and the birth of her children oasis among drunkenness and lies. As for Lucian, he was four precious days in a glorious summer.

It was late January when the baker said Lucian was blown to pieces by a mine. Then Hildy from the post office rushed out. 'He's no dead! He's lost both his legs!' Up and down, round and round, nobody knew the truth. Then like the gent he is he settled the gossip, a telegram arriving at the Dominie's: *To whom it may concern. Fret not. I'm alive and kicking, but no exactly the genius I was.*

Soon he was home, still the powerful soldier but hovering on the edge. Then it was a race to see who would be a good neighbour. Everybody failed the test, Susie Watkins chief among them. She left on the Sunday. Kate arrived at the house the following day to find him suffering. 'Bathe my eyes,' he said. 'They're awful sore.'

She was bathing his face with salt water when he began to weep. 'Sorry for being such a fucking wuss. But it hurts.' She'd never heard him cuss before and was stopped in her tracks. 'Susie's a beautiful girl. You must be heartbroken.'

He'd laughed through his tears. 'She is a beauty and I'll miss her. But the pain I feel is more to do with the rip in my head than the tear in my heart.'

At that she'd simply gathered his face in her hands and kissed his mouth.

The taste of him! So sweet! Next thing the salt-water's flying. She's spread-eagled on the table and he's ripping off her drawers. She'd never had an orgasm like it. Her cries rivalled the peacocks strolling in the grounds. They met the following Monday and the next. The fourth meeting was the last. Kate's anxiety tonight was jealousy. Who wouldn't envy the girl Lucian loved? Yet it wasn't all jealousy. It was concern for wee Daisy too, grand as he is Lucian is not one to make her happy.

Kate nurses a secret – the man is the tidiest ever born or he doesn't live at Drummach Hall. She's been cleaning there for six years. In the early days it was okay but now things are amiss. His stuff is there, every item hung in the closet or folded in the drawer, the same in the bathroom, never a towel out of place or a line round the bath. Sure, there's music in the racks but it's never played, the TV too is silent. From the trailer she had direct view of the house. She saw all the comings and goings except there weren't any. The jeep in the garage was only dragged into service when Daisy arrived.

At first Kate assumed neatness the habit of a soldier who'd spent years in barracks. The kids had their own thoughts: Leon says SAS, Sean ET. Kate knows what Sean meant, the fey quality, the golden glint in Lucian's eyes when watching people. It's as though he sees inside them knowing their hopes and dreams – it's what the sex was about, a response to *her* need.

Lucian Nairne is a mysterious being, maybe even dangerous. Daisy doesn't deserve danger. Kate's first knowledge of Daisy came years ago via a Ouija board. Some mates knew of a woman in Duke Street who did séances. They went for a laugh and ended up sitting round a circle made of scrabble tiles getting messages from spirits via a glass. Nothing much happened until someone started taking the piss, 'do ghosts have sex and if so do they use invisible condoms?'

The glass went mad, whizzing around the table: a message for Mahonia;

'*A man with ice in his heart and death in his hands will bring Mahonia's children close to the Valley of Shadows.*' The woman said for a fiver she'd get a message from an angel. Kate gave the fiver. The woman closed her eyes: 'a *girl with life in her hands and fire in her hair will lead Kate's borrowed child out of the Valley.*'

She asked who the feck was Kate. The woman said. 'You.'

At the time Kate was thinking of changing her name. Giving two fingers to séances and scary old women, she went for Kate. Over time she forgot about the séance. Then Jason arrived, a man with death in his hands if ever there was. Now there's Daisy with red hair and life in her hands and Tulip able to hear and suddenly the prophecy feels like a warning and the borrowed child Sean. Kate doesn't know what it all means and isn't prepared to find out.

Even a trailer is better than a Valley of Shadows.

CHAPTER ELEVEN

Campaign Medal

The alarm went off at precisely four am. Daisy rolled out of bed. 'I'm up.'

The alarm kept ringing, a wailing noise like an air-raid siren.

'Bloody hell! Are you deaf or something?' she yelled. 'I'm up!'

She opened her eyes to find she was inside another's nightmare. She was inside a soldier's head, thinking his thoughts and tasting his fear.

He'd received the call to disable a bomb and the wailing noise a dodgy cable on a jamming device. He was standing next to a mosque, or what's left of it, rafters exposed to the sky. 'A church?' the soldier was thinking in a flash of gallows' humour. 'At least I won't have far to look for St Peter.'

Apart from the jammer squealing all is quiet, other guys standing behind the wire. Using his oppo's back for a desk he is writing a note. Hand shaking and tears smudging words, he takes a deep breath and...Boom!

Daisy woke drenched in sweat. This has been going on for weeks. During the dream the soldier is known. Waking, he's gone. But it *is* Lucian! It has to be!

Nightmare after nightmare, it is relentless, and yet once in a while a rare delight as with flowers singing and sparrows playing sky-hockey.

Thinking she might find a story Daisy offered the dream and Minna's letters to Isla. She laughed. 'I write for kids not frustrated spinsters.' Nights of passion remembered in the letters, body parts lovingly recalled, juicy vaginas and breasts likened to sugar, Minna was no frustrated spinster. Letters aside, two notes were of particular interest, the first because it was sad, the second intriguing. The first note was only a few smudged lines:

Hello, girl with green eyes. I've been asked to leave a note for nearest and dearest. Sad to say I don't seem to have any, but if I did you'd be the one I'd want to say goodbye to. I don't know you but it's okay, I'm no stalker. I saw you once and never forgot. Your lovely face kept me going through a year of hell. I want to thank you and tell you I am here for you. Heaven or hell, I shall find you, and I will love you, and I will keep you safe, God bless and keep us both. Your Wanna-be Guardian Angel.

The signature on the second note is familiar. She's seen it before in one of the group shots. She looks again and this time sees the impossible – two men standing side-by-side, their names printed alongside, Jim and Philip Tree. So alike, they might've been the same man but for a difference: Jamie wears WW2 khaki while Philip is armoured for '*Desert Storm*.'

A photograph taken in the 1940's showing an automatic rifle and fibreglass helmet? How can that be? Once upon a time she'd have gone to Kate but….

'Daisy!' Talk of the devil, Kate's bawling up at the window. 'Get down here! Noah's Ark is at the door again!' Daisy rushed about, changing into shirt and pants. Not good jeans! She's already lost a pair to a goat with the gripes.

The Healing Business, as Kate calls it, started with a goat called Elvis.

'He's got belly ache,' said a lad. 'My gran said you'd help.'

Daisy didn't know how to help but hoping to be left alone laid her hands on the goat's butt. Oops! It vomited over her favourite jeans. 'Is he okay?' the lad asked. She'd stirred the mess with the toe of her boot. 'Even better if you don't feed him Celtic football shirts.' Daisy didn't take any of it seriously but come Christmas she'd look on Elvis as the Harbinger of Doom.

* * *

Kate and kids are moving out. Sean is inconsolable. Daisy will miss him. She's up most mornings at five mucking out the stables. He's always before her. 'Where you going with that?' she'd ask as he barrowed poop away.

'Bagging it, a pound a poop!' Whose entrepreneurial idea but Leon's.

The boy is a worry. The police called the other night, Leon caught setting fire to post-boxes. Kate slapped him but it made no difference. He was a hard ball bouncing from one dodgy situation to the next. Daisy thinks he is stealing from her purse. One way or another she needs diversion. Hopefully she'll get it this evening. She's seeing Bram for a meal and soft-shoe shuffle.

The date in mind she was trying on her new dress when the phone rang.

'Hi, Daze.'

'Oscar?'

'Just thought I'd give you a call to see how you're doing.'

'I'm fine.'

'And your folks?'

'Fine.' He never missed a beat. 'Mother's not well. I've talked with my guy at the Nuffield. He says he can fit her in next week when tests come through.'

'And which mother would that be?'

'My birth mother. We're in touch again.'

'How did that come about?'

'She saw me on telly. It brought us back together. It's what I've always wanted. But then you know that.'

'Do I?'

'Sure, you do! You were the one person who understood. But we shouldn't be talking about this. It's why I called. Channel 4 wants to do a piece on us.'

'Us?'

'You and me.'

'Why would they want to do that?'

'I told them about you. I mentioned the accident and how you're running a refuge and they're keen to meet.'

'I don't run a refuge.'

'I heard you took kids in off the street.'

'I have friends staying but no refuge.'

'I was told animals. Are you sure you're not doing charity work?'

'I have animals on my land but nothing to do with charity.'

'So there wouldn't be any point in me coming to see you?'

'You're welcome any time but not if it's a story for Channel 4.'

'You sure about this? Would be great publicity.'

'For whom?'

'Well, for me...and you.'

'If there's one thing I do not need it's publicity.'

* * *

Bram is taking her to a 'Seventies Night' at the Hopscotch. 'I've hired a tux and frilled shirt,' he said. 'You should wear hot pants.' Hot pants! He could wear whatever century he liked. Daisy is sticking to the 21st and a saffron coloured silk dress with a swooping back that stops just short of criminal.

Scared of becoming a fork-bending voodoo child, she rearranged her wardrobe, removing anything remotely New Age. Tonight's dress is as real as you can get. Does she worry about her wobbly gait? Sure, but it's not going to stop her. Hair whizzed into a million curls and darkened lashes *a la* twenties flapper, Daisy Banks, a total babe! Btw, her hair's never been so strong, dancing about her shoulders like a shampoo ad. Her nails too are unbreakable. Nikki who helps in the stable says it's the gunge they put on hoofs. Daisy doesn't spread gunge on her legs and yet they're so supple she can wear the scarlet Kurt Geiger heels.

It is the Power. 'Go on! Give them a blast!' Sharonda wheedles. 'I'm no asking you to cure somethin' minging. Just give me boobs!' Daisy is adamant. 'I'm no healer. If I were I wouldn't have vet bills.' Sharonda doesn't believe her, neither do the Siamese, hissing whenever she approaches; most creatures give her a wide berth, only Baz, Biddy, and Boff-2 stand fast. Boff might wear a new skin but underneath he's the same soul and so determined to regain a former identity he's reverted to three legs, the fourth having to be surgically removed to arise Boffin Mark 2, aka Lazarus, the Wonder Cat.

* * *

Around one she gave up hope of seeing Lucian – thirty-some-things doing *Saturday Night Fever* not his thing. Earlier today he came to see Kate, saying the bakery she was buying might benefit from a structural survey.

'Bakery?' queried Daisy. 'I thought you were looking for a cottage.'

'Jasmine has a mate at school. His folks are moving to Pit-lochry and leaving the bakery. I thought I might buy it. Lucian's giving me a hand.'

'And the Pudding Club?'

'I'll be carrying it on in Galashiels.'

'And when will this be happening?'

'I was going to talk to you about that,' said Kate, red-faced. 'I was gonna ask if me and the kids could hang on here a while.'

What a cheek! Daisy had a mind to tell them to sod off but out of the corner of her eye saw Sean's new braces glittering on his teeth. 'That's okay,' she found herself saying, 'long as we don't let anybody down.'

Lucian smiled. 'You're a good girl, Daisy Banks.' She told him to sod off instead. 'Calling me a good girl! Who d'you think you're talking to, your favourite niece?' Now she wishes she'd kept quiet. It's odd, other than Oscar she's never really been moved, but with Lucian she has a leash about her neck, and just when she thinks she's free he gives it a tug.

Talking of being on a leash – his ex is here.

'Who's the Jennifer Aniston look-alike?'

Bram looked. 'That's Lucian's ex, Sue Watkins.'

Daisy couldn't take her eyes off her. What's more, when she wasn't searching for Lucian she was watching Susie and Susie watching her.

They collided in the ladies powder room.

'You're Daisy?'

'And you're…?'

'Susie Watkins. I believe you're a friend of Lucian's.'

'We're neighbours.'

'You have donkeys? I see them every time I go by the tollgate. They look happy and well fed.'

'They should be the amount of fodder they put away.'

'And Lucian? Is he happy and well fed?'

Daisy blinked. 'He seemed okay when he stopped by earlier. But other than that I wouldn't know.'

'So you and he aren't…?' Susie waggled her hands.

'No, we aren't…?' Daisy waggled back.

'He's a good man but dangerous.' Susie was gone on a breath of *Chanel* and a question: what could Ziggy from the petrol station have that Lucian had not.

Bram took his jacket from the back of the chair. 'Can you hang on a minute? I've got to see a guy and then we'll leave.'

The group were playing a Stones number. Daisy sat tapping her foot. A soldier pushed through the crowd. Same strong build and height, her heart leapt thinking him Lucian, but it was an American from the airbase.

'Pardon me, ma'am,' he said. 'Would you care to dance?'

Daisy opened her mouth to refuse but was drawn to her feet and, lamblike, followed, the crowd peeling aside as butter to the knife.

Have you ever stood in a spotlight, a circle of light about you but everyone else in darkness? That's how it felt, the real world a moth fluttering against the light, and a man and a woman dancing alone. A muscular arm snaked about her waist, and long fingers enclosed her hand; they danced. 'I'm not sure I can do this,' said Daisy, referring to the encounter more than the dance.

'Sure, you can,' he said. 'Just hold on and we'll be okay.'

'I know who you are,' said Daisy. 'I've seen you in Minna's photographs. You were standing next to a man of the same surname.'

'That would be Great Uncle Jim.'

'How can he be an uncle when the photograph was taken more than sixty years ago and the pair of you like brothers? And even if he were, how is it you wear a fibreglass helmet and he in WW2 serge? I'm no military expert but even I know helmets like that weren't around in World War Two.'

'Jim fought at the Somme.'

'The Somme! You mean as in World War One?'

'It's difficult to understand.'

'It's not difficult. It's impossible!'

He made no comment, only steered her around while humming an old song.

'I know that song,' said Daisy, irrelevantly. 'It's one my mother sings.'

Pressing his cheek to hers, Phillip Tree sang softly, '*I'll be seeing you in all the old familiar places that this heart of mine embraces all day through. In the small cafe, the park across the way...*' A sweet voice, and the clasp of his hand so gentle – Daisy could've leaned against him forever.

'I mustn't listen!' she pulled away. 'I'm confused enough without this Siren song. I've got to do as Minna says and stay real.

I'm no ghost. I'm a flesh and blood twenty-first century woman. I work in the City... used to. I wear gorgeous underwear and a fabulous frock, none of your 40's corsets for me. I go to the gym... used to. And I have my eyelashes curled!'

'It's a real pretty dress. I like the colour. It brings out your eyes.'

'Thanks, but I don't…'

'And I like the way you wear your hair. Makes a guy want to tuck the curls behind your ears and maybe nuzzle that soft indent of your top lip.'

'…?'

'You have a great mouth, Daisy. It's your communication system. A guy can always tell what mood you are in. If the corners are up, good times are coming. If down, batten the hatches!'

'Thanks again, but I believe you're confusing me with someone else.'

'I'm confusing nothing. I know who you are and I know who Minna was, same temperament, same luscious looks but different women. She is Mary, Keeper of the Light. You are Daisy, the total babe.'

'And who or what are you?'

Bending to her ear he whispered, '*Tyger, tyger, burning bright in the forests of the night, what immortal hand or eye could frame thy fearful symmetry.*'

'Please, no singing and no poetry, or I'll never be able to figure it out.'

'Don't try. Do as I do, go with the thermal up-draught.'

'But who are you and why are you here?'

'I'm a rookie completing a maiden flight.'

'Maiden flight?'

'You are it.' Eyes darkly serious, he pulled her close. 'I'd love to set your mind at rest about what's going on but believe me nothing I say will satisfy you – nothing that makes sense anyway.' When she went to speak he pressed his hand across her mouth. 'Please, no more questions. I've little time left and want to use it right. Let me just say that sometimes the Boss hands out a reward for services rendered. You are my reward. And so, sweet-smelling Daisy, keep your delicious mouth closed and let me remember how it feels to hold a woman in my arms, to feel her breath on my face, and know I'm alive.'

Daisy surrendered and laying her head on his shoulder closed her eyes, and with his heart beating in her ear, moved about the floor. When the music came to an end he bowed, kissed her hand and walked away. She stood alone on the floor, her heart aching for that lost soul and for herself.

She was about to return to her table when another airman blocked her way.

'Excuse me, ma'am. I saw you dancing with my buddy. May I also...?'

What could she do other than sigh? They circled the floor until she thought, I didn't get his name. 'Your buddy?' she said. 'What was his name?'

'Phillip, Phillip Tree.'

'And you, do you have a name?'

'Chuck.'

'Chuck!'

'You rang, m'lady?' The American drawl was gone, in its place the clipped British tones of an aristocratic angel masquerading as a ghost.

'I might have known. Was it you sent that sweet American to me?'

'Did you like him? I sent him, because a) he'd earned it, and b) so you'd know the photographs are real. Phillip Earl Wordsworth Tree, known as Peewit, died August 4th, 1997, killed on a training mission.'

'And I danced with...?'

'A memory.'

'And the photographs, the man of 1997 with those of 1940?'

'*Espirit de corps,* my dear Watson! *Semper Fi* and all that!'

Daisy was close to tears. Dancing with that wonderful being had upset her. Such dignity and grace! Where did he go and to what fate? Surely he's more than a handful of dust. Now here's Charley at his acid best. 'Don't be so smart! Treat me with respect and tell me why such a thing would happen.'

'If I told you we'd be here forever which is fine by me but not good for you. I'll simplify and say that years ago Phil's gramps told him of Minna and Chimneys. Then when young Phil was killed he remembered Gramps and Scotland and attracted by the notion drifted along.'

'And Great Uncle Jim?'

'Died at the Somme.' Charley whispered in her ear. 'There was another Tree during the Vietnam War but he pulled through so it was only a vacation.'

Vacation? Daisy fought an image of smiling spectres carrying buckets and spades. 'You mean sick spirits stayed at my house?'

'Not stayed, Daisy, *stay*, as in present tense, though I wouldn't call them sick, more disengaged. They hover between destinations unable to make up their minds. But then you, Miss Delicious

Mouth, know all about that.'

A picture grew in Daisy's mind, soldiers crowding together, some in old-fashioned khaki, others in modern gear. The picture enlarged, a cine camera panning to a wider view, more men, more soldiers. 'Oh!'

Charley nodded. 'Oh, is right. The beings attracted to that seductive whorehouse of yours come from many time zones.'

'If Six Chimneys is a whorehouse what does that make me?'

'Don't take offence, ducky. It's only a turn of phrase,' he said, wheeling her about, the music on fast-forward.

She dug in her toes. 'I don't want to dance with you. Give me back Phillip Tree. At least he was handsome as well as polite.'

'You don't think I'm handsome?'

'Dammed superior is what I think! Angel or not, you can be really horrible.'

'And you,' he said, bending from a great height, 'can be really adorable.'

Then he kissed her, his lips the softest breath of air. She closed her eyes. When she opened them there was only Bram. 'What say we go for an early morning canter?'

* * *

They collected the horses as dawn was breaking. Daisy's horse was up for the trip but Bram's horse wasn't keen. 'Is Connor okay?'

'He's sulking. Not used to be woken at three in the morning.'

Off they went. Gaining confidence, Daisy had dispensed with Baggy's limited services and now rode Gloria, a good-natured piebald, slow in comparison to the high-mettle Connor but an improvement.

'You okay?' said Bram.

'I'm hot.'

'You can say that again.'

Daisy's dress was bundled about her thighs. She had a Barbour jacket about her shoulders, riding boots on her feet and a bush hat on her head.

'Love the outfit, especially the earrings. They go well with the hat.'

She was silent. Though she still felt Charley's kiss on her lips the experience was filed under one-of-those-things. 'Did you see me dancing in the club?'

'You were with a Yank from the airbase. A tall guy, great smile. Why? You're giving me an inferiority complex.'

An hour later and Daisy was worried about Connor. 'We should stop.'

'He's okay. He's being bloody awkward.'

'He's not being awkward! He's ill!' Connor was ill, his coat soaking. Ears switching back and forth, he skittered about. 'We should turn back.'

'Not likely! He's being a pain in the arse and I'm not giving way. Pack it in, you monkey!' Bram slapped the horse.

'D'you think it might be me? Animals and I don't always get along.'

'Don't be absurd. You're the White Witch of Endor, why would you and Connor not get along?' With that Connor side-stepped into a bush all but unseating Bram. 'Maybe you're right. He had that colicky spell a while back and off his feed. We'd better call it a day.'

They took the shortcut back through the copse. But by the time they were on the edge of Drummach fields the horse was wheezing.

'Get off of him!' Daisy yelled. 'He can't breathe!'

Connor went down, front legs buckling, pitching them to the ground.

Daisy was off her pony and at Bram's side.

'Never mind me,' he panted. 'Look to Connor!' The horse was convulsing. Daisy didn't know what to do. Scared of getting kicked but more scared of doing nothing she flung herself at Connor, clamped about its midriff. 'Lord, please help him.' Though the horse bucked and kicked there was nothing she could do – she was within the eye of the storm, and death on the outside.

Conner was still fitting, his eyes rolling in his head. 'Chrissakes do something!' yelled Bram.

'Come on, boy!' she called. 'Help me!' But the damage was done; muscles tearing and a great heart breaking, and all the while Charley on the edge of the copse watching. Not Charley the clown or the impersonator! Charley the Angel of God, his wings folded and hands clasped in prayer.

'Please Charley,' she whispered. 'Don't let Connor die.' Blood seeping from nostrils and ears Connor died. One last kick and he was gone. Daisy lay across the body, still trying to give whatever energy she had into the carcase.

'He can't be dead.' Bram spoke over her shoulder. 'There was nothing wrong with him. A bug, the vet said.' She reached back to take his hand but he threw her off, tears pouring. 'It was a bug! A measly fucking bug! I never would've brought him out if I thought he was really ill.'

Gloria was shivering. Daisy went to her. 'Don't be scared,' she said, stoking her head. 'It's all right.'

'It isn't all right!' yelled Bram. 'That horse was perfectly okay. Sure, he was chesty but I put that down to the heat. He shouldn't be dead. Shouldn't be lying on the ground with flies settling on him! Get off him, you fuckers!'

Daisy placed her jacket over Connor's head. 'That'll keep him safe until we're able to collect him.'

Beside himself with grief, Bram turned on her. 'How can you be so calm? How can you talk about safe? He's dead! He's never going to be safe again.'

Daisy offered the reins. 'Take Gloria. Ride back to the village and get a couple of men to help bring Conner home.'

He snatched the reins. 'I heard you were a healer. You're supposed to have saved all kinds of animals. How come you didn't help Connor? Was it because he was a whomping great slab of muscle and flesh not some flabby spaniel?'

'I don't know.'

'Christ, the rumours I've heard about you! But it was all bullshit.'

'Please Bram. Don't do this.'

'Do what? What am I doing but asking where were you when I needed you? Jesus! Call yourself a healer? You're just a silly bitch who likes being the centre of attention!'

She stumbled out of the copse Bram following every foot of the way.

'I should've known it was bullshit,' he spat. 'If you were a healer you'd have done something about the scars on your legs.'

Daisy ran. 'That's it – run. You could've made history today.

"Can't heal her stunted legs yet brings thoroughbred stallion back from the dead! Quick, roll the presses! Inform the world a new messiah is born!'"

CHAPTER TWELVE

Passion Plays

Daisy stumbled out of the lower field into the lane, pausing only to close the gates (so strong were Lucian's by-laws in her head). Hat in a ditch and dress sticky with blood, she hobbled up the lane, blisters forming on her heels. There was only one place she wanted to be and with only one person.

'Please be in,' she panted shale scattering under her feet. The door opened. 'Lucian!' She leapt at him. 'Connor died and I couldn't save him!'

'I know. Bram called. He said you'd come here.'

'Why didn't it work? I've helped others! Why couldn't I save Connor?'

'Never mind that.' He carried her in doors, and crouching stripped off her boots. 'Right now you could do with a bit of healing yourself.'

'I can't have done it right.' She tugged Lucian's arm, Bram's words cutting deep. 'I should've prayed. Do you think that was it?'

He shrugged. 'It's nae use asking me about prayer.'

'Yes, that's it. I didn't pray enough!' she sobbed. 'But you see, I didn't think I was doing anything to pray about until Charley said.'

'Him again!' Lucian growled. 'He has too much say in your life. Clean those blisters. Use the first floor bathroom where water pressure's good. I'll lay out towels, and…' he glanced at her muddy dress, 'something to get you home.'

Every muscle in her body ached. 'I think I've bruised my ribs.'

Lips a thin white line, Lucian was furious. 'If bruised ribs is all you got then you're lucky. It's a wonder Connor didn't kick you to pieces.'

'Maybe he knew I was trying to help.' Daisy started to weep again. 'And don't you start! There's enough without you bawling me out.'

Lucian led her to the bathroom and left her to it. Daisy flung the dress. She'll never wear it again. Rust-red tinged water gurgled out of the taps. She climbed in and ducked under the water, blood turning the water deeper red.

Blood in her hair! It came again, a vision of a hospital bed, only this time a nurse was pulling glass splinters from a girl's hair.

A knock on the door and the vision crumbled. A sponge to her breasts, Daisy sank down. 'Come in!' Lucian held out a phone 'Yon man wants a word.' He set clothes on a dresser. 'A shirt, shorts and a tie for belt. All miles too big but I daresay they'll do.'

Bram's voice was raw. 'I am so sorry for what I said.'

Daisy bit back her tears but couldn't speak.

'I was wrong to say those things. I never meant...'

'I can't talk about it.'

'Okay. But ring me! Even if it's to say you never want to see...'

She cut him off and getting out of the bath dried her legs. She had thought her scars were fading but no, they are ugly. *She* is ugly! Trembling, she stared in the mirror. Her mouth a means of communication? Lord, if today is anything to go by the world has come to an end.

Another rap on the door. 'Come out and I'll feed you.'

Following the smell of coffee she trailed down the stairs.

'That for me?'

'Uh-huh. Something hot and sweet is what you need right now.'

'Then it's you I need.' The words were out before she could stop them.

He frowned. 'At it again, Daisy? Trying to seduce me?'

'I'm too tired to seduce anything. Can I sleep in your bed?'

'Wouldn't you prefer your own?'

'I can't go back feeling like this. Charley would have me up the stairs and I'll never get back.'

'Then you'd better come with me.' They climbed the stairs, Daisy slurping chocolate. He led her to a room and an immaculate Tester bed. Still in shirt and shorts she climbed into bed pulling covers over her head. There was a rustle of drapes, the click of a belt and the unlacing of shoes.

She stuck her head out of the covers. 'What are you doing?'

'Getting in with you.' He carried on stripping, Daisy watching. A strong body emerged from under the khaki, long muscular legs and a tanned chest. He stripped to his pants and stood looking at her. 'Okay?'

'Okay.'

Legs twined about her and arm across her breast, he pulled her close. 'I'm no leaving you. If anyone's leading you up stairs it's me not Charley.'

* * *

Exhausted, Daisy slept until her spirit began to roam and she sat up out of her body. Asleep, Lucian looked younger, a light issuing from his body. She bent to kiss him, and lips tingling, got an electric shock. He slept on, the living sculpture of a thirteenth-century knight, a sword across his body and his dogs at his feet. And bless! There are dogs! The two Bs lay at the foot of the bed.

'Biddy!' she called softly. 'Basil!'

They wagged their tails.

'It's me, Daisy! '

The dogs smiled in their fashion but stayed held in the same cocoon of light. How strange, some aspect of them is here with Lucian yet their bodies are still in Six Chimneys. In sleep the spirit can do anything. It can leap and sing. It can cross galaxies and boogie with the stars, and all without fear of death. It's only in the waking world death appals; dead as a Dodo – dead as Connor.

Oh no! In remembering, the bedroom disappears and again a horse is dying – or rather a shadow of the same; Conner caught on blackthorn rears in agony, flames scorching his hooves, while the spirit of Bram is of a caricature, a bent and twisted gnome fighting to pull his horse free. Daisy ran to help but the faster she ran the further away they seemed to be.

'There's nothing you can do, Daisy.' Charley was beside her.

'There was nothing I could do back there but at least I tried.'

'I'm sorry.'

'I asked for your help!'

'If it had been in my power to help I would've given all.'

'Then why didn't you?'

'I don't have carte blanche to operate within the world of men.'

'That's not what you said. You said you could do anything, *be* anything, a bird, a plane, Superman! Why couldn't you be

Superman to Connor?'

'There are rules, Eternal Laws that even I must observe.'

'If an Angel of God couldn't help what use was I?'

'You helped make Connor's passing easier.'

'How when he's still screaming?'

'That's not Conner screaming. That's Bram. He knew he shouldn't have taken the horse out and so comes here to punish himself.'

'Hasn't he been punished enough?'

'Bram created this scenario. He must dispel it. Remember Kate and the fire? This is another example of the mind playing games.'

'The children's death felt real. This feels fake.'

'Think charade rather than fake. Bram's pain is real. All human life could be likened to on-going parables.'

'You make it sound like one big theatre.'

'...and with an ever-widening audience! Hard to grasp yet there are many plays being acted out within the mental realms. Humankind creates its own reality, whole continents supported by the power of thought. What is the name of your friend's song?'

'You mean Oscar's *Playground*.'

'Yes, Playground, an apt title for the mortal world, a playground for God's children, an amphitheatre where you might be the star.'

'Yeah, third-rate sitcom.'

'Yes, maybe! Farce does seem to be your level,' said Charley, frustrated. 'What were you trying to do with that horse, pit yourself against God? By all means accept the gift but try to understand the limitations.'

'I don't know my limitations! I don't know anything! I'm dancing with shadows!'

'Dancing with shadows an excellent metaphor for what we do.'

'Well, whatever it is I don't want it.'

'Tough! You've got it.' Suddenly a piano is playing and Charley is talking through his teeth *a la* Bogart. ' "...in all the gin-joints in all the world, why did you have to come into mine?" '

'Stop it!' She slapped her hand over her ears. 'You and your contempt! And stop that screaming!'

Charley clicked his fingers – Connor and Bram vanished.

'Is there a heaven for horses?' said Daisy.

'Yes, as there is for all creatures. Tell me, where's the old dog Biddy?'

'Here with Lucian!'

'Yes, guarding her master, loving him. And when Bram is at peace, there, in that loving heaven, you'll find Connor.'

Daisy sighed. 'I used to think you had to be dead to be out-of-the-body. The idea that a dog could have a spirit never occurred to me.'

'Why should it? You're new to the game.' Catching her round the waist he flew into the sky. Whirling and diving, they flew through stars and planets. 'See this, Daisy?' said Charley smiling. 'This whirling mass of matter is what you mortals call the Milky Way and we in the trade know as God's Eyelash.'

They flew so high Daisy's blood turned to ice. She forgot who she was and what, only knowing she wanted to be with Charley.

Out of a dark sky came a howling noise, '*Daaiiissy!*'

'What is that?'

'Loneliness.'

'No, listen! Someone is calling my name.'

It came again. '*Daaiiissy*!'

The sound brought them diving through clouds and into the bedroom where Lucian was in the throes of a nightmare, and though no sound issued from his lips her name echoed about the room. She reached for his hand. He opened his eyes, grabbed her arm, and pulled her back into her body.

'Ouch!' Daisy woke and he was holding her arm. 'You're hurting me.'

Lucian relaxed his grip, but wouldn't release her. He lay looking at her and then smiled. 'So you're here in my bed and rested. What now?'

'Nothing other than you can let go.'

'I don't think so.' He folded his arm behind his head trapping her hand. 'Not and miss a golden opportunity.' Seeing the set of his jaw Daisy didn't ask what opportunity. Her body was already telling her. 'Given that I've lain in this bed God knows how long imagining such a scenario,' he said. 'I'd be a fool to give up before I've started.'

She opened her mouth to tell what to do with his scenario and he pulled her under his body. 'Hush and let me love you!' He pressed his hand across her mouth. 'I'm going make you beg for mercy.' He loosed the tie at her waist and undid the shirt buttons. 'Then, when you think it's over, and you can walk away and forget, I'll make you cry mercy again.'

As good as his word he pushed Daisy all over the bed, his arm under her head and his body ramming inside her. When she wanted to doze he came at her again, an orgasm turning her to jelly. The third time she was on all fours and he crouched on iron knees, bringing them both to a shuddering climax.

It was powerful sex with powerful results but contrariwise left her unsatisfied. She didn't expect declarations of undying love but where was the tender-hearted man who wept for a beaten dog.

* * *

Exhausted they slept. No sooner was she asleep than Charley was lounging against a bedpost. Back in battered RAF serge, he was at his scathing best. 'Enjoyed that? You made enough noise, scaring the poor dogs away.'

'Must you be everywhere? Can't you mind your own business?'

He yawned. 'You are my business and have been since time began.'

Lucian lay sleeping, the sexual athlete gone and a vulnerable man in his place. Afraid Charley would mock him she tried pulling the sheet over his face but was unable to grasp the physical material.

'Strange isn't it?' said Charley. 'What's real here is unreal in the waking world and vice versa. A bit like those bloomers you're wearing.' Then Daisy saw she was wearing a pair of knickers of the post-war variety they used to call passion-killers. 'I know why you've created those,' he said, smiling. 'You fancy the holy arse off me but rather than submit fence yourself in.'

'Oh push off! You're intruding in a romantic moment.'

He laughed. 'I've seen more romance in water buffalo.' Daisy would've turned away but he had lessons to teach. 'I'll show you romance.' He clicked his fingers and she was watching Minna and the real RAF pilot.

The pilot was trying to get dressed. Minna knelt behind him, her arms about his neck: 'You don't have to go yet.' She drew him back on the bed. He resisted all the way and then, laughing, lay in her arms. Minna sat on his chest, and leaning forward, kissed him. Her lips touched his. Emotion flooding Daisy's heart, she was drawn into the kiss. 'Forget about tomorrow,' Minna said. 'Tomorrow is a million years from now.'

He reached up, his fingers working in her hair. 'You're a bitch,' he said against her mouth, 'a dark and delicious bitch and I am crazy about you.'

'Are you?' she said, running her hands across his chest, smiling as goose bumps broke on his skin. 'Let's see how crazy you can be.' She slid down his body, kissing his belly, poking her tongue into his bellybutton, her hands digging under his buttocks, feeling the muscles tense. 'Will this make you crazy?' she whispered, laving his cock with her tongue.

'Oh Jesus!' he twisted under her mouth.

'Or this?' She took him into her mouth, teasing his with her sharp teeth.

'Do it!' he was shouting. 'Do it and make tomorrow disappear!'

Then she was riding him, head tipped back and hair flowing.

'It's no good!' Penis shrivelling, he lay still. 'I'm scared and I don't know why,' he said. 'I've flown that pig so many times I could do it with my head on backwards yet can't get away from the idea I'm never going to see you again.'

'Idiot!' she said. 'Nothing's going to keep us apart, unless you're seeing someone else and this is your pathetic idea of a

Dear John.'

'Like that's going to happen.'

'It happens. People get tired of fighting for what they can't have.'

'Is that what I'm doing, fighting for what I can't have?'

She stared at the ceiling. 'It's what we're all doing.'

He pulled her close. 'And what are we fighting for?'

'Life….'

'….life.' Daisy woke with the word on her lips and Lucian gazing down.

'You looked to be enjoying that dream.'

'Did I?' she said, the dream splintering. 'I don't remember much other than somebody loved me and I loved him back.'

'I guess that would be Charley.'

'What do you know about Charley?'

'You respect him.'

'Yes,' she nodded solemnly. 'I don't always like him yet I respect him.'

'Who is he and how does he fit into your life?'

'I have no idea! I suppose the only answer is to quote Charley, "where you are I am and have been since the beginning of time."'

'Sounds like a jail sentence.'

'That's how it feels.'

'He loves you.'

'Yes. I don't think there's any doubt about that.'

'And what do you feel for him?' She gazed at the ceiling, so many thoughts but unable to put them into words. For Lucian watching it was revealing. 'If you have to think that long there must be a lot going on.'

'There is.'

'Then I'm sorry.'

'Sorry?' She turned to him. 'Why?'

'Sorry I didn't show you how I truly felt.'

Broken fingernails, she plucked the sheet. 'Wasn't that how you truly felt, because I have heard of Lucian the heartbreaker?'

'If I was that then I'm sorry, because I get a glimpse of how it must feel to have your heart broken. Whatever I was I am not that now. All I want to do is wrap my body and soul about you so that you are safe for an eternity.'

'Oh!' Tears billowed in her eyes.

He bent resting his lips on her fragile collarbone. 'Can I show you how I feel? Can you bear to let me love you as I truly want to love you?' Her eyes shadowed, Lucian held his breath, wondering – as she wondered- if he was shooting a line. Then her shoulders lifted in gesture of surrender. 'Show me.'

The window was open and early morning air soft upon Daisy's naked body. Lucian was making love to her. In the half light, birds shifting under the eaves and rain on the window, he loved her long and ardently, kneeling on the rug, his tongue working deep inside until she was coming in shuddering waves.

'Good morning.' He lay back on the bed and entering her rocked his hips back and forth. 'Good morning.' Daisy closed her eyes, the movements warm syrup in her belly, and the tender smile on his lips made her breathless.

The day progressed, Lucian in skivvies drinking beer from a bottle, seemingly a contented man. The gung-ho approach to sex was gone but not the secret behind his eyes. Daisy saw it and was afraid knowing words trembled on his lips, words she wouldn't want to hear.

'What's wrong?'

'Nothing.' He turned his head to kiss her hand and a stud in his ear flashed.

'That little cross is precious to you.'

'My mother gave it to me.' He turned his head, closing the door.

She sighed. 'Don't shut me out. If you've something to say – say it.'

He demurred. 'Now's hardly the time.'

'There's always time to say what's in your heart.'

'I cann'ae tell what's in my heart. It would take too long.'

'Then a little at a time. It's okay. I'm in no hurry,' she'd said, crossing her fingers and hoping. 'I'm in it for the long haul.' The kiss on the palm of her hand took the sting from his sigh. 'Aye, that's what they all say.'

CHAPTER THIRTEEN

Champions

'Does it come in yellow?' Daisy is thinking of buying a new car. Now that her share in the Pudding Club is bought out it seems the ideal time. A Triumph Spitfire is more than she wanted to pay, but hey, a hot image for a hot girl!

Hot is an understatement. Recalling Lucian's face last night when she did a striptease, she giggled. 'Can I play this?' she'd peeled cellophane from a '*Queen*' Album. Carried away by music and happiness she undid her shirt, waving like a footballer on the terraces: '*We are the Champions, and we'll go on fighting til the end!*' Lucian, or Luca, as she now thinks of him, swept her off her feet for yet more delectable love. 'So what do you reckon, honey bunny?' he'd whispered. 'Is there hope for this Scottish bull or am I still breaking china?' She pressed her nose to his. 'There's plenty Aberdeen Angus but we'll work at it.' When he called her crazy it was in her heart to shout, 'crazy for you,' but the feeling so precious she daren't risk it shot down.

Tonight will be the fourth at Drummach. Every morning she leaves to rush back to Chimneys feeding the animals and catching up on the latest episode in the Khan saga. Then she'll shop for fresh fruit and pasta. She even bakes bread! Basket filled with goodies she'll cycle back to Lucian to show off her culinary skills. They eat supper in the conservatory among the scent of peaches while a blackbird serenades the stars. Night fall, they retire to soft sheets and laughter with nary a dream to haunt them – no angels swinging from bed-posts, only Lucian, the Light-bringer living up to his name.

Today at Six Chimneys she found Sean hiding in the hencoop. 'I'm no going to Galashiels.' She tried reasoning with him. 'This is a great opportunity for your mammy. If she's to succeed she'll need you to help her.'

'I don't care,' he said. 'I want to stay with you and the terrapin.'

'You can take the terrapin with you.'

'Mammy said there's nae room, and it's no just Frodo and Sam I cann'ae take. She says no to the rats, the inspector will close us down.'

'You can keep them here. I'm sure Nikki will feed them.'

'She might forget and they'll die.'

Daisy put her arms about him. 'I'll speak to Mammy and maybe she'll let you stay weekends.' As a sign of goodwill she helped carry a cage of rats to his room. 'Are you sure you won't miss your family?' He blinked behind pebble glasses. 'I got ma family here. I need naebody else.'

The girls played with ideas of staying but found the lure of town too enticing. 'Will you and the big feller be moving in together, Daisy?'

She did wonder where it might go and last night, for good or ill, opened a door. 'Is this your mother?' she'd asked of the photograph.

'Aye, that's Eloise.'

'And the young chap?'

'My brother. More wine?'

Snap! The lock on the family vault shut. She wanted to enquire but fear of spoiling the evening stopped her – then wine loosened her tongue. 'There was a time when I thought Oscar and I were friends as well as lovers.'

Lucian had shrugged. 'I never had that.'

'Nor did I! I only *thought* I did. Do you have any more siblings?'

'Only Ian and he's dead.' Swirling wine in his glass, Lucian shrugged. 'He was killed in a motor accident. I wonder Kate didn't tell you.'

'She never mentioned it. When...what...?'

'They were motoring in the French Alps when the brakes failed and the car went over a ravine.' He'd tugged at an ear-stud. 'This was a present from my mother. She got a pair for me and Ian. It's all I have of them, an ear stud and a trace of my mother's perfume, Lily of the Valley.'

So sad! She'd wept and then tried apologising. 'I'm sorry. I don't know what's wrong with me. I'm never this emotional.'

Lucian had taken her hand. 'What's making you feel this way?'

'Maybe I'm falling in love.'

Why did she have to speak? Now she's staring at a pile of horse shit and wanting to weep again. 'Hell,' she whispered. 'Now, I've really messed up.'

'Talking to yourself, Daisy?' Bram Roberts poked his head round the stable door. 'You know what they say about that.'

'*They* could be right.'

He leaned against the door. 'I wondered if you fancy a canter. I've got Connor's death into perspective. The vet said he'd a brain haemorrhage and I should quit blaming myself. I shouldn't have gone off at you like that.'

'You were hurting.'

'Yes, and you haven't forgiven me.' When she didn't answer he shrugged. 'If there's no point in hanging around I'll be on my way.' Unable to resist a parting shot, he'd paused. 'One thing's sure, it's cleared any doubt I had about healing. I always thought it was shite. Now I know it is.'

Bram Roberts put a hex on the day. After he left everything went pear shaped. Midday she had another visitor in Susie Watkins.

Daisy was milking the goats. She wore jeans and t-shirt. Susie wore Armani and La Mer skin cream. 'I was passing and thought I might pay you a visit.'

'Lovely! Take a seat and I'll make us a cup of tea.'

'Not for me. I'm on a fruit detox,' said Sue, patting a perfectly toned stomach. 'Got to get rid of the love handles.'

'Would you like to have a look round the yard?'

Susie glanced at her shoes. 'Maybe another time?'

They talked of this and that, the weather and Connor's death. Then Susie coughed. 'Perhaps I should get to the point. I came because I didn't want you thinking badly of me. The night at the Hopscotch I'd had too much to drink and curiosity got the better of me. Folks say I dumped Lucian but it wasn't me did the dumping.' Inspecting immaculate nails she spread her fingers. 'I've been called all kinds of bitches, folk saying I left because of Lucian's problem. I did leave but he left before me. All Ziggy Mannering did was be a friend.'

'Can't you stop the tattle?'

'And say Lucian Nairne is a liar?'

'Is he a liar?'

'He never lied to me.'

'Were you engaged?'

Susie grinned, wryly. 'We never got that far. If we had I'd not be here talking to you. Once given his word he wouldn't renege.'

'So no promises were exchanged?'

'He was never there to make promises! We'd arrange to meet. I'd be on time, nothing. I'd phone but could never get through. I'd go to the house but he was never there and I'd no army number to call. I did think he was SAS or the like, but when it got really bad I suspected another woman.'

Sharing bewilderment, Daisy poured them both a tot of whisky. 'And was there another woman?'

'Who knows? I used to drive myself crazy wondering who he was with. Days would go by, then it would be "Hi, Sue," like he'd never been away. But that's not the worst of it. There's another kind of leaving that doesn't involve trains or planes, the kind where he's lying beside you, you've given him a million-dollar blow job, but he's thinking of someone else.'

'So what went wrong?'

'I'm not sure. When I heard he was hurt I was scared thinking him coming back minus arms or legs. But I'm not the bitch they think I am. I'd have stood by him except he didn't want me.'

'He told you so?'

'He said "you're a wonderful girl, Susie, but not my girl."'

* * *

Susie left in a taxi with Daisy wondering if she's next for the chop. There wasn't time to wonder, a policeman stood at the door.

'Mrs Khan?'

'Mrs Khan is in Galashiels today.'

'Can you get hold of her? We need to talk to her.'

'Is Leon in trouble again?'

'That's not the name we have. We're looking for Sean. Seems the lad took a pop at one of they street buskers. Something to do wi' a puppy?'

Sean was sitting in the Royal Free hospital trying not to cry. He had a nasty looking eye and his arm in a sling. 'What happened?'

'He was beating the pup wi' a stick. So I beat him.'

'And the pup?'

'In the pound.'

'Get in!' They drove to the pound where a scruffy looking Airedale, with an even scruffier scarf about its neck, joined the Ark. Despite a black eye and nasty shoulder Sean was thrilled. 'What will we call him?'

'How about if-you-do-that-again-I-will-murder-you?'

He tittered. 'S'bit long. You'll never get him in for his dinner.'

They settled for Elrond, hoping the pup's big eyes would work the magic with Kate. She was in no mood to be humoured, Jasmine and Sharonda bickering throughout the journey back and Tulip with toothache! Leon was the only problem-free area and that because he couldn't be arsed.

* * *

It was dusk before Daisy got away. She'd tried calling Lucian but with both the landline and cell-phone busy she loaded up and was on her way. The two Bs were looking hopeful. It being late, trees casting long shadows, she whistled them up for company, and then, homemade soup and spicy goulash in her basket, cycled down the lane. Once upon a time she fretted over a chipped nail. Now she wears sawn-off jeans and a satin bustier. Behind her she leaves a parcel of trouble – a child she plans to steal, and a house with life-force of its own. Ahead is a man who, according to gossip, is a serial heart-breaker but who she can't wait to see. What happened to the City girl with the DK suits? Has she been taken over by one of Charley's Angels?

* * *

The drive up to the house was in darkness. The dogs meandered round the back. A lamp burned in the porch. 'Hello!' she called, 'anybody home?'

Finding new vigour from familiar scents and smells Biddy raced away through the house. Basil was more wary, wise old eyes surveying the terrain with a look akin to awe. Someone had been busy; Daisy tidied before she left but didn't push the chairs under the table or lower the blinds.

She opened the soup and then looked for a sauce pan. There were pans but they were heavy cast-iron, the handles chipped and rusty. 'Lucian!' She pushed the dining room door. 'Where are the proper pans?'

It was so cold her teeth chattered and any logs gathered earlier cleared from the grate. Passing through the hall she was surprised by a pile of mail behind the door. Newspapers, circulars and letters, some addressed to Lucian, others to Sir Alistair and Lady Eloise, why still unopened?

She climbed the stairs. That's it, she thought smiling, I'll open the door and Lucian will be in bed wearing nothing but a grin. 'Surprise!' She flung open the door. He wasn't on the bed because there wasn't a bed, just a frame. And it stunk in there! What on earth...? A few hours ago it the room was heady with the scent of sex now it looked as if the bailiffs had been in.

He's been called away. It can only be that. It's as he said, '*the army whistles and I jump.*' The army had whistled, and good soldier, Lucian had jumped.

Cobweb lace curtains hung tracked back and forth across the closet mirror. Raking the webs with her nails Daisy hit the door handle, the closet opening to a time capsule, *Life and Times in the Scot's Guards,* uniforms hanging in meticulous lines, caps on the top shelf, boots and shoes on the bottom.

She went to collect her dress worn to the Hopscotch. It should've been in the first floor bathroom but no sign of it or a bottle of *L'Air du Temps* or a *Dove* deodorant – all removed. No dress. No *Dove*. No Daisy.

Close to tears, she ran down the stairs into the kitchen. Since she'd gone to so much trouble she might as well have a cup of tea before she left.

The gas was off at the mains. The same with the electricity!

Too dark to cycle home she thought to call a cab but the battery in her cell phone was flat and the landline pulled from the socket.

Scared now, she stood tapping her fingers on the CD rack, puffs of dust rising. 'What's going on, Kate?' she wondered. 'Do you sit on your bum all day?'

It was nonsense and she knew it. Drummach Hall was a morgue, the air heavy with the smell of rusty roses. When she left this morning it was clean. Dust like this does not amass in a day. The house hasn't been cleaned in years. 'Help me, Lucian,' she whispered. 'Tell me what I'm missing.'

A CD leapt into line of vision, the *Queen* compilation played last night with the cellophane still intact. A sick feeling in her gut was made worse by a photograph album. The album wasn't there last night but now – a flashing hazard light – it stuck out of a magazine rack.

A Mother's loving memories, photographs of the Nairne brothers, gap-toothed and smiling, progressed from football shirts to cricket flannels, one precious moment after another, boys becoming men and men soldiers.

The last photograph was taken in a studio, Lucian and Ian in uniform, a third soldier behind them, his arms about their shoulders. Seeing it, Daisy placed the album back on the shelf and called up the dogs. Desperate to put distance between her and the house she stuffed the photograph in her pocket and getting on the bike raced down the lane. Soon Six Chimneys needle-sharp chimneys prodded a sky where millions of stars twinkled and the stained glass window glowed like flags of all nations. Such a magical sight, Daisy felt she could've put the dogs in her basket, and ET-like, peddled up through the sky and in through the window.

Clip-clip, the dog's claws scratched the ground.

Whir-whir went the bike wheels.

Shuffle, shuffle, came another sound.

The hair on Daisy's head bristled.

Clip, clip! Whir, whir! Shuffle, shuffle, a thread of noise mingled with the sound of shuffling feet, the noise growing until it was the thunder of running feet, and boots marching, and of paws and hooves pounding the ground.

Legs aching – never daring to look over her shoulder – she pushed on the pedals. Voices whispered, the voices becoming a plea, and then the plea a roar, '*take me home...take me home...take me home...TAKE ME HOME!*'

Is this it, she wondered fearfully? Is this what Charley wanted me to do? 'Help me, Charley,' she whispered. 'I got it wrong with Connor. Don't let me get this wrong!'

With the mention of that name there came a new sound, a wild neighing and rushing of the wind. The dogs heard and barked in joyous recognition.

Connor sprang out of the darkness! Head high and ears pricked, the great black horse galloped alongside – tongues of fire shooting from his hooves.

Then Daisy's fear melted away. A fierce exhilaration took over. She punched the air. 'I'll take you home!' she cried, her voice rising above the heaving mass as a Lutine Bell. 'Up you go! To infinity and beyond!'

With the scream of a jet plane taking off – hooves cleaving the air and mane and tail streaming – the horse sprang over her head. The remnants of mortal life went with him, rising up through the starry sky in a multi-tailed Comet to where the window blazed in the darkness.

A Door opened. The True Guardian of the Portal, a Six-winged Seraph, passed them through to freedom. Then the Light was gone. The Knight Templar resumed his place. Glass solidified. And Daisy, tears running down her face, sang and sobbed as she pedalled into Six Chimney's yard:

'*We are the Champions! We are the Champions! No time for losers for we are the Champions – of the world!*'

Part Two

Concrete and Clay

CHAPTER FOURTEEN

Photograph

'Daisy?' Kate stood in the doorway, her newly cropped hair gleaming in the sunlight. 'Will you take a look at Leon? He's getting headaches.'

'Sure, wheel him in.'

Mutinous, Leon was dragged in. 'Load of bollocks!'

Kate cuffed him. 'Mind your manners!'

The moment Daisy touched him she knew the problem. 'He's short-sighted.' She closed her eyes, Leon wriggling under her hands like a worm in the sun. Yesterday a woman brought her dog. 'I know Prince is getting on,' she said, 'but I don't think he's ready to go.' The Retriever lay on the seat of the car. Daisy put her hands on his chest and was almost flattened by the pain. It was like inflating a leaky tyre, the more energy she tried to push in, the more escaped. 'Poor old boy,' she hugged him. Brown eyes hazy with cataracts gazed back. 'Yes,' said the eyes, 'but my mistress needs me, so do your best.'

Trying to help Leon is like turning the tide -such desires careering around in his woolly head concerned with heavily laden shop counters, and friends with itchy fingers, and how to be ahead of the local bobby.

After the debacle with Connor she saw her wannabe healer days over. The house had other ideas when she arrived home the night of the '*Flight from Drummach*' to Sean on the step, his face blotched from weeping.

'My shoulder hurts.'

'Let me kiss it better.' Kiss was all she meant to do but her hands had life of their own. She grasped his shoulder. Crack! He fell across her lap. Scared witless, she hauled him into her arms. Five long minutes passed, then, 'hello, Daisy,' he blinked like a baby owl. 'God says to say howdy.'

Sean will never forget the day he saw God. 'Go back and you'll become a famous explorer,' said God. 'Stay and together we'll explore the Universe.'

'It was touch and go whether I came back,' said Sean.

'What made up your mind?'

'Who'd take care of ma rattys?'

One evening Sean brought home an overweight friend. 'Ma pal, Butch, wants to show you his mole.' Daisy had trembled, wondering what part of his considerable anatomy Butch would unveil. She needn't have worried. The mole in question lived in a cardboard box, a tiny creature with a silky grey pelt and enormous claws. 'He's off his grub,' said Butch. 'I put porridge out this mornin' but he's no hungry. Will you do your stuff, missus?'

Daisy did her stuff on the promise the mole would be set free. They watched it burrow under the greenhouse. 'Come again,' she said, which proved a mistake, Butch returning with pals twice as ponderous.

Tuesdays are spent at the hospice, Nikki supervising pony rides while Daisy and Sean – and Isla when she comes – visit those who can't get about. They take Biddy and Elrond, smart in yellow neckerchiefs.

Sadly, poor dear Basil is no more. He breathed his last on Bank Holiday weekend, Leon weeping. 'Quick! Baz has fallen down behind the aviary.' They'd gathered about him. 'Well?' Leon had demanded. 'What you goin' to do?' Daisy burned to help but remembering past lessons stroked Basil's raggedy ears. 'Nothing,' she said. 'We'll wait with him.'

'Wait for wha'?'

'For the angel to take him.'

Leon was on his feet and running. 'I ain't waiting for no bogey.'

There was no bogey. Trilby came. And perching on a branch in the aviary carolled Basil's immaculate soul into the clear blue sky.

* * *

Daisy was sorting bric-a-brac for Oxfam when the phone rang. 'Hello, Mr Purdie.' James Purdie is a clerk at Somerset and Painswick, the law firm handling the transfer of Minna's stuff.

'The clocks you donated are to be collected from Drummach this afternoon,' he said. 'Will you oversee the transaction, Ms Banks?'

'I'm sure you can manage without me.'

'Indeed yes. We're simply offering the opportunity.' Unimpressed, he rang off. When a person benefits from a will it's customary for the beneficiary to be grateful. Daisy was neither pleased nor grateful. 'You can keep your rubbish,' she said. 'It's no recompense for breaking my heart.'

Minna's bequest is far from rubbish. Treasure among the commonplace, Daisy kept a pair of antique earrings and a cross-shaped medal. The rest is to be auctioned, the proceeds split between St Andrew's and the Sally Army.

Lucian and Charley are notable nowadays by their absence. Daisy hasn't heard from Lucian since the '*Flight from Drummach Hall*'. She is resigned to his loss but had expected Charley to show – if not in life then via dreams.

She peers into the mirror and a face peers back. Did it happen, she asks? Did a woman in ripped jeans become another Moses to a ragtaggle of lost souls, or is that episode of my life like this house, a maze of dreams?

Dreams are unreliable. They mess with your head and leave. It might be better if memories of Drummach Hall did leave since there is no reasonable explanation for that night any more than reason can be applied to the man who lives there. Sheets on the bed and crumbs on the carpet belong to the living. Last year's mail belongs to the dead.

* * *

'Does'nae *want* me?' Kate argued with the man from Somerset and Painswick. 'I always do Mondays. The bin men come Tuesdays, and you know what lazy sods they are. If the bins aren't out on time they won't collect.'

'I'm sure you have your schedule, Mrs Khan, but as I said the house is closed, and, I'm given to understand, about to be renovated.'

'That's okay. I can work round the decorators. I have a key.'

'Ah, that's the other thing. I am to collect the key.'

Kate opened her mouth to argue but saw it was no use. She was being given the bullet. Who'd have thought it? Six years and wallop!

'Thank you, Mrs Khan. Is that the only key?'

'D'you think I'm hiding another? That I'm gonna let myself in and do a bit o' moonlight scrubbing? Get away! I'm sorry to lose my job, Mr Purdue, or whatever your name is, but not so sorry I need a secret fix of *Mister Muscle*.'

'Ha-ha, Mrs Khan, very amusing. Now if you'd sign here?'

'What am I signing?'

'A cheque in lieu of notice.'

'It's for ten thousand pounds!' squeaks Kate.

'That was the agreed loan, the deposit on the bakery?'

'He's still giving me the loan?'

'Plus an extra thousand by way of severance.'

Kate signed. A thousand pounds for six years of washing dirty pants and cleaning his house, Captain Nairne is getting off cheap. Okay she's never washed his pants but did she take care of him. And to pay her off without so much as a thank you! Goes to show, you just don't know folk.

'Leon!' That tricky child of hers was creeping down the stairs, an envelope sticking out of his pocket. 'Come here.'

'I'm busy, Mammy. I haven'ae time for a chat.'

Kate grabbed him. 'What's that you're hiding?'

'Nothing.'

'Give me the nothing!' Leon fought her but she prized it out of his hand, a letter addressed to Strangeways. 'You're writing to Jason?'

'I am,' said he, sticking out his lips the way he does when he knows he's in the wrong. 'And why not? He is ma daddy.'

'He is not your daddy.'

'He is so! He told me I was his home boy.'

'Home boy my arse!' Kate slapped him till his teeth rattled. 'He's no your father. He's an evil shite and I told you to stay away.'

'I did stay away. T'was him wrote me.' He ducked under her arm and ran. By the time he'd reached the gate he was switching into a loping hip-hop gait, jeans hanging on the rim of his butt.

'Get back here...!' Pointless yelling when it was always going to happen. A door bell will chime and Jason will be there, viewing the world through opaque eyes. Oh, Lord, why didn't she kill him when she had the chance?

Kate nearly did kill him. It was the day he did a Michael Jackson, dangling Sean over the balcony threatening to let him fall. That night as Jason slept she took a baseball bat to the bedroom, the same bat that gave her a fat lip the previous week. Reliving the terror in Sean's eyes she hefted the bat anticipating the squishing sound it would make connecting with the hated scull. Then Jason spoilt it, weeping like a kid in his sleep. She couldn't do it – more's the pity, because the following week he set fire to the squat.

Memories of that time are fixed in her mind. A fireman woke her, piercing golden eyes peering through an oxygen mask. 'Let us take you out.'

'My kids! Where are my kids?'

'They're safe,' he said leading her from the smoke filled room. 'They're with my colleague, a bit strung up but coming through.'

They were huddled about a female fire-fighter. Kate ran to them. 'Leave my kids alone!' she shouted. 'You're not taking them anywhere!'

'It's alright,' the woman had smiled, a beautiful woman, tall with the same eyes as the fireman. 'We won't go anywhere until you say.'

'Did you get him?' Kate had grabbed her kids to her heart. 'Did you get that murdering bastard? And will you lock him up and throw away the key?' she'd yelled beside herself in an agony of fear. 'Or will some saggy-arsed judge, who never had kids, let the bastard off with a fecking pat on the head?'

The woman had put her arm about her. 'You and your children are safe. Jason Myers can never hurt you again. So let it go, Kate.'

How could she let it go? There's a purpose behind the letter sent to Leon. Ten-to-one he's due for parole and paving the way to reunion. It couldn't come at a worst time because now she can't rely on Lucian for protection.

* * *

The phone rang again. Daisy answered. It was the post-mistress.

'Hello Hildy. How are you?'

'I'm fine, thanks. You were asking after Lady Nairne? My sister says she and Alistair and Ian were killed abroad. Best talk to Eddy. She knows everything.' Edith Shillingworth, Eddy to her friends, a patient in the hospice, is a mine of information who, between remembrances of youth, speaks of Minna Gray. 'She was a pal of mine. We'd get tipsy together at Hogmanay. Mary loved a wee dram.' Edith's eyes twinkled. 'And other things beside.'

'So I've heard.'

'Been bandying her name aboot, have they? Don't mind what people tell you. Mary Gray was many things, a flirt, a liar when needful – a drama queen, as you say nowadays – but for all that a radiant soul.'

'People say I look like her.'

'Indeed you do. Same pretty face and green eyes.'

'How old was she when she died?'

'Mary was one of those ageless women. She passed in the summer of '73. She was away when it happened. Picked up one of they bugs I expect. The lads brought her home. Ah Mary! I miss her still.'

* * *

Daisy still has the photograph sneaked from Drummach Hall. She had meant Kate to return it, but Lucian giving notice had upset her. 'I never thought to be paid off like a cheap tart.' Daisy saw the cheque and didn't think ten thousand pounds particularly cheap. 'Maybe he's been called away,' she said, offering salve to her own heart as well as Kate's.

'Then why didn't he say?'

'I don't know. I guess it depends on the depth of the relationship.'

'By depth are you referring to your relationship with him or mine?'

'I couldn't say. I never understood yours.'

'It was good!' Kate exploded, her Northern accent overriding borrowed Scots. 'Until you came along it was the best days of my life.'

'I'm sorry. It seems I rained on your parade.'

'You more than rained! You were a fecking deluge!'

Daisy was incensed. 'How can you talk to me that way? Haven't I done my best for you and your children?' Kate paused.

'Aye, you have and I didn'ae mean to have a go. It's Jason. I caught him writing to Leon.'

Daisy was sorry about Jason but furious with Kate *and* Lucian. How dare she speak to me like that? And how dare he suggest a former bed-mate for my cleaner? I thought Oscar was tricky but he's worse. Btw, Oscar is in the news again, a contestant in *Big Brother*, and bored, he escaped, Breakfast TV filming him flirting with the presenter as he sat astride the fence.

It's okay! Let him have his moment. Daisy could care less. Now the Khans are leaving she'll open Chimneys as a Retreat. If pets do well here so can City bankers. It's only what Minna did when she was alive.

* * *

Daisy is at the hospice with Edith Shillingworth. 'Och, thank you, dear! I do so love roses. Now, how are you finding things? Not too many problems?'

'A few but I cope.'

'I'm sure. You're a slip of a lass but strong. You'll need to be if you're planning to stay.' At Daisy's questioning look Edith shrugged. 'I'm ninety-eight. You cann'ae live that long without recognising oddities when you see 'em. That hoos was an oddity when Mary was alive. I doubt it's changed.'

'I rather thought it was Minna that made it odd.'

'Och no! Six Chimneys was a law unto itself long before she arrived. Folk came with faces full of hope but were gone within a year. You need a firm hand to live there. Mary had a small but weighty fist. She wouldn'ae put up with trouble.' Edith smiled slyly. 'I hear you've your own bit of eccentricity.'

When Daisy stayed silent she nodded. 'You're right to be discreet. We live in an age of rockets to Mars but that does'nae mean fey folk like you are fireproof. They may not tie you to a stake but you can still burn.'

Daisy sighed. 'Someone said living in Six Chimneys is living between worlds and to survive I must be real. Trouble is I'm no longer sure what is real.'

Eddy nodded. 'Aye, I know. I've stayed there. You can bide there, talk with a person, and then realise you're talking with shadows. '

'Yes, and worlds that overlap.'

Eddy put out her hand. 'It's no those worlds you need worry about. It's this world. It's not the first time I've heard your name mentioned.'

Daisy sighed. 'It's Butch and co, Sean's friends. I don't mind them coming but they will say silly things like I'm an angel and that kind of rubbish.'

'Mary had the same trouble, fine for love potions but quick to blame. A learned girl, a blue stocking Oxbridge and all, before the war she could be as strange as she liked. Then the lads arrived, the Yanks and Brylcreme Boys, and suddenly she's a tart. Mary was no tart. She was a mystic but found you cann'ae get away from the no-smoke-without-fire mentality.'

'I'd better be careful.'

'Especially with youngsters! That hoos attracts the small and vulnerable. Minna couldn'ae keep Eloise's boys away, especially Lucian. But can you blame the lad with the Brigadier for granddaddy and Alistair for father?'

'Was his father not a nice man?'

'Alistair was a chip off an old block, miserly as Scrooge and a brute withal. Nae physical stuff, but cold as the clay and tongue like a lash. Lucian got oot via the army but Ian wasn'ae so lucky. He was a bit touched in the head. That's why she ran, afraid the father would stick the lad in the army.

'Eloise ran away?'

'Aye, and set up in gay Paree selling gowns, although there were those who said a Yank put up the money. Poor woman, she killed in the mountains along with Alistair and young Ian.' Edith grimaced. 'A terrible tragedy, especially with their elder lad dying! Talk about lightning striking twice!'

'Elder lad? She had three sons?'

'No, just the two, Lucian and Ian.'

'Lucian didn't die.'

'Did he not?' Edith stared. 'Was he no shot in the heed?'

'God no! He was hurt but is okay now.'

'Not dead? Well, I'm blessed. That's the trouble with old age and morphine. You remember trivialities and forget the important stuff.'

'Actually Edith, there was something I wanted to show you.' Daisy opened her bag for the photograph. 'Would you look at this?'

Edith settled specs on her nose. 'I remember this. That's Lucian and young Ian in the cadets. This would be about that time Eloise first ran away.'

'Why didn't she take Lucian?'

'She thought him able to manage. He was on his way to the army proper whereas Ian wasn'ae cut oot for that. She crept oot one night. The husband trailed her back and forth, until eventually all three of 'em died.'

'Poor Lucian.'

'Aye, poor Lucian. He didn'ae have the best of times. Him older, and Ian not so bright, it fell on him to look after things.' Edith stared at the photograph and sighed. 'And there they are, hope in their wee faces.'

'What about the man standing behind them?' Daisy pointed over her shoulder. 'Do you know who he is?'

Edith peered hard at the photograph. 'Is there another man?'

Daisy didn't say another word. It was Charley in the photograph, full military fig, a cap back on his head and his arms about the boys.

In the car park she looked again. It is Charley. Look! He's smiling! And Ian is reaching up to hold his hand! And suddenly for one blessed moment nothing mattered – not empty houses, or horses that can fly, or hands that can heal. Lucian isn't alone, a Guardian Angel watches over him and his family.

She started the engine. 'God bless you, Charley,' she whispered.

'And God bless you,' Charley whispered back.

CHAPTER FIFTEEN

Patterns

Lucian dreamed a dream he'd had many times before. He is sheltering from a storm. Not that this crib offers a deal of protection: what was once a church is now a ruin, the roof open to the sky and snow blowing through smoke-scarred rafters. Cold and confused, he huddles beneath the East window. He has no idea how long he's been here, and with his watch broken has no way of monitoring time. That his unit came under surprise attack is all he could suppose – whatever happened it must've been fast because not only was he minus jacket and boots, radio and sidearm are missing.

'Hey, Jock!' An RAF pilot pushed through the snow, his face through the stained-glass window as blue as his jacket. 'Room inside for a little 'un?'

'Step right in. The door's wide open.'

'Jesu! Talk of devastation! And yet that window managed to survive.'

Amazingly, the East window is intact. Crimson bleeding into blue and gold, it glows through the night like a fabulous Rubens painting. Seeing it through a newcomer's eyes Lucian shared the wonder. 'Yeah, how did that survive?'

'I guess some things are too beautiful to be destroyed.'

Lucian stared. Who's this with the Oxbridge voice and pristine uniform? Silk scarf about the neck and knife-edge crease to his pants, he would be more at home in a Noel Coward play than a war zone.

'So what's HRH's finest doing in this Godforsaken place?'

'Fighting a futile war same as everyone else. How about you?'

'My unit got caught on the hop.'

'Are you injured?'

'My pride is cut to ribbons, but beyond that I'm okay.'

The pilot smiled. 'It would seem that, like the window, you too are impervious to destruction.'

'It doesn'ae feel that way.' Chilled to the bone, Lucian gazed enviously at the pilot's flying jacket. The rest of his gear might look as though it belongs in a WW2 museum yet the jacket is first rate. Catching him looking, the pilot draped it about Lucian's shoulders. 'Here you go!'

'Don't be crazy!' Lucian pushed it back. 'You'll need that yourself.'

'Take it,' the guy sipped from a hip flask. 'I got my own central heating.'

It was like being wrapped in an electric-blanket. 'Okay then,' he said, 'maybe 'til I get warm.' Fog billowed through the roof. 'What's wi' the fog?' he said, the kindness of a stranger inviting tears. 'Lighten up will you God?'

'Lighten up?' the guy laughed. 'I'll be sure to tell Him next time I see Him.'

'Know Him personally, do you?' Lucian grinned. 'Share the odd cup of tea and a cucumber sandwich at the Ritz?'

'Not the Ritz. They cut the bread too thin.'

'Where then?

'The Savoy Grill does great eggs Benedict.'

'Is that right?' The joke fell flat and Lucian's mood with it.

'Yes and a decent cup of tea. I take your point about the fog.

We could be extras in a cheap production of *Gone with the Wind*.'

Lucian wasn't in the mood for word games. 'Tread the boards, do you?'

'I've played a few roles in my time but only am-dram. What about you?'

'I'm useless at that kind of stuff. Too rigid, as my girl would say.'

'Rigid? Is that a problem for a red-blooded female?'

Lucian scowled. He didn't want anyone talking dirty about his girl.

'No offence,' the guy said. 'I was trying to lighten-up as you said.'

Too weary to argue Lucian drank. Fiery liquid hit his central nervous system with the force of a megaton bomb. 'What the heck is that?'

'Holy Water, aka a Bazooka. Go on! Take a pull!'

The flask was passed back and forth; the pilot stayed sober, but warmed by the booze Lucian got loose as a goose and sang of his girl. *'Bonnie wee thing, cannie wee thing, lovely wee thing, wer't thou mine.'*

Embarrassed, he stopped.

'Carry on,' the pilot urged. 'Tell me about your bonnie lass.'

Lucian closed his eyes but be damned if he could remember her name. Come on, eejit, he urged, panicking! This is the one name you must never forget. Then it came to him. 'Daisy! Her name's Daisy.'

'A pretty name. And she's back home?'

Home? Lucian struggled to remember and then for one glorious moment knew precisely where was home – the garden at Six Chimneys, the scent of roses in his nostrils and the lilac tree overhead.

Whoosh! The fog swirled and all knowledge of home vanished.

'I guess home is where your Daisy is.'

'You got that right.' Lucian extended his hand. 'Lucian Nairne.'

They shook hands. 'People call me Charley.'

Lucian couldn't help staring. The guy was powerful-looking. Pure would be the word, a flesh and blood *David*. 'You've lassies crazy for you back home?'

The guy blushed. 'I've had my moments but a long time ago.'

'It can't be that long, not unless you've taken a priestly vow.'

It was a poor joke but well-intentioned. It wasn't a joke to Charley. 'I did take a vow,' said he, 'and celibacy is part of that vow.'

'That can't be easy.'

'It caused problems in the past.'

'What kind of problems?'

The guy was silent for a while: 'A girl.'

'Drink deep, buddy,' the flask was passed. 'I know that, the special face, a love so deep you can't breathe for thinking of her.'

'It was all of that, but as I said, a long time ago.'

'What part of the world are you from?' asked Lucian.

'I'm like the song, "anywhere I hang my hat is home."' '

'You're a regular a regular serviceman then?'

'Yes, sir!' Charley raised his fist in fierce salute. 'A warrior in the Army of the Light in service to my King!' Lifting his head he sang a requiem mass, *'Kyrie eleison, Christe eleison, Lord have mercy, Christ have mercy.'*

An ancient Mass rose above the ruined church and the hair on Lucian's head with it. He'd never heard a voice like it, neither male or female it pierced the fog. Nerves screamed, who is this and why is he here?

The guy seemed to read his thoughts. 'I am about my Father's business.'

'What is it with old men?' Lucian's remembrance of his own father was razor sharp. 'Can they not fight their ain wars?'

'My Father's business is where men lie dead and wounded.'

'So he's into war one way or another.'

'He's into mending war as are my brothers and sisters.'

'I had a brother. He and my parents were killed in '91.'

'You must miss them.'

'I miss my mother and brother. Father and I were never close.'

''91 would have been the Gulf War. You've been a long time alone.'

'It feels like forever. Maybe if I'd been with them they wouldn't have died.'

The pilot shrugged. 'I've heard it said when your number is up that's it.'

'Och away!' Lucian can't stand that kind of talk. 'Is that what it comes down to then, we're a lottery number waiting to be called?'

'I would hope it's a great deal more otherwise why are we here?'

It was a question Lucian was always asking. Why was he always here? He remembers getting the call, a live IED, and getting geared up and writing a last message to Daisy, beyond that nothing. 'Sorry, what were you saying?'

'I was saying my Father sent me to help.'

'What does he do then, your pa?'

'He's an inventor.'

'What sort of things does he invent?'

Charley spread his hands. 'You name it. He makes it.'

'My family were farmers.'

'How come you're in the army?'

'How come you're in the RAF?'

'I like to fly.'

'That I can understand!' said Lucian. 'Alone in that great blue space, banks of clouds beneath and only the stars above – I'd love to do that.'

'That's easily fixed. As soon as this is over we'll give it a go, just you and me and my Pa soaring through the heavens.'

'You guys have your own plane? 'Course you do! I'll bet it's an ancient Spitfire you trot out at weekends for a flip over Cannes.'

'My preference is gliding – Icarus minus the sealing-wax.'

'Gliding? That sounds awful good.'

'If you like the idea of flying why did you join the army?'

'Tradition. Nairne sons are earmarked for the Jocks. The only one who didn't make it was my father; a heart condition, or lack of a heart, ruled him out, hence the need for me and my brother to fill the gap.'

'What is your speciality?'

'The opposite of your pa – he makes, I maim.'

'You don't seem too happy with that.'

'Who can be happy killing?'

'Why don't you get out?'

'I shall when this is over.'

'How long before it is over?'

'How long is a piece of string?'

'Too long and it can hang you!'

'I reckon it's time you rejoined your unit.' Lucian gave back the flask; the guy pisses him off, poking his aristocratic nose into things that don't concern him. 'They must be missing you and your sense of humour.'

'What's the matter? Does the truth disturb you?'

'What truth, Holy Joe, you asking questions that don't concern you? Raking over family business you know naught aboot?'

'My name is Charley, not Joe, and I am imbued with the same degree of holiness as you. As for family business that was your choice.'

'Where my family's concerned I had no choice.'

'You don't believe in freewill.'

'Nothing is ever free. I do the best I can with what I've got and I sleep nights... or I used to.'

'They say a man who sleeps at night is either foolish or fortunate.'

'I don't consider myself especially fortunate so I guess I'm the other kind.'

'They also say a man chooses the family he's born into.'

'Choose my father? I'd have to be crazy to do that.'

'The law says "Honour thy father and thy mother".'

'It's hard honouring a bully.'

'Perhaps your father was also a victim of tradition.'

'Grandfather was a cruel man but did Father have to follow his lead?'

'Mortals are creatures of habit. Your grandfather followed a habit. You follow patterns every hour of every day of your life and every life of your Life. Over and again you dig holes in the earth until they become your grave!' Face pale and his hair seeming to crackle, Charley was on his feet. 'Take this place? Why are you here? There's no battle to be fought and no honour to be won, and yet you continue to haunt a place where no man should linger.'

'We should get out but maybe we need to wait until light.'

'By all means wait for the Light. You'll be able to see clearer.'

'Why talk that way?' said Lucian, 'as if you know things I don't?'

'Because I know things you don't, like right now your greatest desire is to shove that flask down my throat.'

'So what? You don't need to be Svengali to work that out.'

'I also know you are alone and terrified.'

'Fuck you.'

'No, Luca, fuck you!'

Lucian was on his feet. 'What did you call me?'

'I called you Luca. It's how you are known among your friends.'

'How d'you know that?'

'I told you. I know things.'

Lucian leant against a wall. 'I don't get it. I'm sitting here in my breeks. I have nae knowledge of anything but name, rank, and number. Then there's you, who sings like an angel, and cusses like a devil, and is able to read my mind. Can someone please tell me what is going on?'

'I could tell you but I'm not sure it would help.'

'Oh come on don't be so modest! Share the wisdom!'

Charley smiled grimly. 'You are so alike. You both want the truth but shy away from it when it's right under your nose.'

'What's wi' the *both*?' Lucian looked about him. 'Has some other loon joined the party or are you adopting the royal plural?'

'Hush,' Charley held up his hand and energy rolled across space trapping Lucian in a silent cell. Images flashed across his eyes: Daisy by the chicken coop and a dog with a lacerated back. I know this, he thought! This is about the greyhound! Someone had taken a belt to him. Daisy was worried, thinking she should put him down and I lost my temper. No!' Lucian looked at Charley. 'It wasn'ae me losing my temper! It was you!'

It was quiet, a drift of snowflakes like a diadem on Charley's head.

'Who are you?' whispered Lucian. 'Or rather, what, are you?'

Charley saluted. 'Squadron leader, Charles D'angelo, 92 Squadron, Royal Air force, at your service.'

'No! You're not running that by me again.' Lucian shook his head. 'You and your uniform, and your tea at the Ritz! It's some kind of disguise.'

Pulling up an easy chair that wasn't there before Charley sat down. He offered a cigarette case. 'Smoke?'

'Aye, that's you, smoke and mirrors.' Lucian had caught an edge of truth and wasn't going to let it go. 'You said it yourself, amateur dramatics. You're acting a role! You get inside a body like you were inside me that day. It was you losing your temper. You challenging God!'

'No! Not challenging God!' Charley sighed. 'I did get carried away with the dog and wondered why planet Earth was still rolling and why Brother Mick hadn't exterminated the entire species. It hurt. Lord, it hurt! Why do you do it? It's the worst about mankind, hurting a creature that only wants to love.'

'It's never been my way.'

'I know. That's why it was easy to fire you up.'

'You make me sound like Daisy's Robocop.'

'The stronger the man the tighter the hold. You mortals have a saying, "Old habits die hard." And they do, believe me they do.'

'So it wasn'ae me scaring poor Daisy.'

'No, it was Charley scaring Charley.'

'Charley! The name suggests a well-meaning guy but there's nothing well-meaning about you. You're a devil sent to trouble me.'

'Why would I be that? What's the point? Devils are required to tempt the soul into ways of sinning and to enjoy their diabolic selves while doing it. Hanging about a draughty ruin, drinking Holy Water with a self-confessed paranoid schizophrenic, where's the sport in that?'

'There you go again, making me question who I am and why I'm here.'

'So, why are you here?'

'It's the best I can do for now,' said Lucian. 'If I go out now in the fog I'll lose my bearings. Better stay put. At least that way one of us is safe.'

'It's not foggy now.'

'Is it not?' Lucian peered through the window, the hem of the Seraph's scarlet cloak staining his face. 'You're right. The moon's out.'

'You're tired. Why don't you sit down?'

Lucian glanced behind him and there was another chair, a beaten up rocking chair. 'I know that chair. It used to be in the attic in Chimneys.' He looked up. 'I'm dreaming, aren't I?'

'Bingo!'

Lucian sank into the chair. 'Thank Christ for that.'

The angel bowed his head. 'Yes and His infinite mercy.'

'Dreaming? I should've known.'

'Why should you?'

'For a start you've been leaning against soot-stained bricks for more than an hour and there's not a mark on you.'

Charley shot his cuffs. 'It is a nice piece of cloth, Brooks Brothers in the Big Apple, infinitely more stylish than the English version.'

'The flak jacket, is that a Yank job?'

'Naturally. I thought if I was to do this gig I'd better come prepared.'

'This is a gig?' Anger flared in Lucian's head. It didn't matter that he was engaged in a stupid dream. It was this Jackass lounging in the chair got up now as a country gentleman, tweed jacket and corduroy pants! Then would you believe it the Jackass starts to sing,

'*this is the army Mr Jones, no private rooms or telephones. You had your breakfast in bed before but you won't have it there anymore.*'

Lucian hated that song. It really screwed him up. He laid back his head and roared. 'Will someone please wake me? I can't stand much more.'

Charley wagged a finger. 'Now don't get angry. Stay focussed. You'll find it makes your situation easier. Tell me what you meant when you said "at least one of us is safe". To whom were you referring to?'

'Daisy. She's the one I'm anxious about.'

Charley moved closer. 'Why?'

'Because someone needs to make sure she's safe. You can't leave a dead zone unattended. She's got to have round the clock protection. I mean, look at it! There's no cover. I can't leave her vulnerable.'

'Is Daisy here in this ruined place?'

'I don't know.' Lucian was confused. 'She's somewhere close by.'

'So you keep vigil for Daisy. Don't you find that lonely?'

'It is awful lonely but I got company and that makes the difference.'

'All the difference in the world,' said Charley as out of the remnants of fog a dog appeared, two dogs, one following the other, brindled greyhound and ancient Labrador. 'Biddy isn't it?' He scratched the Labrador's head. 'And Basil? Dear old boy you have been busy.'

'So is this a dream? '

'It is a kind of dream.'

'An indecisive angel, that's all I need!'

'So you've dropped the demon idea.'

'Do they give devil's white wings?'

'Are mine beginning to show?' said Charley. 'That means I'm getting weary.'

'Me too,' Lucian sighed. 'I'm so weary I cann'ae think. If I could only sleep I know I could work this out. Can you help me sleep?'

'I can, but if you leave with questions unresolved you're likely to return.'

'I hate this place. Why would I keep coming back?'

'That, as they say, is the million dollar question, still...'

Charley rose to his feet and eyes filled with compassion looked down at Lucian. 'Earlier you referred to this place as Godforsaken. Mercifully no such state exists. His Gracious Presence is everywhere. Yet there are situations where even the Lord God must avert His eyes. This desolate place is of your designing. You built it. Only you can dismantle it. Until you do, you'll continue the vigil.'

'I'm a soldier. I cann'ae leave my post.'

'True.' Charley draped a wing about him. 'Sleep. I shall keep your place. I am the Guardian of the Gate. Nothing will get by me. Your Daisy is safe.'

'Promise?'

'In the name of all that is Holy go in peace.'

The wing about Lucian's shoulder was comforting, like the touch of a brother. 'Thanks.' He closed his eyes and slept. When he opened his eyes he was back home with nothing in his mind of ruined churches or argumentative angels. There was only Daisy and the need to rest. Like a shadow he passed through the house. As he went by switches switched, electricity sparked, and blinds clattered up the window. Dust disappeared. A photograph of a woman and her boys appeared on the shelf. There were clean sheets on the bed and towels in the bathroom. Lucian pulled off his boots and hung his gear in the wardrobe. 'Tomorrow I'll ring Daisy,' he climbed into bed. 'I'll tell her how much I've missed her.'

He closed his eyes and an old Labrador dog and beaten up greyhound jumped on the bed. Sighing, they laid their heads on his feet. As Lucian slept so the lights went out. Gas and electricity ceased to be. Dust grew thick on the blinds. Clothes in the wardrobe vanished. Bed and chairs disappeared. One-by-one the walls fell. All dissolved until there was only a solitary ray of light piercing the gloom, and a man and his dogs dreaming.

CHAPTER SIXTEEN

Promises

'Boys and their stones!' There is a crack in the window about the Knight's shoulder so that from a distance it looks like he is breaking out. 'It wasn'ae me,' said Leon. 'I know,' said Daisy. 'You're a thinker rather than a doer.'

Leon punched Jasmine. 'D'you hear that, a thinker not a doer. So you and Shaz can haul stuff. I'm away with the geeks and anorak boys.'

'Leon!' bellowed a voice. 'Get your skinny black arse up here!' A complex millipede, all parts wobbling in varying directions, the Khans are on the move. Most of their stuff is out. There's only the animals left – and Sean.

Daisy watched for signs of regret. So far not a tear was shed, on the contrary as yet another section of the Khan personality morphed over to Galashiels and 'Fairy Cakes' bakery so Sean's identity began to emerge.

'Am I to call them Willy and Isla?'

'Better not,' said Daisy, who couldn't imagine her father's expression should anyone call him Willy. 'I expect you'll work something out.'

Protective of his daughter, and stickler for detail, William Banks vetoed her plans for Sean, suggesting he and Isla take care of the boy. They put the idea to Sean, Daisy unable to think of his reaction without wanting to cry. Face twisting like a frog he threw his arms about her father. 'Don't let me rattle aboot any more, Daddy. It makes ma head ache.'

Kate is sanguine about his defection. 'I always knew he'd go.' Where the bakery is concerned she tore Lucian's cheque to shreds. When Daisy offered a loan she refused. 'Your ma's offered. A silent partner she calls herself, though she's no so fecking silent.'

The girls came to say goodbye. Tulip is no longer little. In the blink of an eye she's passed from wanting a kitten called Kylie to becoming Kylie. Leon didn't bother to say goodbye but left a farewell gift – a dozen CDs back in the drawer where he found them and her baptismal bracelet.

'Keep an eye open for mail,' said Kate. 'If anything comes bung it on the fire. I don't want bother, especially now I'm seeing Ziggy Mannering. He's no as exciting as some but at least he's sane.'

Daisy climbed the stairs, footsteps echoing throughout an empty house. She's getting calls from Oscar. Though far from interested in him as a lover chatting to anyone is nice. She heard through the Roberts' grapevine Lucian's back. Out for a canter she was stopped at the crossroads: 'Hi gorgeous!'

'How are you, Bram?'

'All the better for seeing you. I hear Kate is moving to Galashiels. Without all those kids running around the place must feel like a morgue.'

'I shall miss them.'

'I guess that means she won't be working for Lucian anymore?' When Daisy didn't answer, he grinned. 'You don't believe in swapping secrets.'

'I believe in minding my own business.'

'I thought he was your business.'

* * *

The phone rang. Daisy set down the currycomb. 'No, the Channel 4 thing is out!' she said, thinking it Oscar. 'And no, I won't marry you!'

There was silence on the other end and then an amused voice. 'I don't recall asking but I'm shocked to think you'd refuse.'

'Sorry,' she said, her heart stopping. 'I thought you were someone else.'

'Clearly you did, poor guy.'

'It was a joke! Nothing serious.'

'Maybe not on your part but are you sure he feels the same?'

'One moment.' Daisy put down the phone, counted to ten, screamed very loudly and picked up the phone. 'How are you, Lucian?'

'Okay until you shattered my eardrums. Can you spare me a couple of minutes this evening?'

The day crawled by. She was applying mascara when Oscar phoned.

'It's me, your favourite TV personality.'

'Not now, Oscar,' she pushed Boff-2 off the bed. 'I've a visitor coming.'

'Have you indeed? Let me guess, some muscular git in a string vest we met at the wedding who lives under a mountain, fucks a goat, and wears a sporran to keep his dick warm.'

'Are you drunk?'

'I might be and then again I might not.'

'You are drunk. What's the matter?'

There was the rip of a ring-pull, a gulping sound, and then he sighed. 'I've got to get away. That Marta bitch is doing my head in. You know, she's been stalking me. Haven't you read about it? It's in all the papers.'

'I haven't time to read newspapers.'

'Too busy with new friends to care about old.'

'I've plenty time for friends who call at a reasonable hour and not three in the morning like yesterday and now when I'm trying to get ready.'

'Excuse me for being inconvenient. I'll call back later when your worshipful presence isn't required elsewhere!' Slam! Down went the phone. Daisy was pressing redial when the doorbell went. 'Hang on a minute!'She opened the door and waved Lucian in. 'With you in a moment. Bit of a crisis!' It was fifteen minutes before she could get away and when she did it was with the knowledge that she'd enjoyed keeping Lucian waiting.

'If you're busy I'd sooner not put you out,' he grunted, as always when nervous or in a rage the Border brogue thickening.

'It's perfectly all right. It was a friend in trouble who needed to talk.'

'He must be in plenty deep to keep you on the phone that long. I tried calling to say I was on my way but the line was busy.'

'Drink? Whisky? Gin? Or maybe a glass of wine?'

It was then he felt the urge to take her over his knee and slap til she stung. Frosty-faced madam! How dare she keep him kicking his heels in her flower-papered parlour while she jabbered with that eejit? It was Curran on the phone. You couldn't miss his wheedling tones. What's he doing in her life?

'I beg your pardon?'

'I said nothing.'

'I thought you asked what Oscar was doing in my life.'

'I don't believe I did, but since you mention it what *is* he doing in your life?'

'We're old friends.'

'You need to be wary of friends like that. He hurt you once. He'll do it again. Can't you do better than a naebody?'

'Probably I could if I so desire, but as I said he's a friend, and unlike you I hold on to friends, even when they're nobodies.'

Things were not going according to plan. What a fool he was to think he could waltz through the door expecting her to love him. 'I'm sorry. I shouldn't have said that. You've a perfect right to help whoever you want to help.'

She shrugged.

Bloody woman was driving him mad. Look at her with cat hairs all over her and her eyes brimming! Ah, but she's lovely! All the time away she was on his mind but he'd forgotten how lovely she was. 'I want to explain about Minna's stuff. I should've let you know it was coming but got called away. I told Purdie to pass the stuff on because it belongs to you. It was left to the notary for the person best suited the house.'

'And you felt I was the one fitting that category? Lucky me.'

Lucian felt his cheeks growing red. He'd never been able to handle sarcasm, and coming from her it was too much. 'D'you not think you suit the house?'

'I don't know. I do what I do. Live how I live. Hope that I don't annoy anyone and expect them not to annoy me.'

'It was never my intention to annoy.'

'I see. Well, thank you very much. As you've no doubt heard most of the stuff went to charity. I hope that's okay with your mother and Minna.'

'Daisy, do you not think you're being a tad unkind?'

'Lucian, do you not think you're being a tad patronising?'

'Excuse me.' He was wasting his time. 'I'll not bother you more.'

'Don't go!'

'Is there any point staying? We'll only be breaking our hearts.'

Then she touched him, her hand creeping over his shoulder. 'Stay, because if you go you'll break my heart anyway.'

He reached round behind him, pulling her close. 'What are we doing, my own Daisy? What is it pulls us together then throws us apart?'

'I don't know,' she said. 'I only know I can't let you walk out.'

He swivelled her in his arms. 'Do you realise we haven'ae kissed yet.'

'Yes.'

'A kiss is special. It's a promise and not to be taken lightly.'

'Yes.'

'I've loved you all my life. Even before we met I knew you'd be here one day, shining and lovely.' He gently touched her lips. 'I shall always love you. Living or dead nothing shall keep me from you.' He kissed her, enfolding every soft millimetre of her flesh. Then he kissed her again, crushing her lips, punishing them both for the pain that was yet to come.

* * *

They had an audience, Boff-2 and Biddy watching. 'Look at the way they sit,' said Lucian. 'They could be a panel of therapists evaluating sexual prowess.'

'Shouldn't they be holding up score cards?'

'And what would my score be?'

'A perfect ten.'

It was a good night with good love and hope for the future. She'd slept with her hand in his. I won't sleep, he'd said to himself. I'll slip away just after dawn – he did leave just after dawn but not the way he'd hoped.

A clock in the sitting room struck four and Lucian dreamt the Angel stood at the bottom of the bed holding up two score cards: 4.9.

'Ah, get away, you finicky bastard!'

'Not finicky, pal, a connoisseur of the finer arts.'

'What do you want?'

Charley grabbed Lucian's hands and pulled. 'To take you on a journey.'

It was weird, like being pulled from quick sands. 'Man, that feels weird.'

'I don't know why it should. Out-of-body is hardly a new state for you.'

'Don't start with the gobbledegook!' Lucian laid his cards on the metaphoric table. 'If you're going to deal with me make it man-to-man.'

'I don't think you mean man-to-man.'

'Whatever strange breed you are stick to it and talk straight.'

'I'm here as councillor. Instructions are to wait a while.'

The quicksand sensation passed. Other than a sense of hovering in space the room felt much the same. He glanced back toward the bed. 'Is that me beside Daisy? I thought I looked younger than that.'

'Don't talk to me about age. When you've been round the block as many millennia as me you'll know how it is to be old.' The room rippled and stretched; Lucian was looking at the same room but in another time and another two people on the bed. The man was tall and fair. Long golden hair and a gorgeous body, the woman was beautiful. Even in the astral state Lucian felt a strong sexual pull. 'She makes me think of Daisy. He looks like you but more likeable.'

'Am I not likable?'

'Can the Angel of Death be likeable?'

'So you do know me?'

'Is that not who you are?'

'There are those who call me Avenging Angel. That of course is ridiculous. Were I to avenge earthly wrongs life as you know it would cease to be.'

The room vanished. They stood in bright sunlight watching two boys kicking a ball. Lucian knew who they were. He didn't want to watch but couldn't look away. The boys played until a voice started shouting. '*Wah! Wah! Wah!*' The words were no more than a rumble but the meaning clear. The elder boy grabbed the younger and they ran, passing so close Lucian could've touched them. Sunlight rippled and they were watching the same boys in their teens. A fight was going on, the younger lad beset by bullies: '*Pissed your pants, did you, moron? Shall we go get your big brother to change your nappy?*'

Lucian's chest swelled with hurt. He watched until he could stand it no more. Overcome with rage, he was sucked into the memory, inhabiting himself of the time. He ran round the corner and clump, swung a cricket bat, smacking the first bully into the rain barrel. Then again, tossing the second aside as garbage. '*Touch my brother again and I'll kill you!*'

Bang! He was back in the bedroom and trembling. 'Why show me that? Why would you want me to remember pain?'

'I want you to remember love. Your love for Ian was a mighty thing.'

'It didn't stop him dying.'

'Do you think death the end of love?'

'It's the end of being able to *show* love. You cann'ae put your arms about a corpse too long. It starts to stink.'

'You're talking of the physical. What about the spirit?'

'I don't know the difference.'

'Come now, who or what is currently talking to me?'

'Maybe it's a part of my brain that doesn'ae shut down when I sleep.'

'Ian would laugh to hear you say that.'

'Ian is a handful of dust.'

'The body may be, as you say, a handful of dust, yet the soul is immortal. Love cannot die. If you want an example look no further than this bed.'

They were watching the same couple. The woman lay on the bed and the guy bending to kiss her, his words passionate; '*I'll always love you. I'll always be here for you. Living or dead nothing will keep me away.*'

Lucian was astonished. 'I made that promise to Daisy.

'Let us hope you live up to it.'

'I don't make promises I cann'ae keep.'

'If you continue to follow your *rules*, Lucian Nairne, you won't be able to keep any kind of promise. Why swear eternal love when you doubt eternal life? What is the point of the promise? Then again, maybe it was a lover whispering sweet nothings and therefore meaningless.'

'You sonofabitch! Call yourself an angel! You're so cutting! If this is how you talk to human beings you should bat for the other side.'

'Steady, Lucian! See what anger does to the world about you.'

The air had changed texture, becoming semi-viscose, twisting in thick undulating waves, and Daisy asleep on the bed twisting with it.

Immediately Lucian was beside her, whispering in her ear. 'Don't fret, love. Nothing can harm you.' Then he was back. 'Okay. What now?

Charley smiled. 'Have you never questioned how you can do that? Move in and out of this ethereal state with such ease.'

'What do I know of such things? I'm a man with human thoughts and feelings. I know nothing beyond that. You say love endures beyond death, I hope it does because I intend to keep my promise.'

'The fellow on the bed made such a promise and kept it.'

'Bully for him! Maybe he could teach me a thing or two.'

'Maybe he could. Are you willing to give it a try?'

Lucian hesitated.

'Whoops!' Charley smiled. 'Fallen at the first fence!'

'Go on then! Do it!'

'It's done.' With that there was the pain and the stench of burning flesh. 'Ah!' Lucian was in a plane, the cockpit ablaze. The hood was stuck. He couldn't get out! Flames chewed his hands and face! Such pain he'd never felt before. It was so bad he vomited even as he fought to be free. The plane screeched toward the sea – the pilot's last thought of the woman he loved.

Daisy woke shrieking.

'What's the matter?' Lucian reared up beside her.

'There was a man falling from the sky!'

'What?'

'A man in a plane! He was on fire!'

'Take it easy! It was only a dream.'

'I know but it was so real. There was a lot more but I can't remember... something about two boys and a cricket bat and...I don't know.'

Lucian was silent.

'Sorry if I made you jump.'

'It's not your fault. You cann'ae control your dreams.'

'It was horrible. I'm frightened to go back to sleep.'

He muttered about it not being a problem. Clearly it was a problem! He got out of the bed. 'I'll take a shower, if that's okay.'

'Please do. There are clean towels. Or if you prefer a bigger bathroom, there's the one along the way the boys used.' He grabbed his clothes and was gone. Daisy stared at his retreating back. What happened to the lover? He's obviously regretting what happened.

She leapt out of bed. I can't be found sitting here. Can't let him think I care. Into her own bathroom she ran. This is Oscar all over again, she thought, despairingly, except with Oscar sex was sex however it arrived.

'Oh shit, shit, shit!' She stood under the shower, frightened to come out. What did I do wrong? Was it because I said I loved him?

'Daisy?'

'Yes?' She crouched, breath bated.

He was outside the door. 'I'm leaving now. I need to be away.'

'Okay!' she called brightly.

'I've left something on the table.'

'Okay!' Hair sopping she leant against the tiles waiting until the outer door slammed and the jeep started up. She was trembling. If there is a goodbye letter on the table she will die.

It wasn't a Dear Daisy letter. It was a jeweller's box, and in the box a diamond ear-stud shaped like a cross.

CHAPTER SEVENTEEN

Sleepers

'Look out below!' Daisy tossed a duvet over the banister. Nobody is home yet the house is far from empty, the *reminders* are having a field day *and* a rep from a holiday rental magazine on her way! Cash-wise, Isla would help but Daisy doesn't want handouts. Independence is what she wants, and close encounters of the poltergeist kind are unlikely to earn Six Chimneys a nod from *Country Bed and Breakfast.* 'So listen, you lot!' She dragged the duvet into the garden. 'Now is not a good time for you to be anything other than welcoming, okay?'

Way up in the attic the echo yelled, '*okay!*'

Muttering under her breath, she hung the duvet on a line and went at it with a beater, trying to knock sense into her heart. Boy, was Sexy Sue right. A whole week and not a call! And what was she supposed to make of the contents of the box? Is the stud 'hello, I love you' or 'goodbye, I don't'?

Back indoors, she was dropping a piece of bread in the toaster when she saw the medal. 'Very amusing,' she snarled. 'Ha-flipping-ha!'

The medal inscribed '*Squadron Leader, CE D'angelo*' was among Minna's memorabilia, Daisy kept it as important to Minna and the man that earned it. However, it's a pest. How many times has she put it and Lucian's earring in a drawer only to find them somewhere else?

Until now the reminders have been low-key, but with the

arrival of Minna's bibelots things took a darker turn, Daisy waking to an open ceiling and dinosaur-bones rafters. Mesmerised, she lay watching the passage of stars until the hole closed up. On Monday the sitting room chimney breast was attacked by a virus and eaten away until she could see through to the garden. Last night she sat watching *Countdown* while less than a foot away a group of invisible men talked crankshafts! It's got so she questions not only the stability of bricks and mortar but her own mental state.

'Cooee!' Mrs MacAllister and Goldie were at the back door.

'Let's go into the sitting room,' said Daisy. In they went, Goldie dragging his hindquarters and Mrs Mac fishing for a handkerchief. The dog lifted his paw. They shook hands, Daisy wincing as twenty thousand volts of pain shot down her wrist. 'Do you think we ought to let him go?'

'I do,' said Mrs Mac, 'I've made up my mind that when my daughter comes next week I'll do what must be done. I need him a wee bit longer.'

Daisy wrapped her hands about the dog's midriff. The air quivered, Charley had arrived. She felt him move into the atmosphere, felt his hands on hers, and heard when he spoke to the dog. 'Come on, old boy. Once round the block and then I'll take you home.'

Warmth powered into her hands. The dog yelped.

'What's the matter with him?' said Mrs Mac.

'He's okay. He feels a bit strange.'

'Look, he's getting up. Wagging his tail! Oh, thank you, Daisy.'

Daisy shook her head. 'I did nothing.'

'You're an angel. You healed my dog.'

'I'm no angel.'

'Then whom do I thank?'

'Thank Goldie for loving you enough to want to stay.'

* * *

The woman from the magazine was late and furious. She said she hadn't realised Chimneys was so out of the way, that she'd been stuck behind a pig truck. 'Two hours of shitty straw showering my car! I would've called ahead but my phone was flat, as I would've reversed but for another pig truck behind.' Daisy offered tea but she wasn't interested. 'Whiz me round then I can get out of here.' She left fifteen minutes later. 'A house like this needs a theme,' was all she said. 'Maybe a spiritual retreat.'

A spiritual retreat? Hah! Daisy went back into the house. Two pig-trucks in the lane? There aren't any pig farms near Six Chimneys.

She dialled the woman's mobile. It was picked up. 'You've a signal.'

'The phone must be faulty.'

Suspicion increased. 'I don't suppose you got a look at the drivers.'

'All I saw was a couple of guys in tatty RAF uniforms.'

'Charley!' Daisy replaced the phone. 'Get down here!'

Silence.

'I know what you're up to!' she yelled. 'And it's not going to work! I'm going to do B&B and you and your buddies are not going to stop me!'

* * *

Lucian was having a bad day. Seven am he got out of bed, reached for his watch, and time shifted forward. Without an obvious progression of thought he was in Northumberland, searching for the identity of one man while trying to maintain his own. How he got to Northumberland he didn't know. He must have driven, the jeep parked on a verge, a heat-haze rising from the bonnet, yet he'd no remembrance of leaving home or of locating the house. All he had was an e-mail from a site called *War Heroes WW2*. On the back was scribbled, in his hand, 'D'angelo, Morpeth House, Northumberland.'

A kid was sweeping leaves; Lucian said he was seeking information about pilots killed during WW2 and that he'd been given this address as a possible source. The kid put down the rake. 'This address?'

Certain he was on a wild goose chase, Lucian nodded. 'And the name, D'angelo. Do you know anyone like that?'

The kid nodded. 'I've an Uncle who was in the RAF, Great Uncle Ed. He was a pilot during the war but he's not dead, he's in hospital.'

'Maybe I could visit?'

'You could but I don't reckon it would help. Uncle Ed's in a long stay unit. He hasn't been able to walk or talk for years.'

Later that day Lucian lay on the therapist's couch. Exhausted, he dropped his guard and told of the blackouts and the out-of-body experiences. To his relief the therapist was neither surprised nor scandalised.

'Tell me again about the plane.'

He described the burning plane.

'And you feel that to be some kind of psychic experience?'

'I'm no sure what it is.'

'Do you dream a lot?'

'One dream keeps on coming, same scenario every time, I'm writing a letter to a girl and then standing at the bottom of her bed.'

'Hardly traumatic, more the kind of dreams had when a lad.'

'I'm no talking wet dreams. I'm writing to tell the girl I'm about to die.'

'It's a stressful life. You can't do what you do and not suffer repercussions. Your mind is on overload. It needs to release tension.'

'Is that what I'm doing with the plane, releasing tension?'

'Visualise the incident and then you tell me.'

Lucian closed his eyes. The pilot died calling for Minna. With that name ringing in his ears the consulting room vanished and once again he is thinking and feeling as the pilot must have thought and felt. There was pain and loneliness and a darkened room, his face and hands bandaged. He is afraid to move, afraid to talk or think because even to think hurts.

'Jesu!' Lucian was back on the couch.

'Tell me what you saw.'

He related the vision. '...and then there's an angel.'

'An angel?'

'Uh-huh.' It was out. Unable to backtrack Lucian told how there are two of them, a pilot, and an angel, and both called Charley.

'That's confusing.'

'You can say that again. I've assigned them code signs, Alpha Charley for the angel and Delta Charley for the pilot.'

'AC/ DC? I sense a touch of scatological humour there.'

'Aye, well, if I cann'ae laugh I'm a dead man.'

'Indeed. With respect to the angel I suggest being careful. Tell that to the army medical officer and you'll be out drawing invalid pay.'

'I know how it sounds. I know what I'd think if it was another guy. But it's not happening to another guy. It's happening to me. Don't you see if I'm to survive I have to believe all this is down to a bullet?'

'I do see. I see more than you realise. And the pilot was alive?'

'He must've survived the fire though how after what he went through is a mystery. Such pain! I tell you, doc, I was glad to wake up.'

'Have you always had such complex dreams?'

'I'm a dull guy. Show me a bed and I sleep. These dreams are the result of a sniper. I guess I've to grit it out until I've a clearer idea of what's going on. You've helped by listening and not calling me whacko.'

'You're as sane as anyone I know. I wonder the Army sent you to me. A priest would've been more helpful, revelation being his field.'

'I don't want revelation. I want my life back.'

'And if the angel turns out to be a divine messenger?'

'Some messenger, him and his double-talk! He's up to all kinds of tricks. Like the name he goes by, Charley, a red herring if ever I heard one.'

'I agree. An angel's name should stir the imagination. It should be Michael or Gabriel, befitting a Warrior in the Army of the Light.'

Lucian drove home. No jump into hyperspace, just a mundane ticket to ride. It was late when he paused outside Chimneys to sit gazing at the window. The shrink said, 'Army of Light.' Alpha Charley used a similar phrase. An image came to mind, the psychiatrist's eyes smiling over tortoiseshell specs. Where had he seen those eyes before? And how come the Army sent Lucian to that practice with an ambience more suited to the confessional box.

He started up the jeep and rove on. Charley is an angel. He can be anybody he wants to be, including a shrink.

* * *

The truth of that thought was made evident later when that night Lucian dreamt of Chimneys window and saw that the glass was damaged and the Knight hanging to one aside. 'What happened to you?'

'Kids and their fireworks,' said the Knight. 'Give us a hand.'

Lucian reached up and it was Charley yanking him into the window.

'I don't know what I did to deserve you,' said Lucian.

'You mean karma, what goes around comes around?'

'Something like that. Why, is it true?'

Charley shrugged. 'Only if you want it to be. My Lord doesn't believe in retribution. He leaves that to mankind. This is what He knows and loves.'

Lucian gazed through Charley's eyes and saw the garden surrounding Six Chimneys and the world before him, cities, mountains and seas, and beyond that countless stars whirling in space – it made his head swim.

'What is this window?'

'A gateway between worlds.'

'Why is it here? Who passes through?'

'Souls that reach the end of an earthly experience.'

'Why d'you need a gate? You're either dead or you're not.'

'Talk about literal!'

'Well, it's true, isn't it?'

'There are people who believe the world can be compared to a dream and men and women the creators of that dream.'

'I've heard that said but don't necessarily believe it.'

'Even so the Gate is here, and dream or not, we wouldn't want those that die to be locked out by an overzealous door-keeper.'

'What would happen if they were locked out?'

'Chaos! Leaves on the track, ice on the runway, a vehicle breaking down in the middle lane on the M25, and a queue back to Budleigh Salterton.'

'I take it that does'nae happen too often.'

'If only that were true. It is in fact a common occurrence. A soul gets his or her spiritual knickers in a twist, creates a glitch in the system, and earnest souls queuing to take their allotted place on Starlight Express have to wait for Mr or Mrs Unfinished Business to sort it out.'

'And you're the one that passes them through. Bit of a nothing kind of job for an angel, isn't it?'

'You think so? Let me show you what's on the other side dying, and I do mean dying, to get through.' With a grinding sound the gate opened. 'Ah!' Lucian covered his eyes. Peaceful souls are not alone in their search for the gate. All passed through, hungry children with overblown bellies, flies on baby's eyes, lambs in the abattoir, a soldier with the bullet in his breast, a stag speared by the hunter's knife – on and on! The Gates clanged shut leaving Lucian shuddering. Charley patted his shoulder. 'Did you learn anything from your time as Charles E D'angelo?'

'I learned about courage. Did he survive the crash?'

'Depends what you mean by survive. Come! I want to show you something.'

They stood by a hospital bed where an elderly lady lay sleeping.

'I know that lady. That's Mrs Shillingworth. She looks in pain.'

'She is but not for much longer.'

The room changed to a vast hall and row upon row of beds where figures lay wrapped in white like line upon line of pale pupae. 'What is this?'

'You're looking at the sick and the comatose.'

'Are they sleeping?'

'Yes, sleeping and dreaming. Some dream of the future, others of the past. Some remember when they were young and beautiful. Others think of their money and how it was spent.'

'Where are the medics?'

'There are none. This is a resting place for the spirit.'

Lucian saw that for every bed there was at least one visitor. 'Who are the people waiting by the bed? Why do they sit so silent and still?'

'They are soul companions.'

A man sat by Edith's bed, his face reflecting pain. Then, when Edith smiled, he smiled. 'Edith dreams of her husband,' said Charley. 'Her dreams make her happy thus her companion is happy. He is what you might term a soul-mate. When she was born so was he. When she passes, so will he.'

'Is it one soul per mate?'

Charley rolled his eyes. 'D'you think this is Sainsburys' check-out? Love isn't on ration. A soul has as many partners as needed. There's no short supply. The soul flies to its counterpart. You have soul mates as do I.'

'Is the pilot a soul mate of mine?'

'You want him as mate? You want to suffer as he suffers?'

'No!'

'I didn't think so.'

'The psychiatrist thinks I'm haunted. He suggested a priest.'

'It's an idea.'

'But not a good one?'

'Bell, book, and candle is never a good idea. I loathe exorcisms as does my Lord. Tossing a lonely shred of life out into the void! So unnecessary! Think how you'd feel if you were floating about the ether recollecting your time as a man and some bibulous bloke in a scruffy cassock throws salt in your eyes and tells you to go up to the Light. Amateurs! Who needs them?'

'So what must I do?'

'I can't tell you what to do. You must find your own way. I can assist but not allowed to make your choices. What do you think is happening to you?'

'I'm two people.' Lucian struggled. 'A soldier who goes to barracks, eats, drinks, sleeps, and loves, and a me who's trapped some place.'

'Can that be sustained? Can one half of an egg exist without the other?'

'I wouldn'ae thought so. Sooner or later the egg will addle. Maybe that's it. Maybe my brain is screwed.'

'You and Charles D'angelo have a common cause; you could say the life of a twenty-first century hero is being compared to that of the twentieth century. Two men with different lives and both split in two? What is it about their individual lives that causes this to be?'

'Both fighters? Is that it?'

'Partly. There is a profound cause of their dilemma. Ask yourself why both choose to remain divided. What is it they seek to accomplish?'

'Is that what I am, a divided soul?'

'Don't get stuck on a word. Look beyond that and ask, if you had to give up your life to save another who would that someone be?'

'That's easy,' said Lucian, smiling.

'Isn't it,' said Charley, smiling back.

'I'd give it up to Daisy.'

CHAPTER EIGHTEEN

Eddy

The hospice called. Edith Shillingworth was asking for Daisy.

'Would you come, Miss Banks?' asked the matron. 'I appreciate it's late but she is a sick lady.' Bonfire Night and Sharonda's fourteenth birthday party, when Daisy left the house was rocking. 'It's too small here at Mick's to do much of anything,' said Kate. 'Could the girls invite a few friends over?'

The few turned out to be many: Goths from the University, leggy teenagers from the College and punk rockers from Sharonda's band, they were rapping to music downstairs, gobbling food in the kitchen, and clustered about the landing smoking pot and talking Existentialism and the Dada movement.

It was as well Leon and Tulip were in Galashiels and Sean with her parents. Most of the partygoers looked to be over thirty never mind eighteen so it was difficult for Daisy to complain other than take Jasmine to one side. 'Don't do anything you regret. I know there's booze and stuff being passed around but I'd prefer it if you two didn't smoke or drink.'

'Chill out, Daisy!' Jasmine did her ghetto-princess head wobble, long fingernails carving the air. 'Me and Shaz have it under control.'

Daisy left them to it.

Edith had been moved. Another old lady occupied the bed by the window. She smiled sweetly and called Daisy 'her daughter.' Unable to pass by Daisy spent a little time chatting. By the time she got to Edith it was dark, lamps had been lit beside the bed. 'How are you?'

'I'm all right but you, why are you looking so frazzled?'

'Kids smoking pot in my parlour might have something to do with it.'

'Rubbish! It's your heart you're worried about not your three-piece suite. So what's happening with you and the Nairne lad?'

'He came to the house, said he loved me and then scarpered.'

'Oh dear.'

Daisy shrugged. 'I can't worry about it anymore.'

'Perhaps it's for the best. You dinna want to be wasting your tears.'

Edith struggled for breath, the morphine pump in constant use. 'Fancy me thinking he was dead. Poor lad alone all these years in that drear old house, I wonder how he manages the upkeep on his army pay.'

'Is he short of money?'

'Most old Scottish families are struggling. Impoverished gentry, Brigadier Alexander and kin were broke but hell bent on keeping up appearances.'

'And yet Lucian recently offered to lend a friend of mine money.'

'I hope she didn'ae take it. We don't want the lad on the rocks, because that's what he is to me, a lad. I cann'ae think of him as a man, only a shy lad quite overthrown by his younger brother.'

'Overthrown?'

'He spent his youth getting between Ian and the world. He had to be strong; his mother needed it, his pa expected it, and Lucian demanded it.'

'You were close to him.'

'I spent a lot of time at Mary's hoos. Ted and me had a strip of land nae bigger than a cabbage patch so we helped at her garden and saw and heard things we weren't supposed to. Eloise was always with Mary in those days. Bosom pals, they'd picnic in the garden, play games and such. Lucian looked on the hoos as his own. It was the one place where someone other than him kept an eye on Ian. Then Eloise stopped going and that was the end of that.'

'Why did she stop?'

'There was a falling oot. Mary suspected Eloise was about to up sticks and leave Lucian behind and so had a go at her.'

'How old was he when that happened?'

'He was in his teens when she first went. Alistair fetched her and Ian back. She stayed awhile then fled to Paris. Then there was an accident. It caused a deal of talk, the usual gossip-mongers raking old coals, talk of suicide. Alistair was a sick man. He hadn'ae long to live. The motor accident seemed awful convenient.'

'Oh my God!'

'Aye, that's what we all thought. Oh!' Edith clutched her side.

'Better not talk,' said Daisy. 'I'll sit and you take a nap.'

She'd brought knitting. While still at the stage of dropped stitches she was persevering. The clock ticked. Time passed. All was quiet but for the hiss of oxygen and chug of the morphine pump. Then Edith opened her eyes. 'Did you do as I told you? Kept your head down about the healing?'

'I'm trying but it's not easy. People keep coming.'

'You must protect yourself. Mary knew that. It's why she started the B&B. It was cover for the real stuff, the medicines and poultices. I'd ask what was in the poultices. She'd tell me to mind my biz. I wanted to be involved but she wouldn'ae let me. "No, Eddy. You have a life. Cherish it." '

'Did she have a man of her own?'

'There were a couple she favoured.'

'Did you ever meet the favoured ones?'

'Maybe. It was a long time ago. There was a Yank she was crazy bout, a real dreamboat. Oh, aye, and there were the Brylcreme Boys.'

'Brylcreme Boys?'

'RAF lads. That makes her sound a tart but this was wartime. You took love where you found it. I was one of the lucky ones. My man came home in one piece. Mary wasn'ae so lucky. Ted's been gone a long time. I felt cheated when he died. But if I'd had Mary's life I could never have had Ted.'

An hour later Edith sighed. 'Looks like I got you here on false pretences.'

'Don't be silly. I was pleased to come.'

'Now, lovey, afore you go you should know matron's had complaints about folks coming to your place with their dogs and all.'

'Really? What's it got to do with the hospice?'

'Nothing but that doesn'ae stop 'em interfering. There's a strong church background to this place. Folk like you give church folk the heebie-jeebies.'

'What do I do here that's different to any other visitor?'

'Nothing. It's not the inmates complaining. It's one of the tea-ladies, a Mrs Roberts. You and her son had a falling out over a horse.'

'Bram Roberts' mother! I might've known.'

'The matron didn'ae take any notice but prefers you not to come.'

'I thought people looked forward to Tuesdays.'

'They do but they won't be asking you, your mammy, or that sweet laddie Sean back again. How is Sean?'

'He's in Surrey with Isla which is as well if what you say is true.'

'The Roberts woman is saying dogs spread germs. Silly cow! We're dying. What do we care about germs?'

'What does matron think I'm doing, holding evangelist meetings in the sun lounge, ordering everybody to take up their beds and walk? I'm an ordinary person. I'm not like Mary. I'm no miracle-worker.'

'That's not what your angel told me.'

Daisy stared.

'Charley, your beautiful angel!' Edith's face was aglow. 'He came to see me in my sleep. Told me I'd be seeing him shortly.'

'Charley came to see you?'

'He did. And I'll tell you something else. The Yank, the favoured one I told you about, the one Minna fancied during the war? He's the spit of Charley.'

Daisy wasn't at all surprised. It would be like Charley to flit about in the '40s looking like Errol Flynn. But she was surprised by what Edith said next.

'He told me you were his special darling. He said he'd loved you all of his long, long life and that you'd help him take me across to the other side.'

* * *

There was a car outside when she got home. Jasmine and Sharonda were waiting. One look at their faces said there was trouble. 'It wasn'ae our fault. We told them not to fool about but they've made the window worse.'

A firework had smashed the glass detaching lead fillets down the side of the centre panel so that now the Knight was threatening to fall.

Sharonda shivered. 'He looks right angry. I'll no sleep tonight.'

Aware of the strong smell of booze Daisy felt sure both girls could have slept on nails. 'Whose car is that outside?'

'Ziggy's. Mammy asked him to pick us up.'

'You'd better go.' Daisy locked the door behind them. The cats began to trickle in, and Biddy, her face wrinkled and anxious. 'It's okay.' She shook Dog-o-Bix into a bowl. 'They've gone now.' Then she set about cleaning up. As always Lucian was foremost in her mind. She didn't dwell on Edith's dreams, if Charley gave the old lady comfort then well and good.

The light was fading by the time she was done All three cats were curled up in the wood basket but Daisy couldn't rest. Taking a jacket from the cupboard she went to check on the animals and then she carried on into the copse. Biddy shot ahead, nosing out the best scents and trails. They were on the way back when a fearful racket set Daisy's hair on end – an animal was screaming!

'Hold on! I'm coming!' Crashing through bracken, birds shrieking, she ran with no idea where to run and found a rabbit in a trap.

'Oh no,' she went down on her knees. 'Who did this to you?' The snare had chopped through its forepaws! Petrified and in pain, the poor creature thrashed about. 'Be still,' she whispered, 'and I'll help you.'

She was too late. The rabbit died. She ripped the snare apart. Damn the people that make these filthy things! Unable to leave the rabbit for flies to consume she gathered it up where it lay in her hands, delicate and torn.

Hurt by the cruelty of man, Daisy closed her eyes and prayed.

It was hard to decide whether she prayed from love or from hate, she only knew she'd never prayed so hard, 'help me, Lord. Help me.'

The wood fell silent. Not a bird cheeped or a leaf trembled.

Bang! The Power came upon her knocking her to the ground, translating hurt and frustration into energy. Heat like molten lava poured through her body with only one point of impact. The rabbit twitched and as Daisy watched great gaping holes in its body sealed. Then flick! Her hands were empty. The rabbit was gone. Cold and shaken, she knelt on the ground. Time passed. Biddy licked her hand. Daisy dusted down her knees, put the remains of the snare in her pocket and went home.

* * *

The telephone rang three-thirty am. 'Come as quickly as you can,' said a male voice. 'Mrs Shillingworth is asking for you.' A coat over her pjs, she was in the car and away. Dawn was breaking when she arrived at the hospice. She ran into the foyer, a woman at the desk, her face haloed by a lamp, waved Daisy on. 'First on the left. Hurry! She's waiting.'

Daisy entered the first door on the left but the bed was empty, the sheets stripped and blankets folded. 'Oh no!' she gasped. 'I'm too late.'

Heart aching, she gazed at the empty bed. A man came into the room. Plain white pants and top, he moved about the room straightening the locker. Then he smiled. 'Who are you looking for?'

'My friend Edith.'

'Ah yes, Eddy. You won't find her here.'

'Where will I find her?' said Daisy, thinking mortuary.

He smiled. 'Don't be sad, Daisy. She is saved.' With that the room was filled with light, and there was a sound, like a mountain crumbling, so fierce she covered her eyes. When she looked again the man had gone.

Weeping, she stumbled from the room. 'Cooee Daisy!' a voice called. A pretty woman in cardigan and slacks waved. 'I'm over here.'

Daisy gaped. 'Eddy?'

'Aye, do you no recognise me?' When Daisy bent to kiss Eddy pulled away. 'No, lovey, not yet. I'm not strong enough.'

The same man came toward them. 'Is your bag packed, Eddy?'

'It's here. Daisy will carry it for me, won't you, love?'

They walked out into the light, Daisy carrying a small attaché case. It was a well organised bus-station with shiny buses. Men, women, and children of all ages and nationalities waited in orderly lines.

Buses arrived, passengers got on, but nobody got -off.

It was a one-way trip.

'This is your stop, Eddy,' said the man. 'Your bus will be along shortly.'

'Thank you, sir,' she bobbed a neat curtsey.

'You're welcome,' said he, and then to Daisy, 'and you're welcome too.'

Following Eddy's example she made a curtsey. He laughed and leaning forward kissed her, lips of butterfly wings and breath of roses.

An old-fashioned charabanc with chrome bumpers and shiny paintwork drew into the yard. Coloured balloons and streamers flew from every window while across the front hung a banner, Welcome home, Eddy.

'Look Eddy!' cried Daisy, but Eddy had lost newfound vigour and leant against the wall old and in pain again. 'Is my Ted there?' she panted.

The bus was empty but for a driver and a grey-haired gentleman peering from a window. 'I'm so changed,' said Edith. 'When he knew me I was beautiful. Look at me now. He might not recognise me.'

'He will know you. How could he forget?'

'He is coming, isn't he?'

Indeed he was. The doors of the bus swished open. Old and bent, moustache bristling and hands shaking, yet smiling fit to burst, he came down the stairs, 'Oh my dear, Eddy,' he said. 'Are you all right?'

Knees trembling and brown spotted hands clutching, they clung together.

Overcome, Daisy stood aside. The old man said, 'you're Daisy, aren't you? My wife has told me all about you. I'm pleased to make your acquaintance.'

The bus driver tooted the horn. 'All aboard that's going aboard!'

'Are you ready, dear?'

'I'm ready.'

'Come on then. There's a surprise waiting on the bus.'

Daisy carried the case to the bus. She didn't think either of them could manage it. 'Can I bring this inside?' she said to the driver, who smiled, his golden eyes twinkling. "Course you can, darlin'. Hop up here.'

The two old people climbed the steps, getting in one another's way, apologising and clinging, petrified of being parted. 'Here's your surprise!' said Ted, mopping his eyes. The surprise was a tan Boxer dog, a tartan bow about his neck. 'Toby old boy!' Eddy was overjoyed.

It was too much for Daisy. She had to get off. 'I'm going now, Eddy,' she set the case on a seat. 'Take care and be happy.'

'Oh we shall be happy now. We have each other.'

'Goodbye! Safe journey!' The doors slid to and the bus moved off down the smooth white road. Two handkerchiefs appeared at the window, and fluttered, and fluttered until out of sight, and Daisy woke…

…to the telephone ringing. She knew what would be said. 'Sorry to wake you. I thought you might like to know Edith passed in the night. She went peacefully and with great courage…but then I guess you know that.'

CHAPTER NINETEEN

Two Funerals: One Wedding

They are going to a funeral. Tomorrow, misery me, they have another, Kate's father died. Today dear Edith Shillingworth will be laid to rest.

The church is packed. Sean, handsome in a grey suit and striped tie, is very excited. 'It's ma first funeral. I'm hoping there'll be black horses and plumes.' There were no horses however the church is a riot of colour. Complying with the deceased's invitation to come 'dressed for a party', Daisy wears a green zipper jacket, black thigh boots and a green cashmere beret, Miss Kermit, as Sean says. Isla, resplendent in tartan bonnet and velvet cape, says the congregation look like the cast of the Rocky Horror Show.

The cortege entered to the choir singing Elgar's *Ave Verum*. Edith chose an environmentally friendly coffin. 'It'll only rot like the rest of me and we cann'ae keep chopping trees.' Eulogies were many, the congregation bursting into spontaneous applause. Edith died as she lived, with enthusiasm and wit, said her niece. The enthusiasm was apparent, love of life shining through her eyes even when in pain. The wit became more evident as the day progressed.

'I've instructions regarding the service,' said the lady vicar. 'We shall sing *All things Bright and Beautiful*, followed by choruses from Eddy's favourite opera *Pirates of Penzance*.' Sean was thrilled and in the middle of '*A Policeman's Lot is Not A Happy One*,' asked if they could come again next week.

It was fun until she turned and saw Lucian back of the church.

Isla spotted him. 'Butter-fingers!' she hissed. 'You let that one slip.'

Daisy kept quiet, her thoughts alternating between Edith, Lucian, and the rabbit. She closed her eyes and there was Charley stretched along a pew, his head in a lady's lap. 'Forget the rabbit,' he said, his voice mingling with Bach's *Toccata and Fugue*. 'You've bigger fish to fry.'

Daisy sent out the thought. 'Did I really bring the rabbit back to life?'

'Put it like this, if he's alive then he's alive. If not he's in rabbit heaven.'

So many questions. 'The man at the hospice? Was he an angel?'

Charley was noncommittal. 'He might have been.'

'Why was Eddy's suitcase so heavy? Where she was going she hardly needed to worry about clean knickers and a toothbrush.' Charley shrugged. 'She was carrying her earthly treasure home. All the love she'd ever known or given was in that suitcase. And I can tell you it was full.'

It was snowing when they left. Isla was in the porch signing books. 'Look out!' She nudged Daisy. 'Here comes that Roberts creep.'

'Hi, Daisy! Quite a turn out.'

'Edith was a popular lady.'

'I didn't know you knew her.'

'We met at St Andrew's Hospice where I believe your mother serves tea, shortbread biscuits, and unwanted advice.'

Bram turned to Sean. 'I hear Eddy took a shine to you. How're you doing, laddie?' He tousled Sean's hair. 'You don't have much

243

to say for yourself.'

'He has plenty to say when it's worth saying,' said Isla. 'Daisy, we're off with the Shillingworths for a bite. If you see your father, tell him where I am.' Cloak flapping, she strode off, Sean tight to her waist. Bram watched her go.

'Quite a character, your mother. I didn't realise she was famous.'

'Mother's books sell in twenty different countries.'

'What it is to have talent. I hear you're thinking of adopting that little lad and that Kate's bought a bakery with a loan from your mother.'

'Good grief! What is your pub the village Search-Engine?'

'There's nothing I don't hear about, including the fact that Kate, or Mahonia, as she's calling herself, turned down Lucian's ten grand.'

'Extraordinary!' Daisy marched on to the car park but when she got there the car wouldn't start. 'Oh won't it start?' Bram was grinning. 'I'll leave you to it then.' He walked away. Daisy leapt out and scooping up a snowball lobbed it at him, knocking his cap off. 'Tell that to your nasty gossips!'

She lifted the bonnet and was fiddling with this and that when out of the corner of her eye she saw a pair of polished boots. 'Need a hand?' She opened her mouth to say everything was under control but it was cold, and he only a breath away. 'Are you going to the Shillingworths?'

'I hadn'ae planned to.'

'Could you drop me there?'

'I'm parked over yonder. Stay put while I pick up the wagon.'

A couple of minutes later the jeep rolled around the corner.

Please God, she pleaded, as she got inside, don't let me do anything stupid. It was cramped inside. Every time he changed gear he brushed her arm. She leant so far away she was all but out the window. Once upon a time he would've joked about that. Now he stared ahead, eyes cold as the snow.

Miserable, she gazed out of the window. Snow was in her eyes yet her heart was filled with Lucian. So dear to her: the cut of his hair, dusky black on this dull day, the smell of him, damp wool overcoat, lemon cologne and a whiff of cigarettes. Beyond this was the indefinable essence of the man. Now it was lost to her forever. 'How are you, Daisy?' his voice cut through silence.

'Thank you, I'm well.'

'Sean looks happy. I understand your mother's taking care of him.'

'We think it best. He'll divide his time between them and Scotland.'

Silence fell, only the swish/ swish of the wipers.

Daisy began to weep, small sniffs and then full-blown sobs. 'Oh don't!' The jeep swerving to the side of the road he pulled her into his arms. 'Don't cry, honey bunny.' Chin resting on her head, he rocked back and forth. The windows misted up. Snow fell. Then he sat back, straightened his tie, and raising her hand to his lips – so final and so very sad – said, 'thank you for loving me, Daisy.'

* * *

It seems Eddy left Sean a share of Copperbottom, a promising two-year-old filly race-horse. Needless to say he was beside himself. 'Can we see her now? Is it in Eddy's backyard? Can I ride her?'

'In the fullness of time, my boy,' said William Banks, fondness in his gaze as he straightened Sean's tie. 'Until then you'll have to have patience.'

Daisy watched Sean race upstairs. 'Is he really fourteen, Dad?'

He shrugged. 'That's the medical assessment. We traced the refuge where Kate stayed but none of the staff remembered him. It seems he dropped out of the blue. But we'll stay at it. Your mother's set her heart on him.'

'I'm happy for her.'

'But not happy about anything else?'

Daisy shook her head. Seeing Lucian again a silence had fallen over her heart. 'Thank you for loving me,' he said, as if it were all over. She was so down not even Oscar's nonsense calls could lift her. Even now she could feel the phone vibrating in her pocket and knew it was he.

'Hello, Daze,' she picked it up later, 'I'm thinking of jacking the Smoke for a while and nabbing over to see you. I could be in Edinburgh by ten. I'll bring a couple of bottles of Voddy and we could talk over old times.'

'Sure, but don't come tomorrow! I've a funeral to go to.'

* * *

One ceremony filled with light and hope, the other a hole in the snow, Daisy prayed for Rajeev Khan, a man so disliked only his estranged daughter came to his funeral. The pallbearers seemed to feel the same way; the coffin sliding into the ground so fast sparks flew from their gloves. 'Bloody hell,' muttered Kate. 'If the vicar talks any faster his teeth'll pop.'

'He's cold,' said Daisy, shivering, 'and wants to go home.'

'So do I but a bit of respect wouldn'ae go amiss.'

Kate watched the coffin disappear into the muddy hole. Goodbye you old bugger, she thought, and may God have mercy on your soul. Raj died the way he lived, causing pain and inconvenience. News of his passing came via an aunt. 'It's your Aunt Bharti. Sorry to call early but I came across your number and thought you'd like to know Rajeev has gone. Are you coming to the funeral? We can't make it – we're short at the pharmacy.' Kate was glad she came. With every sod of earth on the pile she knew closure and the chrysanthemums laid on the grave for dreams never dreamt and the father she never had. She is free and the kids with her. 'Oy!' She nudged Daisy. 'When this is over you and me are for a couple of jars to celebrate. When Daisy's eyes widened Kate grinned. 'No, not Raj being dead, me getting wed.'

'You're getting married?'

'Not *getting* married, *am* married. We did the deed last Tuesday.'

'You're kidding me.'

'Nope. Sorry we didn't invite you. Me and Mick wanted to keep it quiet. Just the gasman reading the meter and a passing postie for witnesses.'

'But...but…'

Kate grinned. 'Close your mouth, Daisy. You look like an Angel Fish.'

The vicar turned to stare. Cheeky sod! He's got a nerve complaining about them whispering the way he rushed through the service. Like this funeral the wedding was a rush job. Two pork chops and a bottle of Chardonnay at the Wayfarer, it wasn't a wedding really, poor old Mick never had a choice, when Kate makes up her mind to do something that's the end of it.

A big soft lump of a man with fallen arches and dandruff he was ideal marriage material. The kids needed a father, Sean was sorted but Leon still needed a firm hand. Kate had hoped it would be Lucian's hand but that's never going to happen. The main reason for the wedding is Jason. He's been transferred to Open Prison and is sending visiting permits via Six Chimneys. She told Mick her fears – his answer was a sawn-off shotgun under the bed.

It's there now, oiled and ready. 'Would you shoot him?' she asked Mick.

'Aye, and tip him in a petrol bunker where no bugger would find him.'

'Do the children know you're married?' said Daisy.

'No and I shan't tell them. Let them get used to Mick first.'

They watched the last rites being performed, and then thinking about Lucian, Daisy whispered, 'what do you think of Drummach House?'

'I wouldn'ae want to live there.'

'Why?'

'I'm not saying, you'd think me away wi' fairies.'

'I would not! I slept there. I know what the fairies can look like.'

Kate looked at her. 'What did yours look like?'

'A house closed up for years. What about yours?'

'None of the fairies lived there – just drifted in and oot like dreams.'

'Did the fairies happen to wear size eleven army boots?'

'And liked the odd glass of old and filthy, if you know what I'm saying.'

Daisy knew what she was saying but like Kate, didn't believe it either.

* * *

They sat in the pub having a bit of a laugh until Kate's face turned white.

'Jason's here!' Daisy turned to look. Monk's tonsure of sandy hair, freckles, and skinny body, what's the fuss about? The man with him, a Cro-Magnon type, might've fitted Jason's rep but was an accompanying policeman.

'Hello, doll.' Jason took a seat opposite Kate. 'Sorry we missed the service. Got stuck behind an artic. We caught the end, didn't we, Mr Thompson?'

Kate gripped her glass so tight the stem snapped.

'Oops, careful!' He scooped the broken glass on to the table. 'Let me get you another.' He was up at the bar. 'Another drink, Mr Thompson?'

The policeman nodded. 'Don't mind if I do.' Back came Jason with a G&T for Kate and a flowing pint. 'You didn't see us but we were by a clump of trees. We didn't want to disturb you, did we, Mr Thompson, thought best to wait.'

'Go away.' Daisy found her voice. 'My friend doesn't want you here.'

Jason glanced up and she knew then why Kate was afraid – nothing in his eyes other than the need to identify the bug before squishing it.

'You must be Daisy, the woman who's been looking after my kids.'

'And how do you know that?'

He winked. 'For the price of a beer old Raj would've sold his soul. Not that it matters now. He's gone and we mustn't speak ill of the dead.' He held out his hand. 'I'm Jason. I expect you've heard about me.'

Daisy slid her hand down the side of the seat to grip Kate's. 'Whoever you are you're not welcome. This is a private occasion. Please leave.'

'I'm going nowhere,' he said, mildly. 'I've come a long way to pay my respects, and I ain't leaving because some bitch says I should.'

His hands were so covered with tattoos he might've been wearing gloves. Spider's web in and around his fingers meant nothing, kids in the village, fans of Spiderman, with the same. It was the insects trapped within the web that appalled – torn wings and quivering antennae, they were grotesque.

Jason spread his fingers. 'Like 'em, do you? They're not everyone's taste but an artist has to do what he has to do. Seen her stuff?' He gestured to Kate. 'Two women alone in that house and no bloke to keep you happy? I bet you not only saw where the roses grow you fertilised 'em.'

'Go away,' said Daisy.

He laughed. 'Right little hot-head, ain't you. Speaking of hot I could do something with your face.' He leant back, his hands forming a director's square. 'An orchid around your eyes, or a Tiger Lilly in keeping with your temper, you'd be the hottest fox this side of Glasgow.'

The police guard sniggered. Daisy sat forward. 'You find this funny?'

'It is only a bit of fun, Miss. He don't mean no harm.'

'I don't care what he means. I want to know why he is here.'

'Jason felt the need to express his sympathy. We escorted him.'

'We?'

'My colleague's out back making a call.'

'Then please collect your colleague and escort this man away. Neither I, nor my friend, want him here.'

'Can't your friend speak for herself?'

'No. She's suffering from laryngitis.'

'You looked as if you were having a good old natter earlier,' said Jason.

'Come on, Kate, we're leaving.' When neither the police guard nor Jason moved Daisy lost her temper. 'This is outrageous! My father is a Justice of the Peace, and when I tell him about this, how this man should never have come and how unhelpful you have been, he won't be at all impressed.'

The guard set down his pint. 'No need to be like that. If you want us to leave we will. There was no disrespect intended to you or Mrs Khan.'

'I'm not Mrs Khan.' Kate found her voice.

'Beg pardon?'

'I said I'm not Mrs Khan. I'm Mrs Mannering.'

Jason looked up. 'Mrs Mannering?'

'Yes! I'm married. Didn't you know? But then why would you? We haven't spoken in years.'

'When were you married?'

Kate picked up her gloves. 'I don't see that's any of your business. But if you're asking you'll find us in the book, Mr and Mrs Michael Mannering, The Bakery, Galashiels. Come on, Daisy. We're out of here.'

On the way home Daisy tried not thinking about it. She'd heard of people like that, men and women who live by different rules. Now having met one of the 'waking dead' as her father called them, she knows Kate has a mortal enemy in Jason Myers – and after today, so has she.

CHAPTER TWENTY

Last Ditch Stand

Daisy will always think of December 21st as the *Day before the Siege*. It began with a curry at the Mannerings and ended with Charley playing ping-pong with the TV remote, Daisy's head, and Lucian's soul.

Click! 'Mammy, make Leon give me the remote.'

'Leon, sit down or get out. We agreed *Ghost* was the one to watch.'

'Yeah, but, I thought it was gonna be a real ghost story with bones and things, not stuff about making pots.'

'There are bones in it and zombies with maggots for eye-balls.'

'Yeah and girls showing their tits, but who wants to see that?'

'You do if the dirty mags under your bunk are anything to go by.'

'Chrissakes! Can we not have a bit of peace for one night? You'll have Daisy thinking we live like savages.'

Daisy sipped a glass of Chardonnay. It's okay, Mick, she thought, any noise is better than silence. Good with the kids and an excellent cook, it's easy to see why Kate, and for that matter Susie Watkins, threw in with this man.

'A little more rice, Jasmine?'

'No more, Mick! I'm watching my figure.'

'Good 'cos no one else will,' muttered Leon. 'Ow! What was that for?'

'Being a pain in the butt.'

'Mammy? Is Zig allowed to slap me about the head?'

'He didn't slap you. And he's no Zig to you.'

Ho-hum, maybe silence isn't so bad. Daisy sat on the sofa squashed between Tulip and Sharonda. The girls giggled, Leon and Mick bickered, and the TV toiled away. Daisy stared at the screen. How odd, I'm here watching a fictional ghost-story while back home is the genuine article. The woman from *Country Bed and Breakfast* sent a copy of her write-up: *Spooks Palace, a great place to stay if you want thrills and chills with a breakfast muffin.*

At first Daisy was angry but when people rang for bookings she was less so. Now, she's watching a black-and-white WW2 movie where a badly scarred RAF pilot talks to an off-stage character whose voice is familiar.

* * *

...Click! Lucian dreamt he sat cleaning his pistol. The RAF pilot sat opposite. Not the pin-up boy of bedroom scenes! This was the Battle of Britain version, patch-work for a face and piss-holes in the snow for eyes. 'Here you go, pal!' Lucian sloshed whisky into a glass. 'You look pretty much how I feel.'

'For your sake I hope not.' Grasping the glass with what looked like chicken claws, the pilot hefted it to his mouth. 'Bottoms up!'

They drank in silence, whisky dribbling from the pilot's mouth. 'Sorry about that,' he said. 'The muscles round my mouth aren't what they were.'

'Are you in pain?'

'Only when I breathe.'

'Do ghosts breathe?'

'You think I'm dead?'

'Well, you're no advert for *Ribena*.'

'I suppose it depends on your definition of alive. If this is living then the alternative can't be that bad.'

'I was thinking along those lines.'

'Quite understandable, old chap. Cheers!' The visitor broke into song: 'This *is the army, Mr Green. We like the barracks nice and clean.*'

'Don't sing that! It reminds me of the Army.'

'It's just a song.'

'I don't wanna hear it, so if you're gonna sing do it someplace else.'

'Testy, aren't we.' The pilot clawed up the gun. 'There've been moments in my life when a weapon like this, or a tall building held a definite attraction.'

'What stopped you?'

'I'm a coward.'

'You don't get a medal for being a coward. What really stopped you?'

'I made a promise to stay alive, plus suicides have a bad rep and buried at crossroads unfit to lie with the decent dead. Crazy! Anyone would think the Pearly Gates were turnstiles and Pete a ticket-collector.'

'And he's not?'

The pilot's jaw twitched. 'You're a cool sort of cove. Most chaps thinking they're supping whisky with a corpse would be screaming for a priest.'

'So what happened? Your plane went down and...?'

'I was picked up by a life-boat. Perhaps if they'd found me sooner I might look less like a corpse but I'm not complaining. Afloat in the North Sea the chances of being spotted are less than zero.'

'Was it worth the effort?'

'I say, draw it mild, old boy.' The pilot peered at his reflection in the window. 'I've heard the surgeon, Archie Mcindoe, work wonders.'

'It'll take more than surgery to make you presentable. It will take a goddamn miracle,' said Lucian. 'I don't mean to do you down, pal, but I saw you were on fire. You tried getting out but the canopy stuck.'

'Ah yes, the hood?' The pilot nodded suddenly old and frail. 'Notorious for gumming up the works.'

'I don't see how anyone could survive after that.'

'Don't you?' said the guy mildly. 'Perhaps you need to find out.'

Click! Lucian opened his mouth to argue but found he was in a life-jacket adrift in miles of sea. It was a role-reversal, instead of getting drunk and arguing with an enigma, he *was* the enigma. Exhausted and certain he would die, the pilot thought on the woman he loved. 'Sorry Minna. It looks like our date is off. The chances of me being picked up are pretty thin.'

Waves bat him back and forth. Delirious, he sings, 'rule Britannia! Britannia rules the waves! Britons never, never, never shall be saved.' Then a dinghy comes alongside. 'You were lucky, mate!' A sailor wraps a blanket about him. 'If it hadn't have been for the flare we'd have passed you by.'

'Flare?' the pilot whispers. 'I didn't light a flare.'

The sailor shrugged. 'Well, somebody did.'

* * *

...Click! 'You okay, Daisy?' said Kate. 'You look a bit pale.'

'I'm okay.'

'Do you fancy a cup of coffee or d'you wanna stick with Chardonnay?'

'Coffee please, strong and black.'

'Scared of the bogey man, Daisy?' said Leon.

Daisy isn't scared, she's furious. The nine o'clock movie slot has been hijacked, Charley using the TV as an educational tool, demonstrating a point to Lucian while sharing it with all in Kate's front parlour. 'I think I'd better go. I have a migraine coming.'

'Don't worry,' says Kate. 'Mick will drive you home.'

'Better not. I'll need my car tomorrow. If I could lie down a moment?'

'No problem. Leon! Get up there and shift stuff off your bed.' The blinds pulled, Daisy lay down, and what with the aspirin, Chardonnay, *and* a migraine, was soon asleep, her head on Leon's pillow prey to a teenage boy's joy and fears. '*It's under the bed...! Give it to me...! I want it...!*'

A thought rose up from the pillow pulling Daisy out of her body, through the wall and into Kate and Mick's bedroom and the source of Leon's passion – a sawn-off shot gun. Downstairs the TV rattles on, the Last Ditch Stand continuing from where it left off, only now it's Charley at the breakfast table. 'I knew you were at the bottom of this,' said Lucian.

Charley shrugged. 'It had to be done. The only way to understand another man's point of view is to become that man.'

'I don't see how the guy survived. I saw him die!'

'Are you sure?'

'Well, somebody died that day and it wasn'ae me!'

'Are you sure?'

'Oh, piss off!'

'Two plus two always equals four with you. But suppose it doesn't always add up and the pilot did die, but, like the saying, wouldn't lie down?'

'Are you saying he was rescued?'

'Yes, he was rescued, but don't lose the metaphor, rather think habits! Isn't it a fact a poor little chuck dashes about long after his head is gone? Might mental habits follow the same way? And might a brave man on the point of dying choose to survive for a need greater than his own?'

'I don't believe you. It's all rubbish!'

'Did the waves feel like rubbish? Did the pilot's fear of dying and his love for Minna also feel like rubbish! Charles D'angelo made a promise. He told the woman he loved he'd never leave her.'

'I made a promise like that to Daisy.'

'You did! Now you're learning you can't make a sacred vow and expect it to go unheard. That man promised Minna he would return to her come hell or high water. He experienced high water. Hell for him was yet to come.'

'Oh, come on!' Lucian was ahead of the conversation. 'You're not going to drop me in a dead man's shoes again?'

'No! Not a dead man's.'

Click! And Lucian is in agony, one nurse peels dead skin from his face while another scrubs his hands with what feels like wire wool.

Click! He's back in the kitchen with his head under the cold tap.

'Tannic acid!' said Charley. 'It's what they used in those days to burn off dead flesh making way for new, which, if you hadn't noticed, is precisely what I am trying to do for you.' He held out his hand. 'Come with me, Lucian! Let's look at possibilities.'

Click! They are in Six Chimneys' garden standing by Minna's tomb. Lucian poked the grave with his boot. 'Is this is where the real Charles is buried?'

Charley shrugged. 'It's not yet settled. What we do in the present affects the future *and* the past. It ain't over until the fat cherub sings.

'I don't get it.'

'That's because you don't want to. Tell me, Captain Lucian Nairne, GC, how much more wool must I pull from your eyes before you're willing to see?'

'I don't know what you're talking about.'

'You do. It's as your father said, you are Jackass stubborn.'

Wham! Lucian punched Charley – or tried to – his fist connecting with clouds, and he is falling down, down...

...and sliding into the body of Charles Edwin D'angelo, a man of ninety plus, paralysed and languishing in hospital: Lucian remains Lucian with his consciousness while experiencing Ed's thoughts and feelings.

'I'm coming out!' Ed D'angelo surges out-of-body, and young and handsome and pain free floats down the ward to where Nurse Janet sits filling in a time-sheet. Ed likes Janet, or Puff, as he calls her. She's on-duty all of this week and not happy about it. He can hear her thoughts: her daughter has a ballet recital Monday evening. Janet wants to be there, especially as her ex can't make it. 'I'm going,' she thinks, 'even if I have to pull a sickie!'

Beep!Beep! An alarm is sounding! Janet is up and running. Lights go on and a crash cart-rams the double doors, a weary locum behind it.

It's true what they say about hospitals, they are the noisiest places. Not that this is your average hospital. A specialist unit, nurses call it 'the last ditch stand', the penultimate resting place for the very rich and the very quiet.

Early morning is mortality-rich. Lots of good buddies take their leave around this time when the air is fresh, and birds are waking, and the sky is as clear as Gabriel's Glance. Ed D'angelo loves the morning. When he was a kid he used to go bird-watching. Now unable to walk he watches the birds in an aviary. And sometimes, if he's lucky, he'll do his own form of flying.

Ed didn't learn to OOBE. It was thrust upon him. It was the plane crashing that did it. It was pain, for Christ's sake! The choice was simple, stay in and be in agony, or get the fuck out of it. Ed chose the latter.

That was in the 40s. He's an expert now and has seen it all, from the Rocky Mountains, to the Craters of the Moon, and the ash that once was Mars. Now at ninety-three he's got it off pat, and – pardon the pun – being a down-to-earth guy finds pleasure shuffling off the mortal coil.

'Oh dear!' Squeak, squeak, the crash-cart is coming back. Janet weeps for the deceased. Ed pats her shoulder. 'Don't cry Puff. He's free now'

'*Kyrie eleison...!*' Here comes the priest. Comatose crumblies, RTA's and those maimed in war, poor bloke must regret being shepherd to this fold.

The light is deepening. There are noises from the kitchen and the smell of fresh coffee mingles with the odour of bedpans. Not that many of the clients have need of those. Most are fed via veins and bagged the other end, san-fairy-Ann to bedpans...or as Phil Tree, the joker, would say, who gives a shit.

Phil Tree, the Yank Top Gun died in '97. It's taken this long for him to adjust. The wings he has now aren't as flashy as the F-117, yet they can outrun the wind and outmanoeuvre the stars. Tick tock! Time is malleable in this state. On a good day an hour can be stretched to infinity. Lately Ed's OOBEs have been about looking after a bomb disposal chappie, the young Scot soldier who arrives here every morning at exactly 0400 hours.

Minna was first to spot him. 'Quick!' She fetched the Keepers. 'Go talk to him before others get to him.' So Ed talks to him, asks, 'do you know where you are?' Or, if the chappie is getting too close to the girl in Room 11, he pulls him back, 'let her sleep.'

After the plane crash Ed didn't know what was happening and spent his OOBE's hiding in the one place he loved, Six Chimneys' attics. Much longer there and he would've given up his body and died. It was Minna's outrageous love that persuaded him to try living again. When you're in pain it's no fun resuming the body, even less when you're old and paralysed. Getting back inside is like trying to shove the Encyclopaedia Britannica into a wet sock.

Ed loathes his body. The closer he gets to that old carcase so borrowed youth fades away. He can touch pain, put an invisible finger to a ninety-year-old-face and watch the finger shrivel. He doesn't want to resume the flesh but will until one day, like Phil Tree, he will earn his wings.

The clock struck four.

Click! With the sound of a vacuum sealing Lucian is no

longer trapped inside the mind of Charles Edwin D'angelo – he is looking at him!

'Hello there, bomb-disposal chappie. How are you?'

Lucian couldn't speak. So it's true, is all he can think, the pilot did survive.

'You keep good time,' said the old boy. 'But working with bombs you have to keep an orderly mind. I was like you at first. Talk about disorientated, I couldn't find my arse with both hands.'

'Who are you?' Lucian found his voice.

'I'll show you.' The old boy drifted down a corridor. He pointed to a bed. 'See over there, the chap with his mouth open? That's me, or rather what's left of me, Charles Edwin D'angelo, though no one here calls me Charles, I'm known as Ed or the old fart in Room 30.'

'If that's you,' said Lucian, 'who or what am I talking to?'

'Better to say *what* rather than who and *commune* rather than talk. Talking implies use of the body. Does it look like that poor sod can talk?'

'No disrespect but I cann'ae see any lips.'

'Point taken. I did lose a fair bit of pucker when the Spit caught fire.'

'What am I doing here? And why am I *communing* with you?'

'You don't commune with anyone. Usually you're moving between two rooms, though mostly you stand outside Room 11.'

'Who's in that room?'

'I'm not at liberty to say. You must find that out for yourself.'

'And the other room?'

'Room 12. You can go in there! In fact, the sooner the better!'

Lucian peered through the window.

'Go in!' said Ed. 'Get it over with.'

Lucian passed through the door. It was dark. 'I can't see anything.'

'Look closer.'

Heart crashing, he bent over the bed. A figure lay there but he couldn't see who. Then a light came on. And he saw it was him, Lucian! The shock bounced him back into his body and his own bed in Drummach Hall, a voice echoing in his ear. 'You've got to go back to the start, Captain. It's the only way. Until you do, you'll keep going round in circles.'

* * *

Daisy swung the car into Six Chimneys drive just as a flower-painted van was pulling out, the real world, Woodstock flavoured, had arrived.

A guy leaned out. 'Say man, is this where the psychic lives?'

'Psychic?'

'Yeah, the chick they're all talking about who makes the lame to walk and the deaf to hear.'

Cold dread struck Daisy's heart. 'Is there such a person?'

'I was told she lived hereabouts.'

'Who told you?'

'A woman in a pub, a Mrs Roberts.'

'Oh, you don't want to believe her! She's an awful gossip.'

'Okay, man. Peace and light.'

'Peace and light.'

The van pulled away.

Daisy let herself in and bolted the door. She put her bag

down and sank down to the floor. The telephone began to ring, and ring, and ring...!

Lucian's nightmare might be over. Hers was just about to begin.

Under Siege

Forget yesterday's telepathic trip round Bedlam; the flower-power dude in the Magical Mystery van was a foretaste of what was to come. A guy from the Chronicle phoned. 'Would you like to comment on a piece we're doing for Women's Interest Page?' He read it out, a discreet little piece entitled, '*Angel of the Borders*,' that told of a girl who not only healed her own crippled legs, she cured the deaf! Daisy begged him not to print it, but it appeared in Saturday's edition with her address *and* telephone number.

Sunday there was a queue outside of people pushing wheelchairs and mothers with prams. Nikki, the stable girl, had to fight her way to the door. Notes were posted through the letterbox, sad notes, '*Our Tommy has leukaemia, please help.*' Some notes wrapped about a dog turd or something equally revolting, '*Burn in hell, witch*!' or '*Eat Spunk and Die*!'

The Wayfarer did a roaring trade, needing extra tables outside and a new selection of pork pies. The Roberts grapevine was working overtime, the main contributor, Sheila Roberts, holding court behind the bar. Photographs of Daisy, her legs in close up, past and present, appeared in the *Sun*, banner headlines: *Healer Heal Thyself!* Monday she opened her bedroom window to tents erected in the meadow and Porto-loos installed. Daisy's story, as told by Jazz saxophonist 'Blues' Curran appeared in *OK* Magazine, which led to pairs of her knickers stolen from the washing line.

Wednesday evening the window was target, the Knight hanging over the stair well, broken wire all that prevented him from being dashed to the floor. The fuss gathered pace, B&B bookings cancelled. Then L'il Kim, the pony, was stolen. Though returned that night Daisy and Kate shifted the rest of the animals to safe pasturage on the Drummach estate. It was then Daisy mentioned the shot gun. Kate didn't seem concerned. 'We'll shift it.'

'Good, because Leon knows where it is.'

'Leon would have found it no matter where we put it. If trouble were truffles and him a pig we'd make a fortune hiring his nose out.'

The genuinely needy were the first to leave driven away by curiosity seekers and hot-dogs vendors. William Banks wanted electrified fencing. Ziggy Mannering had other ideas – a local Ruby team and baseball bats. Then the cavalry returned from a book signing tour of Moscow. Fabulous in Cossack hat and leather strides, Isla diffused the situation, inviting the press and leading hangers-on to the house where she plied all with century old Scottish magic. 'Don't listen to the old girl in the pub. Women like that don't have a life so they screw up everybody else's. Isn't that right, babe?' Babe was doing as she was told, Missy Mouse in a modest skirt and blouse she refilled glasses and handed out sandwiches. Isla was incandescent. When they were alone she did what she hadn't done in years – she slapped Daisy. 'Do you want to mess up this adoption? When the newspaper bloke phoned you should've laughed. No need to be confrontational.'

She's right. Eddy's right. Everybody's right! If she's to have any sort of life Daisy must blend into the background, and so now when they come to the door she says, 'better try the church.'

Not once in all that did Lucian come by. Smoke rose from

Drummach chimneys, he was home but not to her. So to keep from being depressed Daisy did what all sensible healers do, healed by stealth.

Sainsburys' is a never-ending source of supply. A child with snot running from its nose will go by; Daisy will pass her hand over the child's fluffy head. Then there's the overweight and the crippled in electric Go-Karts.

'You go, girl!' she passes the time of day. God, the feeling! Like downloading lightning! But you can't keep filling the fridge with cauli-cheese any more than you can accost tubby ladies in supermarkets. Energy built until she was a Blimp bumping against the ceiling and the attic a hot line to the dead.

Last night she dreamt of Eddy Shillingworth. 'I cann'ae say much or I'll be brought before the Boss but you're to look for a man with dead eyes.'

'Dead eyes?' Daisy hadn't a clue.

'He's coming!' hissed Eddy, Delphic Oracle in twinset and pearls. 'And when he does you must make a choice, the man you love or the child.'

No sooner did she leave than the attic window became a picture screen, and Daisy again looking at a woman on life-support. She could hear a ventilator wheezing and see a monitor flashing. Tall figures in scrubs and masks – more the Judges of Nuremberg than a medical team – discussed disconnecting all life-support. Daisy banged on the window. 'Don't turn her off!' she cried. 'She's only sleeping.' At that a doctor turned, 'sorry, Daisy. It's the only way.'

It was the night for visions and none of them pleasant.

Shortly before midnight she looked up from her knitting to

the padre and Minna's RAF pilot discussing a plane. Sound was distorted, voices cutting in and out. The padre knocked his pipe against his boot and sound burst through. '*...watch out for that hood. Fred greased the slide but I wouldn't count on it.*' Then snippets of the *Last Ditch Stand* burst out, Lucian being put through his paces, the RAF pilot rescued from the sea, and the old man with the scarred face, and something Charley said about what we do in the present affecting the past came to mind.

She leapt on a stool. 'Hello!' she called. 'Can anyone hear me?'

Silence. She tried again. 'Charles Edwin D'angelo, one time pilot in the RAF, the padre is right! That hood is more than tricky, it's lethal!' She tried one last time. 'Get the hood fixed or at least take a hammer with you!'

* * *

Six in the morning there was singing at the door. 'Daisy, Daisy, give me your answer do! I'm half crazy all for the love of you...'

Oscar! Several cups of coffee and bacon and eggs later he was still drunk.

'She's driving me crazy. I should never have done it.'

Wincing at his breath, Daisy replenished his coffee cup. 'Done what?'

' Forget it!' He shrugged. 'I need to sleep.' She dragged him upstairs. If ever there was an illusion it has to be her passion for this man. Unpacking his case, she looked up to him in the doorway, water glistening on a well-toned body.

'So what d'you think?' he said. 'Should we give it another go?'

Daisy gazed at him. Drunk he may be, wasted yes, but still

a hunk with a reasonable erection. Then she felt Charley ripple into the room and seeing Oscar from His point of view: the talent that would desert him and the dreams that come to nothing, sympathy overwhelmed her.

'You poor thing! You have taken a battering.'

Oscar sank and his penis with him. 'I thought the TV scene was okay but it's shit like everything else. I've only had a couple of tracks since *Playground* and they weren't any good. I had a spot on Jools Holland but they cancelled. Then there's Christa. I should never have got married.'

'You're married!'

'Yep, a year ago in Stockholm. Her mother and father are in lager and have this palazzo with reindeer and fir trees and fuck knows what. They built us a chalet by the lakes. I thought I'd got it made but I can't be cooped up.'

Seeing he was wiping his nose on her best cotton sheets Daisy passed him a hankie. 'And so what did you do?'

'I ran from the frying pan into the fire, I got hooked up with Mad Marta, a horn player from the band up to her plastic tits in coke. I can't bring Christa into this 'cos I'm scared of what Marta might do. So it's shit-creek minus paddle; Christa wants a divorce and Marta my balls on a plate.'

'You are in a mess.' She helped him into clean shorts and a t-shirt and then under the covers. 'Sleep and you'll feel better.'

He bashed the pillow with his fist then pulled the sheet over his head. 'I should've stayed with you. You always did understand me.'

Oscar stayed and stayed. She couldn't get rid of him. He would've been there forever but for Marta. The phone rang.

'Oscar there?'

'Who's calling?'

'Never mind who's calling, bitch! Bring that creep to the phone!'

If Daisy had sense she'd have disconnected but the trouble with the Power you not only want to heal the sick, you try to heal the fuck-wits too. 'Hello Marta. Where are you calling?' There was silence on the other end, a rattling of change and further obscenities when a purse was dropped. Daisy could see her. She was leaning against a bollard trying to put lippy on, but her hands were shaking so she couldn't connect with her face never mind mouth.

'Are you at the bus station?'

'What's it to you?'

'I'll pick you up in an hour. Stay by the bollard.'

'What bollard?'

When she told Oscar he hit the roof. 'What did you want to bring her here for? She's a crack-head.'

'Crack-head or not, we can't leave her stranded.'

He scrambled into his jacket. 'You might not be able to but I can!'

'Oscar, d'you want to be like this forever? D'you want to screw up your life and Christa's too? Don't you want to see your wife and your son?'

'Son?' He squealed to a halt. 'What you talking about?'

'Christa's pregnant.' Information was pouring into Daisy's head, facts and figures rattling like ticker tape. 'She's expecting your child.'

'Who says so?'

'She does. It's due in a couple of months. And it's not that she won't see you, she can't. Her mother and father have taken her on retreat to Reykjavik. They're trying to swing some legal deal to keep you away.'

White under his St Tropez tan, he stared. 'You're weird,' he said, blinking. 'I always thought you were weird.'

'Okay, I'm weird, but I'm still going to collect your coke-head and you're still going to be here when I get back, and you're going to tell her you love her but aren't good enough for her. You know, "Ciao, babe," the line you shot at me.'

The car pulled in the drive, with Marta – a pallid spectre of eighteen with wounded eyes and the ribs of a horse in the desert – in the back.

A star worthy of his namesake Oscar was waiting with arms outstretched. 'Marta! I'm so sorry you had to go through this!' Daisy retreated upstairs with the cats. Biddy stayed behind, the old dog loves a good weepie.

Eventually Oscar poked his head round the bedroom door. 'How do you feel about lending me the car?'

'How do you feel about a boot up the bum? Take a cab, you and your ill-mannered doxy, and don't tell me you're catching a plane to Stockholm because I happen to know you're booked in at the Balmoral!'

'You were listening in on the extension?'

'I don't do things like that. I have Charley, my own personal grapevine.'

'And who's Charley when he's at home?' said Oscar.

Never one to miss a cue Charley materialised. Elegant in jeans and white vest, he stood by the door, wings folded down and eyebrows raised.

'Who is Charley? He's my guardian angel and my friend.'

Oscar stood for a time, his eyes mirroring her face. Then he sighed and turned to go. 'You are one scary woman.' She tossed him the car keys. 'And you are one silly fool. Drive carefully and make sure I get it back in one piece.'

* * *

Charley sat with long legs crossed and wings elegantly draped over the arm of the chair. He wears whatever takes his fancy. Today it's blue jeans and a Stetson, ivory handle pistols in his belt and high-heeled boots.

'I like the boots.'

'Good aren't they, the Duke gave them to me.'

'The Duke?'

'John Wayne. He wore them in *Stagecoach*.'

'They're really cool.'

'I am cool.'

'Yes, you are.'

'What are you doing over Christmas?'

'Surely you know that better than me.'

'Daisy, dear, let's not regress.'

'Hush up a minute! I'm trying cast off.'

'Okay, I'll sit and twiddle my thumbs.' He began to sing Gregorian plain chant, his voice trilling up and down the scales like Renaissance castrati.

'Okay!' she said, surrendering. 'I'm listening.'

'Do you believe the future is set in stone?'

'I thought it was pretty much mapped out for us.'

'Where's the freedom in that? You might as well be a rat in a maze.'

'That's exactly how I feel, a rat in a maze, and this house, and this world, a laboratory where technicians watch my every move.'

'You don't believe that. You're the eternal optimist. You believe in Santa Claus and ET and raindrops on roses and whiskers on kittens. If for one moment you really saw yourself a Pavlovian dog, you'd shrivel and die.'

Daisy kept her gaze on her knitting. Something was building inside, a sweet sorrow that wanted to spill over. 'Is the future not set then?'

'Certainly not! How does a river know where it will flow until it flows? How does a daisy know how it will grow until it's grown?'

'Doesn't a daisy grow the same as the others?'

'Do you grow as Kate Mannering grows? I'm not talking looks. The outer covering is only wrapping. I'm talking individuality, the essence of self.'

'But for one essential aspect Kate and I are very different.'

'What d'you mean in *essential aspect?*'

'We love the same man.'

'Ah yes, Lucian.' He sighed, and sat contemplating his boots. 'Do you know one of the sweetest moments of my life was spent watching that man? He was seventeen. A moth was stuck in a curtain. He spent ten minutes persuading it to jump onto the leaf so he could carry it to the sun.'

'And did it jump on the leaf.'

'Yes. He put it outside, turned away, and it was eaten by a bird.

'Don't tell me things like that! They are so disheartening.'

'It's life, dear Watson, but it was a good deed on his part. God was pleased. Talking of My Lord, how d'you feel about spending His birthday with me?'

'It's not Christmas yet.' Daisy ventured a question. 'I'd like to ask you a question but I don't want you getting moody if it's not exactly PC.'

'Is it going to be one of those half-arsed questions?'

'Probably. Why do we celebrate Christmas? How do we know the date of a person's birth when he lived thousands of years ago? What if Jesus wasn't born on that day? What if it was more than two thousand years ago?'

Wings folded over his chest like funeral weeds, Charley was snoring.

'You're right,' she said, grinning. 'It was pathetic.'

'Yes, but said with such charm I'll allow an answer. It wouldn't matter when the Lord was born. I would still celebrate His righteous birth.'

'I don't get it.'

'You should read Mahatma Ghandi. When asked if he believed in Jesus he said, "I would believe even if I didn't." Now that's an enlightened man.'

'I still don't get it.'

'Never mind. I get it and that's enough. Ding-dong! School's in session!' He chimed like a bell. 'The lesson for today is where do rivers rise?'

'I don't know, the mountains, or from the rain, or....'

'And where do they return?'

'Back the way they came, I suppose.'

'And a daisy? If a little daisy dies, do the other little daisies die with her?'

'Not unless someone forgets to water them.'

'So if a plant returns to the whole, and rivers rise and return to the source, tell me, Grasshopper, where did Minna go when she died?'

'I've no idea.'

'Let me offer you a clue.' Charley waved his hand and a wall became a Natural history lesson, a slice of earth and a plant seen above and below the soil. A shoot pushed up through the soil. It flowered and died. As it did so another grew off the main plant into the sun and then another, and another.

'Isn't that beautiful! Have you seen a better metaphor for reincarnation?'

'Is that what we're watching?'

'Would you rather see Venus rising from the waves?'

'If you're asking me if I believe in things unseen how could I not. I'd like to ask another question, half-arsed or not. Where is Lucian?'

Golden eyes opaque, Charley was silent. 'I can't speak about that other than to say wherever he is he is not alone. Words carry weight. They give meaning to matter. Once spoken they hang in Time forever. I am a Servant of the Light. I must aid Lucian in his fight, not impede.'

'He's not alone, is he?' she said, suddenly afraid.

'No, I am with him.'

She opened her mouth to ask how Charley could be in two places at once but bit it back. He is an angel. He can be wherever he is needed.

'Eureka! Break through! Bless its little daisy self – it's learning!'

'If you're going to be silly I'm off to bed.'

He grinned. 'Okay. Let's drink and get wasted.' A glass appeared in his hand. He offered her the glass. 'Cheers! Here's to saying silly things!'

Daisy sipped, delicious warmth spread through her belly. 'What's this?'

'Holy water, aka a bazooka.'

'I shouldn't be drinking bazookas. They make me do silly things.'

He replenished her glass. 'Here's to doing silly things.'

Daisy sipped again. 'This is what Lucian drinks.'

'Och, it's not is it? We don't want to drink the same as that wee laddie.'

'Don't be nasty.'

'I'm no being nasty. I merely wonder why he need be brought into the conversation. Aren't I enough?'

'Of course you are. What an absurd thing to say.'

'Tonight we're discussing the Lord's birthday. We can afford to be absurd. But seriously, tell me what you think of me as a man.'

'You're not a man.'

'I was once.'

'Yes and you didn't like it. You said so.'

'That was me being jealous.'

'Of what?'

'The greatest experience within the sentient Universe. Nothing has skin like mortal skin, nor the receptors for pain and pleasure. Nothing in the whole of God's creation is equal to a kiss.'

'I know what you mean.' Daisy wriggled her toes. 'That moment when skin touches skin and your heart leaps in your mouth.'

'Oh, yeah! Here's to kisses and hearts leaping into mouths!' He leaned closer, his perfect profile an inch away. 'Leap into my mouth.'

Lips sizzling she pecked his cheek.

'No! Kiss me like you mean it.'

Daisy hesitated and he began to pass through rapid mutation, his image morphing into a variety of forms: his cowboy-booted self, then the RAF pilot, and Minna, radiant and wild, and Sean, his dear little froggy face, then Isla, William Banks, Bram , even Connor, the black stallion and Boff-2! And then finally, but no means least, he became Lucian, the same steady gaze and blue eyes, and the same muscular structure imprinted over Charley's self.

'I don't like you doing this. I don't know who I'm talking to.'

'You're talking to me. You're looking at me, the man and the angel.'

'But which is which?'

'Ah, well there you have it.' He kissed her, his lips warm.

'What are you doing?'

'Doing, honey bunny?' He tucked a curl back behind her ear, his voice Lucian's and his hands Lucian's. 'I'm no sure I'm doing anything.'

The conversation was so familiar. Unable to tear her glance away Daisy stared at him. Then he touched her arm, gently. ' Sorry.'

'For what?'

'Trying to seduce you.'

Daisy shook herself. These were her words when in Drummach Hall, except for a reversal – Lucian's words became hers, and vice versa. Even knowing that, she couldn't seem to halt the process. 'Is that what you're doing?'

"Fraid so. But clearly not making a very good job of it.'

Caught in the never-ending cycle of life and love she laid her cheek against the face she loved. 'Don't worry. If you're not up to scratch, I'll allow you plenty of practice.'

CHAPTER TWENTY-TWO

Classified

With her parents, and Kate, Mick and the kids arriving later Daisy spent Christmas Eve day decorating the tree. Taking long treasured baubles from the attic, sipping mulled wine and giggling over earlier times, is the only way to dress the tree, not a woman alone. Snow-heavy clouds lie on the roof flattening smoke from the kitchen chimney and pushing it back down the flu. In this white world everything leans toward the house: willows from the pond and frost burned lilacs, while the wisteria clings to the walls seeking warmth and listening…though there's nothing to hear.

Lucian is home, a light shining in the East wing of Drummach House.

Her parents are taking L'il Kim home on Monday and so Daisy collects her today from Drummach stables. She prays Lucian will be out; she couldn't bear it if seeing her collect the pony he feels the need to speak. She'll phone beforehand and give him the chance to hide behind the sofa. Talking of phones, Susie rang; she's off to Barbados with a chap who owns a diamond mine. 'Hello Daisy,' she said in that breathy voice. 'I thought to ring to say goodbye and wish you all the luck in the world.'

Daisy is grateful. If anybody knows about needing luck it's Susie.

Chimneys went on the market yesterday, the realtor positively gloating. 'It's got mystery and people love mystery.' Daisy doesn't care, if she can recoup some of the money ploughed into the house it can go to the first bidder. A flat in town is what she wants. No more country living. I mean, why keep Six Chimneys. It's not as if Kate comes anymore, nor the girls. Sean is with her parents, public school is where he's heading. 'We've had him to the tailor's twice,' said Dad. 'I don't know what's in his porridge but if he's not a world class prop-forward one day my name's not Willy Banks.'

Sean had his own ideas. 'I'm to be an explorer.' Daisy asked how he can be so sure. 'My pa told me,' he said. She thought he meant her pa, but Sean remembered the day he fainted and a prophecy.

'Move over, you sod!' The goat is chucking its weight around. She did think it had got over its dislike of her but Mephistopheles is consistent. From the goat she went to the aviary watching the last few birds flit about. Then Trilby began to sing. Head tipped back and golden wings fluttering, the heart's roller sang of good-bye to love. Daisy wiped her eyes on her sleeve. Crying because a bird is singing, who would believe it of a City girl? But then who would believe making love to an angel would break your heart.

They made love on her bed, Biddy turning away allowing privacy. Daisy was more than a little apprehensive. If an angelic choir had sung, or cannons boomed, she'd have been running down the road. There were fireworks but mainly of the orgasmic kind. She loved not knowing whom she loved and kissed not knowing who she kissed, yet every kiss a seeming goodbye.

* * *

She left with a torch to light the way, Biddy gazing through the window, wanting to come but preferring the warmth of the stove.

Head down and hands in her pockets, Daisy pushed through drifts praying he wouldn't be there. She needn't have bothered. He wasn't home and neither was L'il Kim, a note from Nikki pinned to the stable door. 'Check your phone. I tried calling but couldn't get through. Took L'il Kim with me. Happy Christmas, Nikki. '

She was turning back when a shadow flitted by into the house. Biddy! The little devil has followed. The door to the conservatory was off the latch, and the house as remembered, dusty and foul smelling, and once again posing the question – who or what is Lucian?

Daisy sat on the stairs, torch light bobbing and the house in shadow. As she got to her feet so a shadow detached from the rest to settle over her in a silken web. She shuddered. 'Ah come on, Daisy,' said an amused voice in her head. 'It's only me.' The *me* was Minna Gray wriggling for space, stretching mental and physical muscles Daisy didn't know she had.

'Now wait a minute!'

'Hush.' Obeying Minna's thoughts Daisy's hand rose in a restraining gesture.

'We can't do this in tandem. It's too risky. One of us must take the lead and since I claim knowledge of this house and this world, it had better be me.'

Light from the torch a bubble in which they moved, they climbed the stairs. The bubble wobbled as did Time. Grim oil-painted faces stared down from the walls and there was a Turkish carpet and rods on the stairs where before there was none. The hand that carried the torch is narrow and pointed, a gold bangle at the wrist. Daisy's jeans became dungarees and an apron suitable for digging taters. Doc Martin's thick with mud trod the carpet.

Daisy doesn't have boots like that nor does she braid her hair. The body overlaying hers was slim and muscular, used to chopping logs and tilling ground.

'Wow, Minna!' she whispered. 'You are one tough woman!'

'To inhabit my world you need to be. Keeping the Light isn't easy.'

Every step took Daisy away from the twenty-first century. She was drawn into a complex mind with an interest in fifteenth-century art, and Leonardo da Vinci's theories of time-travel. She glanced through a bulging mental diary that carried names and addresses from every corner of the world, and knew an undercurrent of excitement about a rerun of a Salvador Dali exhibition in Edinburgh, and of a film on at the Odeon – Federico Fellini's *La Dolce Vita*. Along with such thoughts was anxiety for the dog Fatima and her pups, and for broccoli and aphids (to spray or not to spray) yet above and beyond all this was fear for the man top of the stairs.

With Biddy scratching at the door to the linen room Minna's anxiety overwhelmed Daisy. 'What's wrong?' she asked. 'Is he in there again?'

The door opened. A man sat in the window seat, his hand pressed to the window as though to break the glass and fall to the ground below.

'Why do you do this?' She took his hand in hers, wrapping her fingers around a thick welt of scars. 'You can't stay shut away. You must get out.'

He shrugged. 'Why must I. There's nothing out there for me.'

'That's not true. You have a lot to give.'

'Like what, lessons on how to fall like Icarus?'

'Don't be melodramatic. Icarus's wings were stuck together with wax. Yours are bonded by love. You can't fall but neither can you hide.'

'Why can't I? Others hide in here why not me?'

'They have no choice. You have a life and consequence.'

'What life is that? All I'm good for now is a freak in a side-show.' She threaded her arms about him. 'You're no freak, Charley D'angelo. You're brave and strong and I love you.' He turned, light falling on a mass of cobbled flesh, a hole where a nose used to be and bruises for eyes. 'What's left to love?'

Daisy fainted. Minna and Charles vanished. The carpet on the landing rolled up, the past melting away until there was only Daisy on the floor.

Nauseous, she dragged upright. Then ever-so-slowly Minna slunk back, a different Minna, one who wept under her breath. It came to Daisy that it wasn't she that fainted seeing Charles' face, it was Minna.

'That must have been an awful moment.'

'I thought I'd die.'

'You had a shock and are in pain.'

'Yes, but nothing compared to my poor boy.'

'But Minna, the real Charles is still alive and in a nursing home. He talked with Lucian. At least...'Daisy hesitated. 'I thought he did.'

'It's okay, Daisy. I'm aware of your travels.'

'Sorry if I sound muddled. I've seen so many strange things since moving to Chimneys I get confused.'

Minna snorted. 'You're confused? Try my life for a couple of hundred years. Working in the Light is confusing, one man's reality being another man's cloud-cuckoo.'

'Is Charles real to you? I mean, who or what did I just see?'

'You saw the essence of the man through my eyes.'

'And what do I see, or rather what do I feel, when you're with me?'

'You are aware of the essence of a woman through your own inner eye.'

'And why was Charles...do I still call him Charles?'

Minna laughed. 'That or Ed. It's his name. What else would you call him?

'It's that word essence. It makes me think of vanilla.'

Minna laughed again. 'You are so funny. When I say essence I mean the heart of the man, the quintessential Charles E D'angelo. That's what I see when I see Charles D'angelo, that's what I feel when I touch Charles D'angelo. That's what he is. My heart. My mind! My soul!'

With every 'my' Minna thumped her heart and so doing thumped Daisy.

'Steady on, Minna. I need to breathe. Why was he in that room?'

'He was never in that room. I'm afraid I sparked that particular memory. It's not one I'd hoped to repeat. Charles used to hide away but not here in this fearful place. He'd steal away to the attic in dear old Chimneys.'

'Does he still hide?'

'He's old and his body is weary. There is more than one way of hiding.'

'You didn't hide. You toughed it out.'

'I did as you say – tough it out – but don't make me a hero.

I've had my moments and admit that when I first saw what was left of my boy I was shaken to the core. You were shocked when you first saw your legs.'

'My situation is nothing compared to you and Charles. I think that he and you and Lucian are the bravest people.'

'I'm not a person.'

'Are you actually dead?'

'Define dead.'

'Your heart has stopped beating.'

'A true heart never stops beating but if that's how you define death then, yes, I am dead. Never mind my courage, or lack of it I hear you're leaving.'

'Seems that way.'

'I had hoped to offload this particular burden onto younger shoulders but it seems that hope is a non-starter.'

Daisy felt a flash of irritation. Minna is so bossy. She's spent too many millennia under Charley's tutelage. 'What exactly is it you do?'

'I am Keeper of the Light House. Tell me, what does a Lighthouse do?'

'Keep ships from crashing on the rocks, I suppose.'

'And so what would a Keeper do?'

'Keeps the light from going out! And the ships you save from the rocks? Are they human souls?'

'Forget the word human. It's limiting.'

'You save souls?'

'The Lord God saves. I polish the light.'

Argumentative so-and-so! Daisy's hackles rose. 'And the rocks?'

'That's classified. The Light House Project is a need-to-know basis. And it's no good getting riled, Daisy. The situation is of your own making. You had the right to know. Now you don't. You've given up.'

'Would it be so bad if I did give up? Before I got into this mess I had a life.'

Minna snorted. 'What with Oscar Curran!'

'Oscar has faults but at least he's human. Anyway, who are you to criticise my life? You spend an awful lot of time smoozing about in it.'

'*Noblesse oblige!* One must occasionally stir the dregs.'

'If there are dregs it's what you've created. Why must there be a lighthouse? Surely a person can find his own way when he dies.'

'Classified.'

'Handy word. Politicians use it when about to lie. Those unhappy souls, soldiers and airmen, it's not a lighthouse you keep it's a lunatic asylum.'

'Even if that were true, which it isn't, one must still dish out pills.'

'You scare the life out of me.'

'Somebody needs to! Dripping about like a wet Sunday. Wake up! Get your juices flowing otherwise you're going to be in trouble. We had hopes of you. We thought you were the real thing, but you're like so many of your generation, no staying power. If you're going, go, and good riddance!'

Cut to the quick Daisy exploded. 'Why you ungrateful...!'

Phut! Minna was gone. Daisy's torch went out. Then, briefly, Minna returned. 'On the subject of what is dead and what isn't, ask yourself how I am able to smooze in and out of your life? If

I'm dead, and Charles is paralysed, and Lucian is where Lucian is, where, and what, are you?'

'Oh, clear off! I've had enough of your double-talk!'

Phut! Daisy was alone in pitch black, no one to wind her up or to criticise, or to warn of the danger that is coming. Anger left her trembling and afraid.

Hands outstretched, the torch lost when she fainted, she started along the landing. Downstairs the front doors creaked opened. A presence slid across the threshold and began its creeping way to meet her. Darkness and the stench of sickness rolled up the stairs and across the landing in an oily fog.

Thinking it better not to look Daisy closed her eyes. Endeavouring to be brave she started to sing. '...*when I'm lying in my bed, with thoughts going through my head, and I think that love is dead, I'm loving angels in...in...*'

The words stuck in her throat.

It is coming! It is next to her. She can feel it breathing!

It is dark and dreadful with teeth and claws. It maims the strong, suffocates children, and steals the souls of men. Terrified, she began to cry. Someone took her hand. 'Don't cry, honey bunny. I'll guide you down.'

'Lucian!' She tried to open her eyes but he said, 'keep them shut. You don't need to see what's here. I'll guide you through.'

Down the stairs they went, Daisy clinging to his hand. 'Where have you been?' she sobbed. 'I have missed you so.'

'I've missed you too.'

'It is you?' she said, afraid of shape-shifters. 'You're not something else.'

'It is me. I told you I'd be here. All you have to do is call.'

They were down the stairs and walking through the kitchen. She could smell wilted chrysanthemum. They went out into the snow. It was icy cold but she didn't feel it. The wind battered her face but she only felt the hand holding hers. She wanted to open her eyes but afraid of seeing someone other than the man she loved kept them closed.

'I love you, Lucian.'

'I love you too, Daisy.'

'Will I see you again?

'Cross my heart and hope to die.'

She opened her eyes. She was outside the front door. The porch light was on when she left but now all was darkness, and neither Boff-2 nor the real Biddy – not the dog of yesteryear – waited at the window.

Her mobile phone rang. 'Where have you been?' said Isla crossly. 'I've been trying to call you. There's an overturned lorry at Scotch Corner. Traffic is stacked back a mile. God knows what time we'll get to you. I've rung Kate. Told her we'll be late picking up Sean. So we'll see you when we see you.'

Isla rang off and then Kate called – Sean had been staying with the Khans this week, tying up loose ends before the move. 'Something's wrong with your phone. I've been calling all day. We've exchanged contracts and are taking the girls for a burger to celebrate. Sean and Leon are at Butch's place. His dad will drop 'em off at yours. Ta-ta for now.'

'Ta-ta for now!'

Daisy put the key in the lock, opened the door, and closed it behind her. Someone flicked the lights on. 'Happy Christmas, Miss Daisy.'

To Be or Not

Jason Myers leant on the banister thumbing a text message with one hand while gnawing a turkey leg with the other. Daisy tried to run but was cut off when a burly fist slammed the door shut. 'Meet Bevin, a former cell-mate and fellow good news bringer.' A sweaty gorilla of a man smiled, 'Hiya Red!' and carried on spooning trifle into his mouth from a bowl earlier prepared.

Frightened, yet at the same time furious at the invasion of her home, Daisy snatched the bowl away. 'What do you think this is, meals on wheels?'

He slapped her face. Then he ruffled her hair. 'I love redheads, all that fire and brimstone. Daisy glared, a bruise developing on her cheek. 'Nothing to say? Don't matter,' he scooped up trifle. 'I'll find out later.'

A draught was blowing through the back of the house, and there was broken glass trailing through the hall. They'd got in via the conservatory.

'What do you want?'

'What have you got?' said Jason.

'She's got a great pair of tits for starters.'

'Yeah, if you don't mind the attitude.'

'Nothing wrong with attitude,' said Bevin stroking Daisy's cheek. 'I like it when they struggle. Makes it more tasty when they give in.'

'Try it!' Daisy dashed his hand away. 'You won't find it easy.'

Jason finished gnawing the turkey. 'Here, boy!' he whistled, presumably calling Biddy. 'I got a nice bone for you!' Thank God, there was no sign of Biddy or Boff-2. Daisy knew that if she showed affection to anything this psycho would make them pay. 'If it's money you want I can get some.'

'I know.' He tossed the bone. 'I was so taken with you at Raj's funeral I Googled you – *Best-selling author's daughter hurt in crash!* Now what does best-selling mean? It means mucho wonga. So, I'm thinking free booze, Santa Claus and carol singers, tra la la, so here we are for a visit.'

Bevin yawned. 'Where's the booze?'

'There's whisky in the cupboard and tray of drinks in the dining room.'

'Ooh, la-di-dah, a tray of drinks in the dining room!' He peered inside the hall cupboard. 'Scottish malt? Very nice!' Breaking the seal he took a hefty pull, belched and wiped his mouth. 'That's better. Drop of malt, Jace?'

'I don't drink so much these days. I used to but saw the error of my ways. Fill your boots, old mate,' Jason sat on the stairs. 'I'm in no rush.'

Daisy's mind was racing. Between frantic calls for Charley and mixed blessings that Lucian didn't accompany her indoors, she thanked God for overturned vehicles and the exchanging of contracts. 'I don't know what you think you're doing,' she said. 'My parents are due any minute. You can knock me about but won't be able to take on all of them.'

Jason smiled. 'Tut-tut, Daisy, you mustn't tell lies. Your ma's stuck in a traffic jam and Katy's stuffing her face with her old man.'

'How do you know that?'

He tapped his cell phone. 'I have my sources.'

'Charley!' She cried in sudden panic. 'Charley help me!'

Jason leapt to his feet. 'Somebody in the house?' Bevin carried on eating. 'I've been from top to bottom. Ain't nobody here.' Jason scowled. 'You sure?'

'I'll have another look.' Bevin clumped up the stairs, trashing the ivy wreath wound about the banister as he went. 'Who's Charley?' Eyes like poppy seeds, Jason approached. 'Got somebody stashed away?' She shook her head. He grabbed her chin, turning her head from side-to-side. 'Bev's right, you are a babe and if you're a good babe I'll work a bit of magic on your face,' he said, his nails scraping her eyes, the threat real. 'And not hidden away like that old whore, Kate. It'll be up front for the world to see.'

'Get lost!'

He laughed. 'Spunky little babe. I bet you're great in the sack, a real tiger.'

Breath sour, he leaned closer. "*Tyger burning bright in the forest of the night, what immortal hand or eye, could frame they fearful symmetry.*" '

'How different you are to the last man that said that.'

'What d'you mean different, bigger dick?'

'He isn't a man. He's a..!' A penny dropped from a great height. Phil Tree isn't a ghost. Neither is Six Chimneys an insane asylum. It's boot camp for trainee angels, and Phil Tree, the padre, the old man in the hospital, and all the others, are rookies in the Army of the Light. How wonderful! And how stupid was Daisy. The truth was there right under her nose.

Tears threatening, she turned away. 'What's up?' said Jason. 'Scared of the bogeyman?' She shook her head. How can she explain the miraculous to this man? 'Look out, Bev!' Jason shouted. 'Red's got her own personal spook. Better not poke this particular grate. You might end up on the fire.'

Bevin clumped downstairs. 'I wouldn't be surprised what goes on in this dump. It's weird up there, noisy but no one there, if you know what I mean.'

Daisy knew what he meant. But where is Charley? Why isn't he reducing Jason to cinders? Perhaps this is another Connor situation, Daisy being taught not to pit her wits against God. 'Have you broken out of jail?'

'Broken out? I don't think so. I'm on parole, a changed man.'

'Changed man?' she scoffed. 'You wouldn't know change if it jumped up and bit you. A leopard never changes its spots or a rat its scabby sores.'

Jason lit a cigarette. He blew out a cloud of smoke. 'Keep going, motor mouth. That's the girl we all know and love.' She fought for control. Be quiet, Daisy, you are not helping. Jason's phone rang. 'That'll be my business partner.' He grabbed Daisy's hand, holding a cigarette over her palm. 'One word.' He opened up the phone. 'Hello, little mate, where are you?'

The voice on the other end was excited, and the words were unclear there was no mistaking the exaggerated home-boy lisp. Daisy's stomach churned. Leon! Then, there was the creak of the side door. 'Daisy!' a voice called.

Sean! Eddy's warning leapt to mind: '*You're going to have to choose, the boy you love or the man.*' 'Run, Sean!' she yelled. 'Run!'

Jason ground the cigarette into her palm. She screamed. The pain was dreadful but the sight of Leon and Sean in the doorway more so.

'Why d' you bring that moron?' said Jason, reaching through, pulling the boys into the house. 'Had to,' whispered Leon scanning the room, his face drained of colour. 'We was at Butch's. His dad dropped us off.'

'Run, Sean!' Daisy cried. 'Stupid bitch!' Jason kicked her legs from under and stood with one boot in the small of her back. 'Lie still or you'll have a busted back! Come here, kid.' He made a come-on gesture to Leon.

Leon didn't move. 'What you doin' to Daisy?'

'Don't worry about that. Just show me what you got in the bag. Then Daisy knew what was in the bag. 'Leon!' she cried. 'Go home and take that with you!' Jason slammed his boot down. There was a crack and Daisy fainted.

Sean ran at him. 'Get off of her, you fecking bully!'

Jason swatted him against the wall. 'Bev? See what the kid's brought.' Bevin took the bag from Leon's nerveless hands removing the shotgun. 'Good on you, little mate.' Jason nodded approvingly. 'You did well.' Bevin was not so sure. 'What's with the shooters? You said nothing about no shooters.' Jason shrugged. 'I didn't know there was one. The kid thinks he's Rambo. He said he had a shooter but for all I knew it was a fucking peashooter. '

Leon started to weep, his sobs echoing about the stairs. 'Shut up!' snapped Jason – who ached for the gun but couldn't move because of the bitch under his foot. 'What's the problem, Bev? I thought you were up for a giggle.'

'This ain't a giggle.'

They argued. Through a fog of pain Daisy thought of Eddy's words. She loved Sean. She loved Lucian. Lucian isn't here and so no choice to be made. There's only Sean and a gun, and everything falling apart.

Lucian, she sent out a prayer! Please stay away!

* * *

'*This is the army, Mr Jones, no private rooms or telephones. You had…*'

Lucian is battling demons of his own. Stuck in a mental loop he relives the same memories: a Counter IED expert he's taking off his helmet and kneeling examines the IED. He knows what he's doing but can't think why.

'*This is the army, Mister Green, we like to keep the barracks clean…*'

Then, a rat in a maze, he's inside what's left of a church with visibility down to zero and thick fog closing in. He's stripped to the buff, no armour, no sidearm, and he is waiting for relief that never comes.

'*This is the army, Mister Brown. You and your baby went to town.*'

He's standing guard outside a door. Nurses whisk by. Doctors chat. No one sees a soldier in combat gear, no one except the old guy with the scarred face – Oh and of course the nuisance, the angel. He is here at every loop in the chain. Even now Lucian can feel him at his shoulder. 'Who are you?'

'Captain Lucian Nairne, Counter IED Force.'

'And why are you here?'

'It's so dark in here I'm not sure of anything.'

'Then open your eyes and look.'

Lucian opened his eyes. He is in Room 12. There is a body on the bed and a great deal of blood, his blood! His face! His body!

'No,' he fell on his knees. 'For the love of Christ no more!'

The whirligig stops. His head is empty of sound. There is only him and the angel, Charley – no noise, no exploding IEDs, no sniper's firing, just silence.

'Do you remember what you saw?'

'Me laid out as a corpse.'

'What else?'

'Bits and pieces.'

'Let's help the bits and pieces along.'

Charley clicked his fingers and Lucian was in Six Chimneys. It is springtime, blossom on the trees and the wisteria heavy with buds. A woman is peering through the window, her lovely face a fingertip away. 'What about this?'

'How could I forget?'

'And this?' Base Camp, New Year's Eve, they got the call, two men down, one dead, one wounded, and an IED to be defused. He was getting geared-up. Sergeant Nobby Clarke, his aide, is asking if he wants to leave a message. '*Wanna say something, sir? You know, last words to the missis telling her how much you'll miss her and her cooking, all that kind of shit.*'

'*I've nothing worth saying and no one to hear it.*'

'*What about a prayer to Him upstairs asking to reserve a seat?*'

'*I'm pretty sure I've a place booked down below.*'

'*Don't you believe in Divine Intervention?*'

'*I believe in myself. Then if things go wrong I've only myself to blame.*'

'Do you remember that conversation, Lucian?'

Like the slivers of a stained-glass window the last moments

of his life slide into a recognisable pattern. 'I remember thinking what man has no one to share his last wishes. My Will is drawn up, the house and a few thou to my cleaner and her brood. I figured the government could pay funeral expenses.'

'And the note?'

Lucian shrugged. He wrote to a stranger, a girl with green eyes. He recalls how, hands shaking, he leant on Nobby Clarke's back and wrote: *Hello, Girl with the green eyes, I'm asked to leave a note for nearest and dearest. Sad to say I don't have any. Even if I did you'd be the one I'd want to say goodbye to. I don't know you and you don't know me but don't be afraid, I'm no stalker. I saw you once and never forgot. Your lovely face kept me going through a year of hell. I want to thank you and tell you that alive or dead I'm here for you. Heaven and hell, I'll find you, and take care of you. God bless and keep us both, your wanna-be Guardian Angel.* How he then removed the stud from his ear and wrapped the note about it. *It's the only thing of me worth having. Get it to her via the MO David Gilchrist.*

'It was a good message, Lucian.'

'It's schoolboy drivel. I chucked it away. I'm glad she never saw it.'

'She saw it.'

'How?'

'It was delivered,' said Charley.

'Who took it?'

'I took it.'

Then they are inside the ruined church, stars shining through the rafters and a blackbird serenading the night. The sound is so fragile and so beautiful Lucian had to curl his fists not to weep.

Death felt as fragile and as delicate as that song. No trumpets and no pain, only the knowledge that life is over and the things he wanted to do he can't.

'Do you have any questions?'

'Why did I keep finding myself in a church?'

'It is your sanctuary. It is how you perceive holy ground. You feel the same way about Six Chimneys. A safe place, a holy place, where else would you seek safety for the woman you love?'

'Is that it?'

'It is that simple and that beautiful. Any more questions?'

'What else is there to know? I went out on a call and was unlucky.'

Then he is out with the team retrieving poor Kieran Wallace, hands from behind the wire reaching to take the body. Then it's back to the IED. He removes his helmet. No heroic gesture, he's hot, and in a situation like this a helmet never saved anybody. A good crew, steady hands and a prayer to a God he doesn't know, are what stands between him and annihilation.

Then he sees it. Some bastard's idea of a joke, a pipe filled with shit and tied with Christmas tinsel. But it's a decoy! A sniper fires! Knees buckling, Lucian falls, trips the wire and the decoy explodes showering him with shit. Next he's looking at a ceiling. He feels a thud in his chest. Someone says, 'we're losing him!' Lucian remembers thinking he should put up a fight but he's out, and rolling and rising, and the last glimpse of life is of a body on a surgical table and a thought, 'and a happy Hogmanay to you too.'

* * *

Jason's happy, talk about '*Lock, Stock, and Two Smoking*!' He hasn't had so much fun in years. Fate or whatever, the gun is gonna get him noticed. With this to his name he'll be happy going back to the nick. The way Bev's knocking it back he'll drop the gun and then what larks Pip!

Greasy thoughts slide up and down his mind: I've never killed a woman. I've done other stuff, cats and dogs, whatever's handy. I did Ma's Pekinese, dirty little sod shitting all over the place. What was its name, Gumdrops? That's a laugh! Wasn't gum made it puke over the settee, it was rat poison. But animals are no good. They curl up and die. They don't beg. Will she? He crouches beside her hauling her to sitting position. Breathing in snatches she leans against him. He gropes her tits. When she winces he does it again, his hand between her legs – he'll teach her to poke her nose into his business.

'Pack it in, Jace. She needs a doctor. You've busted a rib or something.'

'I ain't getting no doctor. One look and we'd be back inside.'

'Why me? I've done nothing.'

'Who's gonna believe that?'

So many thoughts whirl about the room. Through a mist of pain Daisy can hear them. Sometimes it's Bevin missing his kids and wishing he'd never set eyes on Jason. Sometimes Leon: 'He promised no one would get hurt!' Sean's thinking, 'I'll get that gun. He'll never hang another kid out of a window.'

No, thought Daisy, I can't let you do that. Anyway, it's not necessary. Any minute Charley in tights and gold silk boxers will spring through the door. 'Enter stage right, thunderbolt in hand.' The pain was bad but the image so absurd she laughed.

'What you laughing at, silly bitch!' spat Jason. 'Don't you know you're in trouble?' She laughed again. Little twerp! Her former self would've knocked him down with a flick of her hand. 'God, you're pathetic!' Minna blasted through, taking Jason – and Daisy – by surprise. 'No wonder your mother couldn't bear to look at you. Poor woman thought she'd given birth to a weasel.'

'Why you..!' Jason threw Daisy across the floor. She fell against Bevin. He dropped the gun. Daisy grabbed it and held on. 'Fucks sake, Red!' Bevin scrambled off the stool. 'Look where you're pointing that thing.'

'S'okay!' says Jason. 'She ain't gonna do anything.'

'But that thing is loaded!'

'I know but she won't fire it. You don't know how, do you, Daisy.'

It's true, thought Daisy. Minna might have known but she hasn't a clue. In the movies they hold it to their shoulder because it jumps when fired.

Gasping with pain, she shuffled against the wall, and bracing her knees brought the butt of the gun up to her shoulder.

'Daisy!' hissed Sean. 'Careful!'

'It's all right, Sean,' she said, struggling to sit up.

'It's no alright,' he said, face ashen. 'Put it down or you'll hurt yourself.'

'I can't. He'll get it.'

'That's right,' said Jason, yawning. 'I'll get it.'

'Give it to me, Red,' said Bevin. 'I'll make sure he gets nothing.'

'That's right, Calamity Jane, Give it to good old Bev,' snorted Jason.

'Shut your fucking face!' said Bevin. 'This is all your fault! If it wasn't for you I'd be home with the kids having a drink with my feet up. We should've taken the money and left. Now there's this girl dying on our hands.'

'She ain't dying. She's quietly passing out.'

'Yeah, but what about when you get the gun? You gonna leave them alone? Kids and sick woman to terrorize, it's your winning lottery ticket.'

'What's up with you? A minute ago you were having a go at her.'

'I wasn't! Okay, I slapped her but I didn't mean it.' He turned to Daisy. 'I didn't, honest. I was just...just..'

Daisy couldn't think. This is all wrong! The wolf is at the door threatening to blow the house down and where is Charley? And Lucian? Didn't he say he'd always be there? 'Lucian, please come and save us.' Then she remembered Eddy's warning and prayed him back again. 'No! Don't come!'

'What she doing?' said Bevin, his hand on the door. 'Who's she talking to?'

'Who you talking to, Daisy?' said Jason. 'Your ghost?'

'The...the angel that lives here.'

'Oh, we've moved on to angels now.'

'There 'is' something here,' said Bevin. 'I knew it the minute I came in. I could feel it in the walls. We should get out of here.'

'Ghosts! Angels!' Jason threw the mobile across the room. 'What's next, Gandalf and Lord of the Fucking Rings? I've had enough of this. You're right, Bev. A couple of kids and a sick woman to terrorize, it's my lucky day.'

He punched Leon sending him flying.

'Don't!' Daisy pointed the gun.

'Why not?' Jason was bored. 'What you gonna do about it?'

'I will shoot you.'

'You won't.' He hit Leon again, blood spurting. 'Who's next?' He turned to Sean. 'What about you? You always did get up my nose.'

Daisy pulled the trigger, the kick throwing her backward. The bullet moved so slowly, carving an upward path to Sean. Ticktock! The Grandfather clock struck once, twice, three times, and then paused, pendulum quivering.

* * *

'Do you remember being shot, Lucian?'

'Sure. Shoot and scoot from up top of the mosque.'

'Do you know where you went then?'

'I went looking for Daisy.'

It is New Year's Day. He is hovering over a row of houses. A door opens and a girl dashes into the road, and then she gets down on her hands and knees in the gutter. She's weeping, her tears a needle in his ears.

He drops down beside her. 'Why are you crying?'

She doesn't hear him and carries on crawling about the road.

He hears a motor. 'Get up, Daisy. There's a car coming.' She runs to the path and safety. But then she sees her cat in the road and runs back.

'For God's sake!' Lucian shouts. 'Get out of here!' He leaps in front of her but the car goes through him and hits her. He's on his knees trying to hold her. People are coming out of houses. Paramedics arrive. Lucian gets in the ambulance with her. He leans over her, begging her to listen. '*I know this is neither the time nor the place but there are things I need to say!*' He doesn't know if she can hear yet keeps going, putting his heart into the stumbling words. '*I get it you've no fondness for me. You don't know me...miserable man teaching other miserable men to kill... waiting for you all of my life.*'

Here with Charley, his soul stripped bare, he pleads again, a shadow of the same man, their lips moving in time. '*If you need me I will come...heaven or hell I'll be there.*' The memory fades to the beep-beep of flat line and of him saying, '*Lord, if you must have a life, take mine.*'

He's back inside the church. 'So much for my promise.'

'It was a very big promise.'

'And bound to fail.'

'Do you understand what followed?'

'I understand I'm in hell.' Lucian didn't care. Heaven or hell as far as he's concerned he's done. 'What now.' It isn't a question – it is capitulation.

'A man can't sleep and dream forever. Sooner or later he must awaken.'

'Is that what I'm doing, dreaming her into my grave?'

A younger angel dressed as a US pilot stepped out of the shadows. 'More like wishful thinking – a multi-screen, full Dolby sound romantic dream.'

Pain hit Lucian. 'How can my love for her be a dream?'

'Everything you feel is real. It's her feeling for you that is unproved.'

'She told me she loved me.'

'You're the author of this romance,' said Charley. 'You wanted her to love you and she latched onto your need. Your fantasy became her life-line. It stopped her drifting away.'

'I don't believe it.'

'Look for yourself and tell me again you don't believe.' The window shimmered. They were outside the hospital room. 'Please!' Lucian grabbed Charley's sleeve. 'Don't take me in there. Not knowing what I know now.'

'You need to see the fold where you kept your lamb safe. You patrol it night and day and have done since you were shot. St Jude's is where Daisy was removed when she slipped into a coma.'

A clock gleamed through the darkness. 'The clock's wrong,' said Lucian.

'In the Lucian and Daisy world three years have almost gone. In St Jude's no such time has passed. Sustained by modern medicine and love of her parents she sleeps and dreams and is kept from death's door by you.'

'How long have I been dead?'

'Ah well, this is where you learn the answer to one of your own questions, ie, how long is a piece of string. You and your love are as two ships of the night drifting toward that Bourne from which no soul returns, except you did return, big ship towing the little 'un.'

'But how can that happen?'

'When you were shot you went where your heart would take you, tracking Daisy through time and space. You've been with her ever since.'

'What about the things we did, the loving and laughing, the real things like the jeep and bikes and people...and, I don't know, the cats?'

Charley smiled at the younger angel. 'Bikes, cats, and jeeps? Interesting don't you think to hear what mortals regard as real?'

'Old habits, my Lord.'

'Indeed.' Charley turned to Lucian. 'If by "real" you're asking if you drove an imaginary jeep and helped with imaginary animals then the answer is yes. But if by "real" you mean did you drive a metal jeep and help with flesh and blood animals of the mortal world, then the answer is no.'

'I thought Daisy needed help. I wanted to protect her. Beyond that, the holes in time, the repetition, I knew it couldn'ae be as it should. But surely I didn't do this on my own – concoct a circus of people and animals.'

'A very creative circus with significant help from the Divine. You're a good man, Lucian. You function within a strict moral code. You knew she was not yours. That's why you moved in and out of the dream, trying to release her. And you did safeguard Daisy, no doubt about that. I couldn't have done better myself. Trouble is, in so doing you forgot the basic rule of soldiering.'

'And that is?'

'*Quis custodiet ipsos custodies!* – Who watches the watchman? You've fought hard and long. Now the time has come to move on.'

'So where do I go from here?'

'Well, unless you get a hold of yourself pdq I would say under the lilacs in Minna's garden. Room 12 is your room paid for by your regiment. It's where you've lived and breathed these last few months.'

'You said I was dead!'

'No, *you* said you were dead. It is Daisy's life that is under question.'

'What can I do?'

'Think Shakespeare, Spielberg, Disney, and the best story-tellers! Grasp the fact that a story well told continues to grow within the listener's mind long after the narrator is silent. Dreams develop a life force of their own. How many times have you heard it – characters come alive, jump off the page, gain life of their own. You and Daisy are no longer a simple love story. You're a three act opera with as yet an unwritten finale. The opera is being watched from Above *and* Below. Right now Above, the Army of Light and the Lighthouse Keepers, is batting zero. Unless you agree to help, there'll be a tragedy that many living in the physical will take beyond the grave.'

'Nae pressure then.'

There were many voices in his head: earth voices, medics shouting and people long gone, his brother, Ian, climbing the Cuillin Ridge: '*Come on, bro*! *I'm waiting!*' There is the wheezing of life-support machines that are keeping both Daisy and him alive, and ever and above a sound akin to jet engines. 'What is that sound and why do I keep hearing it?'

'It is your soul begging a gift.'

'What gift?'

'Your life.'

'If you mean in exchange for Daisy's, take it! Take it now!'

'We don't want you to give up your life. We're asking you to loan your life for a space of time.'

'To whom?'

'Fellow human beings.'

'I don't understand.'

'You will when the sacrifice is made.'

'It's no sacrifice to save the one you love.'

'Indeed in that you share the Lord's Own Thoughts.'

'Bring it on.'

'There will be a cost to you.'

'Show me.'

The window shimmered – images flew across the panes of glass, fast and infinitely complex, yet Lucian saw and understood.

'Are you willing to help?'

'I am.'

'It will bring pain and sadness yet if you hold true a great prize at the end.'

'I don't care about prizes.'

'You'll care about this one.' With that they are looking into Daisy's room and her bed surrounded by doctors. Isla and Will Bates are weeping.

'They're gonna pull the plug!'

'It is moving toward that choice.'

'Take my life! Surely if I die I can be of use to her here.'

'You are of use to her here because you maintain a thread of physical consciousness. Once the line is cut only the Lord can help Daisy.'

'And if I do as suggested?' Behind Charley's back the younger angel, thumbs rising, mouthed the US hell-raiser. 'HOOYAH!'

It was all Lucian needed to know.

It was the window – always the window. He began to run. As he ran pieces of armour materialised about his body – a Kevlar jacket about his torso, heavy boots on his feet, and a helmet with visor on his head and Sig in his hand.

'No Lucian!' shouted the angel. 'Leave your defence system

behind. It's of no use to you on the Other Side. Be your own true self. You are enough.'

The armour melted, leaving Lucian in skivvies. That same sound rumbled through the air, whump, whump, whump, his heart a Viking Jet engine struggling to fire. It was a noise familiar to Lucian. He'd heard it before and always associated it with his death – but no, laddie! Not this time!

There were steps now leading to the window, every step higher than the last. As he ran the staircase behind him melted into emptiness.

The window shimmered. Daisy came into view, propped against a wall with a shotgun in her hands. 'Jesu!' he almost fell. 'What's going on?'

Then he saw it, small and lethal, suspended in space between Daisy and Kate's foundling boy. 'Has that got my name on it?' he panted.

'If you are willing.'

'I'm willing but I'm not gonna make it. It's too far!'

Golden eyes afire, Charley ran alongside. 'Take this!' he thrust an object into Lucian's hand. 'It is the Lord God's gift to you. Do not let it go! Such things are beyond price.'

Lucian's hand closed about the gift. The window was still a million miles away yet the colours were brighter, the Seraph's cloak glowing like a scarlet banner and the screaming of his heart rising to crescendo.

Charley grabbed the back of Lucian's shirt. 'Your Scots Guards motto, *Nemo me impune lacessit?* How does it translate?'

'Nobody gets in my face and lives!'

'So be it!' Charley drew back his arm, and like David's slingshot threw Lucian up the stairs and onto the window ledge.

Tick-tock, a minute hand moved, a pendulum swung and struck for the fourth time. The window exploded. Lucian leapt through the broken shards, and pushing Sean aside braced his feet to take the bullet.

A red cross blazing on a white shirt, it struck his chest.

Part Three

On Loan

CHAPTER TWENTY-FOUR

Keeping it Real

'Did he just pop back?' whispered Janet, holding him on his side, his face pressed into her apron. 'I was off duty at the time so missed all the fun.'

'Yup. Bang! Eyes wide open. Gave me a fright I don't mind telling you.'

'You sure it wasn't the sight of Doc Williams in his new toupee. That's enough to bring anyone back from the dead.'

'Or send 'em in the opposite direction. Okay, roll him!' They rolled him onto his left side, the therapist massaging his shoulder. 'I thought he was a goner.'

There was a polite cough. A soldier stood at the door. The therapist waved him in. 'Not that he deserves to be brought back from the brink, the run-around he's given us and his gorgeous friend all these months.'

The officer blushed, took off his cap, and smiled.

'Yeah, he is gorgeous. I love fair-haired guys.'

'Me too, poor bloke! Been treated rotten, he has, kept hanging about while his buddy made up his mind to pop his clogs.'

'You two madams!' Lucian rolled back onto the bed. 'Don't listen to 'em, Gillie. They'll drive you nuts.' He tugged at the shrunken gown. 'If you've done with your torture for the day get me something better than this thing forever riding up and showing everything I've got.'

'And you've got plenty to show,' said Janet.

'You shouldn't be getting out of bed,' said the therapist. 'You're supposed to buzz for help. Not stagger around like a drunk.'

'I'm no buzzing ever again. It's a piss I want, not you two sadists.'

'Language, Captain Nairne!' Captain David Gilchrist – MO and loyal friend frowned. 'Show a little restraint before these tender blossoms.'

'Tender my ass! Goebbels had nothing on these two. They put a man through hell, guzzle a couple of Iron Brus, come back to do it all again.'

'You know you love us,' said Janet, drawing back the screens.

'Aye, like a man loves the morning after the night before.'

'So cruel and yet so beautiful.'

'Clear off the pair of you. Go enjoy yourselves, you sadists, give some poor sod an enema or stick a needle in his ass.'

Gillie shoved the pile of books off the chair and sat, one stiff leg outstretched. 'Staggering around like a drunk?'

'I guess I do look like that. It's to do with motor function, or so I'm told, getting body and brain in sync again.'

'Is it likely to last?'

'I have no idea. The medics seem to think I'm doing okay.'

'Do you think you're doing okay?'

'I'm alive. That'll do for me.'

Gillie picked up a notebook and started reading. 'What's this, your memoirs? If it is I know publishers who'll pay plenty.'

'Gi' me that,' said Lucian, snatching the book away.

'Why? Is it private? Looked like kiddie's stories to me.'

'If it is private it'll be the only thing that is in this dump.'

'So are you then, walking when you shouldn't?'

'Take no notice of those girls. They love to wind me up.'

'They love you full stop. You've quite a fan base, Captain Nairne.'

'Och, none of that! I just want up and out.'

'What's the rush? Not so long ago you were hell bent on dying.'

Lucian shrugged. 'I've things to do and it's on my hind legs or not at all.'

'Looks like you're up for another gong.'

'Oh for crying out loud!'

'Don't panic. It's only an add-on, the army and government presenting a united front. No need to fret yourself.'

'I'm no having photo-ops! There are folk in here hanging on by a thread. The last thing they need is a camera shoved in their face.' Lucian shuffled to the edge of the bed. Heart crashing, he straightened. 'Do you know who had the frigging nerve to come see me the other day? Oscar frigging Curran!'

Gillie grinned. 'Do you know what you remind me of when you do that, what's his name, Robocop, half man, half machine.'

'More like Elmer frigging Fudd.'

'What's with the cussing? You never used to cuss like this.'

'Men like Curran are enough to make a man swear.'

'Never heard of him.'

'And you're nae likely to, he wrote a couple of pop-tunes.'

'So why would a nobody like that cause you to cuss?'

'He doesn't.'

'Okay.' Gillie got to his feet. 'Well, Captain Nairne, if you've nothing other to do than moan I'll be on my way.'

'So long.' Lucian shuffled to the sink. 'What was it you

wanted anyway?'

'Only that I sold Drummach and bought the other house with the proceeds.'

Lucian's face lit up. 'That's the best news I've heard all week. Was there anything left? I'm no expecting much. Place was a dump. Cann'ae imagine anyone wanting to knock it down ne'er mind buy it.'

Gillie leant on his cane. 'As a matter of fact there's a fair bit over. Can't be sure until the final reckoning but your man Painswick says even after expenses you can expect in the region of two hundred thou.'

'Wha..?'

'Land and house was bought by a golf consortium.'

'I bet that's gone down well with the village.'

'On the contrary they're quite taken with the news. It'll bring business to the area. Your post mistress, Miss Hilda, told me she's thrilled at the notion.'

'What can I say. But I am pleased about you getting Six Chimneys. I've a reason for wanting the old place, and not for myself.'

'Who then?'

'Like I'm gonna tell you.'

'*A bientôt*, Lucian, *mon frère*.'

'*A tout a l'heure*, Gillie.'

As usual the wheelchair was far enough away to be a problem and close enough to make a man try. By the time he was in it he'd knocked over a water jug, scattered a bowl of hyacinth, and dropped the jeweller's box.

'For the love of God!'

'Now go steady!' Her mother was in the doorway smilin, the

jeweller's box in her hand. 'Is this what you're looking for?'

'Thanks.' He folded it in a towel. 'I'm no coordinated yet.'

'Don't worry about that. From what I can see, that gown being a bit on the skimpy side, you're coordinated enough for any red blooded girl.'

A blush rose from his toes to the dent in his head. 'Right then, I'm away to the bathroom to get myself sorted oot.'

'D'you need a hand?'

'No, thanks.'

'Be seeing you will we later?'

'Aye, in a minute or two. I'm just ..?'

'Going to the bathroom to sort yourself oot.'

* * *

'Cooee!' Isla buzzed through into next door. 'Wakey-Wakey! Mother's here! Daddy sends his love and says he'll be along short-ly.' She tossed the parcels on the table and unzipped her jacket. 'You're in the best place today, sweetheart. It's brass monkeys out there.'

She unpacked the basket. 'Now, what have we here, shampoo, conditioner, Kirby grips. I saw yesterday your hair was mussy so I bought a satin pillow cover. My mate, Audrey, who lives in the cottage over the way, says it's good for stopping mussing. But then this is Aud, lives in Tra-la-land, believes in healing and all that. So it might work and it might not. Remember the copper innersole she gave P that gave him bloody great blisters?'

It was about now, following the first rush of energy, that despair falls over Isla's heart. It's Daisy so still and the noise of

315

the life support.

Isla went to the cupboard taking yesterday's nightie and bed socks home for washing. She hates Daisy wearing institutional stuff. 'I don't care if it does split up the back. You're used to better. Look at that poor sod next door, six foot odd tacking around in a mini-skirt!'

She rolled up her sleeves filling a bowl with water. 'Not too hot, nor too cold, just right.'

'All right, Mrs Banks?' A nurse popped her head round the door.

'Fine, thank you, lovey. Just gonna do our laundry.'

'She had a good night last night.'

'Oh good! Not too much of the eye movement then? I don't like it when she does that. I worry she might be having a nightmare.'

'You shouldn't think that, Mrs Banks!' the nurse smiled. 'That's REM and shows she's dreaming, which suggests brain activity.'

They're good girls, these nurses. They do their best, but they're not your mum. Isla went to the back of the bed, a special bed bought with royalties from *Blue Roo and the Thief of Time*. Isla bought this and one for the hospital – first dibs to the lad next door. In those days he was carved of the same marble as Daisy, a Scottish chieftain with Harry Potter lightning flash scar on his head. I asked him, 'how did you manage to come out alive.' He said he'd no idea but somebody up there must like him. Flat on his back he was when he said that but interested in Daisy, so interested Isla was worried.

Well, you don't know, do you? After what he's been through

you'd expect him to be a bit odd. But he's not odd. He's a hero – not that he likes to talk about it. He likes to talk about Daisy, more to the point he talks *to* Daisy.

Last night he wheels his chair to the bed, gets out a book and starts reading about chicken coops. I said why would Daisy want to build a chicken coop? He said it was the only one on the WI trolley. But it didn't have to be a chicken coop. It could be a rabbit hutch. I said that's alright, Daisy loves animals. That was gonna be her thing, a rescue centre of some kind. She was saving for something like that. Not that she'll do it now.

He didn't like me saying that. He said I had to stay positive. Then he pointed to the bobble hat he wears to hide sutures. Look at me, he says. I should be dead. But I am alive and Daisy can be the same.

It's true his situation is nothing short of miraculous. They'd given up on him, the doctors saying the machine was to be switched off, the army had run out of cash and he was to transfer to an NHS place.

'Me and your pa put a stop to that. We saw what a good influence he was and paid for his stay. But don't tell him that! He's the type that walks sooner than be obligated – not like that other useless streak.'

Oscar Curran crept in last Friday. Seems he's been abroad and got engaged before the girl's parents saw through him and gave him the bum's rush. Your pa was for letting him in. He said Oscar doesn't like hospitals. I said, I don't like hospitals but I don't clear off without saying goodbye.

'Not that you care, my lovey, in your twilight world.' She stroked Daisy's hair. 'I don't know how the nurses do it. Working here would depress the hell out of me. Angels all of them, the good, bad, and the six-footers.

'Hello, lovey. Sorted yourself oot?'

In he came in a decent pair of strides and sweatshirt with an army logo. He's good with the wheels, manoeuvring corners, careful not to bump the bed, his big hands deft as any seamstress, especially with Daisy.

'So, what's that on your jumper?' Isla spelled it out. '*Angele Dei, qui custos es me* – is it some of your naughty army slang?'

'It means guardian angel or some such. It's a joke. I lent a pal a couple of quid to start her own cookery school, that's all.'

'Is she your girlfriend?'

'Och no! She's a neighbour who had trouble wi' some skanky bloke. Took away her home and left her wi' a couple of bairns. You know the type.'

'I'm sorry to say I do. My daughter has one just like it.'

'Oscar Curran.'

'That's him. Know him, do you?'

'I know of him.'

'Then you know nothing good.' Isla took out the hair brush. 'Can I do that?'

'Of course!' Isla sat down. So stressful watching the child of your body take leave of the world. Look at her, skin like tissue paper. You can see her veins through it. 'Things aren't going well. The doctors think she's failing. She's not responding. What do they want her to do, sing a bloody song! She's unconscious, what can she do but lie there.'

'It's words. Don't let them talk you into anything you may regret.'

'That's what I say to her dad. Let her get well in her own time. Don't pester the girl. But he will keep saying he's not sure she might be better off.'

'Better off how?'

'Switching the machine off.'

The brush hung in the air. Eyes like bullets, he turned. 'And why would he want to do that?'

'He keeps saying you wouldn't let an animal live like that.'

'Don't give up. Keep fighting her corner.'

'I'm gonna, don't worry.' Thinking she was being disloyal she changed the subject. 'I don't know what to do. The doctors say one thing, my heart says another. I'm making it up as I go along. Anyway, I've a bloke coming in later to trim her hair. Your pal, Katy, recommended him.'

'He'll be okay then. Katy's girls are up to all the latest styles. I used to bring 'em bits when I was on leave.'

'Have you no family then?'

'My folks died in a car crash, my brother as well.'

'That's awful.'

'That's life. We love them and we lose them.'

'Yes.'

'But not today.'

'Not today.' With him here, his quiet strength and gentle ways, Isla could have slept. She is tired. Rotten dreams! Last night she dreamt she was talking to a horse – what's more the horse was talking back, saying Daisy will get well but mustn't pit her wits against God! Not that Isla thinks much of God these days. Someone said they should be grateful Daisy's alive; to whom should they be grateful, the same God that leaves your child little more than a doll and lets the bloke that did it walk free?

'D'you know that bloke with the TVR2 is suing us.'

'You're kidding!'

'He reckons Daisy shouldn't have been in the road. *And* he's claiming damages! Not that he'll get anywhere. A flea in the ear, is all he'll get.'

'He'll get more than that if I come up against him.'

Isla stared. Why say that when he doesn't know Daisy. 'Can I ask you something? You and my daughter. You were never...?'

'No.'

'Then why the interest?'

He didn't fool about, no blush or bashful smile or cover up. 'I love her.'

'How can you when you've never met.'

'I did see Daisy. She came to a hoos I used to mind, her and Curran. That's when I saw her. Most beautiful thing ever. I heard him say her name. I heard her voice. I love her voice, a kitten purring. I want to hear it again!'

'Me too, lad.'

'Anyway that was it. I lost my heart, Mrs Banks, for good and all.'

Isla's heart wrenched. 'That's a good way to fall in love.'

He tried to smile. 'It's the only way.'

'How come you ended up here, two crocks side-by-side?'

His big shoulders lifted. 'I know why I'm here, public opinion, government shame and a bolshie regiment – not that they'll keep me, cut-backs and all. I'm surprised they haven'ae kicked me oot already.'

'The house where you saw her? Was it Chimney Stacks?'

'Six Chimneys. Aye, that's it.'

'She wanted that house.'

'It's mine. I bought it.'

Isla leaned forward. 'Why?'

He grimaced. 'You'll think me dumb when I tell you.'

'I know why. You bought it hoping one day she'd be there with you.'

He nodded, a single tear slipping down his cheek.

'Looks like you've got a damaged tear duct,' said Isla, fumbling for her hanky.

'No,' he said. 'No damaged tear duct. Just a soldier weeping for a kitten.'

* * *

'You can beam back in now, Scotty!' the nurse called.

Lucian limped back in the door. He was always agitated when they were clearing the tubes. It looked so dangerous and so brutal.

'Got to do it,' said a nurse. 'Can't have your Daisy choking on her own spit.'

'She's not my Daisy. She's just a pal.'

'If this is how you are with pals, lucky the girl you love.'

'Daisy's no so lucky.'

'No,' said the nurse, straightening the sheet. 'She's not.'

'How does she seem to you?' he asks and always gets the same answer – her condition is stable. It's not true today and it wasn't true yesterday.

By the time he was positioned, book open at the right page and the buzzer at his elbow, it's twenty to twelve. Nurses come every two hours to do their stuff, even when they say scoot he bides outside the door.

You forfeit privacy in this place. Faulty material, you're required to turn yourself over to strangers and to put up and shut up. Daisy's vulnerable to all, who better than the man who loves her to get between her and idiots?

Mrs B asked why he felt this way. He could point to the day Daisy came to Chimneys but that won't explain the depth of passion. It's months since he was shot. That he is alive is a miracle – that he is alive next door to his heart's desire is more than a miracle, it is by Design.

It was Ed, the old boy in the side ward, who said she was here.

The day after regaining consciousness Lucian went for an MRI and got caught in a bottleneck, a crash-cart flashing by and his gurney pushed into a side-ward. This old boy heaves up. 'You there, bomb disposal chappie!' Nurse Janet said, 'that's Mr D'angelo. He's a dear but inclined to wander.'

A porter was for moving them on but looking down at the desiccated shell hunched in the bed Lucian felt sadness. 'Something I can do for you, sir?'

The man hooked a claw. Lucian bent closer, one war-ravaged soul overlaying another. 'She's here. Honey-bunny, the girl you love.'

What d'you say to that, especially when it turns out to be true.

Christ! His heart when he saw her! Not a mark on her face but her body held together with superglue. He asked what happened. 'RTA. She was transferred here not long after you were brought in.'

The rest, if you like, is history. Flat on his back is no use to her. Amazed to find he still had a body and the family jewels intact, he persuaded surgeons to get cracking, and here he is, as Gillie would have it, Robocop.

Talking of idiots, earlier today Curran chose to stick his aquiline nose round the door and stand with hands in his pockets eyeing the monitors.

'I hate hospitals. I would've bought roses but Isla said not to bother.'

'Uh-huh.'

'Nurses shorthanded, no time to fiddle with flowers and stuff.'

'Uh-huh.' Lucian took an emery board from his pocket. You gotta watch rough edges on her nails, skin like paper, it can tear.

Curran perched on the bed. 'I brought grapes, silly shit that I am. How's poor Daze gonna eat grapes.' He began to talk about being on TV. It was in one ear and out, until a sentence caught Lucian's attention. '...nabbing down the M3 to see if it's still for sale.'

'You talking aboot Six Chimneys?'

Oscar turned to Lucian. 'Ya, that's the one, an ugly stained glass window taking light in the hall. The first thing I'll do is have that out and put a nice piece of reflective glass in its place.'

'It's no for sale.'

'Don't tell me it's sold! The time that's been on the market and yet the minute I want it someone buys it. You never know, the right price I might make a deal. D'you happen to know who bought it?'

'I do.'

Curran examined his nails. 'You bought it.'

'Like you didn't know.'

Anger flashed across Curran's face. 'Isla may have mentioned it. She can't stand me. She'd do anything to keep me away from Daisy.'

'A mother generally knows what's best for her child.'

'And that's you, is it? And why are you here? The papers call you a hero but who are you really and what do you want from Daisy? I don't like you always being here, doing her nails and stuff. You like playing with dolls?'

Lucian was on his feet, hand locked about the other's wrist. 'Shut your mouth,' he spat. 'She doesn'ae need you talking like that.'

'But it isn't her. The Daisy I knew, her walk, her voice, her hair springing about her head, was alive. That's not my Daisy. That's a...a dead body.'

'Out!' Lucian bundled him into the corridor. 'And don't bother coming back if that's all you've to say!' Then as though whispered in his ear he added, 'and why call her yours when you're married?'

Curran was taken aback. 'Who says I'm married?'

'Never mind who. You've no right to Daisy. She's not yours to disappoint, so clear off back to your wife, desperate though she must be, poor lass, to be saddled with an eejit like you.' Lucian shut the door and found he was on his feet, unaided, trembling, about to piss his pants but upright nevertheless.

Now he's watching the clock. He should be in his own bed but can't. It's this time of night when Daisy seems close to surrendering. Hours of the Wolf, they call them, when the spirit is at its lowest.

Opening the box he drew out the cross. It used to be an ear-stud. He thought he'd lost but it turned up in his locker. Now he's had it hung on a chain and winds it about her fingers at night, hoping it will keep her safe.

Taking her hand he whispered, 'sleep easy, Daisy.' Now for the book, the *Velveteen Rabbit*! This was Ian's favourite. Mother would read it. It is a good story. It made a kid feel safe. Daisy needed to know she was safe, because, although he didn't like what Curran said, Lucian understood why he said it.

Opening it at the page he began to read: '"What *is real?" Asked the Rabbit one day when they were lying side-by-side near the nursery fender, before Nana came to tidy the room. "Does it mean having things that buzz inside you and a stick-out handle?"*

"Real isn't how you are made," said the Skin Horse. "It's a thing that happens to you. When a child loves you for a long, long time, not just to play with, but REALLY loves you, then you become real."

"Does it hurt?" asked the Rabbit.

"Some times," said the Skin Horse, for he was always truthful. "When you are REAL, you don't mind being hurt."

Closing the book Lucian took Daisy's hand. 'Come home, bonny lass,' he whispered. 'Don't hide in the dark. Come home to me.'

The Doll's House

Daisy thinks she hides in a cupboard in the attic, a walk-in cupboard that holds four tins of white paint, a box of candle stubs, and a dog basket. She's been there since the accident – she thinks of Lucian being shot as the 'accident' because she can't bear to think of it any other way. When she was knocked down by a tipsy Santa Claus in a TVR2 she rose out of her body to music. No one sang when Lucian was shot. There was silence and a smoking barrel.

'Oh, my God!' she whispered. 'What have I done?' For a moment (a soldier in or out of uniform) he stood still, multi-coloured glass falling about him. Then he sank to his knees, red staining his breast. 'Oh, darling!' Mad with fear, she thought to save him but as he sank, so did the house.

There was a screeching sound, a giant sheet of cardboard being ripped apart. Then cracks appeared in the ceiling and walls began to move inward.

She threw herself over Lucian to protect him from falling masonry but the stuff that fell had no more weight then polystyrene tiles, and then – a lake of parquet lozenges twisting and writhing – the floor began to emulate the ceiling.

'What's happening? Is it an earthquake?' Lucian did not speak. Fingers like ice, he gripped her hand. And Sean? And Leon? What of them? Daisy looked over her shoulder. 'Sean...!' Her voice died in her throat; though she'd often doubted Six Chimney's provenance she could until a moment ago at least pretend it to be a flesh and blood world. Now it is a surrealist nightmare, a book closing, the crackling sound the coming together of heavyweight pages – and the people once considered to be mortal now paper cut outs that, bit-by-bit, fold down within the book.

A lingering image is of Paper Sean, crayon freckles patterning a paper nose. Lucian was flesh and blood, and so remained, until the form under her hands dissolved, leaving a handful of rose petals on the stairs. 'No!' She snapped her eyes shut! Let's hide in the cupboard! Better not to have eyes than witness the death of love.

There is life on the other side of the cupboard and a sense of a house nested within a house and whispered memories of people of long ago, ladies in hooped skirts and men in periwigs, the oak balustrade visible through their diaphanous forms – Six Chimneys 3-D cinema showing a twenty-four hour newsreel on the distempered wall. Thai and Ming are kittens with a notice attached to a pen, 'ready for re-homing.' The canary, Trilby, lies stunned on the conservatory floor, and then in rewind is backing away from the pane of glass that stunned her until a woman is poking cuttlefish through the bars of a cage while calling her, 'pretty Jenny.'

Daisy suspects the car New Year's Day killed her and that she and all inside the house are ghosts – the idea being too much to bear she sleeps, dropping a veil over pain, separating one layer of reality from another.

* * *

Tick-tock, time passes. One day the cupboard door opened and a face looked in, a beautiful face, pure and good. 'Don't you think it's time you came out?'

'I don't like it outside, it's too busy.'

Wings taking up space, the angel climbed inside. 'I know what you mean. A Light House does take some getting used to.' Daisy couldn't see the point of leaving the cupboard. She was safe in there. Why go out? It's a waste of time...bit like Oscar.

'You remember Oscar?'

'I remember my cat. He died the same time as me.'

'You think you are dead?'

The door pushed open, Boffin hopped in and sat on the angel's knee.

Daisy stared. 'If Boffin's here and sitting on your knee I must be dead.'

'I'm of the celestial realms. An elephant could sit on my knee.'

'What's your name?' said Daisy.

The angel shrugged. 'I have a million names. What would you like to call me?'

'Charley's a nice name. Can I call you Charley?'

'Sure, Charley will do. Come on! Out you come.'

She crawled out. The house is as it should be, curtains at the windows, chairs to sit on and a fire in the grate – all was right but for those living there. 'Hush!' she whispered to the angel, 'those men are ghosts.'

'Why do you say that?'

'I can talk to them but can't touch them.' People and things are constantly on the move. One day the dog went missing. One minute she was by the stove and the next an empty dog-collar. 'Where did she go, Charley?'

'Her master needed her. Your cat was killed in an accident.

He's here because like Biddy he wanted to be with the one he loves.'

Tears filled Daisy's eyes. 'Boffin stays because he loves me?'

Charley brushed a curl behind her ear. 'We all love you.'

She cried then. 'What am I doing here?'

He stroked her face. 'That's something you have to work out. But I can tell you the beings you call ghosts are working their way up a ladder.'

'What's at the top?'

'Heaven. This is a reception centre or as Minna calls it a Halfway House. It is a bridge between worlds and because of its temporal history draws those who die in service of their country.'

'Is Minna an angel?'

'God seems to think so.'

'Can the people here leave?'

'They are volunteers, and as such can leave whenever they choose.'

'Do they want to leave?'

'Ask.' She asked a handsome RAF pilot. He shrugged. 'I'm only a part-timer so it's different for me. Soon I'll have my wings and then if Minna goes, I will.'

'I always thought ghosts were tormented souls.'

'So did I but I know differently now. I'm a beginner at this. A man who in life only flew a Spitfire is hardly in the same class as Charley but fliers die and helping is better than razzing about with a sheet over my head.'

'Yes, ma'am!' said a sailor. 'The only tormented souls are you and the soldier. Can anybody tell me why he comes? The plumbing hasn't worked in years. And do ghosts care if the pipes freeze. It's not like we're gonna catch a chill.'

The soldier comes every day at four. The first time he stepped through the window *and* Daisy. She should've been hurt but the sensation was more of a kiss than a blow. She ran to tell the angel. 'There's a man in the hall.'

'That's Lucian searching for his girl. She was knocked down by a car. Look! He's thinking of her again.' As they watched a figure grew out of the air, a woman with hair red as autumn leaves and skin as pale as milk. Then the image collapsed into a million pieces as though he was unable to sustain it.

'Why does he come?'

'He's doing what he always did, taking care of the house.'

* * *

One winter morning the men brought in a fir tree and began hanging crystals on the branches. Expectation was in the air. Charley was excited, his wings fluffy white. 'It's Christmas Eve, Daisy, and that's a big day for everyone.'

He spoke and the light-fitting blew out the ceiling.

'Big enough to cause this kind of commotion?'

'Big enough to turn the world upside down! Mortal calendars end December 31st. In this house the calendar begins with the Lord's birth. You might take advantage of that, Daisy, since Christmas is best spent with family.'

'I'll stay here with the others.'

'There are no others. They've returned to be with their families.' The angel consulted his watch. 'Lucian is late. I'll go look for him.'

'Can I come with you?'

'Hop on the bike.' With that a Harley Davidson appeared by the stairs. The angel climbed aboard, Daisy behind him with Boffin on her knee. 'Where are we going?' she said. Charley revved the motor. 'Straight through the window and so hold on! As Bette Davis said, it's gonna be a bumpy ride.'

* * *

They landed in a dismal house where the shimmering forms of children darted about the walls. 'A house is a living entity. What you see are memories. Everything that happened here, every joy and every sorrow is registered within these walls.'

'They children seem frightened.'

'They were once. Their fear has passed but the house remembers.' They went into a kitchen where a woman sat at a table. Eyes heavy with sadness, she leafed through a photograph album. The kitchen rippled, a further shape settled over the woman, the same face and faded elegance yet a happy woman who, smiling, looked at a photograph of a soldier and a young woman.

'Who are those people?' Daisy whispered.

'You and your husband.'

'Me!' As she watched a child appeared in the photograph, a pretty dark-haired little girl perched in the man's arms.

'That is your daughter, Emma.'

There were so many photographs and every picture filled with smiling faces.

'What are these photographs?'

'Probable lives.' Charley flicked his hand and the kitchen, the photographs, and Daisy's memory of them ceased to be – now there was a staircase that led to another staircase and another ad infinitum.

'We're between worlds, Daisy. Make your choice.'

'But how do I know which stairs to take?'

Boffin leapt from her arms and ran to a staircase. 'Follow the cat. He knows.'

They climbed the stairs. Charley paused at a door. 'All beyond this door has at some time been dreamed into being.' He opened the door onto a doll's house that had countless rooms, in which the sun shone, the rain rained, grass grew, and people and creatures lived. There were worlds, skies and stars!

'It's a Universe.'

'It's a series of universes, each representative of a life.'

'Whose life?'

'Yours.'

Daisy was awestruck. One moment she was a giant observing an anthill the next a tiny Daisy living in a colony with a million other tiny Daisies. She stepped into one room and she was Daisy Banks who worked in the City and had a boyfriend called Oscar and cat called Boffin; memories of that life – of her parents and friends – was so strong it rushed through her soul as spring water.

'I feel like I am a doll in a doll's house.'

'Is that how this appears to you?'

'I can't describe in another way.'

'Don't try. It's a survival technique. As you give me wings and a halo you have given the ineffable a manageable symbol. It helps cope with the mystery.'

'If you don't see a doll's house what do you see?'

'Atoms whirling!'

'There are so many rooms.'

'You've led a long and colourful existence. You know how to be a leaf. You know how it is to be a star. One day you'll remember how it is to be an angel.'

'How can there be more than one life when I haven't finished this.'

'How can you live in Scotland when your body lies in England? If you want to know more choose a room.' There was power in the angel that gave strength to Daisy. 'I remember you,' she said. 'But I see you as a cockney Hell's Angel.'

'I played the fool in the past to lessen your fear but the time for foolishness is past.' He pointed to the doll's house. 'Look and see how this began.'

Every room in the house was as a theatre stage with props and actors, and centre-stage Daisy gazing through a window at Six Chimneys. The scene shifted. A car sped down a road. There was a squeal of brakes and a hospital room. A couple sat by the bed, the woman attaching tinsel to the bed rail.

'My poor mum! How long have I been there?'

'In your parents' world a year draws to a close. They come every day. Your mother washes your hair and cleans your teeth, doing things she did when you were a child. She hopes you'll come back to them. Your father has no such hope. That is why tonight at midnight the machines will be switched off.'

'Daddy, don't do it!' Daisy ran to her father only to pass right through him.

'He can only hear you in his heart and that he is hardening against you.'

'Why? I'm still his daughter.'

'He fears for your mother. He believes it's time she, and you, moved on.'

'What can I do?

'Choose a memory and learn.' There were so many. One room was like Six Chimneys hall. Crossing her fingers she stepped into that. A gun fired. She screamed. 'I killed Lucian!'

'You killed no one. It was a dream. Thought is the basis of all creation. Your mind mixed with the minds of others to create that particular room.'

'I remember a dream where Kate and her children died.'

'I tried to show you what the power of thought could do.'

'I *thought* I'd moved to Scotland. I *thought* I was happy. I even *thought* I'd fallen in love. Now that life is slipping away. Was it all fantasy?'

'Does your love for Lucian feel a fantasy?'

'I don't know anything other than I want to be with him.'

'Then hold onto that because when you return to the physical, *if* you return, all prior knowledge of him will vanish.'

'Why do we go through all of this only to forget?'

'It is a mortal condition. It happens before the font and after the grave. A fog descends. Most mortals choose not to remember other lives. They prefer not to know. Man believes he cannot survive and remember heaven.'

'So Six Chimneys, Kate and her situation, Connor, the shooting, it's all a dream?' Daisy was afraid. Is all life a dream? Could these people, so dear and precious vanish as she would vanish when machines are switched off?

'Kate and her children are real people in a real world,' said

Charley. 'They share your dream as you share theirs. In other realities Lucian wasn't shot so Leon and Sean will not face a lifetime of regret. Equally there are lives where you choose not to return and a switch is pulled. You should look at one of those.'

'I'm afraid to.'

Charley took her hand and they were in a room that stunk of booze. A woman slept at a computer console, light from the screen falling on a haggard face. 'In this life Isla never got over your death. She drank and shut herself away from the world. The books that you see on the shelves are her escape.'

'Where's Dad? He should be here! She leant on him. He was her tower.' With that, Daisy was in a crematorium staring at a plaque in a wall. '*William Banks. Beloved husband and father. Left this world August 4th 2009.*'

'Alas,' said Charley softly. 'In this world the tower has fallen.'

'My dad is dead!' She burst into tears. 'My darling daddy passed away and I didn't know. But why? He wasn't old.'

'He blamed himself for switching off the machine.'

'But he shouldn't have died and left poor mum alone!'

'She isn't alone.' A young man entered the room. Sean! He cleared away dirty cups and plates. Then he led Isla to the bathroom, to shower, and to bed.

Daisy was distraught. 'My bright and beautiful mother! And Sean is so kind!'

'And hag-ridden! See what happens when a boy blames himself for a sister's death. See him blackening his face with axle grease. He is getting ready to fight for the animals he loves: rats injected with cancers, monkeys stripped of glands, Beagle pups with severed larynx, their lungs filled with smoke so a mortal can fill hers.'

They saw a building enclosed by fences and figures crawling toward wire enclosures – cages, animals peering out. Alarm bells rang. Guards appeared. That world faded with a close up of Sean's face, his eyes reflecting the chaos.

'The tragedy doesn't end there. All were affected by the supposed shooting. As with all actions the consequence goes on forever, even in dreams.'

'This is my fault! If I'm the dreamer I'm responsible for the outcome.'

'A life is not governed alone. You had a part but others share responsibility. The burglar doesn't need to steal or the gun to fire.'

'No, but I forgot the most important character.'

'Because your love was never for a living man! You loved a dream, or rather, you loved his love of you. Would you like to see him as he is, alive, human, and all that that means? He is by your bed, reading from a book, his heart bleeding.'

Daisy peered through a window into a room. So familiar, the same bed, the monitor bleeping, but beside the bed a stranger. 'He's in a wheelchair.'

'Temporarily. Nothing too much will keep this man away from his goal, whether it is to disable a bomb or to save the woman he loves.'

'So this is Lucian. I don't recognise him.'

'Why would you when you've never met. Do you recall Lucian of your dreams?'

'Yes, a real tough guy, tall, blue eyes and dark hair, a hero, decorated.'

'You describe Captain Lucian Nairne GC.'

'The man by the bed seems quiet and gentle.'

'The difference between men is not the colour of hair or what medals they wear. It is what you know in your heart. Could you love the man sitting by your bed?'

'I might if he hadn't broken his promise never to leave.'

'Has he left you?'

'He's not exactly fighting off death.'

'Is he not? Then who is this?' Bang! Lucian is shouting, his words taking the shapes of bullets that rip about the room shattering glass and causing the air to vibrate. '*What d'you mean better off!*' he's yelling. '*And don't give me that mercy rubbish. You're talking about killing her! You're talking murder!*'

'Oh don't,' Daisy covered her ears.

'See how he struggles, even now when you fight him all the way.'

'I don't fight him!'

'You don't fight to live! You're afraid of the future, and while this man, the one who broke a promise, fights for your life as he once fought for your soul.'

'My soul?'

'This man who professes not to believe in God did what few mortals dare to do. He passed through the Gate. You died once in the ambulance. It was science then that gave you life. But you'd had a taste of heaven and died again on the surgical table. In his desire to save you Lucian opposed your will – he crossed the Great Divide and drew you back. "Greater love hath no man than he lay down his life for a friend." He did more than lay down his life, he offered his immortal soul.'

Unable to bear it she stared at a window in the hospital room, a stained glass window. 'I know that window. It's a copy of the one in Chimneys.'

'The window in Six Chimneys is glass and stone. The window we rode through exists on a spiritual plane. The void between symbolises the world of possibilities.'

'And when it's open all possibilities are open.'

'And when closed possibilities harden to become realities. Lucian made a choice. He chose to remain between you and the Other Side.'

'Can a man do that?'

'Maybe not, but an angel can.'

'Are you saying Lucian is more than a man?'

'Any man is more than the sum of his physical parts.'

In the silence that followed Daisy stepped from one room to a ruined church where snow drifted through an open roof, and where a stained glass window glowed against the sky. 'What of Lucian Nairne lives on earth?'

'His idea of his mortal self.'

'And what here within the Gate?'

'I could say a part of his soul.'

'Can that happen? Can a man live without his soul?'

'There are those walking the earth whose souls have not yet woken.'

'Is Lucian's soul asleep?'

'You cannot Guard the Gate and sleep.'

'So what will happen to him?'

'That's up to Lucian. He must decide if the stronghold he built can be sustained.'

'Is it painful doing what he does?'

'Sacrifice is not meant to be easy.'

Daisy struggled. 'You're an angel, Charley, can't you do something about it?'

'I told you there are situations over which I have no control. His was an act of love, a sacrifice. The Lord understands sacrifice. Such a deed will remain in His Mind long after the stars have fallen.'

'Can I go back?'

'The spirit is disinclined to re-animate a sickly body. The future is a process of becoming. Things seen are probabilities. Believe me, Daisy, life is within your own hands, the slightest change and the path is altered beyond recognition.'

'I must go back.'

'You understand that you'll not recognise him. No saviour of souls, no armed hunter keeping the wolf from the door. He'll be but a man.'

'That's okay,' she said wearily. 'I've had enough of supermen.'

'And angels?'

'And angels. What must I do?'

'No need to do anything. Just take an angel's kiss and sleep.'

'And the "poor things" seen at Six Chimneys? Who or what are they?'

'Sorry, Daisy, that you'll have to work out for yourself.'

Suddenly the room is full of people, she can feel their thoughts pressing. Familiar faces from a dream, Kate and her children, Edith Shillingworth, Sean, even Bram Roberts and the animals, Connor, Trilby, the canary, the Siamese, and of course Boffin and Biddy. Standing around them in a protective phalanx were the padre and the novice angels – the men in RAF blue and the soldiers in khaki, and Minna, and all looking at Daisy with the same searching expression in their eyes.

'I remember this. It's how they looked when they sat on the grass. At the time I thought they sought salvation. They do but it's not their salvation they seek it's mine.'

'And mine,' whispered Charley. 'And Lucian's. And all those of the past, present and future in need of sanctuary.'

'So you're not asking me to die?'

'We're asking you to be brave and happy.'

'I can't promise to be happy. But I will try to be brave.'

Charley drew her close. 'No Minna and no ghosts in the attic to drive you crazy, for a time you will feel alone. Try to cling to that you know to be real.'

'How will I know what's real?'

'I'm real.' Minna undid the belt in her pants and buckled it about Daisy's waist. 'Take this. If you need me call, and no matter what Charley says I shall come.'

The window glittered beautiful and deadly. Words filtered through the glass, words from another reality – a child's bedtime story told by a loving man: ' "...*does it hurt, asked Rabbit. 'Sometimes,' said the Skin Horse, for he was always truthful. "When you are Real you don't mind being hurt."* '

She was at the top when a soft chirrup made her turn. She knelt, cradling Boffin's furry face. 'You can't come. You must stay with Biddy.'

'Knight Templar!' Tears threatening, she turned away. 'Let me pass!'

Silence. The gate remained shut.

'It's Lucian you must ask,' said Charley. 'He's the one barring your way.'

'Lucian?' She reached out, stroking the armoured foot. 'Please, let me pass.'

Metal screeching, the window swung aside. There was darkness and then a hospital room and doctors about to switch off life-support.

'See you, Daisy,' said Minna.

'See you, Minna.'

Daisy stepped into darkness.

Undercover Robocop

'Please don't worry! It's quite warm in here and I don't feel the cold.'

'You should wear them.' He carried on easing her feet into the sheepskin slippers. 'You never know what's on the floor.'

'I shall be fine,' said Daisy, cheeks flaming. 'There's warm-air heating and it's not as if I'll be putting my feet on the floor today.'

'Not today, but tomorrow you will be.'

It was like arguing with a bus, a double-decker bus at that. Didn't matter what she said, if it didn't fit in with his ideas on the matter he wouldn't budge.

'How long have you been a volunteer?' she said, gazing down at him, resisting the urge to tidy his hair after the bobble hat. She knew why he wore it, to cover the scar that ripped through the right side of his head.

'Not long.'

'Do you like being a helper?'

'I don't know that I help so much as act as go between.' He straightened, rising until she was staring at a taut midriff and a star on his belt buckle. 'I spend time in the paraplegic unit. Guys there can use help working out to get what they're entitled. My buddy, Gillie, is big on forms. We get together.'

She asked about the star on his belt, was it a military thing? Though not in uniform one can tell he is a soldier. It's not just the upright bearing, it's the way he stands still and says little. 'You remind me of Dad. He was an army man.'

'Aye, the Coldstream Guards.' He smiled. 'By rights we shouldn'ae be talking.'

'Why's that?'

'Your father's an ex Grenadier and a Surrey man. My family's had a bit of bother with both.'

'Oh really? When was that?'

'September, 1513, when the Earl of Surrey and his family hacked most of mine to pieces not far from my home.'

'You recall the incident?'

He smiled again, a rare sight. 'I am a Scot. It's my duty to remember every Sassenach slight upon my life and land.'

'Oh, my word, and I thought *Braveheart* was over the top.'

'So it was. Gibson did an awful drear job of dying.'

'He did rather drag it out but then that's Hollywood heroics. Do Scottish heroes not die like that, slowly and cleanly with a blissful expression on their faces?'

'No,' he said, the smile gone. 'They die as soldiers die, thinking of home.'

'Sorry. I shouldn't have said that.'

'My fault. I shouldn't have led you there.'

'Speaking of heroes,' she said. 'I did hear a whisper you were one such.'

'Only a whisper?' The smile returned to his eyes. 'I'm shocked. I thought my gossip status to be more in the nature of a roar.'

'That may be the case where Nurse Janet and Co is concerned.'

'Away wi' that,' he rolled his eyes, closing off the conversation. 'Is there anything else I can do for you, Miss Banks?'

She thought to jest. 'You might call me Daisy. Having knelt

at my feet shoving my toes into my slippers I think you entitled to that at least.'

He nodded, his expression closed. 'I'll do that then.' Then he was gone.

Daisy breathed out. Male volunteers are okay yet females more welcome. With a woman you don't have to worry about medical paraphernalia. Most of it is disconnected, thank goodness, but there are still the titanium screws that hold flesh and bone together while giving her the legs of an armadillo.

What's on today, a trip to the MRI wing, and then the audiologist, followed by a visit from the dietician? 'Lucky me!' She gazed out of the window watching sparrows fly. It must be nice to fly, she thought, to climb higher until you're no more than a speck in the blue. It's normal to be depressed after major surgery, so she's been told. A year in a coma, surgery and morphine, it's no surprise she's so down her chin is alongside the pink sheepskin moccasins.

That she is depressed hasn't escaped notice. 'Omigod, look at this!' Six am this morning, Nurse Janet shoved a mirror in front of Daisy's face. 'What?' she'd screeched, thinking her nose had fallen off. Janet had sniffed. 'A face most women would kill to own. Shame it's so miserable.'

Daisy feels lost. For a time everyday on waking she has no idea where she is. Then it comes: 'Ah yes, St Jude's long-stay unit. This is my body, and the scar about my waist is...' Pop! It's gone and the sense of another life with it.

People say they remember a near death experience as bright lights and tunnels. Not Daisy, her last memory is the car slewing round the corner, Boffin in the headlights, and a man trying to push her out of the way.

'I think one of the neighbours tried to help,' she said to Isla.

'Really?' said Isla. 'Would that be the same neighbours queuing up to say you were on your hands and knees drunk in the middle of the road?' The chap that knocked her down is suing for damages. Maybe that's why she feels sad, the injustice. She'd better snap out of it because tomorrow is physiotherapy and anyone getting through that deserves a medal. Lucian Nairne said that. The nurses think he is sexy whereas Mum thinks he's son-in-law material. 'Giving his time to the sick,' she said yesterday. Daisy was scornful. 'What's this, a biblical parable and he a holy man laying hands on me?'

Isla grinned. 'I dare say he'd like to lay hands on you, though not in a biblical way... but then thinking about it – *exactly* in a biblical way.'

Isla is up to something. Daisy can read the signs. 'Don't be doing anything silly. No match-making, not while Oscar's trying to make amends.'

'How can he make amends when he's never here?' said Isla. 'And why bring him into the conversation? We're talking about a man not an excuse for one.'

'Mum, please. I know you don't like Oscar but he is my partner.'

That was when Dad spoke up. 'He's partner to no one.'

'Daddy, can't you try to like him?'

'I don't respect Oscar and I can't like a man I don't respect. He's fickle! He's shallow! And he's married.'

It seems Oscar is married to a dancer he met in Sweden, and who, according to gossip, is already suing for divorce – Dad read about it in an *OK* magazine at the barber's. 'Stupid face grinning up and a girl with bosoms spilling out! I've no respect for him and less for you if you don't get rid of him.'

* * *

Daisy lay on the bed trying to get into a pair of jeans. She puffed and panted until, disheartened, she kicked them away. 'I'll never get into these.'

Janet picked them up. 'You will when the swelling goes down.'

'And how long is that going to take?'

'Soon enough. Be patient! You're on your feet. What more do you want?' She took a pair of cargo pants from the wardrobe. 'What about these?'

'Yeuch! Isla bought those. I don't like them.'

'They're fabulous.'

'Then you have them. I want pants that slim me down, not make me look like an elephant.'

'You don't look like an elephant. There's nothing of you.'

'Only ten pounds of titanium.'

'You can't expect things to heal overnight.'

'I'd hardly call ten weeks overnight.'

'You've come a long way in that time. Look at yesterday! You spent pretty much the whole afternoon on crutches and only stumbled twice. Oh, give yourself a break! You're never satisfied. I can't do this, can't do that, there are women coming through these doors that have no legs to put into jeans.'

'I know and I'm not complaining about the treatment. I want to go home.'

'You are going home on Thursday.'

'I'm not talking about Surrey. I'm talking Scotland!'

* * *

Isla brought a letter from the Scottish solicitors. 'He's offered a year's lease.'

'Why a lease when I want to buy it?'

'He must have reasons. Your pa and I went down to have another look. He's got workmen doing stuff but then on old house needs renovation.'

'I don't want it renovated. I like it as it is.'

'What, mice in the egg house and a tomb in the garden? Even so, it's better than the tip we call cemetery. If I'd a choice I wouldn't mind lying there.'

'I'll bear that in mind, Mum, for when I get the house, if I get it.'

'You'll get it. The owner's just being considerate.'

William Banks coughed. 'We should talk about that. My man says it's a pig-in-a-poke, the house entailed by articles stretching back to the middle-ages.'

'Your pal doesn't know everything.'

'What's to know? I don't know why you and Daisy are so set on the place.'

'I have to be independent, Daddy.'

'Can't you be independent closer to home?'

It's a question Daisy can't answer. She has no idea why she wants it only that she does; the memory of the house – willows drooping and the scent of roses wet with rain as vivid as the clock

347

on the wall.

Later, she was with the old man in the side-ward, and sighing asked how she could describe a matter of life or death. He shrugged, his claw-like fingers flickering across the phone. '*no cn do jst is.*'

Daisy likes to sit with Ed D'angelo. It's peaceful, they play scrabble and sometimes chat, Daisy doing the chatting and Ed texting. He rarely leaves his room, lies in a state of the art bed or sits in a chair overlooking an aviary.

'That's a wonderful aviary! So many beautiful birds!'

He nodded: '*wf bort avry so I cn rmbr flyg.*'

Janet translated: 'Ed was a fighter pilot in WW2. His wife paid to have this installed so that he can look at the birds and not be lonely.'

'*Ys!*' Ed nodded, his amazing golden eyes alight. '*Minna luv me 4vr.*'

Janet shook her head. 'Poor old boy,' she whispered. 'His wife's been dead for years and his care here sponsored by the Lighthouse Association.'

'What's that?'

'I don't know but where he's concerned it has bottomless pockets. He was here long before I came, the aviary arriving the week he was brought in, and the bed and the rest constantly updated. There's even a small cinema where he and other patients can watch movies and all paid by the Foundation.'

'Must be a very wealthy organisation.'

'I'd say so. Being nosy I tried researching and got as far as some big American bank and a Scottish firm of lawyers. Then I got an e-mail from a bloke called Phillip Tree the Third, who thanked me for my interest, and quote, "I know of your devotion to Ed, and would I please accept enclosed cheque."'

'A little bit of praise goes a long way.'

'And a five hundred quid cheque every Christmas goes even further.'

With that Ed's fingers flew: '*U lk my wif Dsy. Sm rd hr. Sm sml.*'

'You look like his wife,' said Janet.

Daisy nodded. 'Yeah, I got that.'

'*My wf Angel.*'

'I'm sure she was.'

'*No! Nt ws! Is, hony buny!*'

'Who or what is honey bunny?' said Daisy, confused.

'You,' said Janet. 'That's his name for you.'

His fingers flew again. '*Wif servant of Ang Gab. She kps lite.*'

'His wife is Angel Gabriel's servant. She keeps the light.'

'What light?' said Daisy.

'I have no idea.' Janet drew Daisy aside. 'Most of the staff here think Ed's a crazy old man. I don't think that. Yes he wanders! He's in pain most of the time and on morphine and what he says doesn't always make sense, even so, there's more to him than a wandering mind.'

'Can't he speak?'

'Yes, he can. I've heard him. I think it was painful back then he couldn't manage. Now he doesn't try.'

'All those burns!' Daisy shuddered. 'I wonder he's still alive.'

'I've stopped wondering. A power beyond flesh and blood keeps Ed alive. I think he's one of those people who've learned to get beyond the body.'

God bless the man. Daisy looked at his shrivelled carcase and saw a chrysalis. Some sense of what she was thinking must've communicated because he smiled, his fingers tapping out a message: '*ecce homo, ecce papilion.*'

* * *

'Hiya, babe!' Oscar threw his jacket on the chair and grabbed the remote control. 'Don't mind if I watch this, do you? I'm on Breakfast TV. It should be good,' he gave her arm a squeeze. 'Kevin Spacey was in the Green Room. We got to chatting about *K-Pax* and maybe a spot in one of his movies.'

'That sounds like fun.'

'It was.' He broke open a pack of chewing gum popping a wedge into his mouth. 'I had a fantastic weekend too, non-stop dancing at EJ's.'

'EJ's?'

'Elton John's place... well, not in his place, a marquee in the garden. Me and a couple of lads got a jazz combo going. We didn't leave til five. Couldn't move for an hour when I woke up, still nissed as a pewt.'

'Sounds fun.'

'It was except Marta, the horn player, decided to strip in the middle of one of the flower beds. Awful sight. Scared most of the guests away. Shush! It's on.' The programme came on, Oscar nodding and grinning from both sides of the room. When it was done he snapped off the remote. 'What d'you reckon?'

'You look good.'

'Yeah, I thought so too though,' he peered in the mirror, 'I might go for a new hair style, maybe a modern Mohican.'

'You could do that.'

'And perhaps a stripe cut into the back, a Johnny Depp look.'

'Perhaps.'

'Better be breezing.' He shrugged into his jacket, flicking the collar and rolling back the sleeves,' thanks for the advice. I knew I could count on you.'

'Always.'

'I see you finally got into your jeans. You look good.' He patted her bum. 'You always did have a great arse. See you, then, darling!' He was gone, striding down the corridor whistling his latest hit, '*Sinners Playground*.'

* * *

Daisy's not a dreaming person, or didn't think so until today, however during the early hours this morning she had the mother lode of all dreams.

It began the moment she closed her eyes. It was about the house, Six Chimneys always on her mind. She was taking biology lessons, looking at drawings on a blackboard. No earthly blackboard, it could manipulate the drawings *a-la Studio Ghibli* so that the subject could talk, or walk, or fly.

There was a lecture on the Life of Water, sounds issuing from a funnel wave not unlike the Bore on the River Avon describing the passion and pain of a river and those watery individuals that dwell therein. From then she learned of the growth from Stone, a millennia millennium. From there eyes of rich and vibrant hue told of the formation of colour, the class given a short (and rather risqué) insight into Yellow's desire to become like Scarlet. It was very personal, and judging the laughter, very funny. During the dream she laughed with other students yet now doesn't know what she found amusing.

During class she conversed with a tiger who took her on a whirlwind tour of his jungle domain. Panting, she ran alongside through tightly woven grass – hunting or being hunted she couldn't tell. On and on it went, every experience both enchanting and disturbing, yet not once did she consider herself to be dreaming. The encounter didn't feel like a dream! She felt as though she was learning of a life she never knew existed where creatures seen only in a nursery book lived and flourished – fairies with wings of silk, dragons spouting flame, and mile high energies moving through cornfields like monster Dyson vacuum cleaners whose sole directive was the filtering of pollution.

One lesson told of a moth that lay dying, wing ripped to pieces. Had she seen this when awake she might've killed the moth ending what she saw as suffering, yet this moth knew nothing of pain, and sang of the sun and air, and the Lord of All Creation, and was grateful for the opportunity.

The last image before waking was of a rabbit with wounded ears. He sat beside her relating the *Velveteen Rabbit*. 'To be really real,' he whispered, nose quivering, 'you must do the best you can with what you've been given.'

She woke thinking there was no one she could tell of the dream unless it was Ed D'angelo. She hurried down to tell only to find he already knew.

'*U bin lite-hs,*' he texted. '*tlkg wiv my wif.*'

Her thunder stolen she went back to her room and found, to her surprise, she could tell Lucian Nairne. '...the teacher was dressed for the Land Army in heavy boots and jodhpurs. Hardly befitting an angel, wouldn't you say?'

He grinned. 'Don't ask me. The closest I've been to anything remotely good was an old Dominie back in Sunday School.'

'Was he like an angel?'

'Not unless angels are handy with their fists and real fond of old and filthy.'

'Old and filthy? That sounds disgusting.'

'Not at all! It's a Scots coverall for a glass of something hot and tasty.'

'You mean like you.' It was out before she could stop it. She sat with eyes wide open and hand clamped across her mouth – shutting the gate after the horse had well and truly bolted! 'I'm so sorry,' she said.

Mouth curled in amusement, he continued to gaze at her.

'I don't know why I said that. I think I was caught up in the general tide of Scottish magic. You know, all the nurses trying to seduce you.'

More silence.

'And obviously making a rotten job of it.' Sighing, she did a swift change of conversation. 'Mother says we're on the same plane Friday.'

Click! He came alive. 'Uh-huh. 1300 hours Friday.'

'You've business in Edinburgh?'

'Close by.'

'Bit of a coincidence us travelling together?'

'Business trips to Scotland are not unheard of and I am a Scot.'

'Of course! So what are we reading tonight?'

He held up a battered book. 'This is the only book on the

WI trolley that wasn'ae about making flaky pastry or how to line a drawer wi' scented paper.'

Daisy hadn't seen Lucian for a while and had missed him – which is probably why she'd made such an ass of herself. 'You've been away.'

'The army whistled and I had to jump.'

'Can you be a little more specific?'

He smiled. 'That's classified.'

'Classified? And I thought you an honest man.'

'Am I not?'

'Isn't classified the word politicians use when about to lie?'

'Aye, and the MOD when they tell you it's a necessary war.'

Oh! The smile vanished. She'd caught him on the raw.

'Let's not do this, Daisy?'

'No, let's stick to where the book takes us.'

'Let's do that.' He stretched out his long legs and leaning into the pool of light began to read: '"*Do you really mean, sir,*" said Peter, "*that there could be other worlds – all over the place, just round the corner.*" '

Daisy smiled. 'CS Lewis, The Lion, Witch, and Wardrobe.'

'You've read it. Is it worth the reading?'

'Yes, if you like fairy tales.'

'They have to better than tales of war.'

'How did you get that scar, Lucian?'

'I got it doing what I thought at the time was a necessary bit of policing.'

'Are you okay now? I mean, is the wound healed?'

'The wound in my head is healed but I'm no sure about my heart.'

'Is there anything I can do, or is that also classified?'

'I was only teasing, Daisy.'

'I did think you were.'

'Good, because where me and my life are concerned there's nothing closed off to you.' Startled, she gazed at him. Glance steady, he held her gaze, a line being drawn, an invitation, or challenge, for her to cross over. 'I am an open book. Everything I am is for you to read. You need only open me.'

The world shrinking to a pool of lamplight and a man with truth in his eyes, Daisy couldn't breathe. 'My cat died.' It seemed important to tell him.

'I'm sorry. Had you had him long?'

'A few years. Boffin only had three legs but was ace getting around.'

'A brave cat then. I had a dog back home. Biddy, was her name. Fat and inclined to smell, but my dog for all that. She died while I was stuck in here.'

'You mean she pined away?'

'Christ, I hope not! My neighbour looked after her. A good woman, Kate wouldn'ae let anyone down, not even a dog.'

'Do you think there's a heaven for cats and dogs, Lucian?'

'I'd like to think Biddy's somewhere else buried in the garden.'

'You had her buried? '

'My pal Gillie saw to it. He laid her in a garden close by.'

'I wish I could've done that for Boffin.'

'Not to worry. He'd have known you loved him.'

'Will you get another dog? I've heard the best way of showing love for your animal is to get another. When I'm in my house I shall get a cat. In fact, I plan to have lots of cats, and dogs, and donkeys. I mean to have an animal sanctuary, that's if the old misery that owns my house will let me.'

'And your man, Oscar, how does he feel?'

'Ah, well, that's another story.' She sighed. 'Why do things have to change?'

He shrugged. 'I don't know. I guess life is about moving on.'

Drawn to the topic they moved closer. He was a fingertip away, Daisy's face reflected in his eyes. She wanted to look away but couldn't. 'Don't look at me.'

'Why not?'

'I'm not a very nice person. I thought I loved Oscar but now I'm thinking of him going and not feeling a bit sorry. What kind of a woman does that?'

'A sensible woman,' he said. 'A woman who rather than make a poor choice sets both parties free to choose again.'

'Sensible?' she smiled. 'I've been called many things but never sensible.'

'You are so.' He set the book down and took her hand. 'You're beautiful, and bright and glorious. You're also a woman who's a privilege to love. As for seduction, and clumsy attempts, let me tell you, if you're in need of practice I'm your man. All you have to do is whistle.'

CHAPTER TWENTY-SEVEN

Still Undercover

'No lifts installed,' said Lucian to the electrician, 'I'll be running a marathon by the time we're in so you don't need to worry about that.'

'As you say, Captain, though I was thinking of your missus. The back stairs is on the dark side. Maybe spotlights on the stairs and skylight for the outhouse?'

'Okay but no contractors. I want you doing it not eejits like Fairbrother.'

The electrician snorted. 'Bring that man in on a job and I can wave goodbye to years of a good reputation. Getting back to your missis – it's a big hoos wi' lots of stairs. You might consider a lift.'

Lucian wandered into the conservatory. This was Minna's favourite place. A Turkish cigarette, a glass of whisky on the side and feet on the fender, she was one tough lady. The kids were fascinated by her. They'd squint through the hedge, imagining witches' spells rising in the wood smoke. 'Dinna go in there,' they'd say to passers-by. 'She'll turn you into a frog.'

He needs to go through Drummach attics before handing over the key. The terms of the Will are curious yet Painswick reckons they are watertight, the contents of the house and personal effects *'bequeathed to one who deserves them.'* Six Chimneys has sold several times since Minna's death but no one stays. When asked why they say the same: 'The house doesn't want us.'

* * *

Lucian can't seem to stop sleeping. He used to be a night bird, four hours sleep was plenty, but since being shot he could sleep on a rail. Apparently it's normal to drop-off after surgery. Maybe it's the same with dreams, 'cos, Jees, he could fill a book! Last night he dreamt he saw Nobby Clarke getting into a lift. When he asked where he was going Nobby said he was off to see Celtic play Rangers in the cup-tie. Lucian said he thought the ground was sold out. Nobby had grinned. 'I prayed in advance,' he says. 'Got my seat booked.'

That's some dream considering Staff Sergeant Clarke was blown to pieces in Basra along with Clyde Bassett when their lorry hit a mine.

Nobby dying got to Lucian. He hears of another lad or lass getting killed and his guts shrink. The psychiatrist he's seeing quotes John Donne: '"*Any man's death diminishes me.*" ' Last time he chose to do so Lucian lost his temper. 'They weren't just anyone! They were my buddies. And you're damn right their death diminishes me! They are under the sod and I'm still here!'

His mobile buzzed. 'Hi, Mrs B. How are things?' Off she went, talking ten-to-the-dozen. He held the phone out offering the odd, 'uh-huh'. He understands. She's anxious for Daisy. 'It's a long way to Scotland! Will she be safe?'

'We're no Planet Zog, Mrs B. We wear kilts, not bones through our noses.' He mentioned Kate might help out. 'She's a good woman but a rare gossip.'

'That's okay,' says Isla. 'Her gossiping will make up for my daughter's silence.'

Daisy's better now at talking but withdrawn from the moment of waking.

My Lord! The moment is imprinted on his soul. He slides off the chair and down on his knees. 'Thank you, Lord.' Then he sees the electrician is watching. 'I'm thinking there's damp down there, Archie,' he says, fooling no one.

Archie Basset's a good lad. Clyde Basset was Archie's Uncle.

'You got your Uncle's stuff sorted yet?'

'He left instructions where to be buried – not that there was anything to bury.'

'I imagine not.'

'He was home Christmas. Asked after you, Captain. Said you were the finest officer he'd ever served.'

* * *

Lucian took a couple of days off to visit the cemetery in Saint Malo. They're all there under a marble slab. At the time of the accident he wanted to bring them home but Grandfather Nairne wouldn't hear of it. '*I'm no laying down good money for that! What did they expect driving on foreign roads?*'

Visiting the grave stirred up old pain. Last week he dreamt of Nobby Clark, last night it was Ian. They talked of Mother and Chimneys and then Ian was smiling and shouting his favourite goodbye, '*see you later, alligator*!'

'In a while crocodile,' Lucian whispered, his eyes suddenly full of tears.

Better get a grip. Can't have Major Nairne weeping.

Today at a review board he learned he'd been promoted. He

also learned he was heading back to Afghanistan and Camp Bastion. It's what the promotion is about, and the newspaper coverage '*Wounded Hero returns to Killing Fields*,' the Army making use of Lucian's situation to embarrass the government.

He is tempted to resign his commission but after what he's been through figures he's going to die sooner rather than later and might as well get on with it. He still can't believe he was out all that time being fed through tubes and nurses washing his body. The shrink asked if he recalled being shot; he made the appropriate responses. What he didn't say was that he remembers rising out of his body and taking Daisy for a spin on a motorbike, her cat, and his old dog, Biddy, in a sidecar. Crazy! Come back Wally Disney, all is forgiven!

* * *

'Okay then, get a lift installed.' Lucian's on the phone to Six Chimneys.

'You're right to do it, sir,' says Archie. 'Your missis won't have to climb all of those stairs.' Archie refers to Daisy as Lucian's missis and he's not the only one! Porters at the hospital do it and the old chap in the side-ward. Meeting him was a real wake-up call. Those burns! You can hardly complain about headaches when you're looking at him.

Poor old chap's holding on for something. His latest text, '*not log 4 wgs.*'

Whatever wgs are, apparently he's not long for it.

Daisy isn't Lucian's missis. Other than a hospital volunteer she's no idea who he is and that Six Chimneys is his. To be honest, these days he's not sure who he is. There's a scene in a movie where a guy is heading for the electric chair and his girl waits by the phone for news of a reprieve. The camera closes in on a calendar, days of the week peeling off like petals, then on the second hand of a clock moving round the dial – Lucian's the guy strapped to the chair waiting for the switch to be pulled. He tends to think there is no reprieve.

* * *

He's had another call from Mrs Banks. She worries. The night Daisy regained consciousness, poor woman, she was on her knees by the bed, face white as a ghost. 'Thank you for coming back!' Then there's Daisy's father with hands like grappling hooks wanting to heft her back from death. Nice enough guy but at the time Lucian was for killing him. Now the guy blames himself for being wrong and a stranger for being right. Mrs B thinks it too. There's distance between husband and wife that wasn't there before.

If she can keep her mouth shut Kate Khan will be good for Daisy. 'I don't think I can do it,' Kate would've refused. 'How's it gonna look? You doing all that to the house and her not knowing?' With that he pulled rank, 'is that your business, Mahonia? If you don't think you can do it I'll get someone else.'

How she stared – you could tell she didn't know whether to walk out or whup his ass. They two had a thing going for a while. Wow! Zig Mannering doesn't know what he's in for. Some woman, you never knew if she was going to lick your balls or bite them off!

* * *

Lucian sits above the hospital physio department and there's movement back of the gym. Daisy's here with Janet and Yusef, the muscle.

He can hear Yusef talking. 'I know you're tired, Daisy, but a couple of minutes won't hold you up.' Up she gets out of the chair, her knees making that wavering side-to-side movement only a fellow sufferer would recognise.

A quick glug of coffee and Lucian scrunched down in the seat. Janet knows he is here, that woman's got eyes like a hawk.

'He's here again!' Look at her whispering to Yusef. 'How many times has he been? Is it seven weeks on the trot? I call that committed.'

'I call it stupid. You wouldn't catch me doing it.'

'Yeah, but then you're a regular misogynist, Yusef.'

'What are you two talking about?' said Daisy.

'Never you mind! Get your ass in gear and start walking.'

'Brute!' Daisy doesn't really care what they're whispering about. She wants to get this over and be on her way. 'So what do you want me to do?'

'I want you to walk to the end of that line without once saying it hurts.'

'You're a hard bitch, you know that.'

'Yes I do know that, but if I was any other way would you have got out that chair and walked?'

'We shall never know,' said Daisy, pushing down on the bars.

It wasn't easy. Pain was there before first step but she kept at it. Janet might be a dragon but she's a great nurse. If it was a choice between redundancy money or Janet in a suitcase, there would be no competition. But nurses can't up sticks when you want them to, plus the chap who owns Six Chimneys has sorted a neighbour to help out. 'I suppose I should be grateful.'

'Grateful to whom? Watch that ankle, and don't think I didn't see you scrape the floor. You're to lift not slide. Sliding's not walking. It's cheating.'

'Grateful to the old misery that owns Chimneys for hiring a cleaner.'

'Is he old?'

'Has to be. Some regimental old buffer who thinks he's Winston Churchill.'

Janet sniffed. 'Sounds pretty tasty to me.'

'Did you see the latest letter? He wants to know if I'm getting a dog. I expect he's a farmer and can't have the sheep bothered.'

'Then again he might be concerned with your safety.'

Daisy executed a neat turn, swivelling on her heel while bringing her foot in line. 'He still won't sell. A year's tenancy is all.'

'Sounds like a good idea to me. You get to test the ropes. Trouble with you, you can't see the wood for the trees, you blind wee bat.'

'Wee bat? Where have I heard that before? And what's with the phony accent? Since when did you become a lover of things Scottish?'

'Since she set eyes on him up there on the mezzanine.' Yusef pointed. 'The bomb disposal geezer all the nurses are mad about.'

Daisy looked up. 'Oh, you mean Lucian.' Uncertain for a moment, the tension between them altered, she waggled her fingers. 'Hi, Lucian!'

He nodded, got to his feet, and was gone.

'Yusef!' hissed Janet.

'What?' he said.

'Never mind. If we're done here I guess you can go. Apart from slurping your feet you did a reasonable turn so it'll have to do. Who's picking you up?'

'Mum. I've to give her a call when I'm ready. She's with her publisher. The new book is out.' Daisy dug in her bag. 'She sent a signed copy for your daughter.'

'Thanks very much. Shar loves her books. They remind her of that lovely velvet rabbit thing. Lucian used to read that to you,' said Janet, pocketing the book. 'I'd clock on night-shift and hear his voice whispering through the wards. I'd have the best night's rota. Even my Ed would be listening. I'd do my rounds and all I'd see were eyes peeping over sheets. That's some bloke, you know.'

'So people keep telling me.'

'Well, bear it in mind.'

'I know he's a lovely man. I just don't see why I should make more of it.'

'For the future, I meant. Just in case.'

'Alright then, just in case.' Daisy held out her hand. 'Thanks for everything.'

'Only too glad to help. You take care. Don't forget to see Ed before you leave.'

* * *

Daisy got back to the room to find Oscar waiting. 'Hello. I didn't expect you today. Is everything okay?'

'Er well, I've had the offer of a gig.'

'I see.' She could feel it coming. It was hovering on his lips, growing like a cartoon bubble. She could almost see words forming. '...the ...only... problem...is ...it's... in...!'

'...the only thing it's in Germany.'

'You must be thrilled.'

'I am but I feel bad leaving you.' He went into a long protracted speech about how he didn't deserve her. Midway through Daisy lost patience. 'Okay, then, don't let me keep you. I'm sure you're in a rush to get off. I know I am.'

'Why, where you going?'

'Scotland.'

'You're still going through with it!'

'Of course! Why would I not?'

'I thought with me not coming you might change your mind.'

She smiled. 'Oscar, you've been looking for a way out for weeks. This gig in Germany makes your situation, and mine, easier.'

'So, no matter what I said or did you were always going to go.'

'I think it's the other way round, don't you? No matter what I would've said or done you were always going to go.'

'Bloody, hell, Daze, what's got into you? You're not the girl I used to know.'

'I should hope not. Pathetic carrying on as I was before.'

'What was wrong with before? You had friends, money in your pocket and your own house!'

'Nothing, forget it.'

'I'm not forgetting it. I was part of your life then.' Furious, yet enjoying the drama, he paced the room. 'I guess with me out of the way you're strong.'

'I'm not referring to physical strength. I'm talking mental strength.'

'Of course you are! When women get hormonal and want to kick a guy in the nuts they use words like mentally strong. "Oh, it's not you, darling, it's me"!' he adopted a high falsetto. "I need to find inner peace and so I'm going to a spiritual retreat, taking time out to find myself."'

Daisy laughed. 'Maybe that's why I'm going to Scotland, to find myself.'

'Jees! The way you came back from the dead bang on the stroke of midnight, I'd have thought you'd more than found yourself.'

'Well, you know me, Oscar. I love to make a dramatic entrance.'

'You did that alright! You scared everybody half silly,'

'Were you scared? I thought you were away that night trying to mend your marriage. Or were you getting a divorce? Things move so fast nowadays.'

'Oh, I get it, the Scotsman been talking! The bloke's some kind of nutter. You should have seen him when you were out cold, busy-busy, brushing your hair.'

'Don't be silly.'

'I'm not being silly. The bloke's crazy about you.'

'He's a volunteer.'

'A volunteer? Is that what he calls himself?'

'I don't think he calls himself anything. He's shy and keeps to himself.'

'Shy? The face of *Help the Heroes*? Don't make me laugh.'

'Whatever.' Daisy had had enough. Time is getting on and she wants to say goodbye to Mr D'angelo. 'Lucian didn't say anything. It was Dad.'

'Your dad never liked me.'

'My dad likes everybody until they prove less than likable. But never mind!' She kissed his cheek. 'Go, Oscar, wherever you're going and have a good life.'

He went without a backward glance, relief written all over his shoulder blades.

'Bugger it!' She flopped on the bed. 'I should've left the closing speech until I was outside. Now I'll have to carry my own bag.' She fastened the chain about her neck. Such a lovely thing! A small diamond studded cross on a chain, it was left on her locker one day, apparently a gift from an unknown admirer.

There was a rap on the door. 'Need a hand with that bag?' Lucian was at the door. So tall and straight, he made Daisy smile. 'You're never off duty, are you?'

'I hope so. I'm gonna make a boring companion if I am.'

'You mean on the plane?'

'I mean anywhere.'

'Don't you think it strange, you and me on the same plane?'

'Not at all. I heard you were going to be on that flight, and since I'm going in the same direction on the same day I got a seat.'

'Next to me?'

'I couldn't be that lucky. Is this the only bag?'

'Dad took the rest yesterday.'

'So that's it, you're booked out.'

'Signed, sealed, and delivered.'

'You're officially no longer a patient.'

'I'm an out-out-patient. Why, is it important?'

'It makes a difference.'

'In what way?'

'The hospital has a policy.' He took her bag and offered his arm. 'Volunteers are not allowed to fraternise with patients.'

'Fraternise?' Daisy's breath caught in her throat. He was smiling, blue eyes dazzling. 'You intend then to fraternise?'

'You betcha,' he said. 'Like I've never fraternised before. And if that doesn'ae work I'll allow you to try your latest moves.'

'My latest moves?'

'Uh-huh, seducing me.'

Fraternising

'Please stop,' she said, her mouth bruised from kissing. 'You're a stubbly man. I'll have no face left if we go on like this.'

'I cann'ae help it.' He patted her lips with his handkerchief. 'The barbarian lies only so far beneath the surface of every full-blooded Scot. It comes to fore in the height of battle.'

'Are we battling?'

'What d'you think, honey bunny?'

'It certainly isn't peaceful. I'm quite worn out.'

'That's okay. You can sleep on the plane. I'll make sure no one bothers you.'

'You included.'

'Me especially.'

'But you'll be in another seat so the promise isn't difficult to keep.'

'Don't worry about that. I feel sure I'll be able to charm myself into the seat next to you. I have my ways, you know.'

'I do know.' With her release as a patient the quiet man in the background was done and Operation Ravishment in progress. Not that she's complaining. It is wonderful. *He* is wonderful and she can't believe it's taken so long to see it.

'I'd like to pop along to see Mr D'angelo before I leave,' she'd said, the hospital a million years ago from now.

'Good idea,' he'd taken her arm. 'I'll pop along with you.'

They'd knocked on Edwin's door. 'Hello, Ed,' she'd said. 'I've come to say goodbye.' His lips moved but no sound came out. Janet, who specials Ed pressed his phone into his hand. Claws clicked over apps. '*No g'by ltr gatr.*'

'What does it mean?' whispered Daisy. Janet shrugged and passed the phone back. Lucian nodded. 'I think I know what it means.' He wrapped his hands about both of the old man's hands. 'In a while crocodile,' he said.

The old man nodded and began to weep.

'Bye, Mr D'angelo,' Daisy kissed his cheek. He muttered in her ear. She nodded and walked away. Lucian stayed for a couple of minutes, and then, 'come. I'll treat you to a cup of coffee,' he'd said to her. Next, he's hailing a cab and they're pulling up outside a hotel.

'You stay here?'

'Tuesdays until Thursdays,'

'Tuesdays and Thursdays?'

'Uh-huh. You do fatigues on Tuesdays and Thursdays.'

'Oh,' her heart did a flip. 'You stay here because I...Oh!'

'Uh-huh.'

'And we're here to have a cup of coffee.'

'Uh-huh.'

'Oh, *that* kind of cup of coffee.'

'Uh-huh.'

It's difficult from then on to recall the exact train of events. They got as far as the lift. He put down her bag and leaning her against him, turned and punched the stop button. 'Will you no look at that,' he said. 'The lift's broken.'

'Oh dear,' she'd whispered, drowning in blue. 'Perhaps we should call for help.'

'Aye, but not yet.'

Much is said about kisses being sweeter than wine; to be sure his kisses had an intoxicating promise that minutes later his body amply fulfilled. It wasn't how she'd planned to spend the day. Gauging the startled expression on his face it wasn't his plan either. 'Are you surprised, beautiful Daisy?' he said.

What could she say other than yes but she lied when she said it, because though the situation is new, the passion is known. Strange and bewildering, it felt like a transfer of time – another man and another time.

'Do you believe in soul mates?' she asked the following day.

'You women and your spooky vibes.'

'No, truly. Do you think there's a special person for everyone?'

'I have no idea, though I doubt love is on ration, least not in my case. You can have all that I have. Sure, I've buddies like Gillie, and Kate and her kids, but you're my honey bunny. The difference is not how many you love as how you love.' He drew her closer. 'You thinking maybe we've been together in the past, you a Sassenach milkmaid and me a Scots Laird about to ravish you?'

She slapped him. 'Don't give yourself airs! Why should I be the female about to be ravished? How about a role reversal, me Tarzan and you Jane?'

'Hmm,' he mused. 'It's no a situation I'd given much thought, but if you're willing to wear the loincloth I don't mind having the nuts.'

* * *

Isla was at the airport looking decidedly smug. 'I was beginning to wonder if I should send a search party.'

Daisy refused to be drawn. It's easy to let things pass when you're happy. The way she feels today God can give her a scolding and she wouldn't mind.

'Btw, you're wanted back here a week on Tuesday,' said Isla. 'The feller in the TVR2 has managed to get a court hearing.'

'Okay.'

'And your pa will be putting you on the stand.'

'Okay.'

'And the opposite side have a shark for a lawyer.'

'Okay.'

'And I'm dying my hair bright blue with purple spots.'

'Right.'

'And Six Chimneys is falling down.'

'What!'

'Forget it. I'll see you a week Tuesday.'

'Aren't you coming with us?'

'And be embarrassed by all the kissing and canoodling? I should say not. I'll shimmy on back to Surrey. Your pa's not feeling so good.'

'What's wrong with him?'

'Overdid the duck last night.'

'Maybe I should stay. What do you think, Lucian?'

'Whatever you want. '

'No, your pa won't like you changing your plans. If you are home he'll put on a stiff upper lip. If not he can slob around a bit. It'll be easier.'

'But if he's not well.'

'Don't fret, hon. Your mother knows what she's talking about.'

'Alright, darling, if you think it's best.'

'Oh, my God!' Isla yelped. 'You sound and look like an old married couple.'

Daisy snuggled against Lucian. 'Yes, we do rather.'

'Well, I couldn't put up with that for a day never mind a week. It would drive me mad. Anyway, before you go I must tell you we've met the cutest kid when up here measuring curtains. It's the boy, Sean, one of your mate's brood. He and your pa were out together fishing more times than they are in. I do believe he's invited the lad to stay a couple of days in Surrey!'

'Really? Well, he can't be that ill then can he?'

'No, I told you, he overdid the duck,' Isla kissed Daisy. 'Have a good time and take care of one another. And don't get lost,' she said, her eyes suddenly solemn. 'You know what that house is like.'

* * *

A strong head wind, it was an uncomfortable flight. Daisy slept through it. Lucian was content to sit. So, here they are, through gun shots and car accidents and out the other side! Shame she can't rely on him altogether, as suspected the review board recommended him ready for active redeployment.

'What no quibbling, Major?' said the OC.

'What me, sir? No, sir. I'm an accepting kind of person. Stick around and you might even hear me break into a couple of choruses of "*Que sera*."'

'Well that's good to know. We did hear you were settling down.'

'You shouldn'ae take notice of rumours, sir.'

'But you are so often the focus of rumour. What was it I read in the *Sun* newspaper yesterday? *Major Lucian Nairne, the brightest star in the martial firmament to be married.*'

'*Firmament!* That's a terrible lapse of grammar for the *Sun*.'

'So is it not true then, you preparing to marry.'

'As I said, you shouldn'ae take notice of rumours.'

'But we do, and ever in need of recruits felt we couldn't pass up the opportunity of deploying our star to a fairly visible sky.'

'And to fairly visible snipers.'

'The price of fame, Major Nairne.'

There it is, tick-tock, that clock again. What was it he said to her last night about wrapping her in his soul to keep her safe? Looks like that's all he'll be able to do. What can you do to make the people you love safe? He can take out insurance on his ass. 'But it won't keep the wolves from the door.'

'Wha..?' she blinked. '...say something?'

'It's okay. Go back to sleep.' So what does he do? Get wed; sign on the dotted line, pension and funeral costs readily available. At least then Chimneys would be secure. Yesterday, when she saw the letterhead, she put two-and-two together. 'It was you that bought Six Chimneys.'

'Uh-huh.'

'You're the miserable old curmudgeon who wants to know everything about my life including the colour of my knickers?'

'Less of the old!'

'You're the nasty, very ancient Scottish person who wouldn't let me buy the house! The chap who is never in when phone, and who instructs Pip and Squeak his mouldy solicitors to say he's out of town?'

'That's because...' Here we go, he thought. Cut the crap, man, or you'll sound like a Bunny Boiler. 'I wanted you to have the house with no strings attached.'

'And what if I wanted strings?'

'Do you then?'

'Not telling you now.'

She was pink in the face and so he played his brave-little-soldier card. 'The plan was not bother you. I was to bide a while in a trailer...'

'You planned this with my mother.'

'We discussed it.'

'Discussed it my reconditioned bum! It's a master plan. You put your two crafty heads together and worked it out to the last detail.'

'I wouldn'ae say master plan, exactly. It was by chance really. And then Gillie, my pal, he's good at bargaining, sold Drummach to a golf consortium, and...'

She slapped her fingers over his mouth. 'You're fibbing. I know because when you do your accent's so thick I can't understand a word you say.'

'How d'you know?' he drew her hand about his neck. 'You've never heard me fib, least not until today. I'm maybe being prudent with the truth.'

'No need to try,' she slipped between his knees. 'I think my mother's an interfering old bat but I'm used to that, whereas you, my gorgeous man, were willing to give up the home you love to live in a miserable trailer...'

'It's nae miserable.' He nearly blew it. 'It's comfortable,

shower room, all mod cons. I leased it to Kate Khan for a while, Mannering, as she is now.'

'What, the fabulous Miss Katy. I understood she's very beautiful and very... what's the word?' He kept silent. Nothing on earth would have persuaded him to open in his gob at that moment. Nuh-Huh-Way!

'Voluptuous. I believe that's the word. What d'you think, Captain Prudent.'

He drew her into his arms. 'Major Prudent to you.'

* * *

Eight o'clock this morning she's perched on the edge of the bed brushing her hair, her legs like a badly stitched bendy doll.

'Come here, dolly,' he said, 'and let me gi' your legs a rub.'

'No thanks. I know your rubbings and have the bruises to show for it.'

'Gi' me that brush! You're no taking away my job. I've signed up for this, a lifetime commission.' Springy silk, he used to brush her hair late at night with only the monitor beeping. He'd tell of his childhood, that not only did his parents loathe each other they didn't care for their kids. Mother made an attempt but in the end even she abandoned them.

A well-kept skeleton, Lucian learned of his mother's double life in '91 when he paid a surprise visit to the boutique on *Rue de Bac*. It was he that was surprised finding Ian in the shop and Maman and a Polish General out back. Looking back he knows he was harsh, stomping out of the shop with never a backward glance. A tough guy in those days he sent her letters back unread.

Loving Daisy he knows he was unkind. If he could go back he'd do different telling Maman how he loved and missed her.

Lucian's phone beeped. Daisy opened her eyes. 'Who is it?'

'One of Ed's wee tappings.'

'What does he say?

'I don't know and don't care.' He pulled her close, breathing her in like oxygen.

'Go back to the start is an odd thing to say don't you think?'

'Ed's an old man close to dying. What time is it?'

'The plane's about to land.'

The plane taxied up the tarmac. They waited for a wheelchair to arrive. 'Awful,' she said, cheeks burning. 'People having to wait while I'm taken off.'

'I'd make the most of it if I were you. This time next year you'll be prodded along wi' the rest of the herd.'

'Won't you be there to save your missis from the ravening hordes?'

'Of course, from this day until the end of time.'

'Good,' she said. 'I love a happy ending.'

* * *

But for one thing the house was everything Daisy could have wished.

'Where's Robocop?'

'Here,' said Lucian, lugging bags up the stairs.

'Not you, Robocop, the window Robocop.' The glass above the stairs, the very thing that brought her, was gone, and in its stead a sheet of plain glass.

'Stone throwing kids did for him.'

'Can he be mended?'

'I'm not sure. The guy in Melrose reckons the window is centuries old treasure. The struggle me and Gillie had getting it oot! We had to use a crane.'

'Poor chap.'

'What me and Gillie, d'you mean, or Robocop.'

Daisy dimpled. 'Why you, of course, my love, and your friend.'

'I should think so. Lifting that almost did away with my ain centuries old treasures.' She went to him and while he had a suitcase under each arm, and thus defenceless, slid her hand between his legs. 'Ah, diddums! Did we nearly lose the family treasures?' With that, he dropped the suitcases and carried her up the stairs. 'Aye, and we wouldn'ae want that.'

* * *

'If you're no fussy the attics are full of Minna's belongings,' he said that evening. 'Chairs, tables, and lamps, that kind of stuff.'

'Minna is the lady in the tomb?'

'Uh-huh. She left her belongings in trust and her money to an American charity. She was a wealthy woman when she died though how naebody knows. It's said she wrote books and translated documents.'

'Were you related?'

'She was friends with my mother. Nae kids of her own I reckon she took to Ian and me. If you're interested her journals are still back home?'

'Are you sorry about giving up your home?'

'I regret nothing of that house other than it was built.'

'I take it you didn't have a happy childhood.'

'You might say so.'

'Well,' she said, 'we shall have to make sure our children have the very best childhood. That way we will hopefully make up for yours.'

'So you're willing to have my kids?' he said, drawing her into his arms.

'I want no one else's.'

'Maybe we should make a start.'

'I thought we already had, but say no more – lead on Mac Duff.'

'Ah, Daisy!' He snatched her up. 'Don't you be another one goin' in for misquotes. It's "lay on, Mac Duff."'

'Who cares? You're so bossy, especially when making love.'

'If you mean I take the leading role, isn'ae that what a man's supposed to do?'

'No.' She pushed him on the bed and sat astride him. 'Not all the time.'

'Yeah!' he said, his eyes sparkling. 'Is this you being seductive again I'm bound to say you were a mite stingy praising my technique.'

'I did think blood curdling screams were praise enough.' Daisy did her best to please. Legs less than supple it wasn't easy wriggling about a bed, but the response to her hands and lips, his stomach muscles rippling, were encouraging. Even so, it wasn't long before he took the lead.

'See?' she whispered against his lips. 'Bossy.'

'Be quiet, honey bun, I'm concentrating.'

Daisy loved the way he concentrated, the wrinkled brow and the softening of his mouth. She loved the way his hands covered her breasts, the sensitivity of his finger tips. Lucian is a heavy man, tempered steel, she appreciated the way he kept his weight away while at the same time causing her delight. She loved the way they spooned together, drawing her into his belly. She loved the way when he laughed a boy shone through. She loved the way that when sad he stood close, drawing comfort from nearness. Most of all she loved his kisses, his hands about her face as though saying, 'keep away. This is mine.'

Such a powerful sense of possession and with it an echo of yesterday, an anxious echo that muttered, *'hold this, see this, now! And now, because....'*

'Because what?' she said that night, as they lay watching the stars shine over the willows. 'Why do I get the feeling you're waiting for a phone call?'

'Does it seem that way?'

'Yes. As though you know any minute you'll be called away.'

'Because that is the case. I've been in the army all my life and a practical man plan ahead, but even then there's always the call one doesn'ae expect.'

'I know and I'm not complaining. It's just that I want you to enjoy the hours as well as count them.'

'Aye, well,' he drew her close. 'That's what we must do. We must hold onto the day because in the end it's all we have. The rest is dreams.'

CHAPTER TWENTY-NINE

Mouth of Babes

The scratching at the door grew more frantic.

'I'd better get out.'

'Lean forward and I'll rinse the soap off your back.'

Daisy leant forward and the necklace broke. 'Oh, catch it quick before it goes down the plughole!' Lucian caught it and placed on the dresser. 'It's okay.'

'Is the chain broken?'

'The top of the cross is worn. I'll drop it off at the jewellers.'

'Good, 'cos I'm fond of it and wouldn't want to lose it.'

'The chain's left a mark on your neck.'

'Like mould you mean?'

'No mould, just a mark.'

'I think it must be gold because the stones are definitely diamonds.'

'Checked it out did you?'

'Of course! I mean diamonds, how exciting!'

'So what's that on your finger if not a thumping great diamond?'

Solitaire flashing she waggled her fingers. 'Yes but I know who bought me this, my husband. Where's the excitement in that?'

'Cheeky madam. Lean forward again.' He rinsed soap off her back. 'And you've another mark round your waist that looks like a wee plaited belt.'

'That's what the surgeon said.'

'Did that happen when you were knocked down?'

'I've no idea and stop finding fault?' she said. 'Auditioning for Michelin Man is making me self-conscious enough.'

Threading his fingers through her hair he eased her onto his arm, wet hair darkening his shirt. 'I am your husband. It is my duty, wife, to assist you in your struggle for perfection by pointing out your good and bad points.'

'Nairne women don't have bad points. We are the blue blood of all Roxburgh.'

'Is that so.' He took a towel and wound it about her head. At present they're using the small bathroom, the other bath too deep for Daisy to get out without a struggle. 'You ready to get oot?'

'I will get *oot* under my own steam. I don't need you to... Oh, Lucian!'

He lifted her out and set her on the mat. 'There you go.' He rolled down his sleeves. 'That's one and a half females sorted. Now I can sort the next.'

'In "next" are you by any chance likening me to a hysterical bitch?'

'Well Biddy is a dog, and she is scratching at the door, and you...!' He ducked to avoid the sponge, but Daisy was a good shot. The sponge caught him middle of his shoulder blades. In retaliation, he opened the door. 'Go get her Bid!'

Biddy-pup hurtled in, all paws and excitement.

'Oh, no, darling, look she's peeing!'

'Hell! So she is!'

'And on you by the look of things.' Daisy started to laugh until she needed to pee. 'Oh get out,' she shoved them out the door, 'leave me and the bump in peace.' Still laughing, she sat on the loo. There were more paws on the stairs, Basil, the rescued greyhound, not wanting to be left out. 'And don't give Baz any more chews!' she called. 'Little and often, the vet said.'

Lucian rattled the door knob. 'I gi' you little and often if you don't get oot that bathroom. It's cold in there and your chest isn'ae strong.'

'That's not what you said last night.' Daisy dragged a pair of bloomers over her stomach, passion killers like granny used to wear – not that passion is in short supply with Lucian on call for overseas duty and no idea yet when his tour might begin. 'Leave my chest alone. It's never been so generous.'

'You can say that again,' he said. 'Talk aboot the milk of human kindness.'

'Yes, and as of now that particular nightcap is off limits!' she shouted. 'I don't know what you think I am, your friendly local delivery man?'

He was gone, running down the stairs, accompanied by assorted cats and dogs. 'Hardly a man, 'was the comment that floated back.

'No,' muttered Daisy, 'if I were I wouldn't be toting this. Oh, Emmy, move over!' She tried shoving the bump aside to do up her boots but can only see her own protruding belly button. She looked in the mirror. That scar about her waist? The surgeon suggested it a friction burn. Now there's this mark round her neck like punk choker. What is it? Why is she branded?

Suddenly, for no real reason she is afraid. Tossing the pillows she attempted the bed, knowing that no matter how neat a job she did Lucian would remake it. 'Heaven's sake,' she said last night. 'You're not in barracks now.' With that he'd climbed in and pressing his iron belly against her said, 'if you're registering a complaint, Private Nairne, make sure you present it in triplicate.'

She knows she's being a pain but can't help it. Isla is livid. 'You about pop and all alone in this house?! Can't he get compassionate leave?'

'I'm sure he could but he won't. He thinks if the others have to do then so must he. But I did want him with me when Emma's born.'

'Why are you so sure she's a she? You've not had the test.'

'Emma's a she alright. Only a female would be in such a hurry to be born.'

Daisy is sick of the whole business. She hadn't realised how all-consuming pregnancy can be, puking and peeing through the Merry Months of May, June, and July, heat-rash and indigestion until November. Now with the winning post in view and Lucian is called away. Poor darling, he feels guilty about it and is forever on the phone asking how she is. Then there are the text messages, if not from Lucian then from Ed. '*lo hunbun r U restn.*'

Apparently Ed's not doing too well. Nurse Janet called to say he has a chest infection and that he's now marked *not for resuscitation*. Certainly there's something wrong. Mr D'angelo used to send the '*go bk 2 strt,*' message once a month to Lucian. Now it's every day! And what was that he mumbled in her ear the day she left hospital, '*tanks 4 th hammer*'?

It made no sense then. It makes no sense now.

It seems people don't trust Daisy to look after herself. The other day Isla came up from Surrey recently with a pair of Siamese cats. 'I thought they'd be company for you while Lucian's away.' Then there's Kate and her husband, Mick, and the girls always popping in. And if they are not guardians enough there's always Robocop!

He's back. 'You've had some new side fixings,' said the glazier. 'I told your man once the seal is broken they must be replaced straight away or the whole thing will fall apart.' Fact is the chap's ruined it. Where once was delicate pastel motif patterning the side panels there are now rows of leprous coloured Smarties. Daisy is horribly disappointed, which is silly really when you think about it, since she's never seen the window this close up before.

'It was beautiful,' Kate added salt to the wound. 'Men with scythes cutting corn and all the angel wings and fluffy clouds like souls rising.'

Oh well, at least he's here. Robocop is Lucian. Without him the house will fall.

* * *

Daisy and Kate are at antenatal classes.

'I'd forgotten how painful this is,' said Kate, lowering her bulk to the floor.

'It's certainly not the dreamlike experience I was promised.'

'Is it not the best time of your life then?' Kate hiked her voice into high Edinburgh treble. 'Are you no a blooming rose of a pregnant laydee?'

'No,' Daisy snarled. 'I'm a mass of screaming nerve centres with swollen feet.'

'All that stuff is bollocks.' Kate stretched out on the mat, her belly Mount Popocatepetl. 'It's just men trying to keep women docile.'

'Docile.'

'Aye, docile.'

'Docile means compliant! Since when were you ever compliant?'

There was a moment and then Kate nodded. 'I was for a while when I was a lass. Compliant to a pervert father, compliant to ten or twenty skanky blokes, compliant to a murdering bastard called Jason, on and on...'

'Sorry, Kate. I never knew you before and so tend to see you as strong.'

'Good, 'cos that's how I want people to see me. I was a victim before but not now, thanks mainly to your man. I'll no lie about it, I love Lucian. Ziggy is a good man, and after that bastard Jason a total relief. But he's not Lucian nor ever will be. Does that bother you, Daisy?'

'I'd be lying if I said I wasn't envious of time gone before when I wasn't with him but I try not to lose sleep over it. But what happened to Jason? You told me of the fire, but you never said what became of him.'

'Nothing much to tell! Firemen said he'd likely tripped on the stairs and knocked hisself out and was burnt to death in the fire. I near drove myself mad thinking it was my fault. Then I let go of it. Now I have Zig. The kids like him. We run the pub and we have food on the table. I can't ask for more.'

'And Sean?'

'Oh aye! Seems we're losing him to your Ma!'

'Yes, sorry about that. Isla does rather take over.'

'That's okay. She'll gi' him a great start to life, that's enough for me.'

'Mum adores him. She says he's very bright.'

'He'll be okay.'

'And Leon?'

Kate shook her head. 'Sharp as a needle but driven by demons. I can only do my best. They say God looks after fools, drunks, and kids, so I live in hope.'

'Fools, drunks, and kids much covers us all.'

'Except Lucian.'

'Yes.' Daisy sighed. 'Except Lucian.'

* * *

Lucian sits on the stairs of what used to be his home. He's here to retrieve the last of Minna's belongings. The house cold and unwelcoming as ever he can't wait to get out, but knowing he is soon to leave Daisy, talks with his lawyer on the phone, making sure everything is in place. 'I received a copy of the Will through the post this morning. Thanks for moving things along.'

'You're welcome, Major Nairne. Let's hope this is simply a safety measure.'

'Yeah, lets. One question, what exactly does "in perpetuity" mean?'

'It means the house and land belong to your wife to manage in whatever way she chooses. She can sell, rent, or break the whole into apartments. It means that at least where her finances are concerned you may rest in peace.'

'Okay, that's all I needed to know.' He stretched. 'Thanks again. I must be going. I've had word I'm to be shipped out on Monday.'

'And it almost Christmas!'

'Aye well, Santa Claus and bombs don't heed one another.'

Flipping the phone, Lucian dusted off his coat. It's filthy on the stairs! Spider's webs everywhere – you'd think it had been empty for a hundred years ne'er mind days. Grandfather's hang-dog face lowers over every corner. Strange, Lucian can't recall a time when he, or Father, used physical violence and yet they knew how to cut the weakling from the flock, and Ian with his childlike mentality easy prey. Lucian spent most of his teens trying to get between the knife and the cut, hence before he was twenty his heart was in ribbons.

It won't happen to his kids. Lucian's children will be happy and he'll be happy knowing they are. Hefting his bag over his shoulder, he walked out into the cold air, slamming the door on the house and all that it meant.

* * *

The phone rang. 'Daisy Nairne?'

'Speaking.'

'Used to be Daisy Banks?'

'Yes.'

'Friend of Oscar Curran?'

'...er yes.'

'The name's Marta. I need Oscar's address so I can return his stuff.'

'I don't have his address. We lost touch months ago.'

There was a pause and the flick of a lighter. Getting a mental image of a skinny girl high on speed and low on sincerity Daisy tried offering advice. 'Oscar is like Slinky Dog in Toy Story, he stretches in a million directions.'

'I didn't ask for your advice, bitch! You're yesterday's news, so don't...'

Click! So much for advice.

The phone rang again. At the fourth ring Daisy picked it up: 'This is the ghost of Six Chimneys speaking. Another word, ducky, and I'm over to that squat where you and your filthy lags hang out and having your guts for garters! So piss off, have a good life, and don't worry Oscar, or my friend, again.'

Click!

Good grief! Daisy stared at her reflection in the mirror. Was that me? Silly question, but since living in Chimneys she feels as if she's several beings under one skin – Daisy, Emma, and a third, who hopefully, will remain anonymous.

* * *

Shoulders hunched against the wind Lucian entered the ruin that is the Church of St Jude the Less. Down a side street stinking of cheap wine and vomit, the door should've been booby-trapped never mind on a latch. But then, worm-ridden pews that serve as beds for winos, what is there to steal.

Doffing his cap he went inside. Once upon a time this was a holy place, now it's a doss house. Earlier, he went to S&P's office to sign papers. What papers d'you sign here? Will an angel lean out of the wrecked darkness, saying, 'sign here, Major Nairne, and that's your Daisy safe in perpetuity.'

Sighing, he dropped his head in his hands. What's the deal,

big man? You fought in the Gulf and in Serbia, why so fussed? Marriage is the fuss, marriage and love. Until now he had no one to worry about other than himself and a glass goddess – a girl with green eyes, the girl in the letter.

That girl is gone, sand-blasted away by a flesh and blood reality, his maddening, drive-him-crazy, sex-and-sugar, honey-bun of a wife.

'Get a grip, Lucian.' He hunted about for a smoke. Then remembered he'd given up. 'Mustn't smoke, sweetie,' she said. 'It's bad for the baby.' So, now he chews gum and cusses out the rookies. Last night he was so wired-up he phoned his mate for a chat. Gillie's a great bloke. They've known one another years and can talk about anything – almost an older brother. Bozos at the garrison reckon he's gay. It's bollocks! They didn't see what Lucian saw at the wedding, Gillie gazing at Daisy with his heart in his eyes.

So he cares for Daisy, that's okay, it makes his promise to protect her while Lucian is away the more sacred. Isla says the Army should have a heart, that her son-in-law should plead compassionate grounds. He can plead all he likes but won't make an atom of difference – a year was all he was ever going to get. How does he know this? Brother Ian told him via Sean.

This was Sean at the wedding, too much champagne, his eyes intense and his legs rubbery. 'D'you think I'd make a soldier?' he says. 'I'm nae tough guy.'

'There's more to a soldier than being tough,' says Lucian.

'Aye, but havin' a six-pack helps.'

Having drunk his own share Lucian's gaze was just as earnest and his legs as rubbery. 'Your good soldier isn'ae made. You can pump all the iron ye like but if your heart isn'ae in it, it's no gonna happen.'

Sean nods. 'My Pa says the difference in men is not the colour of their hair or what medals they wear; it's what they have in their heart.'

'There you go then.' A memory had crept to the surface. Didn't Sean attach his ass to Kate in a woman's refuge? Maybe he's found his real father. 'I'm glad you and your Pa are getting along, Sean. Does he come to see you?'

'He usually sends somebody; one sich gi' me a message t'other day.'

Lucian thought to humour the lad. 'Oh, aye, and what was that?'

'He said, "Tell my brother I'll be seein' him sooner than later alligator."'

Jesu! Remembering that moment – the honesty in Sean's eyes – Lucian's blood runs cold. Never knowing the effect of his words the lad had continued. 'He said to tell you he'd see you on mare's birthday.'

'Mare's birthday? *Anniversaire de ma mère*? Is that what he said?'

'Uh-huh. Mare's anniversary and no a minute later.'

There's a saying 'lightning never strikes twice' as there's another 'out of the mouth of babes.' Sean's no baby yet he carries the same innocence as the lad whose message he delivered, and now, knowing the date referred to – Hogmanay, Mother Eloise's birthday – the odds of lightning striking Major Lucian Nairne twice are greatly reduced.

* * *

It was cold in the church. Lucian slept and woke shivering. He called home but only got his service. Then he remembered that it's clinic day, Daisy will be with Kate. Last week he went with them. The only man among pink-cheeked ladies – and them all in T-shirts printed bearing pictures of a pregnant male angel – he felt a bit of a fool. But it's all good fun even when he and Daisy fight, and though there was no church wedding they know they are blessed.

'Daisy said if God wanted he'd be there, registrar's office or no.'

'Which is aboot right I'd say,' a voice came out of the gloom.

'Excuse me?'

A tramp shuffled out of the shadows, last night's Vindaloo preceding. 'I heard you say if God wanted to be there, He'd be there.'

'It was something my wife said.'

'Aye, and your wifey is right. The Lord God takes nae notice of gobshite preaching. He knows what's real and that's where He goes.'

'You're an authority on his movements, are you?'

'You bet your bonny ass! He and me is like this, reet tight.' The tramp clenched his fist. 'Warriors in the same army!'

'Aye well.' Lucian was on his feet, he'd not the time or inclination.

The tramp held out his hand. 'Afore ye go can ye no tap us a snout, Guvnor?'

Lucian made a show of patting his jacket only to be surprised by a mangled carton in his left pocket. Two cigarettes, and Oh, boy, could he use one.

He offered the packet. 'Will you look it!' The tramp took one by the tips of filthy, tobacco stained fingers. '*Gauloises Blond! C'est magnifique.*'

He went into a spiel about the difference between Gauloises or Gitanes and in a neat Parisian accent. Lucian grinned. '*Vous parlez en parfait, vieil homme?*'

'*Bien sur! Je suis un homme voyage. Et vous, mon fils,* get aboot much?'

'You cann'ae tell by the army claes and bonnet?'

The tramp wheezed a laugh. 'Jest windin' ye up, Jock.'

'Well, use a lighter hand. I'm fit to bursting.'

'Aye, and bigger and noisier than any of they bombs you lads dismantle.'

'How d'you know I dismantle bombs?'

'I seed the badge on your arm and your face in the paper.'

'You want that cigarette?' said Lucian.

'I don't know that I do. I'm trying to gi' it up.'

'Is it working?'

'Nah!' The tramp lit the fag inhaling like it was attar of roses. 'Away, soldier blue,' he says. '*Avez-vous un drag!* God willn'ae blame ye for wantin' to make yoursen feel better. This is the Man we're talkin' aboot, no crabbit dominie.'

Oh, the temptation. 'Maybe if I go outside.'

'If'n you do you'll be up to your oxters in snow.'

'I'll nae bother with the snout. It's a dump but still a church.'

'Wise move. Playin' wi' bombs you need to keep on His good side.'

'Hah!' Lucian smiled, remembering Nobby Clarke and the

dream. 'I had a buddy who took out insurance on a place in heaven. '

'Better to keep paying your dibs. No late bets.'

'In that case I won't have the snout for I am a man charged with redeeming other men's mistakes. I cann'ae afford to make many of my own.'

'Wha' mistakes you made?'

Lucian sighed. How d'you list things you shouldn't have done when you no longer remember what they were. 'The thing is does God forgive them?'

The old man nodded. '"I think that if God forgives we must forgive ourselves.' CS Lewis said that, your Lion, Witch, and Wardrobe man.'

'Is it so?' Lucian gazed at the tramp. What happened to bring him to this? He opened his mouth to ask but was beaten to it.

'So what's a lad like you doin' in a dump like this?'

'It don't matter why. I doubt God is here to listen.'

'This dump may be abandoned but it's nae forsaken. See the bloke in the winder back there? That's Micky, the Medicine Man. Pray to him. If He cann'ae heal it then, trust me, there's nought wrong wi' it.'

'I thought it was St Jude. Isn't that what the church is called?'

'Nae such saint exists. There was a feller a couple a hundred years ago but nobuddy special. These days anyone can cast to the fore. One of they spin doctors and you'd be wearin' wings.'

'Will they be taking that window out? Surely whoever's in charge won't leave it here to be abused along with everything else.'

'It will abide. It's like you, indestructible.' A sparrow flew down from the rafters, pecking at some dried bread. "Are not two sparrows sold for a farthen' yet none shall fall without your father knowin'.'"

'CS Lewis again?'

'Wisht, no! A story-teller way better than him.'

The sparrow flew back into the rafters. 'God speed little sparrow,' said Lucian, wistful. 'I wish you a better Father than mine.'

'Is that why you come here, to think on your pa?'

'Never mind why I'm here, why are you?'

'You mean apart frae snitching snouts? I'm thinkin' on my Pa.'

'And what is he up to?'

'Everythin'. He's a busy chappie. But you niver answered my question, why are you here? I seed ye here last week and the week before.'

'I like a bit of peace and quiet when in town.'

'Me too.' The old man dug into a pocket bringing out a bottle. 'Fancy a nip?'

'No thanks.'

'Go on. Have a swally! Your man at the pub gi' it me. A genrous soul is Ziggy, got his place booked on high even though he keeps a shooter under the bed.'

'Ziggy keeps a shot gun?'

'He's never used it, nor ever will.'

' Zig is solid. He took care of a friend of mine when she was unhappy.'

The tramp sniggered. 'I'll bet he did.'

'Not like that. He's a good man.'

'I know, I was only tryin' to lighten the mood. So do you wanna drink?'

'I must go.' Lucian was overwhelmed with fear for Daisy and

the baby. Why blither with old men when he could be home? 'Why did we bring a bairn into the world? We should've known the odds stacked against it.'

'Is a soldier serving God and King not allowed happiness if only the while?'

The question leapt from Lucian's mouth. 'Is it only for the while then?'

The tramp looked at him. 'I don't know, Lucian. You tell me.'

'Why do you call me Lucian?'

'Is that no your name?'

'It is but how do you know it?'

'It was in the newspaper, Major Lucian Nairne, George Cross and bar, *the brightest star in the military firmament.*'

'Och, none o' that!' said Lucian sharply.

'As you say.' The tramp was affronted. 'No need to come wide wi' me! I meant nae harm. I thought you might like a chat seein' you was low.

'I'm sorry.' Lucian fished a twenty from his wallet and laid it on the seat. 'Get yourself another bottle or maybe some socks for your feet.'

'Thank you. You're a good man.' The old man pocketed the twenty. 'But hold on! Is this no yours?' A small diamond cross glinted in the gloom.

'But that's off my wife's necklace! I must've pulled it out when I gave you the note. I was taking it to the jeweller's, wouldn'ae want to lose that.'

'No, neither you would. It's a gift beyond price.' The tramp melted into the shadows. 'Sich things dreams are made of.'

CHAPTER THIRTY

Visible Material

*'Angels from the realms of Glory wing their flight o'er all the earth,
Ye who sang creation's story, now proclaim Messiah's birth..!'*

Daisy let them finish and then brought out a tray of biscuits
and hot punch. Probably she shouldn't be giving booze to teenagers, but, backsides hanging out of their jeans they looked so cold.
'Thanks, missis.' They drank the wine, scoffed biscuits, patted the
dogs, and then rattled a tin. 'Gi' us a donation?'

'Who what are you supporting?'

A shared look and a suggestion: 'The hospice doon the road?'

She offered a fiver and they shuffled away.

The package from the solicitor arrived as she was 'preparing
the nest', as the midwife, would say. 'Once you start wanting to
scrub the house from top to bottom you know things are moving.'
Scrubbing floors is not Daisy's idea of fun. There are nicer things
to do, like sitting in the conservatory reading a book on Leonardo
da Vinci, a glass of wine and a cheese and pickle sandwich on the
side, and the occasional toke of a Turkish cigarette.

'Since when did you smoke?' said Lucian the morning he
found her up in the attics. 'And what the heck are you doin'
heaving things aboot?'

'I'm getting rid of clutter! And I'm not smoking – I'm tasting.'

'And what does it taste like?'

'Vile.'

'So why are you doin' it?'

'I fancied it. I've been to the library reading about when this was a B&B. Talk about eye opener! I thought Minna was a sweet lady. Not true, most of the village was up in arms against her, you know, "pitch forks! Burn the witch!" '

'She had her troubles but nought so Gothic.'

'She was busted for selling pot!'

'It wasn'ae pot! It was a herbal thing for women's complaints. My mother used it until Father banned her from using it. He didn'ae like the smell.'

'Banned? What is that a Nairne throwback to the Dark Ages? Men telling women what to do with their lives, what to eat and what to wear...'

'Daisy! You're goin' into one of your wobbly things again.'

'I am not going into anything. Banned sounds pretty heavy handed to me.'

'Heavy handed was his way and that of his father. Now, I'm your modern metro-man, hence, my wife does pretty much as she likes. Right now I need her to float back to Planet Earth and say why she's sucking on a cigar.'

'I bought a pack.'

'And you're going to smoke it?'

'Of course not! Smoking is bad for the baby.'

'I should think not after forcing me to quit.'

'Did I force or was it that being a loving father, you saw the sense of it.'

'You forced me.'

'Anyway, I was telling you of Minna. The librarian said she kept a bawdy house for men at the air-base. I was really p'd off about it, I can tell you, referring to our home in that way. Suppose she says that when Emma goes for books?'

'If it's Lottie Baird you're referring to she's aboot to fall off her perch ne'er mind scold a bairn not born.'

'But people talk and I wouldn't want our daughter hearing such things. I left but was in two minds whether to go back and punch Lottie's lights out.'

'Lottie's in her nineties. She'll have nae lights to punch. Daisy, come here.'

'No.'

'Come here and have a wee coory.'

'I'm busy,' she kicked a lampshade across the floor. 'I can't be cuddling now.'

'Come on, honey bunny.' He held out his arms. 'Gi' your old man a hug.'

With that Daisy was done for. Trying to keep back the tears she laid her head on his chest. 'You shouldn't have to go. You've done your bit.'

'So have others.'

'Yes, but you've already been hurt. You deserve a rest.'

'I've had a rest here with you and a whole, good year of it.'

Seven o'clock he left, pausing to look up at the window where she stood unable to wave. The dogs followed him to the jeep. He patted Baz, rubbed the top of Biddy's head, slung the bag in the back and was gone.

And slowly but surely the heart of the house ceased to beat.

As with everything he did he'd put a brave face for their last evening. She did the rounds, checked the coops and closed off the meadow. Then she'd found some idiot left a goat tied to the rain barrel. It took her ages to persuade the beast to the barn. By the time she got in she stunk of goat.

'I got us a Chinese!' he called.

'I must have a bath first,' she squelched up the stairs. 'Nae problem,' he'd said. 'I've run it already.' He had too, candles dotted about and clean towels from the cupboard. The meal was tasty, not that she ate, the stone in her heart too heavy for the passage of prawn crackers. He'd bought a bottle of wine. 'Tears of Christ, Gillie called it. He said it would be good for you.'

David Paorach Gilchrist, in Gaelic his name translates as the power of Christ. A nice chap, elegant, Lucian thinks his buddy's the biz. They're always on the phone, Lucian with the easy voice he has with someone he likes. Daisy gets a different tone, Isla calls it his 'Are you still here, honey bun?' voice.

'It's like he can't believe you're with him.' Isla laughs. 'It's the writer in me,' she says. 'I'm always looking to see what I can pinch. And FYI I'm writing a book about Sean, as a boy with special talents.'

'Too late, Mum. It's already been done.'

'I'm not talking Harry Potter! I'm talking a direct line to Venus.'

That he is unsure of her bothered Daisy. Last night he sat with his eyes closed and glass of wine drooping. She thought how tired he looked and was about to suggest bed when the candles flickered and he flickered with them.

'Lucian!'

'Huh?' He looked up, smiled, and was whole again. Now in the attic clearing a trivia she relived the moment. It was a trick of the light, of course, yet for a moment he faded away as a painting fades when left too long in the light.

She asked if he was okay. He lost his temper. 'How can I be

okay when you're alone and this place bursting at the seams? Chickens, a pony, and now a goddamn goat! Had you no enough animals without a zoo takin' hold?'

'I always wanted a sanctuary.'

'Yes, but there's a time and place!' Alert to changes in the atmosphere the Siamese slid round the door. He exploded again. 'And now you've yon mangy cats under your feet! What if you fall and naebody here?'

'They're not mangy, they're beautiful. But to answer your question I'd sound the alarm.' She'd tugged the bell-pull. The call was put through: '*Sentinel Alarms! Are you in need of assistance?*'

'See!' She switched it off. 'You don't need to worry.'

'I do worry. I suppose you could always get Kate to pop over?'

'I can manage. I don't need anyone to lean on.'

'Okay, but there'll be stuff you won't be able to manage. I've left a list of addresses you can call on. Top of the list is Captain Gilchrist.'

Daisy let him speak. It had all been said before and in softer tones, under the blanket, her arms about his neck and his lips to her breast. 'I love you. I shall always love you.' The words were said last night. The note he'll find when he's far away, and with it the jewelled cross keepsake from an anonymous admirer.

* * *

Camp Bastion, Helmand Province.

Lucian found the stud while trying on a smaller size flak jacket.

'Been on a diet, sir?' said Kevin Wallace – the late Kieran's brother.

'It's the wife,' said Lucian. 'She's got me on the scales.' Surprised by how much weight he had lost he set the jacket aside. Stiff, it would chafe his neck. He'll stick to the old one. He opened the box and there it was, a note wrapped round the tube, the ear-stud taped to the note. She said it the last night he was there. 'I put aloe vera in the bag. It will help with sunburn.' He made a joke of it, after years of lugging a heavy Bergen about it would take more than sun to scorch his ass. Now he sees the jewelled cross and all humour ceased.

'This is not what I wanted.'

'You say something, Boss?'

'Give me five will you, Sergeant.'

Kevin left and Lucian read the note: *I collected this from the jewellers. As you know it was given to me by a stranger. Now I'm giving it to you because it kept me safe. I'm praying it will do the same for you. I love you, your wife, Daisy.*

Ps, as you see I had the cross converted to an ear-stud. I thought it fitted your image of a Macho Man. Pps, Emma sends a kick and a kiss.

It's wrong. He can feel the wrongness creeping into his mind. While she wore that cross she was protected, and not only by his love, by his mother.

Sighing, he slipped the note into an inner pocket. He'll do as she asks and wear the ear-stud. No one will think less of him. Most of the team have some form of talisman. With Kevin it's a Shaun-the-Sheep key fob belonging to his son. Addie Faulkner has a ratty pigtail hanging over one ear. Cpl Ginger Flynn has black cat earrings, SI Josie Moore red lace underpants.

Nobby Clark tied one of his wife's handkerchiefs to his belt. Lucky charms, if you think it keeps you safe maybe it does – it didn't do much for Nobby.

The ear-stud doesn't make Lucian feel safe. He thinks of the Juvenal crib, *quis custodiet ipsos custodies,* and wonders who guards this particular guardian.

This tour is about recognising borrowed time. If he were honest, if he stood before God and God said, 'I offer you a gift, Lucian, a year of love.' He'd have to think before replying because it's not about the having – it's about losing.

He mentioned his fears to Gillie. That guy never cusses unless really riled, neither does he pass judgment, but he sure cussed Lucian when he said that. 'So you find it hard to sleep nights. Love's no sedative. Neither is it a cure-all. Real love offers joy and pain in equal amounts. I know. I've been there.'

Lucian said it's tough having another person's life in your hands, and that he wasn't complaining. He was glad of the time he'd been given. Gillie still wasn't impressed. 'Love is a choice. Take it or you can leave it, heartsease direct from God or scenes from a Soap Opera.'

* * *

'Deck the halls with boughs of Holly, fa-la-la-la-la-falalalah..!' Kids from the caravan park are shouting through the letter box. They think because she gave them money once they can keep coming. Daisy opened the door. 'Clear off, you bunch of layabouts!' They skipped away, laughing, one of them wearing the holly wreath from the unmarked grave. She was a mind to go after them but went back inside, double locking the doors.

All of this last week she's slept with the light on. 'Don't worry,

Baz,' she'd said, the old dog blinking in the light. 'It's only so I can see to go to the loo.'

It is this time of year when she misses Boffin most. All the delicious smells and lights on the tree, he loved Christmas. They have a tree here in Six Chimneys but it's not a fir tree, it's an artificial tree so to avoid pine-needles falling.

Mum and Dad arrive tomorrow with Sean. The Mannerings are coming here for Boxing Day lunch while Daisy and her parents are to dine in the pub on the Monday. It's all very seasonal, but nothing without Lucian.

Lucian called to say the Army had arranged a TV link on Christmas Day. Daisy was aghast. 'Don't let them talk you into that! Seeing you would kill me!'

He'd snorted. 'Don't worry. If the choice is to disable a bomb or be seen on the box I know what to choose.' Now she feels selfish. He might have liked to chat and talking *has* to be better than the silence hanging over the house.

The moment Lucian left she didn't want to be here. A feeling of dread has been building for days. Six Chimneys was everything she wanted but now with him gone there is a hole in the house that every day gets bigger.

The focal point is Robocop's window; sooner than pass she uses the back stairs. The animals feel the same way, the Siamese stay downstairs, while poor old Baz hangs what's left of his tail between his legs. Biddy-pup is the opposite and sits on the landing, head on her paws and eyes fixed on the window.

Daisy doesn't ask what she sees. She doesn't want to know.

* * *

Three o'clock the phone rang. She dashed to pick it up. 'That you, darling?'

'Sorry, Daze, it's only this darling.'

'Hello Oscar.'

'Hello Daze. Happy Christmas, may all your troubles be wearing a diaper.'

'How are you, Oscar? Or rather, how's Marta? Is she still stalking you?'

'Nah, she's found some other poor sod to put through the grinder.'

'That's good then.'

'I suppose, though I miss the crazy bitch. She was at least consistent.'

He went on to talk of his disappointment with the music industry, the latest musical flop and how his agent wasn't answering his calls.

Five minutes of that Daisy broke in. 'Are you busy at the moment?'

'Well, I'm actually calling to let you know me and Christa are back together again. We've settled our differences, ain't that right, sugar?' A muttering in the background told Daisy she couldn't look to him for company. 'Anyway, gotta go. Slash! Slash! Poor pussy-whipped, Ossy! Ciao, angel, be happy!'

* * *

Camp Bastion, Helmand Province.

'Hark the Herald angels sing, glory to the newborn King, peace on...'

The General jabbed a thumb. 'Shut that noise up, will you?'

The aide stuck his head round the Mess door. 'Turn the radio down!'

The Shadow PM, the US Under-Secretary, and various other minor officials are clustered about the heaters. It's the annual *Support our troops this Christmas* photo-shoot and Lucian the unwilling focus of attention.

'Now, where were we? Ah yes, tomorrow's TV interview!' The General bared his teeth. 'Can we count on you, Major?'

'For what, sir.'

'An interview.'

'No thank you, sir.'

'You don't want to talk to your wife...what's her name?'

'Daisy.'

'Pretty name that. I used to have a liver Pointer Bitch called Daisy. Soft mouth, she could bag a brace without breaking the skin. Don't you want to talk with your Daisy, Major?'

'I do, sir, very much, but not wi' the world looking on.'

'But it's a simple process. Someone asks how you're enjoying your day and would you like to speak to your family. Then they roll the cameras.'

'Not even that nowadays, General,' said the aide. 'Most of it is pre-recorded.'

'There you are then! Nothing to it, as Captain Jenkins says.'

'Then maybe Captain Jenkins would like to do it.'

The Shadow PM smiled. 'I rather think it's you they want to see.'

'Yes, sir,' the aide nodded. 'The George Cross, don't you know.'

Lucian managed not to shrug. 'Then they'll have tae go

away disappointed.'

The silence was broken by more smiling and more shuffling. Lucian looked to Tabby Gates, the AO. 'Is that all, sir?'

Tabby Gates smothered a grin. 'That's all, Major. '

* * *

'All is bright, round yon Virgin, Mother, and Child, Holy infant...'

It's Christmas Day 0130 hours and they're beyond drunk. Josie Moore is in the corner sobbing over a picture of her mother. Kevin's on today's TV link, and though out of his skull on whisky, tapes a message to his stepson while trying to explain football's off-side trap to an equally pissed camera man.

Cpl Ginger Flynn, the beauty with the eyes of a vixen and the soul of a dove, has passed out twice and is now painting Lcpl Shaw's toenails while Lucian, the reluctant TV Star, bows to pressure agreeing to the interview. Tabby's for a bollicking if he doesn't. He just hopes Daisy won't be watching.

'*...so tender and mild, Sleep in heavenly peeeace...*'

'Will you no have another wee dram, sir?'

'*Slainte mhath, Kevin!*'

'*Alba gu brath!*'

'*Slainte don Branrigh!*'

Never mind God saving the Queen, somebody needs to save Lucian's head because as well as the customary buzz in his ears there's a vice about his brain and a gorilla applying the screws. Right now the gorilla takes the saggy form of Addie Faulkner and his war against a neighbour's Leylandii.

'I says to him, either you take a chainsaw to that effing eyesore, pal, or I'll be takin' a chainsaw to you.'

'And did he take somethin' off the hedge?'

'Did he hell! So I went out next morning and chopped the bugger down.'

'Tha's telling him.'

Lucian's blackberry buzzed. Even knowing it wouldn't be Daisy he took a quick look. It was Ed's usual giff-gaff: '*U go bck 2 strt.*' Some bloke! What is it they say, 'old soldiers never die?' Certainly true of RAF pilots. Every time Lucian calls the unit it's the same reply, poorly but still hanging on. 'He's waiting for something to happen,' said Janet, his carer.

'Like what,' says Lucian, 'God to say his number's up?'

'Whatever it is, its driving him mad.'

'Why d'you say that?'

'Because he can't wait to be with his wife! Believe me, if he could go he would. You should hear him talk to her. It's heart-breaking.'

'Poor old boy trapped in that body.'

'I'm not sure about trapped. I think he does those out-of-body things.'

Lucian thought to joke about it. 'Have you seen him floating by then wi' a catheter bag under his arm?' She wasn't amused. 'You may laugh, Major, but when you work in long-stay you see things – especially on nightshift.'

He'd shuddered. 'If I wind up in a place like that make sure you get me out.'

Janet thought him joking. 'And how should I do that?'

'Anyway you can! A pillow over my face, an air-bubble in the veins, the shortest route the best.'

She'd snickered. 'I wouldn't dare. Your Daisy would be popping a pillow over my face.'

'No, she wouldn't! If she knew how I felt to be like poor old Ed she'd be there before you, kissing my lips while she pulled the trigger.'

This was said months ago when Lucian felt indestructible. Now he shakes such thoughts away – when you do what they do, suicide is not the best topic.

* * *

'Angels in their realms of glory winging light all over the world...'

Kevin is telling Lucian of his troubles back home. 'If me and Jenny can hang together and not let her ex interfere with Jamie, her kid, we'd be okay.'

'You'll be fine, Kevin. I'm sure you know what you're doin'.'

'Thanks for listening. Great bloke. All the lads say so.' Kevin staggered back to the cameraman and secrets of the off-side trap making room for the next.

Over the last twenty-four hours they've all singled Lucian out for an ear-bashing. He listens but might as well not be here, his real self focussed on Six Chimneys. Isla will be there now which means Daisy's got flesh and blood for company and not the silver folk that float in and out of the attic.

They're up there. As they are in Drummach, Lucian hasn't seen them but knows they are there, some are friendly, and some are not...

...and some like Lance Corporal April Shaw in need of sleep. 'Hello magical, mind-blowing, Major Luca Nairne!' A muscular arm is flung about his neck cutting off circulation. 'How are you?'

'I'm okay, Lance Corporal Shaw. How's yourself?'

'Pissed is what I am, pissed, horny and lonely.'

SI Josie Moore sways toward them, mascara smudged eyes, but other than that looking fabulous. 'Wha's-up, Major Nairne! You look terrible.'

'I'm in trainin' for a corpse.'

'Good luck to you! It's a good cause.' The girls sway away, lovely in their cups as they are sober. 'Eat your porridge, Luca,' Josie calls. 'Napoleon said an army marches on its stomach. Come the call we got some marching.'

She sees it too, how Lucian is losing weight. Tabby Gates reckons Lucian has the makings of a romantic hero, pale and interesting. Reading is one of the things he's missing. At the moment they're doing Wuthering Heights, Cathy coming back from the dead. 'I'd do a Cathy if I went first,' says Daisy. 'I'll hang about the cloisters moaning and being a general pain in the butt.'

'Nae different than usual then.'

'Oy! I'm just saying if you hung back I'd come and get you.'

If weight loss and fatigue are signs of the physical times – or if Sean and his mysterious pa have anything to do with it – Lucian will be there first.

He has a theory about his loss of weight. It's an abstract theory that would have him locked away were he to share it, yet the more he thinks on it – and the more he drinks on it – the less abstract it becomes.

It's about VM – visible material. If you got it, use it. They talked about it in their last briefing – ideas meandering from rivers and pontoon bridges, to bivouacs, dug-outs and adobe huts.

Adobe huts are made of sticks and shit held together with spit.

Click! A boozy light flickers in Lucian's head: Six Chimneys is lath and timber, other materials, cement and steel girders, added over the centuries. There is another Six Chimneys that is made of fire and air and held together by love.

'Oh, yeah! Eureka, Archimedes, baby!'

Lucian knows how it sounds but he's working on it, trying to compute function and cause. At the mo' – JD flowing – understanding eludes him, yet he seems to think that as of now he is the spit and shit that holds everything together.

'*The first Noel the angels did say was to certain poor shepherds in fields...!*'

'Away the lads, Luca!'

'Awa' the Jocks, Tabby!'

'Let's hear it for the Kiddies!'

'*Nemo me impune lacessit!*'

'With nobs on!'

'*We are the stuff dreams are made of.*'

'Isn't that what Wally Shackspoke said?'

'It is, Tabby. It's from The Tempest. '*We are such stuff as dreams are made of and our little life is rounded with a sleep.*'

Lucian is the stuff Six Chimney is made of – he's always known it, but until now, in this goodly company, passing the bottle, he was unable to internalise. 'It's to do with supporting the infrastructure, Tabby.'

'Of course it is.'

'It's why I'm losing weight. Every second of every day spent away from the house drains me of energy.'

'Is tha' right?'

'No, I'm wrong.' Lots of finger waving. 'It isn'ae the infrastructure I support.'

'It isn't?'

'No, it's Daisy and my idea of Daisy. She's the infrastructure. And the VM, the visible material, is my need of her.'

''Course it is! She's a beautiful girl, your Daisy.'

Two bronze Buddha they smile and nod – Lucian is smiling and nodding but he's not really there. He's perched on a camp stool in the bottom meadow flicking a line. He's looking to catch a tidy wee mouthful and so acute is his hearing – so tuned into the infrastructure – he doesn't need to cancel out Tabby to beam in on Radio Daisy – she's there, live on band VM.

CHAPTER THIRTY-ONE

Merry-go-Round

Edwin D'angelo, or rather his carer, sent Daisy a message.

The phone rang. 'Hi, Daisy. It's me, Janet.'

'Oh, how nice! Happy Christmas, Janet! I was thinking of you and Sharon and wondering if she liked the tyger bonnet.'

'She loves it. She was wearing it when I left, two striped ears sticking up. Made me laugh. When I get back I'll send you a pic via my mobile.'

'And I'll try and receive it. I'm useless at such things.'

'Me too! I'm surprised I haven't electrocuted myself, death-by-Janet.'

'At least you'll know how to perform CPR. How is Ed?'

'It's him I'm calling about. He wouldn't rest until I called.'

Daisy's heart sank. 'Am I going to like this?'

'Well, Ed and his messages. He says, "hun-bun watch Luca TV at two." '

'Nothing about going back to the start?'

'Not that I know of.'

'Okay then TV at two. Does he say which station?'

Janet laughed. 'Don't be silly. This is Ed. You have to work for it.'

Daisy said nothing to her parents but made sure that the TV stayed on.

'Come on, Daisy, the food's getting cold.'

'Hang on a minute! I'm looking for "Christmas with the

Troops." It's here somewhere. Oh, here it is.' A picture switched in, the camera panning over a bleak terrain, and then bagpipes are playing and the show is rolling.

'US guys put your arms about the UK gals! That's it! Huddle up real close. Hold it! Now look dangerous!' The Director punched his fist. 'Hooyah!'

Click! Click! Click!

'And cut! Thank you guys and gals, or should I say ladies, beautiful as you are.'

A US newsreel-station films combined UK and US troops at their Christmas lunch, which is okay, but the Director better stop referring to Ginger and Co as girls or he'll be getting his head punched. They are girls, yet first and last they are soldiers, and what with all this pussy-foraging – and everyone suffering a hangover -tempers are apt to fray.

'All this hanging about is getting on my tit,' growled Lucian. His head! He needs to sleep but the pallets are thin and his bones sharp. In the showers this morning he found bruises on his chest the shape of defibrillator pads, but then, the way he feels a touch of CPR wouldn't go amiss.

'Okay, boys and girls!' The guy is at it again. 'One more take!'

'Oh for Chrissakes!'

'It's enough to drive a man mad.'

'Or a woman,' muttered SI Moore.

'Or a lady,' said the US pilot, grinning.

Once again they huddle together, sighing and kicking up dust.

The director points to Lucian. 'Hey, big feller!'

Silence.

'You! The UK officer on the left!'

'I think he's talking to you, Boss.'

'Is he by God?'

'Hey, big guy!' The Director waved his arms. 'Could you get one of your people to give you an AK47? You'd look great holding one of those.'

'As opposed to a stick of celery, I suppose.'

'Did you hear what I said, feller?'

Lucian eyed him. 'You talkin' to me?'

'Yeah.'

'You talkin' to *me*?'

'Yeah, I said can you get an AK47 or somethin'.'

'You saying I need a machine-gun? That I'm not badass enough?'

There are sniggers from the USAF fliers.

The Director, no fan of *Taxi Driver* scowls. 'When you've had your little joke, Mister Robert de Nero.'

'When you've had your little joke, sir, Major Nairne, sir!'

'Yeah, when you've had your little joke Major Nairne, sir, can we get on?'

'I think not. We're done with your shoot. Company, step out!'

A burst of humour then all falls flat again. They then line up for the TV newsreel. Tabby is on first, spluttering all over the place. Now it's Lucian's turn. He steps up, takes a deep breath, and it happened – one minute he's staring into the camera hoping he's remembered to shave and then all is darkness.

* * *

415

The programme opened with the Shadow PM talking. '...*with that in mind may I on behalf of her majesty's government thank you all for your dedication to duty, and for the sacrifices you and your families made.*'

The scene shifted to huts and soldiers, hands behind their backs and shoulders straight ready for the fray. One by one they come forward. First it was the girls, who, smiling and embarrassed talked to their loved ones.

'Cracking looking girls,' said Isla.

'Beautiful,' said William.

'I'll bet the lads have trouble keeping to their own bunks with that lot.'

'Do you mind!' said Daisy. 'Soldiers sharing bunks is the last thing a soldier's heavily pregnant wife wants to hear.'

'I don't see Lucian,' said William.

'You won't,' said Isla. 'He wouldn't be seen dead talking to the press.' Then, his tall figure unmistakeable, he came into shot. 'There he is!' Dad pointed. 'There's our boy!'

There's our boy. Long after they left Daisy held that remark to her heart, not only what was said but the pride in her father's eyes. Even so, it was a terrible interview, static cutting Lucian's face to ribbons. One moment he's saying, 'my wife,' so clear, and then a blank screen and another voice talking: '...*if you need me I'll be there...if you need me I'll be there...*'

The same words over and over, it will stay in Daisy's memory forever.

Isla was on her feet. 'What the hell is that about?'

'I don't know,' Dad had shrugged. 'Some poor sod recounting a nightmare.'

'Turn it off! Turn it off!' Unable to bear it, Daisy left them all to it, and running upstairs hid in the bathroom.

'What's up with Daisy?' said Dad.

'She's missing Lucian.'

'He's missing her,' said Sean.

'Same thing,' said Isla.

'No,' said Sean. 'It's not.'

* * *

They met together in the pub. It was a good lunch. Kate's a great cook and Ziggy generous, maybe a little too generous with the wine, everyone tipsy.

Sean remained sober as did the other lad, Leon.

'How are you, Leon?' said Daisy, thinking he looked lost.

'I'm a'reet, thanks.'

'It's nice to finally be able to put a face to a name. When do you go back?'

'Tomorrer.'

'For how long?'

'Another six months.'

She patted his arm. 'It'll soon pass. Then you'll be home for good.'

'I won't,' he said. 'You'll no catch me here agin. I'm for the navy.'

'Oh, the navy! It's a good life so I'm told. Are you old enough to join?'

'Old enough for the sea cadets.'

'I wish you luck. I'm sure you'll do well.'

'Reet.' He ambled away, brow lowering and jeans doing the same.

'Don't worry about it,' said Kate. 'He's angry wi' me. He thinks I shouldn'ae have had him put away. But what was I to do? I couldn'ae let him go on as he was. He'd have ended up dead down a back alley.'

'The navy could be the making of him.'

'Or the breaking.'

Isla and Daisy and Sean are looking through Minna's photograph albums. 'These pics are of blokes that stayed here during the war?' said Isla.

'I believe so.'

'Look at the uniforms! God, it's like a convention. That's a Yank, see the cap? And that's a Polish uniform, I know because a friend of mine married a Polish captain. Wow! What do you? Lucky Minna! That is some way to spend your war bivvying up to a new bloke every night.'

Daisy pointed to a portrait photograph. 'That's Minna.'

'Great looking woman but I don't think much of her taste in clothes.'

'This was taken in '43. I suppose they had to make do.'

'D'you know who she reminds me of?'

'People say I look a bit like her,' said Daisy.

'You do, but I was actually thinking of me. Mysterious Minna reminds me of me when I was young and beautiful.'

'You are still beautiful.'

'Maybe, but not young.'

'Can i have a look?' said Sean. Daisy pushed the album toward him. She stifled a yawn. She is tired and wants to go home.

Isla saw her yawning and nodded. 'This is your own fault. If you'd stayed with us you could have sat around all day resting instead of looking after a zoo.'

'It's not a zoo.'

'It might as well be. I know Lucian worries about it.'

'That's because you tell him too much!'

'We're all worried.'

'No need to be. I'm okay here.'

'Then why the leaflets from the house agency?'

'Just keeping abreast of house prices. Good grief! Can't a person look at a few things without other people drawing assumptions?'

'Alright, if you say you're okay then fine because by the looks of that snow your pa's thinking of leaving tomorrow.'

'Fine! I wouldn't expect you to stay if the weather gets worse. I'm not going to be on my own. Nikki who helps with the pony will stay over.'

'Are you sure? Only it's the last chapter, lovey, and you know what I'm like. I can't settle til I've written it and I can't write unless I'm home.'

'It's alright.' Daisy kissed her mother. 'You go do what you have to do.'

Isla wandered away to stare out of the window at the snow.

'Daisy, have you seen this?' Sean pushed the album forward. It was a group shot, a dozen or so people circled about Minna.

'Oh yes, that's a nice shot. It's the first one I've seen with girls.'

'Uh-huh. Notice anything about them?'

'Nothing other than they're gorgeous.'

'Look again.'

Daisy was drawing the album toward her when suddenly everybody's on the move. And no wonder, snow is blasting down.

Ziggy is talking to Dad. 'Start now, Will, or all bets are off, and you know what happens in the UK when it snows, the world comes to an end.'

'Hear that, Isla?'

'I heard. So, Daisy, are you coming? We can squeeze her in, can't we, Sean?'

Sean was looking at the album. 'She cann'ae go. She's needed here.'

'Do you think I should go with you?' said Daisy. 'I don't have to stay. I can always get someone to look after the animals.'

'And who'll look after Lucian?'

'What?'

'Who will look after Lucian?'

Daisy laughed. 'Why, the Army, of course.'

Sean nodded. 'Aye, but what Army?'

* * *

Her parents left early morning. 'I'll stay,' said Isla. 'You and Sean go.'

'No! That's fine!' Daisy didn't want to be alone but neither did she want her pregnancy managed. 'Bye!' she waved them off to a last glimpse of Isla's head bobbing and Sean's smile.

Sean the Sphinx? He is aptly named. One glance from those sea-green eyes and you're under his spell. It's only a few months since she last saw him yet he is changed, and neither the love of terrapin, or Berwick Rangers football club, can bridge the gap between him and his former family.

Kate, who's seldom fazed, had stared. 'He's no my kid anymore.'

'How came he to be with you?'

'It's a long story and a bit on the spooky side.'

'How d'you mean spooky?'

'I heard about Sean and your ma long before I met him.' Kate gave Daisy a sideways look. 'It was one of them séances, where they've a table with cut out letters and a glass spelling words? Sean was in a message along with a warning to stay away from Jason.'

'No!'

'I cann'ae recall all the details, only that it was a warning about a man wi' a cold heart and death in his hands will bring Mahonia's kids into danger.'

'Did you take it seriously?'

'You bet I did. The woman couldn't have known my name was Mahonia.'

'Neither did I. I thought you were called Kate.'

'That's where it gets more spooky. This woman, real old witch, hoop earrings, and all – and I remember this because I know now she was talking of your ma and Sean – said, "a woman wi' life in her hands and fiery hair would take Mahonia's borrowed kiddie away."'

'And you think that was Isla with the fiery hair?'

'Who else can it be? You cann'ae get hair redder than you two, and think o' the books she writes? If that isn'ae life in her hands I don't know what is.'

'God yes! And you took it as a warning about Jason?'

'Aye, just in time, thank God, to stop him murdering us in

our beds! When I look back I think I must've been blind. If ever there was a man wi' a cold heart it was him. It wasn't until he got nasty with Tulip I remembered the message. You see, we had a fight that night. He stormed off then came back later and set fire to the squat wi' a can of petrol.'

'Oh Kate!'

'Aye, but this is the spooky bit. Somebody woke me. A voice said, "get up! Take your children doon the fire escape." '

'Oh, that is so...!'

'I know. The place was full of smoke. I grabbed the kids and left.'

'Thank God for the voice.'

'I do. I thank Him every day. I'll tell you something else, though you'll probably think it's just me. I know the voice. I didn't then but I know it now.'

'And whose voice was it?'

'Lucian's.'

* * *

Camp Bastion, Helmand Province.

'How are you, Lucian?' Tabby Gates leant against the door.

Lucian covered the letter. 'Nothing wrong that having my guts washed out wouldn't cure. Three days and I'm still pissing pure alcohol. '

'You reckon that's what caused you to fall?'

'I don't know.'

'Cos, you know, you went one hell of a fall. Hit the ground, wallop. Scared the shit out of the TV crew. They thought you'd been shot.'

'I thought I'd been shot. I felt my knees go and thought, here we are again, another six months masquerading as a cabbage.'

'You look okay now, a bit pale maybe, and still underweight.'

'That's from fending off crap from the girls.'

Tabby grinned. 'Giving you a bad time are they?'

'They would if I let 'em.'

'I guess they are concerned about you. The MO found nothing wrong so I'm guessing your cure is the same as mine, lay off the JD.'

'Aye-aye, sir.'

Tabby left and Lucian sat down. He's writing to Daisy. The last time he did this he was leaning on Nobby Clarke's back. Trouble is, he can't seem to do it right. No matter what he says it comes out as mush and so he starts again.

My dearest Girl, while I've got the time I thought I'd tell you how much you mean to me. I'm not the most romantic of men, not best at showing my feelings, too rigid for the gentle stuff. I don't know why. The past, maybe. What is it they say, 'give me the child til he is seven and ...'

'Oh, wha' the ...!' Another in the bin.

He starts again. *Dearest Daisy, I seem to remember you saying I had a reputation as a heartbreaker. I don't know what I was before I met you. Deaf, dumb, and blind, I think. All I can say is if I was such a man I'm sorry for it because I get a glimpse of how it is feels to have a broken heart...*

'Chrissakes!' He screwed the letter up and dropped it in the bin.

Taking a fresh piece of paper he began again and arrived at a compromise. It wasn't what he wanted to say but he stuck the note in an envelope. He's sick of thinking. You can't do this job and worry. Life is risk. Mend washing machines and you risk aching knees. Be a lion tamer and you risk getting your ass chewed off. If you sign up to defuse bombs... di-dah-di-dah.

If the call comes he'll go. If he dies he'll take it up with St Peter.

Tabby asked what happened at the interview. Lucian feigns ignorance but knows only too well what happened. It can be summed up in a series of moves.

1) The cameraman moved closer.

2) Lucian saw his reflection in a mirror attached to the camera.

3) The interviewer posed the question: 'Who are you, sir, and what would you like to say to folks back home?'

4) Lucian began his spiel: 'I am Lucian Nairne. I would like to talk to my wife...'

5) He stops because not only has he forgotten his wife's name – he doesn't know he has a wife.

6) Not knowing Daisy he doesn't know himself.

7) If a man has no knowledge of himself he ceases to exist.

8) If the mirror that once showed a human face is empty a man has no reason to stand and so he falls.

* * *

Kate phoned. 'What are you doing for Hogmanay?'

'Nothing much,' said Daisy, the phone propped against her ear while watching TV and picking polish off her nails. 'I thought I'd have an early night.'

'D'you fancy spending Hogmanay wi' us?'

'That's kind of you but I can't leave the animals. Baz is afraid of fireworks and there are bound to be fireworks.'

'Fetch him with you. Fetch the lot! Mick will pick you up, "lock, stock, and two smoking"....nae danger.'

'Can I see how I feel tomorrow? Give you a ring about lunch time?'

'Sure! What are friends for if not to look after one another?'

'Thanks Kate. You are a good friend.'

'Lucian's been awful good to me and my kids. If I cann'ae take care of the one thing he loves then I'm an ungrateful bitch.'

During the conversation Daisy never once took her eyes off the TV screen. It was like when she little watching the *Daleks* in Doctor *Who*. She'd hide behind the sofa but couldn't resist peeping over a cushion.

She'd rather not watch but every morning is prompted by Ed via text: *U wtch Luca TV 2dy*. The picture is scrambled every time and the same unhappy man mumbles the same unhappy words.'...*all of my life...night or day... grabbed my courage to tell you...I will come...heaven or hell... I'll be there.*'

That night an angel woke Daisy. 'I've come to show you the window.'

Daisy protested. 'I don't want to see it.'

'Too bad! This tragic business has gone on long enough.'

Then Daisy was on the landing looking at the window. Such a beautiful window! Despite a ham-fisted glazier it remains a work of art. As she watched the window changed, the Knight Templar faded away to be replaced by Lucian.

'Oh my God!' Daisy shrieked. 'Get him down! Please, get him down!'

'I wish I could,' said the angel. 'Left to me I'd blast it out of the skies and you with it.' She dragged Daisy closer. 'Look and tell me what you see!' Daisy didn't know what she was supposed to be seeing which made the angel angry.

'Look again!' she shouted, her voice cannons firing. 'Tell me what you see!'

'I see the branches of a tree holding him back.'

'Is it a tree?'

Daisy's sleeping eyes scanned newly soldered panels. 'Oh!' Then she saw it, as clearly as though the angel switched on a lamp. They weren't Smarties securing the panels. They were finger nails. Her fingernails! Her hands!

'It's me,' she whispered. 'I'm holding him back. But why when I love him?'

'Because you love the story more and rather than wake to an unknown future you cling to the story-teller and go round, and round.'

Music began to play and with it the noise of a great hurdy-gurdy. It was a fairground carousel with animals, horses, and dogs, and cats, and people turning round and round, going faster and faster, until she screamed.

'Stop!' And woke.

CHAPTER THIRTY-TWO

Is This the Day

Camp Bastion, Helmand Province.

The morning began badly with a text from Ed. Usually any messages are aimed at Lucian. Today Daisy is in the crosshairs: '*2nite hun-bun go bck 2 strt.*'

Furious, thinking Ed might've sent the same message to Six Chimneys, Lucian tried calling home but couldn't get through. Anger left him with a massive headache. He opened the locker and was swallowing a fistful of pills when in the locker mirror he saw what looked like a bird's wing.

He went outside, no bird, just piercing sunlight and a headache.

The pain in his head got worse and then the fingers of his left hand went numb. Christ! Cold funk washed over him. Scared, thinking he was having a stroke, he pulled on running shoes and went out jogging the perimeter.

Gradually the headache eased, his fingers regaining feeling. Fool, he thought, it's only a headache. Then passing by the oil-dumps he got the same giddy glimpse of feathers, only this time it was a glistening angel wing. The wing flexed and a gust of wind picked Lucian up and threw him down.

He was helped to his feet by a guy who rolled back the cuff of an immaculate shirt, pointed to a Rolex, and said: 'This is the day, the hour and the moment. Look for me, Lucian Nairne, and wait.'

A passing squaddie asked if he was okay.

Lucian brushed down his knees. 'I'm good, thanks.'

The squaddie jogged on. 'Maybe take more water with it, sir.'

Lucian returned to the hut, poured a hefty tot of JD, and then knowing he needed to be sharp dumped it for water. Showered and dressed, he rewrote a letter to Daisy, dropping the ear-stud inside the envelope. Then he went to the mess and, a condemned man, ate a hearty breakfast. Now, armed and ready, he sits crammed inside a Chinook-47 along with Tabby and the rest.

According to his watch he has three hours, eleven minutes, and forty-three...two seconds to live. Some angel! Sizzling with power, and with a perfect Eton knot in his tie, he might've stepped out of Esquire. The boots that straddled the dust shone, and the hand coming down from a cloudless sky was firm and the nails clean. He'd helped Lucian to his feet, and smiling, said. 'All you have to do is keep your eyes on me.'

At the time Lucian understood the words and why they were said. Now only the voice reverberates in his ear. He'll never forget that voice. Can you hear God and not know He calls on you? 'Does'nae matter. It is as it is.'

'Sorry, Major, did you say something?'

'No, Corporal Faulkner, nothing that matters.'

It's a big team on the way to do a little house-cleaning. They sit either side the Chinook, Bergens on the floor and boots planted square. Camouflage gear is meant to diminish individuality and lend amorphous fuzz – today, despite camouflage, every man and woman shines. As a team Lucian knows what they can do and what to expect. At the base they share a beer and a joke under the mantle of in-it-together yet as individuals are closed to him. He can't see into their hearts anymore than they can see into his

– today, knowing this the last time they'll serve together, their unique individuality is palpable.

Sun slants through the forward windows transforming the clunky metal carrier to an exotic Chinese kite while reminding Lucian of the stained glass window on the stairs. These warriors wear fibreglass helmets and blast-proof vests. They carry Glocks, machine guns and rocket launchers. They don't wear white tabards nor are their breasts crossed with scarlet. It's doubtful any one will be immortalised – yet today they are brave as any Knight Templar.

There's beauty in every one and not only the feminine beauty of Corporals Shaw and Flynn, lashes dipped in gold and mouths like delicious plums. There is nobility in Thomas Gates' profile. The same is true of Andrew Faulkner, enemy of overgrown hedges. Fingers splayed, his hand rests on his knee. Sunbeams play upon that hand revealing the bones beneath. A hand enables a man to paint a Sunflower to sculpt a Kiss or copy the Koran. Andrew's hand risks the wrong move and Sunflowers and kisses are gone forever.

* * *

Nikki is on the phone. 'I won't be able to come today. My battery's flat.'

'Don't worry about it. I've shoved all the animals together in the barn. With them all under one roof it's easier.'

'I don't like letting you down.'

'It's okay. I'll be seeing Kate later.' Daisy carried on with the Hoover. She's been chasing non-existent dust since six this morning, and when not cleaning is checking rental property. She needs to get out of this house, *and*, she needs to burn the damned photograph albums!

Daisy had a nightmare last night where an angel with Minna Gray's face accused her of holding Lucian back. That Daisy's worried about him is obvious, that she scolds herself through Minna is hardly surprising since she'd spent the previous day putting a folder of the WW2 photographs together for Isla.

The BBC is running the Army link again today. Though she hates what she sees the TV program is all she has. Last night, as a result of the nightmare, she prayed for help. It's said the Lord Jesus looks after children; six-three and 220 lbs is hardly a child, nonetheless, Lucian had a mother who would want him to live and thrive. She prayed. 'Keep my husband and those serving with him safe. And if you can please help that other chap who seems terribly lost.'

The door bell rang when Daisy was in the nursery looking at all the pink and wondering if she hadn't been hasty. They hardly talked of boy's names. She suggested Alistair but Lucian wouldn't hear of it. 'I'm no having a son of mine with that name.'

Daisy protested. 'Isn't it customary to name a son after his father?'

'Not mine and not my grandfather.'

'Well then he'd better be named after you or my dad.'

'Or Ian! If we have a boy he could be called after my brother.'

Then the door bell rang, Basil's ears telegraphing the news. A baby hippo in leggings and oversize t-shirt Daisy lumbered downstairs, averting her eyes when passing the window. She opened the door to a curtain of snow.

A woman smiled. '*Bon jour, ma chere,*' she said. 'I am collecting on be'alf of charity. May I ask a donation?'

The snow was thick. The woman was dressed in a Shearling coat and hat to match but Daisy wouldn't leave her on the doorstep. Glad of company she offered coffee. There was a bit of a moment, Baz howling and Thai and Ming suggesting porcupines. Daisy shut them in the kitchen and peace restored served coffee and shortbread in the sitting room.

They talked of the usual things, the weather and difficulties getting about in the snow. 'How do you manage?' said the woman. 'You are cut off from the world, and,' she gestured toward the bump, 'most *enceinte*.'

'Indeed, *très enceinte*.'

'When is *bébé* due?'

'Just under three weeks. I had hoped my husband would be here but he is a soldier and goes where he's needed.'

'A brave young man.'

'The bravest.'

The woman drained her cup. 'I must leave.'

'Oh, please stay a while!' said Daisy.

'I would like to but I cannot. I am 'ere on – what is it you say – a wing and a...'

'...a prayer. That's a pity. As I said I am alone and glad of company.'

The woman smiled. 'You are not alone. The One who loves you is with you.'

Daisy sighed. 'That's good to know. Are you here on holiday?'

'I know the area. I used to live not far from 'ere.'

'Really? Do you know..?' The phone clicked into service, Oscar's voice! Daisy tried ignoring it. 'You have family here?'

'No, I too am without family.'

'I'm sorry. It's a rotten time to be alone.'

The woman shrugged delicately. 'When a woman is alone any time of the year is bad, even when, as with you, she is greatly loved.'

The phone started up again, shrilling through the house.

'You are busy.' The woman walked to the door. 'Thank you for the donation. It shall be put to good use.'

Daisy peered at the cruciform label on the tin. 'TAL? I don't know that charity.'

'It is the Army of the Light.'

'I haven't heard of that. Is it like the Salvation Army?'

'The word salvation is appropriate.'

'Then well done to you for coming out in this lot.'

'It is my duty and eternal pleasure to do so.'

On impulse Daisy gave her a hug. 'I wish you a happy new year and a safe journey home. The snow is heavy. Have you far to go?'

'Not so far.' Blue eyes brilliant against a white back-drop, the woman drew the collar about her throat. '*Adieu!*' She gestured to the bump. '*Et toi, petite Emma.*'

'Oh, you know she is to be called Emma?'

The woman made a sad moue. '*Je ne sais pas...perhaps at last.*'

Daisy waved goodbye. She didn't ask about the perhaps, didn't understand it, but then guessed the woman had heard about Emma in the village. She returned to the sitting room to find a posy of lily-of-the-valley on the table, a sweet perfume pervading the house making Daisy feel a little less lonely.

* * *

One hour, fifteen minutes, twenty-seven seconds and counting, the sappers have cleared a path. Two isolated IEDs located and dealt with. Now, machine guns at the ready, the escort walks through narrow defile FOB.

A radio pings, Kevin Wallace takes the call. A crofter's son from Mull used to hauling sheep between his knees, he shambles forward removes his helmet and wipes his brow. Sandy in complexion, he's the image of his brother yet unalike in disposition. Kevin Wallace is a decent guy, whereas Kieran – though one shouldn't speak ill of the dead – was a foul-mouthed slob who took pleasure out of other people's pain, his motto, 'if he couldn't kick it, drink it or fuck it, it didn't exist.'

A cloud passed over the sun. Light hit Kevin's pale eyes and suddenly Lucian didn't know who he was looking at, the guy with a stepson Jamie back home, or hell-raiser Kieran, killed in action a year ago to this very day.

Kevin grinned. 'It's like the effing song, sir, *memories are made of this*.'

'What?' Lucian gapes. He'd heard those exact words before but not from this man. 'Say again, Sergeant?'

'I said it's like the song! No matter how many times you ask those effing Sappers for precise effing co-ordinates, you never get the right effing data!'

Whoah! This is what Kieran said seconds before he died. Ah, but wait a minute! It's familiar because this sort of thing is said all of the time. Eighteen years he's fought alongside guys like Kevin and Kieran who have the same habits and use the same battle-zone

433

argot. It doesn't have to be weird. It's like the other song, '*This is the army, Mr Jones. No private rooms or telephones. You had your breakfast in bed before but you won't have it there anymore.*'

With the memory of that song a division occurred in time. Lucian knew where he was and what he was doing, yet overlaying today like some delicate embroidered gauze was yesterday's Lucian listening to yesterday. There it was, two brothers separated by death, two ends of a year drawn together by time, and two worlds – that of the living *and* the dead – coming together.

Whoosh! The world stopped turning. The Team stand or crouch in varied attitudes, Kevin with mouth open and dental work exposed and Corporal Shaw shunting a machine gun onto her shoulder. Lucian can think and hear but the thoughts in his head are not his own. A bead of sweat hung on Kevin's nose. '... *I'm telling you, Jenny, your effing ex comes near Jamie again I'll not be answerable for the consequences. He's leading the bairn in tae bad ways.*'

Tabby Gates thinks of his wife and the girls. He worries about school fees and is fearful: '*No, Sarah, it can't wait til I get home. You get that lump seen to!*'

There's Ginger. '*Patsy's never on time with rent...she thinks I'm made of money...and it was her who got nail-polish on my dress.*'

Addie Faulkner and April Shaw share the same sadness, '... *miscarried last year... sorry, April, I'm a married man... Bets mustn't find out!*'

Pain and fear, truth and lies, he hears and feels it, and beneath every thought, like an underground river, the same anxiety, and same anguished prayer, '*I must keep up...don't let them see I'm scared...be brave...be strong!*'

Sound multiplies, thoughts multiply until with a pop and inrush of air the vacuum is filled. He can move – and the world – and the war creak into action.

* * *

Daisy received a special delivery through the post from Lucian's lawyer, a photograph and a small sealed package. 'I think you'll find these interesting,' was the lawyer's scrawled comment, but with another link from Afghanistan about to begin she set the package aside for later.

The screen ripples and there they are, soldiers standing in line, bright sunlight reflecting through the camera as brilliant rainbows. The presenter smiles:

'*Good evening ladies and gentleman. Here we are again at Camp Bastion. It's time to introduce the team. Up first we have Colonel Thomas Gates, GM, known to his colleagues as Tabby.*'

Daisy remembers Thomas Gates. He was at the wedding and very drunk danced with his young daughter in his arms. Today, hands behind his back and jaw set, the man is very sober and very English. '*Sarah, if you're seeing this then you'll know what's happened. What can I say other than thanks for putting up with me. We had a good life, better than most, and I am grateful. Kiss the girls for me and tell them I love them. Give my parents my best wishes and please, go see the doctor. Don't ignore it. The girls need you now more than ever. Goodbye, my dear, until we meet again.*'

Next to speak was a Sergeant Wallace. He was talking to his little boy.

' *Hello, son. You're only little and can't understand why everyone is sad, but not to worry, you'll know in time. Right now Mammy needs you to be man of the family. You're to do what she says and take no notice of your other pa 'cos he don't know what he's talking aboot. Shaun-the-Sheep sends you a kiss. God bless and keep you, love from Daddy Kevin.'*

Next to speak was a beautiful blonde: *'Hello Mum and Dad, it's me, Geraldine. I don't want to say too much because I'll start blubbing. I just want to say you're not to worry. When I took this job I knew what it meant. I never had any doubts so don't you have any. These last years with the team have been the best years of my life and if it had to happen so be it. Say hi to Patsy for me and then tell her to get the hell out my flat! It's to be sold and the money to go to you. I send my love to my friends in Chiswick. Love you all, kissy, kissy!'*

Daisy is crying. This link is not like the prearranged stuff. These people speak from the heart, especially Geraldine, who she seems to think she knows.

Then, finally, Lucian made his way to the front. The presenter spoke. *'We have another member of the team. Who are you, sir, and what would you like to say?'* Lucian began to speak. *'My name is Lucian Nairne.'*

Daisy waited for the link to break-up but it held still, and though the words were soon those of a stranger, it was Lucian, same lock of hair at the crown of his head that no matter what he did always stuck up as a question mark.

'Hello Girl with Green eyes. It seems I'm required to leave a note for my nearest and dearest telling my last wishes. Sad to say I don't seem to have a nearest or dearest – I guess I lost them on the way – and even if I did you'd be the one I'd want to say goodbye to. I don't know you and you don't know me but don't be afraid, I'm no stalker.

I saw you once and never forgot. Your lovely face has kept me going through a year of hell. I want to thank you and tell you my wish is for you to know that, alive or dead – heaven or hell – I will look out for you, and find you, and love you.' God bless and keep us both,

    Your wanna-be Guardian Angel.

Army of the Light

Until this moment Lucian thought he was a sensible man thinking and behaving in a sensible manner. There's nothing sensible about today. He has grit in his eyes and dust in his boots; so many irritants, so many aches and pains of this world, and yet walking beside him is a being from another world.

The angels – if that's what they are – began appearing about an hour ago. First there was Kevin who gained Kieran, his dead brother. Ginger was next, a light growing about her heart until a winged man gathered about her.

One-by-one they came blossoming like flowers. Lucian didn't know how he stopped from weeping. St Wenceslas' pages, they followed on the heels of every member of the team, only they didn't follow – follow suggests separation – these beings were part of their host, within and away from the flesh.

Now twenty or more such beings escort the Team. An elfin creature leads Tabby. That's a thing to see, Thomas Gates, GM, a machine gun on his arm and grenades sprouting from his belt, being led by a slip of a lass!

A few minutes of that and Lucian had to ask. 'You okay, Tabby?'

'What d'you mean?'

'Are you feeling okay?'

'How the fuck d'you think I feel after three fucking hours of this!'

Okay, Lucian got the picture, only he can see them, and this is the Day. If the Messenger was right, and the presence of angels would suggest it so, then Lucian is in the last thirty minutes of his life.

The phone buzzed in his thigh pocket, a text from Ed, and in clear script, none of the usual shorthand: '*This is The Day, Lucian, the hour and the moment, for me and for you. Keep your eyes on the Boss.*'

Unreal! This has to be a dream or the worse kind of nightmare. With that the angel now walking beside Lucian turned his head. 'It's not a dream.'

Blind fury rolled up. 'Then who or what are you!'

'You know who I am.'

'I know who you look like! You look like my pal Gillie, but you're not him. Medical Officer David Gilchrist promised to stay and care for the woman I love while I'm stuck here with this mob and would never go back on his word.'

'David is a busy fellow and can be in many places at many times.'

'Are you saying my Daisy's not alone?'

'Your Daisy is my Lord's Daisy and therefore can never be alone.'

Lucian saw the compassion in the eagle eyes and bit down so hard his lip bled. 'I must be out of my mind. You say you're a man that I thought of as a brother. You tell me you can be in two places at the same time and that Daisy is safe, and God help me I believe you, but it doesn'ae stop me fearing for her.'

Lucian struggled to understand. 'Can the others see you?'

'No one sees me as you see me. Awareness varies. Some receive a mental image of help. Some feel the touch of a hand or hear a voice telling them they are not alone. All know they stand in extreme peril.'

'Who are your companions? *What* are they?'

'They are friends.'

'Are they – are you – able to read minds?'

David smiled. 'I've known you all your life but still wouldn't know which way the ball might bounce, and friends don't drop in unannounced. They wait for invitation. How do these friends appear to you?'

Lucian couldn't find the words. 'I think of them as angels.'

'What do you see when you look at Thomas Gates and the rest?'

'Human beings.'

'And what do they see when they look at you?'

Lucian shrugged. 'I've no idea.' Right now he's more concerned with Kevin. Every warrior has a ritual when preparing for battle. Some daub their bodies with paint others wear amulets. Kevin does a dance. He's at it now singing Champions while spitting in the eye of the Devil. He can't dance at the best of times. Now with heavy gear on he looks like a puffa-coated troglodyte. 'Sergeant Wallace! Get your arse over here!'

'He can't hear you, Lucian.'

'Of course he can hear me!'

Kevin can neither hear nor see him. Lucian Nairne might believe he's a key player in the league but as far as the team is concerned Lucian Nairne isn't with them. He never was with them. Who is Lucian Nairne?

'Lucian Nairne?' A thought drifted through Kevin's head.

'*Wasn't he the ATO killed along with Kieran a year ago?*'

'Jesus!' Lucian was knocked sideways. 'Did I just imagine that?'

Gillie shook his head.

'He thinks I'm dead?'

'Yes.'

'Ah, for Chrissakes!' A door opens and memory is restored, Lucian is in hospital looking down at the body in Room 12. A year of sacrifice is confirmed, and this is the day the twelve months on loan to the world ends.

Needles pierce his heart. Bubbles carrying dreams rise in the air and for twelve long months float and dance and then pop, a house with six chimneys vanishes. There's a wedding, a man and woman joined together, pop, another bubble gone! The bride dances with new-found friends, pop. The magic words, 'I love you, Lucian,' are never spoken. Hot sex, pop! A child, Emma, never conceived, pop! A year of love, pop! Daisy. Pop! Daisy. Pop!

'Kill me.'

'Lucian.'

'If that is me in a coma pull the plug.'

'Lucian!'

'Shut the fuck up! Don't talk to me, Charley, Gillie, whatever you are! Don't say my name! I'm back where I started except it's worse.'

Time spent together with people you love is treasure. Small things, a Chinese takeaway and a bottle of beer watching TV, are the underpinnings of love. They open doors that once were shut. Even the elite club of misunderstood men, buddies moaning about the missus, was Lucian's for the asking. So many things, the smell of home when opening the door – cats and the dogs getting fur over your clothes – and the scent of her hair as you breathe her in.

It's back-to-back, she for you and you for her. It's home. It's gone.

'Kill me.'

'I do understand.'

'You don't or you wouldn't have done it. If a thirsty man is given a mouthful of water he wants more. How could you give me Daisy and then take her away?'

Charley made no comment which is as well because Lucian loathed him. And what's with the battle fatigues? And the Glock! Who's he gonna kill, Tweedledum and fucking Tweedledee? 'You've taken my self-respect. I used to think I was a decent guy. I must've known in my heart I was on a short lease and yet even believing she carried my child I had to play hero.'

'Then again it might be that you knew the year had to end and chose to end it by returning to the start.'

'Yeah right, like I know anything anymore.'

'If you don't know why you're here then no one does. A near-death experience feels like a dream yet is infinitely more potent. You decided the route and how it began. Now you must find the end.'

'Are you saying I wanted this, my hopes and dreams in tatters?'

'I'm saying you wanted *this*, the conversation we are sharing. *This* is your will not mine. You didn't have to waken to the truth. You could have passed quietly into Eternal Sleep. You didn't have to take up arms again. You stayed true to the soldier and took the battle to the enemy.'

'But what use am I? See?' Lucian tried touching Kevin, his hands passed through him. 'What weapon can I carry? What enemy can I hope to fight?'

Charley turned. 'This enemy.'

* * *

Daisy is in the attic frantically searching through the photographs.

The newsreel was worse than the other. Not only did Lucian speak as though he didn't know her, she didn't know him. He looked like her husband but the more the camera homed in, the more he became a stranger. The structure was there, tall and well-built, but this soldier had an arrow head razed into his left eyebrow, cute, sexy, but not Lucian. Same with the hair, the sides were indented, fashionable, but not Lucian. The mouth was different, a scarred bottom lip. Daisy knew her husband's mouth, had kissed every plain and hollow and that wasn't him. Then there's the ring. Soldiers often remove their rings. Lucian might have removed his but might there not be a tell-tale ring of white flesh. The real difference was in the eyes; if eyes are the windows of the soul then the stranger's soul was hidden behind blue stained-glass.

She searched through the photographs without knowing what she was looking for since all were taken during the Second World War. It was when looking at the photograph Lucian's solicitor sent she knew where she'd seen the blonde from the newsreel. She's there! Geraldine Flynn, with her Kate Moss mascara eyes and L'Oreal lipstick! And Oh my God, she's here again in the 1940's shots!

Daisy stared open-mouthed: every picture was the same, men and women of the 40s – the Brylcreme Boys and Land Army Girls – and pictures of twenty-first century soldiers with modern weaponry! And in every single photograph – old or new – Daisy Banks! Yes, truly! Every linked arm, every smile, was directed to the girl in the middle of the crush, the one in jeans and satin bustier, the one fiddling with a diamond stud in her ear that flashed as the camera flashed.

Hands shaking, she set the photographs down. Then she was up and on her feet. Cameras can lie. What about the web search engine? All fingers and thumbs she switched on the computer looking for Geraldine Flynn, Counter IED Force. A headline flashed: *Another British Soldier Dies of Gunshot Wounds*!

She cleared the screen and logged in again. Up it came: *Corporal Geraldine Flynn, known to her friends as Ginger, killed this day when a mine exploded.*

Hands shaking, she fed another into the search: *Breaking news, Lieutenant Colonel Thomas Henley Gates, GM, killed today when a...*

Terrified now, she fed in the one name. The screen rolled, flickered, and then: *Major Lucian Nairne, Scots Guards, was killed today while defusing a...!*

* * *

Charley touched Lucian's hand. 'What are you feeling right now?'

'Nothing. I'm beyond feeling.'

'Then look for that, look for despair, perceive it as an image and you'll see.'

It took a while. Drowning in his own misery Lucian was

unable to see anyone else's. Still he looked and eventually saw. 'Och hell.'

If he'd found angels difficult to describe then these... things... were nigh impossible. Humanoid daubs of paint, thick and glutinous, they crawled out of the earth, ashes-to-ashes, dust-to-dust, wretched, and infinitely pitiable.

The noise hurt his ears. Appalled and disgusted, he was desperate to help, to cure, or to kill, as in compassion a man would step on a wounded moth. 'What are they?' It didn't occur to him to say who. Who implies a person.

'Memories of how it felt to be human.'

'They look and sound as if they are in pain.'

'There is no *they*. This *is* pain, or rather the *imprint* of pain. But would you speak of this, now, Lucian, with the clock is ticking! Time moves on and though I and my companions have dominion over such your colleagues do not.'

'What do you want me to do?'

'I want you to do your best! You felt the year with Daisy was your sunset on the porch. I want you to leave this incarnation sure of another sunset.'

'I thought you didn't read minds.'

'You and I share the same love, thus everything you know of Daisy is known to me, as everything I know of her is shared by you. But now, do what you can for Kevin Wallace. He's a dear little man, and his brother, though not so dear, has fought to save him.'

'From what?'

'From death! Kevin is an excellent technician. He'll do his best to disable a murderous weapon but he doesn't have eyes in the back of his head. Neither he nor any other member of the team can see what you can see.'

Charley said that and again Kevin was rendered immobile.

'Now what? Why is he standing about like a dummy?'

'You caused it to happen.' Charley sighed. 'You fear for the team and rather than let a bull run loose in a china shop you caused time to freeze.'

'I did that? What about Daisy? I have to know she is safe.'

'Daisy is as Daisy was a year ago, unconscious and on life-support.'

'And the bairn?' Fighting tears, Lucian held up his hand. 'I know! There is no baby and no wife. Does she know this is happening, that it's all a lie?'

'She has her own version of the truth. It's how mortals perceive life, a single life with a beginning and an end.'

'She'll suffer.'

'If that is her choice.'

'Does she have a choice?'

'Yes as do you, Lucian. You can help your dream Daisy if you're willing.'

'I'm willing! Of course I'm willing!'

'Then trust me when I say the only way to help is to complete your path.'

'Is that why I'm here with the team?'

Charley nodded. 'The power of love is great. As I said, Kieran Wallace did everything he could to save his brother, including beckoning you.'

'What must I do?'

'Find the problem and resolve it.'

'With no hands to fight?'

'You must find a way. This is your domain. You make the rules.'

'But you're an angel. You're here and in battledress. Why can't you help?'

'We can and will but in our own way. As for battledress it's your soldier eyes that have given me a Kevlar vest.' Charley smiled. 'Our weapons of choice are love and humility. I don't believe I need a bullet-proof vest for that.'

He said that and the flak jacket was gone and the pistol and hand grenades. Once again it was just Charley. 'I guess I thought you needed them.'

'Thank you for the thought.' Charley drew him close. 'You are brave and beloved of my Lord but the enemy we fight doesn't wield a gun.'

Lucian leaned against him. 'I don't know what to do.'

'Use your expertise as a soldier. Do as you are trained to do.'

'And keep my eye on the Boss.'

'That above all! Go where He leads and love will sustain you.'

'Are you not the Boss?' Lucian was talking to himself. Charley stood on a ridge about 100 yards away. The enemy is at hand.

'Agh!' It came at him in rolling waves of fetid smoke, the fear and pain of the lost and lonely. It knocked him off his feet. He couldn't see what angels could see only that it caused their wings to crackle and the earth to quake.

The Charley he knew – man and one-time buddy – was a pyramid of fire that burned so brightly Lucian was not alone in covering his eyes. An old man in a hospital bed, cried out, 'Puff! Turn the light down or I'll go blind!'

Dummies

Daisy must have fainted. When she opened her eyes it was dark and bitterly cold. The dogs were with her but no sign of the cats. 'I must phone Lucian.'

Then it fell on her, Lucian is dead. 'No!' She didn't believe it. The army wouldn't release that kind of news without first informing the family.

Biddy-pup and Basil trembling, she crept down the front stairs. All was silent but for the dogs whining. Even the grandfather clock had stopped ticking.

Kaboom! Eyes tightly closed, she stepped onto the stairs and was plugged into the National Grid – energy charging the soles of her feet, rising through her body and out through statically charged hair!

'Agh!' Teeth chattering and breath forced from her lungs she was at one with the Light, and for a moment could see the multi-coloured vortex that was the Window. A whirlpool, enticing and dangerous, it reached out to pull her in. The need to follow was so strong she had to hold onto the banister.

The dogs thundered down the stairs and yelping with fear and excitement leapt into the Light. The doorway, for that's what it had become, had a Guardian. Wings flexed and barbed, a sword in one hand and fisherman's net in the other, he bestrode the sill. 'Come on, Daisy!' Golden eyes ablaze, he crooked a finger. 'I'll take care of you.'

'No,' she whispered. 'You're not real. You're make believe like this house.'

'*Housee*,' the echo sighed. '*Housee... homee...housee...homee...*!'

Other creatures were drawn to the Light. Wisps of smoke came from all corners of the house, phantoms, shreds of life, men, women, and children with pallid faces and hungry eyes crawled up the stairs. Then, with a scratching of pincers and claws, small life wriggled from cracks in the floor and walls – the remains of many-legged beasties that spun webs in the dark.

'*House...home...take...me...home...take me...home...home take me...*'

Such a piteous cry! Such pain! Daisy longed to gather them in her arms, bones, tentacles and fur, and rush them out into the night and freedom.

'Eeeyah!' A cry ripped through the air, an eagle calling her chicks.

A tremor, alertness, passed through the shadows gathering in the hall.

'Eeeyah!' Swish, the angel began to whirl the net over his head.

Daisy ran. 'Excuse me, sorry, excuse me!' Hurdling left and right she ran out through the front door. A blast of icy air brought her to a skidding halt. Reason reasserted, she turned to go back but the door was shut.

'Please let me in!' she hammered on the door. 'Don't shut me out!'

'Out! Out! Out!' The cry echoed back. She tried to start the car but the battery was flat. The only place to go was the new golf club and that closed for the holiday. Cradling her belly, she struggled through the snow, were it not for Lucian's parka in a grain bin she'd have frozen to death.

All was dark at the golf club. Teeth chattering, she pounded on the door. An old man shone a torch through the door. 'What d'you want, Missy?'

'I need help. I've locked myself out.'

'Silly lass, out on a night like this in your condition. Come away in!' He locked the door behind her. 'Wasteful woman that she was my wife was always leavin' doors open.'

'May I use your phone?'

'Don't have a phone. Haven't had one for years.' She felt she'd been walking for miles, the flickering torch showing muddy wallpaper. Eventually he showed her into a back kitchen. 'Sit doon. I'll be back shortly.'

She sat before a miserable fire adjacent to another room that might've been a photograph from Minna's scrapbook, a gentleman's club circa 1910.

It was quiet, snow deadening sound. There were faded pictures on the wall, soldiers, familiar in a sepia-tinted way, and a Vettriano print of a couple waltzing with a baby in their arms. She was trying to make out their faces when the old man poked his head round the door. 'What d'you want, Missy?'

'Oh... er... I need help. I've locked myself out.'

'My wife was always doing that, leaving doors open.'

'I have to get to my friends! Please! I looked on my computer and saw...'

'Computer!' He snorted. 'My youngest was always fiddlin' wi' one of those! Useless things! A man should be outside walking not wasting his time messing wi' paints and crayons. But then what can you expect wi' a Frenchy teaching 'em bad ways. If you knew the struggles I've had...!'

He went on a rambling tirade aimed at his wife and how she'd ruined his life. Daisy couldn't bear it. Her heart was breaking. She needed help but this man could help no one. 'And you've no phone,' she cut across the words.

'No, but I'll walk ye hame and see if mebbe your lights are back.'

She wanted to say don't bother but couldn't stay there. 'Your wife is dead?'

'She is.'

'I'm sorry. And your children? Are they nearby?'

'They're dead.' There was pain in the faded blue eyes. 'My youngest died in a motor accident and my eldest killed in one of they wars out East.'

Daisy sought to comfort but he limped away. 'I'll get my coat.' Unable to sit she went through to another room where a man, even more ancient, huddled in an invalid chair. 'Excuse me,' she said. 'I didn't know you were here.'

He was blind and more concerned with a biscuit fallen on the floor. Daisy retrieved it, gave it a surreptitious wipe, and popped it back in his hand, whereupon he brought her hand to his mouth.

'*Non, grand-père! Ne mangez pas le main*!'

It was the French lady, the charity collector. 'Oh! It's you!'

The woman tucked a blanket about the old man's knees. 'Grandfather is frail,' she said. 'Any change to the routine and 'e becomes fractious.'

'Sorry to intrude,' said Daisy. 'I locked myself out.'

'Oh dear and in the snow too!'

'The other gentleman said he'd take me home.'

'*Ah, non, ma chere!* Like grand-père, 'e is unable to leave the 'ouse.'

'Then I don't what I'm going to do.'

'My younger son is with me. He will bring you home.'

'Oh, okay.' Daisy didn't understand but was beyond caring. There were footsteps and the sudden sweet scent of roses.

'*Voila*,' the woman turned her face alight. 'My son.'

'Your son?' Daisy stared. 'But this is..?

'Hello, Daisy,' said David Gilchrist. 'It's good to see you.'

* * *

'Do what you're trained to do,' said Charley. 'Use your expertise as a soldier.'

Charley's world is of superhuman beings. The Lord God is their arsenal! Tabby Gates inhabits a flesh and blood world. His team carry Glocks and machine guns. It takes skill and courage to fight a war. Skill can be acquired. Courage can be found, or feigned, but you can't feign fingers.

Lucian walks between both worlds and is help to neither. He hasn't the eyes of an angel or the senses, yet he can feel pain, the enemy's pain merged with his until he lost purpose, drifting through layers of consciousness, vaguely aware of a monitor bleeping and of concern in the faces of those about his bed.

A thought went through his mind, why hang on? Better to give the life that I do have for those that will truly mourn, people like Sarah Gates, Ginger's folks, and wee Jamie Wallace. No one will miss me, not even a green-eyed girl.

Charley said a near-death state is more potent than a dream.

Did he not also suggest Lucian was behind the gift of a Kevlar vest? If he can create armour for an angel he can do the same for Kevin. Here in No Man's land thought is VM, the visible material – it is the machine gun and the pistol. If he can harness thought, he might still be a soldier worthy of the name.

Thought is open to Darkness as well as the Light, hence a memory whispered in his ear and once again a sniper's bullet cracked through the air. He remembers dying and rising out of his body only to drop down into an English suburb and Daisy in the middle of the road – and a car coming.

'*Get up, Daisy!*' She doesn't hear him.

'*Get up, Daisy! For God's sake get out of...!*' He leaps in front but the car carries right on through him and she is left bleeding. The memory of that makes him lose heart – if he couldn't save Daisy, he couldn't save anyone.

Then he feels as if he is dying and some filthy thing sucking his breath.

'Ugh! Get off!' He drags it off and kicks it away, but the whisper remains, 'if you can't save the woman you love, what use are you?'

The creature is at his throat again, stronger than ever. After a bitter struggle he finally beats it off – that's how it works, sorrow thrives on sorrow.

He cried out, 'How can I stop from feeling? How can I defend myself?'

Then he heard it, a voice whispering in his ear, 'you remind me of Robocop,' and he laughed out loud. 'Daisy! You clever lass!'

Click clickety-click, armour fastened about him – miraculous armour – nothing like it in Her Madge's Scots Guards. Round and about him it wound, double-tracking his heart, and so, armoured from head to toe, a Sig in one hand and sword in the other, he laid back his head. '*Nemo me impune lacessit!*'

'Yes, my Lord!' Charley stood astride the Ridge arm raised in salute. Beside him hovered another angel, the US pilot, still airborne yet aboard a craft no living man will see – a hybrid cross between dragon and eagle, it beat the air with massive wings like a fabulous Phoenix rising out of the sun.

Man, thought Lucian, I'd love to ride one of those, and quick as flash a thought comes back, a conversation with an RAF pilot regarding Icarus wings: '*...easily fixed. As soon as this is over we'll give it a go.*'

* * *

The woman draped a scarf about Daisy's head. 'Keep this,' she said, 'for when a real bébé arrives.' Daisy forgave translation errors. You won't have long to wait, she thought, the baby is coming.

Emma's on her way. 'Oh,' she stopped and closed her eyes.

'What is it?' said David.

'I'm tired and in pain.'

'Lean on me.'

They were on their way back when time began to unravel. The new gates were first to go. One minute there, the next replaced by the old gates.

'The gates disappeared!'

'They're still here,' said David. 'We're walking through them.'

'I don't mean these gates; I mean the ones with cherubs on the top,'

'I didn't know they made gates like that.'

'That's not the point! They're not there now.'

David shrugged. 'Which is as well because they sound like junk.'

Then the house lost its glossy covering. Daisy heard a slicking noise and turned to see the paint roll off. The day before he left Lucian talked of men spraying the walls, 'they can pile on all the gloss they like,' he said, 'but they'll ne'er make it white.' As the paint retreated so did the new windows, blink, blink, they disappeared and rotten frames back in situ. 'I don't believe it!'

'What Daisy?'

'The windows are cracked.'

'Och, I know. Stone-throwing lads will always be among us.'

Within seconds, piece-by-piece and pane-by-pane the new orangery was coming down. Head down, she whispered. 'Don't look back, David.'

'Why?' he said. 'Will I be turned into a pillar of salt?'

'I don't know! I don't know anything. I used to call Six Chimneys my home as Lucian called Drummach his. They are nobody's home, no one alive. I don't know what's going on. I don't know what's happened to Lucian. And I don't know what's happening to me other than I'm going crazy.'

'Hold on, Daisy. It is the darkest night before the dawn.'

The house was in darkness. 'The lights are still out.'

'We can't have that.' He spoke and the lights came on, every window ablaze.

Pain hit her again. She crouched over her knees. 'I didn't expect this.'

'What did you expect?'

'I expected to be in hospital with people who know what they're doing.'

'I know what I'm doing.'

'You've delivered babies?'

'Sure. I've been present at so many births I've lost count.'

'I knew you were a medical officer but didn't know obstetrics your thing.'

'Obstetrics, paediatrics, gynaecology, hierology, biology!' He shrugged. 'You name it I've done it, all the ologies in this world and the next.'

Daisy glanced sideways. She was never sure of this chap. Lucian thinks he's great, but she's not sure. 'I didn't know that lady was your mother.'

'I am son to all mothers and mother to the world.' He started singing.

*'Other people's babies that's my life, mother to dozens
and nobody's wife. Other people's babies, cots and prams,
such little terrors, such little lambs.'*

Daisy couldn't sing and couldn't think why he would want to. At first seeing him was such a relief, as though the battle was over. Now she's not sure.

'David? Is it true? Is Lucian...?'

'Hush!' He took her hand.

'Only I read that he is...'

'Hush!' He put his hand over her mouth. 'Such words are like wounds, once said they may never heal.' Then he began to sing again, the words chilling. *'Low born clods of brute earth, they aspire to become gods, by a new birth, and an extra grace, and a score of merit, as if ought could stand in place of the high thought and the glance of fire of the Great Spirit!'*

'I know that, it's Edward Elgar's Dream of Gerontius,' she said. 'The Savoy Players used to sing it. It's music set to a poem about an old man who is dying, but before he can go to heaven must face his demons. Is that what is happening in Drummach Hall, demons and devils?'

'Such things do find comfort in dark corners.'

'In the poem the old man is carried to heaven by an angel,' said Daisy. 'It would be nice to think Lucian has an angel to keep him safe.'

'He does have such a being. You all do.'

The door swung open. 'I must phone Kate.' Daisy tried but the number came up as unrecognised. She tried the midwife with the same result.

David stood watching. 'Oughtn't you do something?' she said, irritated. 'You're a medic and for heaven's sake this is an emergency.'

He produced a phone. 'You want me to call for help?'

'I think it would be a good idea.'

He made the call. 'Hello officer, sorry to trouble you on a night like this, but there's a lady here who thinks she's having a baby. Uh-huh? Well, that's fine. Six Chimneys? It's along the... You know it? Excellent! Thank you officer. '

He flicked the phone. 'They said to tell you it's Hogmanay, everybody in Scotland losing their mind. If they don't come you're to start without them.'

Daisy was about to scream when all the furniture in the sitting room vanished. Then the new butcher's block in the kitchen and the American fridge were replaced by a beaten up Aga and rust-bucket storage heater.

'No,' she said. 'It's not happening.'

David nodded. 'I think it is.'

Then, a scene from Disney's Sorcerer's Apprentice, new rugs rolled themselves into neat bundles and sat outside the door. It was when the lift was taken out, and new light fittings, and she in darkness that Daisy dared to ask.

'Where are the dogs and the cats?

'Safe.'

'And the animals in the barn?'

'Also safe.'

'Safe? ' she said, fearfully. 'And where is that?' Her mobile buzzed. She picked it up, and lo and behold, Ed and a text that said, '*in hun-buns head.*'

* * *

When it comes to the Battle for the Gate words are obsolete. Lucian can describe a onetime idea of an angel, you know, the white-winged individual found in a child's prayer book, but that's not what fought on the Ridge – one moment sounding as the sweetest music the next the howling of wolves.

Hard to tell what in the height of battle stormed out of the sun on multiple wings, diving into all that agony to gather the same to their breast. One thing was sure, while their weapons may be of love and humility, those angels fought like bad-asses, kicking and gouging and rolling in dust.

Daisy, he thought, if you were here you'd be amazed, yet he was glad she wasn't, the cries of grief rising from the chaos would have made her heart burst. Are they devils? Are they the enemy? Sometimes he saw the creatures writhing in mud as nothing more or less than angels fallen along the way.

But a soldier ought not to question the face of the enemy. Safer to stay with stuff he can appreciate, such as the weapons the angels used, some like heavy-duty fisherman's nets that, acting as force-fields, snatched those that wanted to be saved while repelling those that didn't. And what were those that were saved? He thought the haul might be likened to fish and flesh, yet fish that wept as a baby weeps and flesh that burned like acid.

Not that it matters! His task is to search and destroy the weapon that is to kill his friends. He might not know them as friends, might not have laughed with Tabby or felt Ginger's lips on his cheek, yet they are human and in harm's way.

Now, brush in hand, Kevin kneels in the dust painstakingly removing dirt from the IED. There are footprints around the area which means the locals know it's here but didn't give a wide berth. It might be a dud, then again might not.

Mentally, he asked Kevin, what are you going to do?

'*I'm gonna get the sod.*' A couple of careful strokes of the brush and Kevin is laughing and cussing at the same time. The canister is a dud. Kevin dances away but Lucian stays watchful, his inner radar pinging. What was it Charley said, 'words hang in time forever.' If that's so, then Lucian should be able to find the enemy. 'Who are you?' He sends out a thought. 'What did you do with the real stuff and where did you put it?' Straight way he saw hands connecting wires, and heard bitter amusement, '*shit to shit.*'

Jesu! He saw the same hand shake another's hand. Out of that handclasp a silo of death grew – 105 mm shells stuffed with plastic explosive. Lucian knew then the decoy is meant to keep the team happy: '*okay, kiddies, you found this but don't look too closely on your way back because I'm waiting.*'

'Charley!' Hope rising, he shouted. 'I know what it is!'

Even as he shouted he knew he was on his own. It's what Charley meant when he said, 'You started it. You must end it.'

Real

'In hun-buns head! In hun-buns head! In hun-buns head!'

The text became a shout ricocheting back and forth throughout the house. Daisy covered her ears. Gradually the shouting died away. It was no use looking to David Gilchrist for answer. Impassive, he stood in the doorway, yet a conversation of sorts developed between him and Daisy. 'Ed D'angelo! I used to like that old man but now...?'

Ed D'angelo didn't make the furniture disappear. Neither did he strip the light fittings from the ceilings.

'Foolish old man! I'll ring the hospital. Tell them he must be stopped.'

By all means, yet ask yourself, did a foolish man cause the paint on Drummach walls to disappear? Or dismantle the orangery where you and Lucian used to share a glass of wine?

'We never did that. Lucian sold his parent's home to buy Six Chimneys.'

Was that before or after you went to Drummach and found mail behind the door and Lucian's clothes mildewed.

'Lucian's clothes mildewed? Mail piled up behind the door?'

That would be about the time Kate and her kids lived here and you thought yourself Mother Teresa, healing the sick and raising rabbits from the dead.

'Don't be silly.' Daisy laughed. 'I would never think that.'

Is it silly? Then what about all the names in your head, and the people, names and faces of people you don't know, like a tacky relationship with a man called Roberts, and friendship with a lady who went on a charabanc to heaven.

'I don't know any of that. In fact, I don't think I know anything.'

Well, that's a start.

It's true! Daisy's begun to wonder if Six Chimneys is not a house at all but a book written by a woman called Minna Gray, who, part-magician and part-devil used to live here. 'I thought I lived in Surrey with my mum and dad.'

You did live in Surrey.

'...but then I bought the house in Richmond and we lived there, me and Oscar. God! Whatever happened to Oscar? I heard he was working in a bar in Dublin and shacked up with a student from the music school? Yes, because that's when I decided to move up here to be with...with ...'

She paused to stare at a man who stood in the kitchen. 'Are you Lucian?'

The man shook his head.

'Then who is Lucian? And where is he? I mean, as the father of my baby he ought to be here, oughtn't he?'

Still the man stared.

'You'd think he'd be here, wouldn't you? After all, I am pregnant...aren't I?'

'Are you?'

'I'm dreaming, aren't I?'

'Not so much dreaming, Daisy, as imagining.'

'Imagining? You mean none of this is real?'

'Not as real as you want it to be."

'Oh!' Slowly the pregnancy ceased to be, an ache in Daisy's belly replaced by the ache in her heart. So painful, a hole gouged in her breast could not have hurt more. Imaginary child and imaginary lover, she wept for both and knew that somewhere her tears were felt by another.

* * *

The angel made her a cup of tea and mopped her tears.

'Are you a real angel?'

'Never mind me! It's you that's open to question.'

'I did think so but then I thought if I'm dreaming I'll eventually wake up and so what's the point of worrying.'

'What makes you think you'll wake?'

Tea bitter in her mouth, she poured it down the sink. 'What do you mean?'

The angel grabbed her hand. 'Come with me. I'll show you what Daisy saw the first time I brought her to this place.' Then she's on the back of a motor bike, her arms about his waist and mouthful of strawberry tasting feathers. They flew forever yet ended again outside Chimneys.

Daisy gazed through the window and saw men and women sipping tea.

'What are they doing?'

'Waiting to go home.'

'They don't look unhappy.'

'They're going home. Why would they be unhappy? This is a Halfway House. Many here pass on through the Gate. Others get well and go home.'

'Why when I look through these windows do I see sadness?'

'You see yourself.' The angel flicked his hand and Daisy was looking at another Daisy, and another, and another...! 'Oh!' she gasped. 'They're everywhere!'

They were everywhere, multiples of Daisies: Daisy mending socks, a Daisy reading a book and a Daisy polishing a bookcase. It was the same outside, Daisies digging the garden and walking dogs. Some Daisies had a task and sang and were happy, others wandered aimlessly.

'They don't see one another! And the men and women, they don't see them either. 'Oh look!' As she watched another Daisy appeared, carrying a cat-transporter. 'There's another one!'

'Pesky little creature! We need a Pied Piper and a tin whistle.'

'You see them as vermin?'

'I see them and my soul aches for whatever you are, you are suffering.'

'Why do you keep saying 'you'? I'm not one of those things.'

'You are exactly one of those things. You are a dolly, a plaything.'

Daisy slapped her hands over her ears. 'Stop saying that!'

'Sorry, but you are an approximation, a thought-form.'

'I'm not! I'm the real Daisy!'

'You're Lucian's idea of Daisy. You are a dream.'

'No, I, I, I..!'

'Hush.' Charley reached out and all was silent, a doll sitting in a doll's chair.

* * *

Time passed, and slowly and benevolently, the Daisy-doll was removed.

Charley squatted on the floor by the cupboard under the stairs. 'It's okay, Daisy. You can come out now.'

The real Daisy isn't in there. She is where she has been this last year, in a coma. The cupboard under the stairs is a bolt-hole, a vantage point from which she can observe the dream, pitying, enquiring – but not enquiring too deeply.

Charley has infinite patience. Nowhere, and everywhere, he sits in a hospital room and holds a pale and wasted hand – no one sees him but he's there.

The patient is still, no sound other than that of a machine pumping air into her lungs, no movement other than the flicker of eyes under eyelids. Charley is also next door in Room 12. There's no sound or movement there other than of a machine. In Six Chimneys he squats outside a cupboard, takes a book out of the air, a photograph album, and shoves one photo halfway under the door.

For a while there's silence and then pale fingers inch it under the door.

Daisy is looking at men and women in uniform, some old-fashioned cloth and cut, others modern gear. They all stand about a smiling woman. 'That's me.'

'No kidding!'

'What am I doing in these photographs?'

'You're looking at a possible life.'

'Doing what?'

'Keeping the Light.'

'You mean like Minna.'

'Yes, but with your own individual touch. So what do you think?'

'About what?'

'Daisy, you do know you're not here. That your body is elsewhere and that I commune with your dreaming spirit.'

'God, I hope so,' she muttered. 'I wouldn't want this to be real. It's too painful. How could you talk that way to that poor creature?'

'If you think it was hurt in the way you'd be hurt then that's down to you. These creatures are substitute selves. All feeling comes from you.'

'You said they were Lucian's idea of me.'

'So they were initially. He gave them direction according to his imagination. He could do no other. He doesn't know you. The dolls were how he *thought* you'd be. How he *hoped* you'd be, loving, kind, sweet and...'

'....and blisteringly hot in bed.'

'Oh definitely that – sexy as all get out.'

'And a sweetly submissive Stepford Wife?'

'When were you ever submissive?'

'I suppose some of it is me.'

'It's all you. Yours are the fingers that hold poor Robocop in thrall.'

'Minna said that.'

'Minna knows what she's talking about. She was like you at first, Scheherazade, the princess who stays alive by telling her prince a thousand and one lies.'

'Did she make a million Minnas?'

'She had a couple of false starts.'

'Will I have to die to become that person in the photographs?'

'Minna didn't die when she came to keep the Light. The giving up an earthly life is not a requirement. It's the commitment; the soul will do the rest.'

'How is Lucian?'

'Weaker by the second.'

'Really? Oh God!' In room 11 the monitor above the bed showed a sudden rapid increase in heart rate. A nurse in Room 11 buzzes for help.

'Calm down, Daisy! Now is not the time to die!

'Don't tell me to calm down! I don't want him to die.'

'Come out of the cupboard, Daisy, and talk to me properly. I can't hold a conversation with a wooden door.'

'No! I'm staying put! That way no harm comes to anyone.'

'No harm!' Charley grabbed the door and pulled it off its hinges. 'Out!' He reached in, took hold of her wrist and pulled. 'I've had enough of this.'

Eyes big and round, she crept out of the cupboard – ergo out-of-her-body.

'What happened to the house?'

'There is no house. There's a ruined dream and a man choosing to die to save men he doesn't know for a woman who says she doesn't care.'

'I do care! I care very much!'

'Then do something about it!'

'Like what! Tell me and I'll do it.'

Charley rolled his eyes. 'Do you believe this, Lord? She's asking me what to do when for the last imaginary year she's been telling herself and Lucian exactly what to do. Puck is right, "what fools these mortals be!" '

Daisy opened her mouth and every phone in the Borders began to ring.

Charley proffered a phone; Ed D'angelo in perfect Queen's English. 'Daisy! For God's sake, and mine, and Lucian's, and every other soul stuck in this never-ending dream, go back to the bloody start!'

Click!

'Oh,' she said closing up the phone. 'I see.'

'Right then,' said Charley. 'When was the last time you looked at your body?'

'I never look at my body. Why would I want to do that?'

'Because until you do you won't accept the truth.'

Daisy looked. Poor thing, bones broken and reset, jaw rewired and pelvis realigned, no matter what the surgeons do they can't restore life to one who prefers to dream. The machine keeps the motor ticking but it's as the doctors say, even if she recovers consciousness it will be to a vegetative state.

'I am in a mess, aren't I, Charley.' She was alone. Charley had left her to understand, and she did understand, and could feel the old man down the corridor urging her on, 'Yes, honey-bun, back to the start.'

With that thought she was running down a tunnel and into Dunstable Road.

She's on her hands and knees in the road. A car is coming. She wants to run but Boffin's in the road. She stoops to pick him up and from out of nowhere a man pushes her clear of the car and is himself dashed to the ground.

Phut! The image disappeared.

'That didn't happen.'

'Yes it did!' Charley is again beside her.

'Not to me. If it had I wouldn't be the mangled mess on life-support.'

'In Lucian's mind he saved your life many times.'

'But if that's a surrogate Daisy, can't I have that life where Lucian saves me?'

'That dream died. He thought if he couldn't save you he couldn't save anyone.'

Daisy was overwhelmed. 'He must have really loved me.'

'He did and does. Do you think you could love in so generous a manner?' Thoughts grew in her mind: my body is a mess, why would I want to begin again? Surely it would be better if Lucian had a new start. After all he deserves it. The thought became the need and the need a desire. 'I'm ready.'

'To do what?'

'To go back to the beginning, only Lucian's beginning, not mine.'

'And how do you propose to do that?'

'I'm not telling you. It's a crazy idea and you'll laugh.'

'Tell me and I'll decide how crazy.'

'Can I whisper?' Charley leaned down. She whispered in his ear. He frowned. 'Difficult.' Her face fell. 'But not impossible. If you're going to do it, and it will be difficult, you'll have to want it very badly.'

'More than life?'

'Much more.'

'I'll do it, and not because I don't rate my life but because I rate his.'

'That is a good answer.'

Having made the choice she blocked her mind to all else and thought on her City days when she'd employ her favourite ammunition, 4-inch Jimmy Choos, an uplift bra, and a Donna Karan suit. Spiffed up is the only way to die. If you've got it, flaunt it, Isla always says, and in this weightless, whirling world she can be whoever she wants to be, Supermodel, or Queen of Sheba.

Daisy settled for herself and *Rouge Absolut* Lippy. Mentally she looked in a mirror, and disregarding the broken doll, the rewired jaw and thinning hair, she re-established the old Daisy, formally known as Lucky.

It wasn't easy. Fear crept in, her hand wobbled and the lipstick smudged regretting home and Richmond, and her own bed and stuff in the closets, things gathered together over time, things she loved. Mum and Dad! Never going to see them again! Never going to hold them again!

A tear trickled down her cheek. Warm fingers reached out of the darkness and wiped it away. A voice spoke in her ear. 'Don't cry, little Daisy.' A package was placed in her pocket. 'This is a token of My love. You'll find it useful.'

'Thank you, sir.' Daisy curtseyed to the darkness, and then, dressed to kill – or be killed – she emerged for the last time from the cupboard under the stairs.

'You look very nice,' said Charley.

'That the best you can do?'

'You look as you always look, beautiful.

She climbed the stairs and stood under the window. All is quiet, none of the maelstrom. Nervous, she giggled. 'Quiet as the Grave.'

'No time for jokes,' hissed Charley. 'No time for anything but the Lord God.'

'It's okay.' She patted her pocket. 'He told me what to do.'

'The Lord spoke to you? I didn't hear a peal of thunder.'

'It didn't come on a peal of thunder. It came in a sealed package.'

'What?'

'I'll whisper again if you like.' She whispered.

Charley huddled up. 'Wow! That's pretty sneaky, isn't it?'

'I don't know. Can the Lord God be sneaky?' She applied fresh lipstick and then she shook out her hair. 'I'm ready.'

Charley watched her climb the stairs. 'The one you must convince is Lucian. In his mind he's already given up his life. He'll not want you to take it back. Be strong and pray it will succeed. If it does more than one life is saved.'

She nodded.

'You sure about this?'

'I'm sure.'

'Then say the word. You know the one.'

'Amen.'

* * *

Lucian went crazy for a while after locating the shells. 'Kevin!' He tried banging on the guy's head but his fists thumped the air. 'Don't switch off!' he yelled. 'Fuck's sake stay focussed! It's not over!' As far as the team are concerned it is over, a Chinook en route to collect them. Pretty soon they'd be whooping it up, all of them thinking to have a beer and to live, laugh, and be happy.

'No! I cann'ae have it! Cann'ae let them down!'

A thought lifted up, the guy who did this has a cause for which he was willing to die, visible material like that must leave a trail. A ferret sniffing out a rat his spirit rushed ahead and found a silken thread – albeit a twisted thread – leading to a dry wadi. Under pressure, his body on life-support begins to fade.

Lucian knelt in the dust; as Charley said, friends don't drop in unannounced. They need to be invited. 'Lord, there's enough C4 in that wadi to kill an army. I want to help but I don't wanna hurt anyone else. What can I do?'

Then the Lord spoke in his ear, 'Love is the spit and shit that binds everything together. I'll send you help. Look out for him.'

Sighing, Lucian got to his feet. The team appeared out of flame coloured smoke as gladiators, helmets and Kevlar vests gilded by the setting sun.

Exhausted, their minds were open to him, Lucian didn't need to be a telepath to know what they were thinking – shower, drink and then sleep.

The battle is over but the war continues, but it's okay, God said He would deal with it. Lucian watched and wondered how it would happen, would squads of tanks and planes career over the skyline? Then he thought, fool, God doesn't need that, a flick of His finger and the sun, moon and stars will perish.

The team are coming closer, the escort, human and divine, are shoulder-to-shoulder. 'Any time now, Lord,' urged Lucian, 'or they're past the point of no return.' There's the flick-flack of rotors, the Chinook arriving to pick them up.

Lucian's guts are in a knot, his heart beating so fast it leaps in his chest.

'This is C4 packed inside 105mm shells, Lord,' he whispered. 'The blast from that will flatten everything in sight, team, escort, angels *and* Chinook.'

Black clouds gathered, and then, like a dimmer switch applied, the sun dropped below the horizon, and it began to rain, drops bouncing off the ground like machine gun fire.

Tall and still and silent the angels remain apart, their heads turned away as though unwilling to witness the destruction of so much fragile human flesh.

'Oh Jesus!' thought Lucian. 'He's not coming. They're going to die!'

Then a cart appeared over the Ridge. Intent on the idea of Celestial Cavalry heading up the pass Lucian almost missed it. It trundled along the ridge, a lad and his dog inside, the lad prodding a bullock with his stick.

'Oh shit!' thought Lucian. 'It's a suicide rig.'

'Tabby!' He began to run and shout. 'Tabby, for Chrissakes fire on sight!'

But Tabby couldn't hear and kept on walking, the team ambling behind and none of them assuming offensive positions.

What's the matter with them? Can't they see what I can see?

Then it hit him. Idiot! That old bullock cart is the Messenger.

They're saved! Panting, exhausted, he crouched on the ground.

I should have known. It's as Charley said, their weapons are love and humility. Who would He send but an honest boy and his dog?

You see, he'll get out the cart, flick his fingers and the C4 will go phut!

Still the cart kept coming. Lucian didn't care – for the first time in his life his mind is empty of anxiety, no one and nothing to worry about.

'Oh, thank You, Lord. I am so grateful.'

They say that when a man is close to death his past flashes before him. Lucian saw nothing. It's all been done and said. If he had a thought it was to never walk this path again and if he had a prayer it was for Daisy.

The bullock stopped a couple of yards from the target.

God's disguise – a kid and his dog clambered down. From the back the kid looked familiar. Seventeen or thereabouts, slight in build and gawky, he made Lucian think of Sean, Kate's bairn.

Still, the angels stood with faces turned away. Maybe I should do that, thought Lucian. You're not supposed to look on God. Maybe I should be on my knees. Or maybe I should help that kid; Messenger or not he's only a lad.

With that thought the Messenger turned and smiled, and Lucian was undone. 'No', he whispered. 'Not my brother. Not Ian.' It was him, Ian, his face alight with love. And the dog, for Chrissakes, the dog was Biddy!

'No, no, no!'

Biddy wagged her tail. Ian smiled. 'Hiya bro! Good to see you.'

Bent double, Lucian couldn't speak, and couldn't breathe, tears mingling with the rain to soak his face. Heart breaking, he begged, 'don't do this Lord. Not to my brother. He's already been through hell. Don't send him there again.'

The Lord had His intention. Ian and Lucian and the dog were always His Own. Ian stood smiling at Lucian. Then he waved and he and Biddy turned toward the wadi. 'See you later alligator,' the words floating back.

Love and fear giving wings to his feet Lucian began to run. He ran and leapt into the wadi. If his brother had agreed to this, to give his life again, then he's not doing it alone. Lucian grabbed him and held him close, warm flesh and blood in his arms. He hugged him to his heart and with one last thought let go of the rest. 'I love you green-eyed girl, but it's okay, don't wait up for me.'

* * *

Daisy felt it happen, saw a sheet of flame, knew that life-support in Room 12 had been disconnected and felt love trip the Gates of Heaven.

Closing her eyes, she leapt into the Light. Immediately, she was snatched into stronger arms, borne on stronger wings. 'What are you doing, honey-bunny?'

She could see him – knew his wonderful face and blue eyes. She knew the arms that carried her and the voice that spoke to her. 'No!' She fought to close her mind to him. 'Go away. You are a stranger to me.'

'Daisy, love, come gi' me a wee coory.'

'I don't know you. I don't cuddle strangers. Go away and leave me alone.'

'Daisy, honey-bunny, sweetheart, go back and live.'

'I don't want to! Not without you.'

Summoning every ounce of will-power she thrust him away. 'You're a nuisance, a stalker! It's your fault this happened! You've caused so much trouble and given pain to so many. It's got to stop. Can't you get it into your head you're nothing to me.

You're an illusion. Go away and stay away!'

Sighing, he released her, and fell into darkness, falling further and further away, a bright star in the night dimming and going out.

Sobbing, she kicked toward the past. She knew where she had to be, the port-hole, the door into hope, but like the doorway to Six Chimneys the harder she flew the more she beat the air, the further the doorway retreated.

I'm not going to make it! Not going to get there!

The porthole was closing.

'Help me someone! Don't let me fail!'

The prayer flashed through the darkness. A figure stood on the other side of the portal. Minna smiled and unwound her belt. 'Took your time, didn't you, Daisy, girl. I thought you'd never get here.'

Swish, she threw the belt out. It slid about Daisy's waist and pulled her through the door and into bright sunlight. 'Don't speak!' said Minna. 'Hold to the intention. Look to Lucian and hold the love.'

It's New Year's Eve and Captain Nairne, IED Task Force, is turning away from a sniper's bullet. Defenceless, helmet on the ground, he is caught mid stride.

The bullet moves so slowly Daisy might have plucked it from the air.

Oh look at him, so dear and so beloved. He's tired. I see it in his eyes. That's all right, my love. You'll soon feel so much better.

The package, the gift from God, was in her hand.

The bullet advanced, the target, Lucian's head, no more than a sigh away.

A voice whispered in Daisy's ear, an old man in the side-ward: 'greater love hath no honey-bun than she lay down a favourite necklace for her beloved.'

Daisy threw the diamond necklace up in the air.

The cross flashed in the light.

The flash caught Lucian's eyes.

He swerved to look. The bullet passed him. And hit Daisy. And in a hospital somewhere doctors pulled another plug.

CHAPTER THIRTY-SIX

Unintentional Hero

'Boy, did we ever choose the wrong time to come.'

Daisy sighed. 'What's wrong now, Mum?'

'What's wrong? Try this lot coming down the lane bagpipes wailing and drums banging! I told you the place is jinxed. We should've stayed at home.'

It seems they chose the wrong time to come. First there were road-works on the M3 and then the hotel overbooked and spending the night in a pub. Today's not much better, the house agent failing to show which means they can't get inside. Now a funeral is about to take place – Oh, and it's raining.

Six Chimneys is not meant for Daisy. The warning signs were there from the start. She fell in love with the house last year when she came with Oscar to Jenny Millar's wedding. Oscar hated it. 'Why would anyone want to live out here in the sticks with nothing but a haggis to keep you warm nights?'

Anyway, along with her job at the bank, he's gone. It wasn't the thought of living in Scotland that made him run; it was Daisy getting knocked down by a boozy Santa Claus and him thinking he might have to wheel a cripple about.

Poor guy, Mum nearly killed him. 'Get out of my sight, you piece of crap! If you'd kept your dick inside your strides she would've had a happy New Year along with normal people instead of nearly getting killed.'

Yes, a boozy Santa in a TVR2, and, Daisy having thrown a

wobbler, on her hands and knees in the road picking up vinyl! Still, that's all over now. She may have one leg shorter than the other now but at least she's alive.

'No good us all hanging about here,' said Isla. 'Me and your pa will go fill up the car. You and Sean might as well try getting a cup of tea.'

They went to a cafe across from the pub. Sean is Daisy's adopted brother. Mum miscarried in '99, a boy, so the midwife said. That same year Dad did a charity stint at a women's hostel, processing claims pro bono. Sean was the skinny myopic kid who leant against Dad's knee every day, never speaking, just leaning, dumped at the hostel, someone said, by a crack-head.

It broke Dad's heart to leave him there every evening, until one day, along with a three-legged kitten, he brought him home. Now he's a Banks, adored by all, but a true Scot, determined to hold on to his accent.

'Pity we couldn'ae get in the hoos, Daisy,' Sean yawned. 'It would make a great animal sanctuary. There'll be deer in that brae, if some sod hasn'ae already shot 'em.' Sean and animals! He and his buddy, Jason, are always in trouble over animal rights. Jason's a true zealot. One eye, and a badly scarred face from being mauled by a lion, he recently mortgaged his house to fund a trip to the Bay and along with other fanatics ram a whaling ship.

Daisy likes him as does Dad. 'Give the chap a break,' he tells Isla. 'He's like the rest of us, trying to atone for former sins.' Isla can't abide him, she worries he'll get Sean into real trouble. It's why Sean's here on the trip out of harm's way. Daisy used to worry but after last night, and the lovely Jasmine met at the pub, she's less so. Sean hasn't stopped talking about the girl. He's on the phone now fixing to meet with her and her brother, Leon, on R&R from the navy. Animal sanctuary sure, yet Jasmine's the real reason Sean would live here.

Actually, an animal sanctuary is not a bad idea. It's not as if Daisy's anything else to do. Well, there is one thing, but that's proving to be a lost cause.

'HAS ANYONE SEEN THIS MAN?'

That's what she'd like to do, hang a poster on every lamppost in the world. Not that she's details other than he was gorgeous. It happened so quickly she'd no time for anything but gratitude. They'd had the usual row, Oscar generally behaving like an arse. They fought, and she, foolishly, tossed his precious vinyl recordings out on the road, and then, even more foolishly, tried retrieving the vinyl – and Boffin, her cat – and a car heading toward her, pedal to the metal.

She should be dead! But no, there was a squeal of brakes and a guy charging out of the night to scoop them both up, Daisy and Boffin! What a way to meet the man of your dreams crawling about in your SpongeBob Square Pants pjs! The fall broke her leg. The street was buzzing, neighbours staring and the driver in the Santa suit trembling. 'I'm so sorry,' he'd said. 'I didn't see you.'

By the time the ambulance arrived Daisy was near fainting. She had wanted to thank her saviour but he hadn't hung around, all she had of him was a jacket he'd wrapped around her. She still has it. She wouldn't go anywhere without it just in case, Cinderella-like, she finds her Prince.

* * *

Back at the house crowds gather to watch the funeral. Mum hates funerals. 'We might as well go back to the pub for lunch. If the rest of that food is anything like last night's treacle pud the landlady's got my order.'

'I'll stay for the house agent.'

'But it's raining.'

'That's okay.'

'Put this on!' Mum tossed the jacket. 'Give us a buzz when you've had enough.' The car edged away through the crowd, Sean grinning and making obscene gestures through the rear window. Daisy took a turn round the garden. Last time the lawns were trimmed. Now the wisteria's running wild and the meadow gone to seed – and what's worse, Robocop is gone!

Disappointed, she turned away and collided with another. 'Sorry.

'Not at all!' An airman in RAF blues smiled. 'Are you okay?'

'I'm fine, thanks.'

'Were you waiting to get into the house?'

'I was but not anymore.' She fumbled with the phone trying to call her parents back to collect her but couldn't raise the number.

'The reception here is tricky,' said the airman.

'Perhaps if I go round to the front reception will be better.'

'Possibly but then you'll get caught up in all that nonsense.'

'Is it nonsense? I thought it was a funeral and rather a grand one at that.'

'Grand?' he grinned. 'I don't think so. The man in question wasn't especially well known. He was a very reluctant kind of hero.'

Daisy didn't care for that, thought him disrespectful, and

didn't care for him with his snappy uniform and throwaway elegance. 'A reluctant hero?'

'Yes, really quite unintentional.'

'The more reason to respect his passing. Too many people nowadays want to tweet their exploits to the world. Give me a quiet hero any day.'

Suddenly weary, she thought of her own hero and of the way he sat beside her in snow. Robocop, that's how she's come to think of him. It's like this house, the stained glass window was the best thing about it. What did Oscar say when he saw it, 'a good price on e-bay?' Someone had the same idea.

'Shame!' The airman was clearly thinking along the same lines. 'Fifteenth century, I believe. They took it down when the current custodian died.'

'Ah!' Daisy understood that. 'People and their belongings do connect.'

The Airman put up his collar. 'The window gone and the custodian to be buried here in this relentless rain, it is sad day for the house.'

'I suppose.' Daisy was drawn into the conversation. 'Yet even with the rain it's a good place to lie – certainly better than the council tip we call a cemetery.'

'And he's not alone, someone else sleeps here.'

'There's another grave?'

The Airman sighed. 'Yes, a tomb for a ravishing doll of a woman.'

'I'm sorry. You obviously knew her.'

'I don't know about knew. A total enigma, I'm not sure anybody really knew her yet I think I may claim to know her as well as anyone.'

'And love her.'

'Oh yes,' he said softly. 'Love her beyond life and death.' Then he straightened. 'If you want to take a look inside I have a key. And there is a new window! It's really quite charming, almost, if not more enchanting than the last.'

'Why not?' Daisy nodded. 'It's a long drive back to Surrey and I won't be coming this way again.' They didn't need a key; the door to the conservatory was open. 'I never thought to try that,' she said. 'Marching in uninvited seemed a bit of a cheek.'

'I'm certain you were invited. However, if you mislaid the card?' Doffing his cap, he offered his arm, 'I invite you. Mind the step and of course the cats.'

A pair of mosaics, exquisite in detail, the cats were set in the stone floor. 'Birds being my thing I've never really had time for cats,' he said, 'but I could make an exception for these. See their names carved into the stone? Caelum-Chi-Thai, Prince of Samarkand, and Prince Meow-Chi-Ming of Doi Angka. Doi Angka is a mountain in Siam so I'm thinking they are Siamese.'

Daisy laughed. 'But of course! Look at their blue eyes!'

'A canary, terrapin and a horse, I believe there are more.'

'So many animals!' Walking about the hall Daisy was amazed. 'And so much furniture! I had assumed it would be empty.'

'Six Chimneys is never empty even when it is.'

'It's beautifully furnished.' She looked at the red and gold rugs on wooden floor and tapestry wall hangings. 'Did the custodian die here?'

'His body was elsewhere yet his heart was here.'

'One can see the house was loved. It's beautiful, and fragile, and yet at the same time strong.'

'And so, if I may say, are you.'

'Thank you.' She hobbled along the hall and into what looked like a small sitting room. 'How sad,' she said, 'the remains of a Christmas tree.'

'More like a lavatory brush!' The Airman opened a window and threw it out. Daisy disliked him again. The tree may be ugly but had meaning to the owner or wouldn't be there. 'As I said, people and their belongings connect.'

'You think the custodian connected to that?'

'I don't know. I'm not the custodian.' She didn't add and neither are you but he followed her train of thought and fetched the wretched tree back, dusted it with his sleeve and set in the windowsill where it continued to be ugly.

'There you are,' he said. 'Now you are custodian.'

Daisy laughed and so did he.

'The things we do.'

'Yes,' she said, laughter dying, 'and the things we don't.'

'You should sit.' He helped her into a chair. 'Colourful cast. Terrific bit of graffiti. I like the dragon.'

'That's Janet, a nurse in physio. It's coming off next week. I can't wait.'

'I'm sure. So, what haven't you done?'

'Oh, a thousand things.' She looked at his pristine uniform and the medal ribbons. 'I haven't flown a plane.'

'Now that is a loss. To miss out on flying is a real shame. I'd offer to take you for a spin myself but am somewhat hors de combat nowadays.'

Daisy wasn't listening. It was the Christmas tree! Awful thing!

She got up and snatching it from the windowsill threw it out. 'You were right. It is ugly.'

'Hah!' He laughed. 'I wondered how long. The new custodian has good taste.'

Daisy attempted a wobbly curtsy. 'A girl's got to do what a girl's got to do.'

'I feel that way about flying. Recently, I took some chaps for a spin across the Pond. I enjoyed it but one chap said he'd sooner drive a tank through the air.'

'He didn't like it.'

'He liked flying but not in a plane.'

'How else can you fly?'

'That's what I said but then he took me for a trip aboard his craft. We flew across the Alps into the setting sun. Now I'm done with metal wings.'

'I see.' Daisy's attention was diverted by the noise outside. The cortege was passing. Pipes wailing and drumsticks twirling, it was a spectacle. Then out of the rain a lone bugler played. Tears rushed to Daisy's eyes.

'You weep for a stranger.'

'He was a human being.'

'A man, a breath of wind and a little life. Dreams are made of such things.'

The bugle ceased. There was a moment of quiet, no sound, the house, and the world for that matter, in respectful silence. Then, click, the world moved on.

'What happened to your leg?'

'I was knocked down by a car, or rather saved from being knocked down.'

'Greater love hath no man than he lay down his life for the woman he loves.'

'It would be if he had loved me, as it was he didn't know me.'

'A greater sacrifice then wouldn't you say?'

'I would. I'd give anything in the world to meet him again but I don't know his name. He gave me my life and I didn't even say thank you.'

'I doubt gratitude was his purpose. Life and love are gifts freely given. The trick is to have an open heart, that way we recognize the giver as well as the gift. Talking of gifts!' He straightened his tie. 'I need to be on my way.'

'You're not here for the funeral? I thought you one of the mourners.'

'Not me. I've done my share of weeping.'

'Was he a nice man? I mean, the deceased, was he happy?'

'Happy is not a word that springs to mind. Dedicated and loyal, yes, a stubborn son-of-a-bitch, proud to the point of overbearing, all of those things.'

'But not happy.'

'He's happy now that he's free. Like you he was involved in a dispute with a machine. A fighter-pilot in WW2 he got into a scrap with a Messerschmitt. The plane caught fire but he couldn't bail out, the canopy wouldn't open.'

'Was he dreadfully injured?'

'Burns to the hands and face, yet he survived.'

'What other choice is there?' Daisy got to her feet. 'Thank you for talking to me. I was feeling rather down. You've made the trip worthwhile.'

'I'm glad you feel that way, Daisy.'

'You know my name.'

'I heard you were coming and though I can't quite say in the flesh, I wanted to make your acquaintance. The name's Charles. Charles Edwin D'angelo.'

'How do you do?'

'I'm very well now, thanks to you, Daisy.'

'Me?' She smiled. 'I don't see how. '

'I don't suppose you do. Daisy, would you do me a small favour? Would you find and leave a posy of flowers on the tomb I mentioned? People being sentimental there'll be plenty on the new grave, but they'll forget to honour Minna and I wouldn't want that.'

'Of course.'

'I must be off or I'll miss the bus.'

'You're taking a bus in this weather? I'm sure if you're not going anywhere too far my dad would be happy to give you a lift.'

He put on his cap. 'Honey-bun, where I am going you and your family need not follow, at least not yet awhile. But thanks for the offer.'

At the gate he turned. 'You know the Wing Co was hurt in that scrap but not as he might've been. Some careless mechanic had left a hammer where it was most needed. Ed lived a good life and a long life and was grateful, and bearing the debt in mind, offered the mechanic a gift.'

* * *

Inside the rooms smelled of drying herbs and wax polish. A woman lived here cherishing every floorboard and sparkling window pane, Daisy seeming to know that pretty clothes are somewhere in a bedroom closet, as military uniforms in dust proof bags hang in a gentleman's dressing room.

She shuddered. The Airman was right when he said Six Chimneys is never empty. Everyone who's ever slept in this house is here, and as lovely as it is agents will have a problem selling. Women will walk in and straightway say, 'no thanks. I'm not living another woman's dream.'

Sighing, she made her way to the main staircase and there she saw it, the new window, and turning, she made for the door.

Oh, but God is clever and so very sneaky. When He wants to shock mortals awake He schleps on a Director's cap: 'Lights, Action, Roll 'em!' and turning on the sun reveals the commonplace as glorious.

Robocop has been replaced with art worthy of the Louvre. Michelangelo would've applauded the artist. Michelangelo is probably the artist!

Sunbeams pour through the window setting the stairs afire. Gold glass flows into blue and silver, line connects with line, feather with feather, and the new custodian flies down the stairs into the heart of the observer.

It's the eyes you never forget. Emerald green, they scour the soul, asking questions, who are you and what do you want?

* * *

The funeral over, people linger at the graveside reading the labels on wreaths. The tomb is under a lilac tree, a heavyweight cherub gazing down wondering if the occupant being dead is now content to remain so. The stone was almost worn away. '*Mary Gray, loved beyond life and death.*'

That's what the Airman said! It's funny, but Daisy can't recall his name, or if he was even in the house, or if like the window, he is part of the enchantment.

There were masses of flowers on the grave, small posies and formal wreaths.

She reached down to turn a label as another hand sought to do the same.

'Sorry.'

'Sorry,'

'That's okay.'

'That's okay.'

Daisy smiled. 'You next.'

'I was trying to read the tag but the ink's blurred.'

'Perhaps that one, the lily-of-the-valley?'

'Wait,' he said. 'I'll fetch it. You cann'ae bend with that leg.' He offered the posy. She read: 'For Ed, from Janet, alias Puff the Magic...'

'.... dragon.'

'....dragon.'

'We must stop doing that.'

'We must.'

They surveyed the grave. 'So many wreaths?'

'Aye, and such a racket'

'A Scot referring to bagpipes as a racket? Surely that is sacrilege?'

'I think it must be. Let's pretend I ne'er said it.'

'Let's. Were you here for the funeral?'

'I came to look at the hoos.'

'Oh, me too! I was thinking to buy but the agent never turned up.'

'More fool he. The man will never know what he missed.'

Daisy was not averse to receiving a compliment from such a man, a soldier, good to look at and wounded by looks of things and leaning on a stick.

He smiled and offered his hand, 'Lucian Nairne.'

Smiling, she shook his hand. 'Daisy Banks.'

'If you still want a look I have a key.'

'It's okay. I've had a quick tour.'

'It's a grand place. I used to live across the way. Me and my brother spent most of childhood running aboot these gardens.'

'In the rain?'

'Och aye, always in the rain.'

Daisy was tired. Until her parents got back the house was the only shelter. She was loath to return, seeming to know if she did, she'd never leave.

The man beside her coughed. 'If you're against going back in the hoos I've a place nearby. I sold my folks' place to buy this and so for the while I'm bivvying in a trailer. It's not much but you're welcome to shelter there.'

'That's kind.'

'Uh-huh. 'Course there's always the egg hoos here if you dinna mind mice.'

'I don't mind mice. I don't mind trailers either.'

'Good. I can make a cup of tea if you fancy it or something warmer.'

'I'd like that.'

'Then gi' me your bag.' He took her bag and the umbrella. 'Best take my arm. So many treading aboot here they've made the ground tricky.'

Overwhelmed by a sense of déjà vu she said, 'have we met before? I mean, you haven't by any chance been around Surrey lately?'

'No Surrey. Up until a month ago I was getting my leg fixed. After that I spent a while in Paris. My mother had an apartment there. I've taken the lease. Miss Banks er...?' He halted. 'I think I'd better come clean.'

'About what?'

'I said we haven'ae met and it's true but I do know who you are. Last year you were at the Wallace wedding.'

'Jenny Miller's wedding?'

'Aye, Jenny Wallace, as she is now. I served with Kieran Wallace, her husband's brother, who was killed in Afghanistan. Kevin invited me to the wedding.'

'Jenny seems happy.'

'That's good to know. From what I heard it's been a long time coming.'

'It was. Did we dance? Sorry if I don't remember. I got thrown about by so many people that night names and faces are a blur.'

'We didn'ae dance. I'm no dancer and you were awful popular.'

'Yes and the bruises to show for it.'

'Scottish weddings are inclined to be manic. My one regret was not speaking to you. So when I saw you here I thought I'd grab my courage and say hi.'

Daisy smiled. 'Hi.'

Blue eyes glowing, he smiled back. 'Hi, yourself.'

There was an odd moment when Daisy felt that she needed to ask nothing of this man, that all information was known and treasured.

'So the hoos is up for auction. Will you be putting in a bid?'

'I don't think so. I've wanted it for ages, drove my parents crazy. But having been inside I realise there's no room for me. What about you?'

'Nu-huh! There's too much water passed under that particular bridge.'

'I spent my life searching for that house. Now it's as though it never existed.'

'It's a weight off my shoulders. I was always worrying aboot this hoos. God knows why. Naebody asked me to do it. I felt it a duty to my soul.'

'That's it exactly! I knew I had to come back or I'd never be at peace again.'

'I'll probably go back to France. D'you think you could live there?'

'Yes, with the right person, and...' Daisy struggled to free her crutch from a pothole, '...preferably with both feet on the ground.'

'Well that's me oot for a while.'

'What happened to your leg?'

'I was shot.'

'Oh!'

'Thank you for that. A soldier's war wound is all he's got so he tends to put all his eggs in one basket in the hope of a gasp from a soft pair of lips.'

'Are you okay now? No lasting injury?'

'I'm done with the Army. This is me making the most of my army duds. I hope you're suitably impressed.'

'I am impressed. You may put your eggs away now.'

'Good because to return to the subject of the right person, I feel I should tell you I've had a picture in my head of my ideal person since I was a bairn. I've carried her in my heart all of this last year and am more than willing to carry her in my arms for the rest of my life.'

'You don't seem to mind what you say.'

Suddenly serious, he said, 'I do mind, and I'm sorry if I offend, but I've had the words so long in my head I cann'ae stop them coming oot my mouth.'

Then she knew where she'd seen him before. 'You're the chap at the therapy clinic who used to urge me along! It is you, isn't it? I'm not imagining it?'

'Aye, it was me. My regiment has a bed sponsored in that hospital so naturally when I was invalided oot I was put there.'

They were outside the trailer. A dog barked. 'You have a dog.'

'I have two, Biddy, who's been with me forever, and Baz, an old greyhound from the sanctuary down the road.'

'I have a cat called Boffin. He only has three legs.'

'That's okay,' he said softly, 'my dogs get on wi' cats. Miss Banks? Daisy?' He took off his cap, rain dripping on his hair. 'Do you think we could have dinner together some time?'

Daisy was gazing at the tiny cross in his ear. 'You wear an ear-stud.'

'What this?' Blushing, he tugged his ear. 'It's no a thing I'd normally wear but it was a gift from my mother and it did save my life.'

'How did it?'

'I still cann'ae figure it. I thought I'd put it with a note I'd written. I'm in bomb disposal. Long story short, it was hot. I'd taken off my helmet. I'm staring at a decoy. A sniper fires! I turn away thinking I'm a dead man and this flips out of nowhere. I reach to catch it and the sniper gets my leg rather than my life.'

Daisy wanted to tell of the stud in her jacket pocket but knew she couldn't explain a miracle. When the car knocked her down she tried saying sorry to her Good Samaritan, that she had risked his life along with her own. His answer is framed in her heart forever: 'I was offered a choice, to share life or save it. Since you and I have an Eternity together, I figured this time I'd save.'

That was it, though he did leave reminders, an ear-stud in the shape of a cross, and a black silk D&G jacket with a picture of an angel on a motor bike on the back, and the words '*Angele Dei qui custos es mei.*' Now, Lucian Nairne, hangs the jacket about her shoulders. 'According to this you have a guardian angel.'

'More than one now I think.'

The words lifted into rain soaked air and were carried along the lane to settle in the lilac tree. Blossom falls on the cherub's head, flowers from heaven and sweets to the sweet, the cherub smiles. His smile floats toward the house and under the door along the hall and up the central staircase to settle on the soft lips of the new custodian – the Spark that will keep the Light in Six Chimneys.

The sun goes in and the window is once again a window. No angelic force storming the barricades with fist curled to threaten or beguile, just a window, dusty, timeless and irreplaceable. The house is empty now and the windows shuttered. Only the smile remains. A man and a woman driving by might see the house and want to investigate. She, the woman – a pretty red-head with remarkable eyes – might want to peer through a crack in the shutters.

Dusty stairs, and a handful of leaves, is all she'll see, then again perhaps a half-chewed Doggo-Bix and a scrap of paper – a note – dancing in a draught.

'Hello Girl with green eyes. I've been asked to leave a note for my nearest and dearest. Sad to say I don't seem to have any. Even if I did you'd be the one I'd want to say goodbye to. I don't know you and you don't know me but don't be afraid, I'm no stalker. I saw you once and never forgot. Your lovely face kept me going through a year of hell. I want to thank you and tell you that alive or dead I'm here for you. Heaven or hell I shall find you, and I will love you, and I will keep you safe for an Eternity.

God bless and keep us both,

your wanna-be Guardian Angel.'

The End

Bug's Wings

This is how it started. One day in early Spring Pa took the belt from behind the door to administer discipline. When he was done his arm wrung out and sweat in his eyes he gave Gabe a choice, he could work with them that was already killed or he could do the killing. There weren't no choice. Gabe could never work in a slaughterhouse. Cattle so scared, great eyes pleading for mercy, it would've killed him. So he did the other thing, went to work for Simeon Salmanovitz at the Valley Funeral Parlour.

Mr Smith took him back of the shop. 'This is the preparation room where I do most of my work.'

Gabe peered round the door. A couple of metal tubs and a pulley contraption screwed to the rafters, he daren't think what kind of preparing went on in there. That first day he hovered. 'Come on in,' says Simeon. 'No need to be afeard, nothing happening here but folks getting ready for their last journey.'

Coffins propped along the wall, shadows everywhere and a strong smell of lye eight year-old Gabe thought it an awful place. That smell! There were times in later life when he'd get a drift of that and straight way was back in Virginia watching Simeon Salmanovitz embalming a corpse. Skinny old guy, dry as leather, he'd be standing over a drain, an apron about his waist and his feet encased in outsize rubber boots. 'Come close, young Gabe Templar,' he'd be saying, 'and I'll show you how it's done.'

Gabe didn't want to know. Pa said he was to be making coffins.

He said nothing about washing dead bodies. He'd hovered at the door. 'I can't stay, Mr Smith,' he says, 'truly I can't.'

Simeon nodded. 'I'll allow it don't seem fair, the sun shining and me and you and Miss Virginia Ransome here in the gloom. I can see why you'd sooner be some place else as I can see how given the choice Miss Virginia would feel the same. Poor lady dying of dropsy she has no say in the matter, her only hope a Christian burial and to look decent when knocking on the Pearly Gates.'

But for a fly buzzing it was quiet. Still Gabe hovered. Then Simeon had sighed. 'But never mind Miss Virginia's hopes. Cut along home and tell your Pa you weren't able to stay. I guess he'll understand.'

There it was again a choice that was no choice. Gabe stayed. He would like to think it was care of Miss Virginia kept him but there were other considerations, the bank foreclosed on the Mill and Pa out of work and them having to leave Alabama. Of course, there was the two dollars promised end of the week and also the need not be a yellow-belly alone with a dead body. All of those unhappy considerations kept him at the Parlour that day but mostly it was about not having to see Ma's face when returning home empty-handed caused Pa to seek out the belt.

Gabe stayed that day and on til his seventeenth birthday. As for the belt the two dollars earned working from school until late into the night made no difference, discipline was maintained, bloodied wheals crisscrossing his back that by morning would be gone. Yes, there at night yet come five of the morning he'd wake without a blemish. It's why nobody knew overmuch of Pa's fondness for discipline, nobody yelling, 'stop that Hodge Templar! You're hurting that boy.'

Ma said the cuts on Gabe's back looked like bug's wings. The overnight healing she put down to good blood her side of the family, 'Sister Belle always quick to heal.' Gabe saw it different. He saw a miracle, a painful miracle while it was happening yet a miracle nonetheless.

After a beating he'd lie on his belly trying not to weep at the pain. Knowing the miracle-maker was close by he'd stare into the darkness. 'It's okay, little gal,' he'd whisper. 'Don't you fret! I know who makes me well and it ain't Aunt Belle.'

On such a night, his back a fiery furnace and his pillow wet, he would twist and turn every muscle aching and yet his heart filled with love. Most nights he'd try staying awake hoping to catch sight of her but dog-tired he'd sleep to rise in the morning healed. 'Cept for dreams he rarely saw his little gal but now and then when real unhappy, kids at school calling him a dummy and Pa extra busy with the belt, she would visit, shining and perfect, his Other Self, a reminder that she was more than a dream.

So it went year-after-year until there was another world war and a dream was made flesh.

Printed in Great Britain
by Amazon